"THE HORSEMAN IS COMING. . . ."

Richard's statement filled Rocky with a fear he hadn't known since Central America.

Thralls here to correct a wrongness. . . .

Rocky shook his head. There was too much real to fear. He couldn't spare thoughts for fears he had created when he was a child.

"No." Richie stood next to Rocky. He was shaking his head, and his words carried eerie echoes of Rocky's own thoughts. "They don't exist." Richie was staring straight out the remains of the hospital door.

Rocky followed his gaze, and he thought he could see a ruddy glint, like an ember, or light reflecting from an unearthly eye. "Tricks of the light," Rocky said. But the unthinking fear brought back memories of dreams, dreams that had been created by an eleven-year-old Richard Brandon.

"Quinque?" whispered Rick.

With the one word, Rocky knew the four of them shared the same childhood dream, and they all feared the same nightmare. And, as if the word were a cue, the sound of galloping hooves dropped out of the wind.

The hooves became louder, and a horseman's shape cut itself out of the blowing rain. The mount was half again as large as any horse had a right to be, and it galloped in a manner that defied the laws of mass and inertia. Steam poured from its nostrils, and its eyes burned coal-red.

"It's coming for me," said Richard. "The Thrall of Chaos—"

DAW Proudly Presents
These Hard-Hitting, Action-Packed
Science Fiction Novels
by S. Andrew Swann:

FORESTS OF THE NIGHT
EMPERORS OF THE TWILIGHT
SPECTERS OF THE DAWN

The Hostile Takeover Series:
PROFITEER (#1)
PARTISAN (#2)
REVOLUTIONARY (#3)

GOD'S DICE

S. Andrew Swann

DAW BOOKS, INC.
DONALD A. WOLLHEIM, FOUNDER
375 Hudson Street, New York, NY 10014
ELIZABETH R. WOLLHEIM
SHEILA E. GILBERT
PUBLISHERS

Cover art by Romas Kukalis.

DAW Book Collectors No. 1062.

First Printing, July 1997

1 2 3 4 5 6 7 8 9

This book is dedicated to Schroder,
who has no right to complain.

ACKNOWLEDGMENTS

Thanks to all the Cleveland people who plowed though this in the rough: Astrid, Bonnie, Susie, Geoff, Becky, Mary, and Malcolm. Your suffering wasn't in vain. I especially want to thank Charlie for giving me a frame to hang this all in. (However, anything in this book is *not their fault.*) Also, thanks to all the people who saw this before it was a book . . .

CHAPTER 1

JULIA

JULIA Brandon clutched her purse and stared at the building before she went in. She must have passed it thousands of times, driving down Euclid during rush hour, but this was the first time she had ever looked at the place. It loomed above the squat brick industrial buildings that crowded to either side of it. The dark stone walls, the gabled roof, and the beveled glass were all out of place in this part of the city.

She stood next to her car for several minutes, wondering if she was at the right address, although "2525" was not an easy number to forget. There was just something alien about the sun-dappled sandstone. It was from another age.

She was about to rummage in her purse for the scrap of paper she'd written the address on, when she noticed the small, unobtrusive sign: "Devereux House—Dr. Lawrence Kavcheck, Director."

What did Mom have to do with this place?

Julia steeled herself and started walking up the parking lot in front of the house. She couldn't figure out what it was. She imagined everything from some historical society to a high-class drug rehab clinic.

She found herself sniffing as she walked toward the building and muttered, "Damn it, Julie Brandon," as she stopped and searched in her purse for a tissue. She wiped her eyes and nose and took a few deep breaths. She wasn't going to break down in front of a bunch of strangers.

When she felt composed, she finished her trek up to Devereux House.

* * *

She was met at the door and taken to Dr. Kavcheck's office. The office was near the front door, and it didn't give her much time to become accustomed to her surroundings. The interior seemed residential, filled with warm-colored carpeting, patterned wallpaper, and wood furniture. However, the woman who took her to Dr. Kavcheck spoiled the homey effect with her white coat and her laminated name tag.

Julia's guide opened a massive oak door and announced, "There's a Julia Brandon here to see you."

Julia could swear she heard a near-whispered question, *"Julia?"* from behind the door. Then she heard a loud, "Please, Sister, send her in."

Sister? Julia felt more lost than ever.

"The doctor will see you," said her guide. Julia nodded and walked into the room beyond the door.

Behind a wide oak desk sat a thin, bald man whose mustache was much too wide for his face. If Julia hadn't been so preoccupied, she might have found the doctor's appearance comical.

Dr. Kavcheck stood and extended his hand. Julia took it.

"Hello, I'm Dr. Kavcheck, and you're M— Miss Brandon, I presume." Julia noticed the hesitation in Dr. Kavcheck's voice.

"Yes—" She hesitated herself, and after a moment she decided that the only way to deal with this was to dive straight in. "Dr. Kavcheck, I have a whole lot of questions."

"I suppose you do," He looked up at the woman, who still stood by the door. "Thank you, Sister. Do I have anything other than paperwork this evening?"

"No, Doctor."

Dr. Kavcheck nodded. "Good. If anything comes up that isn't an emergency, push it till after six."

"Doctor?"

Dr. Kavcheck shrugged, "So I'll do a little overtime."

"Okay . . ." There was a long pause as she closed the door.

Dr. Kavcheck motioned Julia to a seat. "Sister Magdalene is always worrying about me overworking myself," he said by way of explanation. For Julia, it didn't explain anything.

She took the offered seat and blurted, "She's a nun?"

Dr. Kavcheck laughed.

"I'm sorry," Julia mumbled. She could feel her face flush a little.

"It's all right," Dr. Kavcheck said, "I suppose everyone pictures nuns in full habit— Yes, she is. Most of the volunteer workers here are from the local diocese."

Julia couldn't take much more. She looked the doctor in the eyes and said, "What exactly is *here,* Doctor?"

"Call me Larry."

"Would you answer my question?" Julia pounded her purse into her knees in frustration. She felt on the verge of tears again. She knew she was being irrational, but she couldn't help herself.

"Calm down." The doctor raised his hand. "You're going to strangle your purse." He stood up and began talking in a soothing voice. "What do you want to know about?"

"What *is* this place?"

"It's a semipermanent home for people who have severe neurological or psychological problems, people who can't survive on their own, or even with the help of their family. We're staffed by volunteers, including myself. I'm the staff neurologist."

"And the director."

"Oh, you read the sign. I think all that gets me is this neat office."

Julia looked around; it *was* an attractive office. A warm wood paneling covered the walls. Bookshelves were built into the walls, overflowing with medical textbooks. There was even a silent fireplace across from the desk. The only thing that marred the old-fashioned feel of the room was the view out the large beveled-glass windows. All that could be seen outside was a dirty brick wall and a few green metal dumpsters.

"This place doesn't seem like a hospital," she said.

"It isn't. It's a home, a place for these people to live. They need to be cared for, looked after, but they don't deserve to live in an institutional environment."

She could understand this place now, but she was still trying to understand what Mom had been doing.

A long silence stretched into a longer silence until Dr. Kavcheck finally asked, "What brings you here?"

There it was, the question. Suddenly Julia felt embarrassed, as if she didn't trust her mother—and that wasn't it at all. She needed to sort out everything, didn't she? It was her job, since she was the only family Mom had. . . .

Julia felt weepy again, and she fished another tissue out of her purse. She blew her nose and said, "I'm sorry if I seem out of line. I've had a really difficult few weeks since Mom died."

"I'm so sorry." From the sound, Dr. Kavcheck sounded really moved. "I didn't know."

Julia shook her head and kept talking, "No reason you should, is there? But then I drop out a semester from Case to straighten out everything, sell the house—" She blew her nose again. "—it's such a mess. Then I find out that she's been sending checks *here* for fifteen years, nearly seventy thousand dollars. Mom wasn't a rich woman. That's more than our house's worth."

Dr. Kavcheck walked around and placed his hand on Julia's shoulder. "I think I understand."

"I'm sure you do wonderful work here—"

"But you want to know why she made all the donations," Dr. Kavcheck said.

Julia nodded.

"And Catherine didn't tell you anything about this?"

Julia looked up at the use of her mother's name, "You knew Mom?"

"Yes, I did." Hearing the catch in the doctor's voice, Julia wondered if Mom had had a relationship with him. *How much of Mom's life did I ever really know?*

Julia patted the doctor's hand, which still rested on her shoulder.

"Catherine never told you about Devereux House? About her visits here, or her donations?"

"No." As Julia looked into the doctor's eyes, she felt there was something vaguely sinister about the question.

Dr. Kavcheck sighed and released her shoulder. He walked around to the other side of the desk and began rummaging in a more modern-looking file cabinet stationed behind it. "What do you know about your family?"

That wasn't the question Julia expected. As far as she knew, it was just her and Mom. Mom had told her that Dad had died in a car accident in 1970, and the first thought that jumped into Julia's head was that Charles Brandon had survived.

"It isn't my father, is it?"

Dr. Kavcheck shook his head as he pulled a file from the cabinet. "No, but tell me what you know about him."

"Where is this going?"

"Bear with me, please."

Julia sighed. "I don't know anything about him. He and Mom were in a car accident in 1970. I gather it was a rather awful thing because Mom never liked to talk about it. Dad died, and it was lucky that Mom didn't lose me—she was a few weeks' pregnant at the time. She didn't know until after the accident." It wasn't the first time that Julia thought how twisted fate must have seemed to Mom, waking up in the hospital, learning of her pregnancy and the death of her husband within moments of each other.

Dr. Kavcheck shook his head. "She never told you about other children?"

"No. What are you talking about?"

"I guess there's no easy way to say this." Dr. Kavcheck lowered the file and folded his hands. "You have an older brother. His name is Richard."

CHAPTER 2

DR. BRANDON

DOCTOR Richard Brandon bolted awake. Despite the air-conditioning, the sweat-drenched sheets adhered to his body. He sat upright in his darkened bedroom, breathing deeply, afraid to move. He stared into the darkened doorway that led to the rest of his apartment, imagining that he could still see the nightmare that had awakened him.

The vision was still vivid in his mind. Evil claiming a fifth of the world, everything magic becoming perverse and twisted, the four remaining deities standing by and watching, impassive, inscrutable, and apparently uncaring.

Dr. Brandon tore away the sheet and stood up, feeling disgusted with himself. It was an adolescent fantasy he was dreaming about.

He rubbed his forehead and looked at the clock by his bed. It was four in the morning. He sighed, knowing that returning to bed was fruitless. Instead of trying to reclaim two hours of sleep, he stumbled into the shower and stood under a blast of cold water.

Dr. Brandon hated the nightmares. He hated the thought that they might mean something. *Psychologist, heal thyself,* he thought as icy water drove the fatigue from his muscles. *Constant nightmares involving a fantasy world I developed before I was twelve years old; that can't be healthy. . . .*

The admonition was by rote. He'd thought the same thoughts after every nightmare, and he never carried them to their ultimate conclusion. He couldn't, because admitting that the nightmares represented some sort of problem came too close to admitting that his work might be the problem.

Nightmares or not, he was going to go into the tank tonight.

The campus of Case Western Reserve University was hot and empty. Dr. Brandon spent the day mechanically instructing classes half filled with undergraduate psychology students. His mind was elsewhere.

As he talked on about stimulus and response, he carried on an inner debate with himself. He was afraid to go into the tank, and much of that fear was because he *needed* to go into the tank. He was acting like a junkie, hiding the necessity while at the same time he was beginning to structure his life around feeding the need his sessions in the tank represented.

There was something almost godlike about seeing those other lives, other possibilities, other lives unbound by the chains of time and the past that bound him. . . .

Later, when he was alone in his office, he reached his lowest point. He wondered if his whole project was delusional. What if all his theories about quantum mechanics and alternate worlds were so much rationalization? Justifications for self-induced hallucination? When all was said and done, what objective evidence did he have to prove that his visions within the tank had any more objective reality than his nightmares about Midland and the kingdom of Quinque?

Dr. Brandon stayed in his office, rocking back and forth in his chair and shuffling pages of notes. He sat there, questioning himself, until it was eight o'clock. Then he made his way to the basement where the university kept the sensory deprivation tank.

John was late. Dr. Brandon spent the time waiting, double-checking the tapes and the heart monitor. He filled the tank himself. The water was a dark brackish solution, blood warm. A person floating in it would lose all sense of gravity and friction. The tank itself looked like a sheet-metal coffin.

The tank could be as dangerous as it looked, which was why it was forbidden for anyone to do a solo run in the tank. It was possible for someone to panic in the dark, sensationless environment, and without a monitor present, the person could drown in a disoriented attempt to escape. Dr. Brandon felt he was in no danger, but he still wanted a grad student watching over him.

However, as time dragged by, he began to get nervous. He checked the tank again and again and again.

It was supposed to be the longest run yet. It was hard to get the tank to himself, especially when his experiments were not authorized by the university. However, tomorrow was the Fourth of July, and then the long weekend beyond that. That was four days of use, uninterrupted. . . .

With all that time before him, he shouldn't have been so bothered by John's late appearance. However, every time he looked into the waters of the tank, his hands would shake. He could imagine, reflected in the waters, a pair of blood-red eyes looking out at him. It was as if something evil waited for him in the tank.

He shook his head; he was only reliving the nightmare that had awakened him. Quinque, and whatever fate befell it, was not real.

The others, Rick, Richie, Rocky, Richard—*they* were real. As real as Dr. Brandon. As real as an electron.

Dr. Brandon waited for two hours for his assistant to show up. He began to perceive the delay as a test. A stark decision faced him. Whatever the rationalizations were, whatever new worlds he perceived, physically or psychologically, whatever his sessions in the tank actually meant—he was faced with the question of how badly he *needed* to do this.

Was he addicted? If he had to, could he just walk away?

He stared into the water and felt his hand shake.

Could a solo run be so dangerous? He had done it dozens of times. He had never had a disorientation problem before. He could open the tank from inside if need be.

The red eyes reflected in the water, they were just a fragmented image of the Exit sign behind the tank.

It was cold down here, and Dr. Brandon shivered in his swim trunks as he carefully applied the heart monitor wires to his chest, and began turning on the tape machine.

In a few minutes he was slipping into the blood-warm water, and closing himself into the darkness. In the tank, the only thing he could perceive was his own tape-recorded voice.

Shortly thereafter, he began to dream.

CHAPTER 3

JULIA

AS Dr. Kavcheck led her up to Richard's room, the thought kept running through Julia's head, *I always wanted a big brother*. The thought made her feel somehow guilty, as if the wish could somehow be responsible for this man, Richard Brandon, being here. The strange feeling of guilt was wrapped up in anger at her mother, who'd kept this secret.

Maybe it was something about the accident that made Mom act as if she were immortal—no will, no insurance, not even a letter explaining things. Julia certainly never had thought about it, but she was barely twenty-six.

Those thoughts led to another mantra: *She shouldn't have died, not in such a stupid way.*

Mom hadn't been quite sixty yet. She was in perfect health, with two, if not three, decades in front of her. She just had the bad luck to be driving in front of a liquor store in Warren when two trailer-park rejects tried to kill each other. A stray bullet pierced her aorta, and she was dead before her car rolled to a stop.

Julia wiped her eyes and tried to concentrate on where she was, and what she was doing. Dr. Kavcheck was leading her up a staircase that seemed to have dropped in from some Victorian novel. He was talking about the history of the building, about the demise of Millionaires' Row at the turn of the century, how the building came to be donated to the diocese during the Depression. . . .

"He's lived here how long?" Julia asked, forcing the question through her own fog.

"Nearly eighteen years. He came to us about seven

years after the initial trauma." Dr. Kavcheck shook his head. "That was after being through a number of hospitals and state institutions."

She began to feel a little less anger at Mom. She'd been dealing with this, and somehow still managed to save something to put Julia in college. She stopped at the head of the stairs and looked at Dr. Kavcheck. She had just had an awful thought. "If this costs anything . . ."

"Don't worry," Dr. Kavcheck reassured her. "We operate on donations here; the only reason we turn anyone away is space or lack of proper care here. You don't need to worry about your brother." Julia turned away, and the doctor put a hand on her shoulder. "Are you all right?"

Julia nodded. "I'm just not used to the idea."

"You don't need to see him right away. I understand if you need some time before—"

"No, this is something I have to do."

He led her through another corridor, rich with wood paneling in red and brown. The furniture and the paintings tried to match the antique wood trim and the wallpaper, but Julia could tell that they were cheaper and of a more recent vintage. She suspected that whatever original furniture came with this old mansion had been sold off long ago to help with operating expenses.

Too soon they stopped in front of a door. Above it a small black-and-white porcelain plaque was screwed into the door frame. It read "14" in white stenciled numbers.

"How many patients do you have here?"

"We can handle about twenty-five at a time, depending on the strain on the staff. Ready?"

Julia nodded. "Shouldn't you knock or anything."

"Richard doesn't mind."

Dr. Kavcheck swung the door open on a bright little room dominated by a tall peaked window segmented into small diamonds of leaded glass. It faced the west and the lowering sun, so its shadows carved the room into a grid.

The room had a single hospital bed facing the window, whose essential nature wasn't hidden by the patchwork quilt draped across it. The head of the bed was flanked by a bureau and a bookshelf. Flanking the window were two chairs, one kitty-cornered opposite the bookshelf, facing the bed. The other matching chair obviously went in the opposite corner, but instead it had been pulled out to the foot of the bed and turned around, facing the window.

Julia's brother sat in the chair. She knew who it was the moment she saw him. He had the same tousled brown hair she had, and her mother's sharp nose. She walked into the room, staring at him.

Dr. Kavcheck followed her into the room. "This is Richard."

Julia shook her head, as if at an illusion that might evaporate if her mind cleared. She edged next to the window so that she could face him. His gaze never shifted from the view out the window. She saw more of his face and decided he was a handsome man. There was just a slight dusting of gray around his temples, and it made him look distinguished. However, if she looked hard, she could see that the gray on one side followed a line up the side of his skull, and that point suffered from a slight, almost unnoticeable, asymmetry.

She looked into his eyes, expecting to see blankness. What she saw was much more eerie. He didn't look back at her, but his gaze wasn't that of dead disinterest. It was as if he were looking at something intently and just didn't notice her. Occasionally his eyes would shift, as if to follow something.

She reached out and brushed a lock of hair away from his forehead. He didn't react to her touch, and his unreadable, neutral expression didn't change.

He seems lost. The thought touched something inside her. "What is wrong with him?" she asked.

Dr. Kavcheck walked up to her. "He's suffered deficits in nearly all his higher brain functions. We can't say how much because the primary deficit is in his ability to communicate."

"Was he always like this?"

"No." Dr. Kavcheck walked around the bed and picked

up a yellowed notebook. "He used to draw, and he used to look at these books."

"He can read?"

Dr. Kavcheck handed her the notebook and said. "I don't know if he read. Your mother was convinced he could understand language, but I really don't have any way to determine how complete his comprehension is, or was. His reactions were always very limited. But he would open the books and turn the pages." He tapped on the book and said, "Up until his first stroke this was the only way he communicated. Afterward, he didn't."

Julia felt a twinge of shock, "He had a stroke?"

Dr. Kavcheck nodded. "Unfortunately, his injuries predispose him to have strokes. He's only had one major one since he's come here."

"Good Lord," Julia said, and opened the notebook. When she saw what was drawn there, she repeated herself. "Good Lord. Did he draw this?"

The page had opened to a dark scene that, at first, seemed a random cloud of scribbles someone had done in a black ballpoint pen. But after a moment the shadows resolved themselves into a form. An armored horseman rode astride a demonic horse. There were no straight lines, the scribbles simply became denser to describe the flanks of the horse, became more wispy when describing the highlights on the sword and the armor. It was almost as if the artist had been scribbling over a bas-relief.

"Yes, that's how he drew."

Julia flipped a few more pages. All of them were the same style, childish scribbles that merged to form a realistic portrait of stark light and shadow. The images were fantastic—a horrible dog tried to rear slavering out of the page, a winged serpent curled around a squat stone tower, a beautiful androgynous figure seemed to be turning away from the viewer.

She flipped back to the horseman. That was the most arresting picture, perhaps because the mount's eyes had been drawn in a blazing red, the only color she had seen in the pictures.

"He doesn't draw anymore?"

Dr. Kavcheck shook his head. "Not for over ten years."

Julia held the notebook, and felt the full impact of Richard's isolation. No matter how grotesque the pictures, the thought of only having one avenue of expression and then having that taken away as well was horrible.

"There's someone in there," Julia said, looking at the picture of the horseman.

"Catherine said that a lot," Dr. Kavcheck said. "She came here every week to read to him." His voice trailed off. In a more subdued voice he said, "I tried to contact her when she didn't show up two weeks ago, but the number we had was years out of date."

Julia was shaking her head. She put her hand on Richard's. He didn't react, but Julia hoped that somewhere, inside, he was comforted. How awful it had to be for him. If Mom had come here every week, then to suddenly stop.

"What did she read?"

Dr. Kavcheck motioned at the bookshelf. She craned her neck to look past Richard, at the books. For some reason she had expected to see a shelf full of children's books, Dr. Seuss and such. What was shelved here was much more eclectic.

On one shelf she saw Tolkien, C. S. Lewis, and Mallory, on anther she saw Hegel. Mixed in with romantic fantasy and German Idealism were books of popular science, many of which had "Quantum" as part of the title. Hegel, Schelling, and Fichte didn't surprise her, Mom had been teaching graduate-level philosophy for years. Julia supposed that if Mom was making secret weekly visits to read to Richard, she had the sense to read things that interested her.

She didn't know what to make of the books on quantum physics.

She turned back to Richard, who was still looking passively out the window. It began to sink in that this was her brother. He was the only family she had left. It was probably her imagination, but she felt a connection between them, even if Richard couldn't express it.

She touched the side of his face. His impassive expression didn't change. *"Richard,"* she whispered, as if he were only distracted and the name could call his attention. His eyes kept looking out the window, occasionally following things that weren't there.

Julia could feel her eyes tearing up again. She stood and gazed out the window, so she didn't have to face the doctor. Still, he asked, "Are you all right?"

Would you be all right? she wanted to blurt out, but that wasn't fair to the doctor. Instead she put her hands on the back of Richard's chair, straightened her back, and nodded vigorously. "Yes, yes." After a moment, she asked "Can I be alone with him for a while?"

There was a pause while the doctor considered her request. Then he responded, "I don't see why not. You remember where my office is. I'll be there when you want to talk some more." Another pause, "There's a call button for the nurse on the nightstand, if you need any help."

Julia nodded again, without turning around.

She waited until she heard the door close behind her before she started crying. Julia stood, shaking, tears dampening her cheeks, sucking in irregular breaths. After a while she whispered through the sobs, "Some sister, huh?" She let go of the chair and found her purse, then sat herself down on the foot of his bed and fished for a tissue.

She pulled out an empty Kleenex package. "Damn it, perfect." She sniffed and rubbed her nose with the back of her hand. "I'm sorry, Richard, this is all a bit much." She looked out to see the view that Richard found so fascinating. She was somewhat surprised to see the Terminal Tower from here, most of the Cleveland skyline piled on the western horizon, segmented into diamonds by the leaded glass window. It was like staring through a giant chain-link fence.

She shook her head, rubbing the tears out of her eyes. "I just really miss Mom, that's all." She stood up and patted his shoulder. "It's not your fault."

Richard kept staring out the window, toward the horizon.

CHAPTER 4

ROCKY

IT never failed, every single July Fourth, someone asked Rocky the question, "You don't want to see the fireworks?"

This particular July Fourth, the questioner was a woman sitting at the bar next to him. In response, Rocky shook his head and took a long pull from the Foster's he was drinking. Dusk had fallen, and the explosions had begun outside.

"Reminds me of Nicaragua," Rocky lied to the woman, whose name eluded him. The bangs outside didn't remind Rocky of gunfire, or the *Wisconsin*'s 16-inch guns. The associations were older, less clear in his memory, and more troubling. His denial of the dimmer pain was barely conscious, and almost by rote.

"Oh," she said. She stayed his drinking hand by touching the back of it with her index finger. The gesture forced his attention away from the beer, to her face.

Young, Rocky thought. Too young to be here. She might have just reached twenty, if one gave her the benefit of the doubt. Blue eyes, blonde hair, and a perky smile fresh from the factory.

"Was it bad for you?" she asked him in a low voice.

How did this conversation start? Rocky couldn't remember. "Not really, I was logistics. A glorified truck driver—one of Reagan's Teamsters." He wondered how old she'd been when he'd been driving the Pan-American out of San Salvador. Six or seven? The thought made him uncomfortable.

"My dad was in the Marines, down in Panama—"

"Let's change the subject."

"Okay. Murray said you were a cop."

Rocky glanced down the bar toward the bartender. "Thanks." Murray was filling a pitcher and pretended not to notice.

"What?" she started tracing a pattern on the back of his hand. "You undercover or something?"

"Nope. Just on a little vacation." Rocky disentangled his hand and drained the remainder of the Foster's. He pushed away the glass and waved Murray over. "Is that why you're over here? Because I'm a cop?"

She shrugged in response.

Murray came over, "Yeah?"

Rocky faced him, almost said something about the girl, thought better of it, and asked, "How many is this?"

Murray paused a moment, "Ah—"

"Great, I can't remember, and you have to think about it." Rocky got up with the deliberate caution of someone used to hiding his drunkenness. He fished out his wallet and pulled out a ten dollar bill. He slapped it down on the bar. "Here, I'm going."

"You're leaving?" said the girl, "It's early."

"For you it's early."

Murray picked up the bill. "Catch ya later, Rocky."

Rocky nodded absently, "Be here tomorrow and we can even out the tab. Don't want to think about math right now."

"Sure," Murray said. He was already headed to another part of the bar. *At least Murray still trusts me.*

Rocky slid his wallet back into his pocket as he walked to the exit. It took an unreasonable amount of concentration to do it without looking foolish, which was why he was surprised when he heard a female voice say, "You *really* a cop?"

He glanced over his shoulder and saw her, blonde hair and perky smile, following him. *Just what I need.*

"Yeah, allegedly." Rocky pushed out the door and into the street. After the air-conditioned bar, the atmosphere outside was a steaming wet towel slapping across his face. Rocky had to take a few steps and put his hand on a newspaper machine to steady himself. It was muggy enough that the sodium streetlights had hazy yellow haloes around them.

Somewhere, in the distance, there was a massive cacophony of explosions, followed by the faint sound of applause. His head throbbed, and he was thankful that he only lived two blocks away.

"I didn't see a badge."

Rocky turned around, slowly because the heat made him feel all the fluid inside his skull whenever he moved his head. "What?"

She was still blonde and perky. "When you paid—"

Rocky rubbed his temples. "Oh. Look, three things. First, I don't carry a badge in my wallet. It's got a nice leather case all its own. Second, I don't have it on me right now because the department gave me a two-week unpaid vacation. Third, if I came on to you in there, kid, I'm sorry, but I really don't want any company right now."

"Oh," the perky smile evaporated as she backed away. "Sorry."

Rocky felt bad enough that he almost reconsidered, but he didn't say anything to stop her as she pushed her way back into the bar. *Murray probably encouraged her,* Rocky thought, *trying to cheer me up.*

However, it was the last thing he needed; a few hours with someone just about half his age, especially someone with a thing for cops, someone who would ask him things like "Did you kill anyone in the war?"

He pushed himself away from the newspaper machine and glanced down to see the headline under his hand, all about the Soviet siege of Teheran. There was a large color picture above the fold, piles of Iranian dead. It was just the wrong picture to look at in his frame of mind.

He started walking down the street, away from the bar, away from everything. He forced himself to think of the air conditioner in his studio. The machine was a leaky, decrepit thing, but the thought of a cool breath of air pulled him through the muggy night, no matter how his head throbbed.

Like the rest of his day, he'd timed his exit from the bar just wrong. He took a right and ran straight into a pedestrian stampede. Hundreds of people were returning from the fireworks at Edgewater Park. It was an annual exodus of a third of a million people that choked a good part of the near-west side. It would last until sometime after midnight.

Rocky had been just drunk enough to forget entirely about it, even though his apartment lay only a half-dozen blocks from the lake. He turned on to his street and faced a mass of people walking in the opposite direction. They carried towels, lawn chairs, coolers, and wailing children. The crowd clogged the road itself, slowing the cars to below a walking pace.

He hugged the corner of the street, allowing the mass to break around him. He held his ground, rubbing his forehead. *Why'd I leave? If I had stayed another half hour—*

He stopped badgering himself. He knew why he'd left, and he knew why he'd chosen not to remember the crowds of Edgewater.

"Someday I'm going to go, and I won't freak out," he whispered to himself. "Then everything'll be fine."

As he began moving against the crowd, he muttered, "And tell me another story. . . ."

The crowd was a nightmare. Kids kept running into him. A young woman with a stroller looked at him as if his walking against the flow of traffic were some personal insult.

Halfway to his apartment, he had moved to walk on the lawns. It was easier to avoid the stationary picnickers.

He was stepping around someone's hibachi when a blinding white flash washed everything away. No shadows, no form, only a featureless white light that Rocky kept seeing even as his eyes were clenched shut and streaming tears from the painful brightness. He heard the crowd react, the beginning of a scream. His foot hooked the hibachi, tripping him forward, and the crowd's noise was washed out by a rumbling thunderclap. The noise felt like a heart attack in his chest.

As he fell into the light, he thought, *Someone finally pushed the button over the Gulf.*

Then his face met wet lawn, and someone poured cold water over him.

He lay for a moment, stunned, blinded, tasting mud and grass. The water kept pouring. Rocky started shivering. He blinked a few times, and saw another flash, a weak blue compared to the prior explosion of light. The rumble followed a few seconds later, at about the same time that he realized that it was raining.

It wasn't just raining, he was in the middle of the worst shitstorm he could remember outside of Central America. As he stood up, he couldn't see ten feet in front of his face.

No sign of a crowd—picnickers—anyone.

"What the fuck?"

It was like suddenly standing under a shower going full blast. A river was running down the asphalt next to him, and his feet had already sunk an inch into the sod under him.

Rocky had never blacked out before, and he was certain that he hadn't had that much to drink—but the sudden change in everything frightened him. He began to wonder if he'd hit his head, or had a seizure, or . . .

Rocky looked up at the apartment building next to him. Same lawn— "I collapsed and they just left me here?"

Rocky backed away from the building. Something seemed wrong about it, about everything really. More than just the sense he'd blacked out. He'd lived in this neighborhood for the past five years, and something just seemed wrong about it.

He shook his head. "Just a little disoriented, and legally drunk."

He silently cursed the people who'd left him as a lawn ornament and started home. He dashed up the steps and pushed inside the door before he realized that something was seriously wrong.

Someone had stolen his apartment.

Not just the apartment, but the whole second and third floors, and the roof. His apartment building was a graffiti-wrapped shell, naked and empty to the flooded checker-board linoleum.

"Wrong building," Rocky muttered.

He backed out the door again. This time he saw that it was now mostly plywood. However, the address wasn't boarded up.

It wasn't the wrong building.

CHAPTER 5

RICHIE

RICHIE drove the decrepit VW microbus down the ugliest stretch of East 119th Street. The windows were all open because the VW didn't have a working air conditioner, and because Richie wanted to let out the smell of the pot his five passengers were inhaling.

"S'wat's the plan?" Duke asked with the hoarse wheeze of someone who was trying to retain smoke and communicate at the same time. The microbus hit a pothole, and Duke erupted in a fit of coughing.

Keep telling myself that this is an easy job.

Richie didn't much like Duke, or Duke's friends, but Duke was all he had at the moment. At least, Duke was the only person he knew who was crazy enough to shaft Rico. And, all profit aside, the job Richie had in mind was to shaft Rico.

"I get us in the lot, and you boost the cars." Richie looked over his shoulder at the stoned menagerie behind him. "You got that?"

Five tattooed white guys nodded at him, one saluting him with a pry bar. Richie turned around and shook his head. "Maybe this isn't such a good idea," he muttered.

The microbus hit another pothole and Duke waved a joint in his direction. "Here, have a toke, calm you down."

Richie shook his head. "Nah, you're calm enough for both of us."

I ain't setting you guys up. If you all get busted, it's because you left that brain cell you're sharing back at the trailer park.

In fact, Richie sort of liked the idea of these white trash homeboys successfully making off with the lot. Getting reamed by these Parma potheads would do wonders for Rico's image. Richie pictured the fat asshole stepping off his yacht, after the fireworks, and finding out that his most profitable chop shop had just been looted.

It'd serve the bastard right for fucking with him.

Richie pulled the microbus to a stop a block away from the lot, which was an innocuous-looking shed and a fenced-in yard generically named "Diamond Auto Repair." There were a half-dozen cars in the lot, as well as one nasty Doberman. There were lights on in a small office in the shed. Dirty yellow light leaked through the windows. "Closed," read a yellowed piece of cardboard hung over the front gate.

That sign rarely, if ever, came down. Rico's little operation here was an open secret. Even the local cops knew it, and tolerated it. Rico was a big smelly fish in the stagnant pond of Cleveland politics. You'd have a better chance of getting Mayor Kucinich to admit that the city council had done something right than you'd have of a Cleveland cop busting one of Rico's operations.

Which was why Richie's plan was going to leave such a stunned expression on Rico's fishy little face.

Richie let the microbus roll to a stop. When the microbus' parking brake finally stuck, Duke pushed open the passenger door. Richie grabbed his arm, restraining him. "We wait till dusk, remember?"

"Oh, yeah. Sorry."

It's a good thing you're not the point of all this, Duke.

It was probably a good thing that the cars down there were already hot-wired. Not that Richie cared about the cars, particularly. Duke and his friends were here just to add confusion to everything. Richie's intent was to cause a mess that Rico, the Feds, and the Colombians who owned this microbus would spend forever trying to figure out—as well as causing Rico a minor financial apocalypse and blowing anyone's faith in him being able to hold his little organization together.

If this little enterprise gave one of Rico's lieutenants the balls to cap his boss, Richie'd be all for it.

While his stoned squad of mercenary car thieves waited for dusk, Richie climbed into the back of the microbus and liberated a battered suitcase and a bolt cutter from under one of the rear seats. He pulled it up next to the driver's seat.

"Okay, when I open the gate, you drive in," he said to Duke.

"Jawohl, mon kommandant," Duke saluted him and burst into a giggling fit.

"No prints in the bus," Richie said.

Duke held up his hands. He wore filthy work gloves, a joint smoldering between the fingers, trailing smoke that was as much glove as pot.

What the fuck, Richie thought. *This is* supposed *to leave everyone guessing.*

Richie stepped out of the microbus, allowing Duke to slip into the driver's seat. The sky had turned purple beyond Diamond Auto Repair.

A firecracker went off somewhere, and the Doberman beyond the chain-link began barking frantically.

"Good doggie," Richie whispered. This pooch had a small reputation. Rico had let the dog chew out the crotch of a hood that he'd been particularly disappointed in. Rico made a point of spreading the story around, letting everyone know what a hard-ass he was.

Richie smirked at the bargain-basement Cerberus, guarding the chain-link gate to his little Plutonian realm. *Fuck you, dog,* Richie thought. *I'm armed with a bit more than pomegranate seeds.*

He zipped down the front of his jacket. It was a relief, given the heat. But Richie was dressed for the job, not the weather.

As part of his plan to spread as much confusion as possible, Richie was dressed like a biker—black jeans, motorcycle boots, and Harley Davidson jacket complete with chains. To top off the ensemble, he walked around to the passenger door and retrieved a black cycle helmet from the footwell. With the helmet's visor down, the only patches of skin left visible on his body were on the backs of his hands, through the holes in his driving gloves.

Shortly thereafter, the real fireworks began. The Doberman started barking madly. Richie gave Cerberus some time, time to allow the fireworks display to grow in volume, time to assure him that the one person here wasn't checking on the dog.

As the fireworks began building toward their finale, Richie walked toward the fence, carrying the bolt cutter and the suitcase.

Cerberus went wild with the barking, at him now, not the fireworks. "Good doggie," Richie repeated as he walked to the gate. He didn't smile as he said it. He disliked dogs, and attack dogs most of all.

Cerberus paced him on the other side of the fence. Richie reached the gate with "Closed" on it, and examined the padlock and chain holding the gate shut.

One snip from the bolt cutters and the chain rattled to the ground, almost inaudible for the barking dog and the fireworks. The dog went nuts, jumping at the chain.

Richie carefully laid down the cutters and reached into his jacket. He withdrew a thirty-eight Colt revolver that, according to the man who sold it, had been involved in the death of at least one local drug dealer.

Richie wanted something for the ballistics department to think about.

He timed the shot with one of the blinding-white, chest-throbbing fireworks. The skyborne explosion swallowed the report of the .38 as Richie put a slug through the dog's right eye. One whimper and Cerberus collapsed. It tried to get up once, its legs skittering on asphalt, and was still.

"Could get to like fireworks," Richie said to the dog as he pushed open the gate with his foot. There was no sign of commotion up at the office. As he walked into the lot, a pair of headlights washed over him, throwing his shadow up against the garage. The sound of a protesting transmission told him it was Duke in the microbus. He heard the squeal of brakes, and a rolling stop behind him.

That was all Duke's show now. Richie had another job to do.

He walked into the garage, and into a lighted office that was walled off from the rest of the space. Inside, a balding man was hunched over a computer terminal.

Richie leveled the gun at the man and said, "Open the safe."

The man sat bolt upright. "What?"

"Open the safe," Richie repeated.

"Look, I don't think you know who you're messing with—"

Richie put a shot through the monitor. The picture tube exploded. The guy jumped back far enough for his seat to tip backward, spilling him on the floor. "You work for Rico, your name is Eddie, you live on East 115th Street, and you are going to open the safe."

"I don't have the combination."

"You're the fucking accountant. I want you to picture angry Colombians with straight razors." It didn't mean anything, but it sounded cool, and it would confuse the hell out of Rico if the story ever made it back to him.

Eddie scrambled backward, toward the safe, scooting on his ass. "Yeah, open the safe, sure . . ." He began fiddling with the lock without turning away from Richie.

A bad transformer smell from the shattered monitor was leaking under Richie's helmet. "It might help if you look at it," he told Eddie.

Eddie seemed torn for a few seconds, unable to pull his gaze away from the gun in Richie's hand. Richie motioned with the gun, and the guy reacted as if he'd been slapped in the face with it. His fingers slipped all over the dial, but Richie didn't press the guy any farther. More pressure, and it might take Eddie even longer to open the safe.

"Please, don't hurt me, there isn't a lot of money in here. It's slow, holidays and all—"

"Let me worry about that."

The safe was a large, nearly immobile affair, a perfect cube of pebbled gray metal. Richie suspected it was more fireproof than burglarproof. Rico was not someone to be casually held up. Even so, it looked like forcing the safe could take about half an hour, even with all the tools available in the garage. Richie approved.

The door swung open. Eddie bent forward and Richie cleared his throat. Eddie scrambled back as if something in the safe might bite him.

"Good boy," Richie said.

Predictably, on top of everything in the safe was a gun. It looked to be a nine-millimeter Beretta. Also inside the various drawers were ledgers, papers, and a shitload of other stuff that any honest DA would give his left nut for. There was also a stack of cash, predominantly tens and twenties.

"See, I told you. We don't have much money here—"

"Shut the fuck up, Eddie." Eddie nodded and retreated to a corner next to the wall, the length of the desk away from the safe.

Richie put his suitcase on the desk and opened it. "This isn't about money, Eddie." Richie removed the gun and the cash from the safe, and stacked them next to the suitcase. Eddie just stared from his seat on the floor.

"This is about a whole lot of Colombians who packed a VW microbus full of about five kilos of—well—" Richie hefted a brick of coke the size of a shoebox out of the suitcase. "This stuff."

Richie tossed the brick into the safe. Eddie looked confused.

Richie loaded the safe with four more bricks. They barely fit. "Now they lost that VW, and they're very unhappy about it. And you know, the Feds are also kinda unhappy. You see they were looking forward to this real big bust. They've been setting it up for months. And they lost the VW, too."

Richie closed the safe on the cocaine, and made sure the lock caught. "Shield your eyes, Eddie."

Richie blew off the dial with a couple of well-placed shots. Parts of the lock made a satisfying pinging sound as they ricocheted off of the concrete floor of the office.

Richie checked the shots remaining in his gun and picked up the nine millimeter.

"What are you doing?" Eddie said.

"Why I'm delivering Rico's coke, what else?" Richie put .38 caliber holes through the office door, the window, and the corrugated steel wall. The gunshots merged with the finale of the fireworks show a couple of blocks away. He kept firing until the .38 was empty.

For a brief moment Richie thought of the crowds ohing and ahing at the much bigger Edgewater show, across town. He pushed the thought away.

He leveled the Beretta at Eddie and tossed the .38 out into the garage. The ballistics department would have fun with it.

"I'd suggest a change in career." Richie started piling the cash in the suitcase. It wasn't anywhere near the value of the coke he'd just dumped. "No one's getting that safe open until the Feds arrive, the bullet holes give them probable cause, and I'm sure the papers in that safe will interest them as much as the cocaine."

"You're crazy!"

"Rico's a local bird. I doubt he pulls a hell of a lot of weight with the DEA. Especially when they've been rabid to haul someone in for all that coke— Hell, the DEA *bought* it. They want a return on their investment." Richie closed the suitcase. "But if you're real lucky, the Colombians'll get here first."

Richie picked up the suitcase, pocketed the nine millimeter, and left.

Behind him, he heard Eddie yell, "Rico'll kill me."

"He'll have other problems," Richie said as he walked out of the garage.

The only vehicle remaining in the lot was the microbus. The local church had finished their fireworks display, and all Richie had left to do was to walk away. Richie reached the gate, and was about to remove his helmet, when the sky exploded.

The light was a pure blinding white, even through the tint of the visor on his helmet. It was almost a physical force pushing him. A deafening rumble followed the light a half-second later. The sound tried to shake his rib cage apart, tried to drive him down to his knees. He dropped the suitcase. The world went dark and filled with the sound of ripping canvas.

The shock of the explosion stunned him. It wasn't until he felt the water streaming down the back of his neck that Richie realized it was raining. Raining hard enough that even when his eyesight returned to normal, the world was invisible behind the rippling across his visor.

"Quickest goddamn storm I ever seen." Richie shook his head as multiple chains of lightning exploded across the sky above him. "Fucking lightning was too damn close."

Rain or not, he had to split before the Feds or the Colombians showed. He looked around for his suitcase, but it was impossible to see out of the helmet. He took it off—

The suitcase was gone.

"It couldn't have washed away. . . ."

As he raised his eyes, he realized more than the suitcase was missing. The microbus was missing. The parking lot around the garage was a lake, and there was a pile of broken asphalt and old tires where there'd been four stolen cars parked, barely twenty minutes ago. Richie could see weeds choking the mound, even through the rain.

The chain-link fence was rusted and wrapped in vines.

Most bizarre of all, the garage was not only abandoned, but different. The outline was similar, but it was boarded up and had the doors in the wrong places. And instead of "Diamond Auto Repair," the dilapidated sign read "Esso."

"What the fuck's going on here?"

CHAPTER 6

RICK

RICK was staring at the spreadsheet on the monitor in front of him, so it was a few minutes before he realized that his office wasn't empty, and someone was talking to him.

He looked up and said, "What?"

Leaning against the doorframe of his office was Francine Griffith, his news editor. "I said, 'haven't you ever heard of time off?' Holidays? Independence Day?"

Rick yawned and leaned back in his chair. It sounded old and tired. It, and the desk, were here when he first leased the space for the *Observer*. It was a sign of the financial state of the paper that he had yet to replace them. "So what are you doing here?"

"Funny, I was asking you the same question."

Rick shrugged, "Just shuffling numbers, trying to keep us afloat for another month—"

Francine sighed. "Cleveland's own Quixote. When are you going to delegate some of this crap?"

"When we can afford to hire someone to do it."

Francine sighed again, walked around the desk, and grabbed his mouse. "What are you doing?" he asked, even though it was obvious as windows began closing and the hard drive whirred.

As she saved everything and shut down the computer, she asked, "How long have you been sitting in that chair, staring at that screen?"

"Well—"

The last window closed on the monitor, and she turned off the system. She looked down and said, "Someday, when I leave the office, I'm going to empty out that little refrigerator of yours, or maybe steal all the toilet paper, just so you'll have to go aboveground and see the real world, if not actually go home."

"I'm not as bad as all that," he protested, though, when he stood up, his knees popped loudly enough that he was afraid she'd hear. Worse was the sound of rusty springs decompressing under the green vinyl seat of his office chair.

Francine just looked at him with an expression that said that they both knew he was lying. "You know, Rick, we had a barbecue this afternoon. Everyone from the office showed up. We even had a few of those columnists you've conned into writing for free. . . ."

"Oh, shit!" A weight of fatigue crushed down on him when he finally realized what day it was. "Damn it, I'm sorry. I was going to go. I just forgot—"

"You forgot the picnic?" she asked incredulously.

Rick shook his head, "No, I lost track of what day it was."

She looked him up and down with a growing expression of alarm. "You mean you didn't leave yesterday?"

"I—" Rick's throat caught, and he simply nodded. "I guess you're the delegate to save me from myself."

She grabbed his arm, "Look, boss. You're leaving, and you aren't coming back until Monday even if I have to barricade the damn office." She pulled him out the door, and he didn't resist much. He didn't realize exactly how tired he was until he'd stood up. Now fatigue, and probably hunger, was turning the world fuzzy around the edges.

Francine led him through the offices, cloaked in an almost sepulchral darkness despite the fact that it was probably still light outside. The bare cinder block walls and the concrete ceiling added to the impression. The utilitarian brown carpeting and the empty desks of the editorial staff did little to raise this space out of the ground. The only light left when Francine extinguished the one in

Rick's office was the red glow from the exit sign, above the concrete stairs to the outside.

When they had finally climbed out of the *Observer*'s offices, to the parking lot behind the Kingsbury Building, it was like emerging from a grave. The light caused Rick to squint, even though the sun had just ducked under the horizon.

Francine watched him and said, "Christ almighty, why do you do this to yourself?"

A half-dozen glib answers came to Rick's mind; none reached as far as his lips. He answered only with a vague shrug that evolved into a stretch, then a yawn.

When he lowered his arms, Francine was still staring at him. Her expression was half accusation, half—something else. Rick hoped it wasn't pity. "You win, Francie," he said to her. "I'm out, fresh air, open sky." He walked around in a small circle, opening his arms to the sky. He took a deep breath and said, "No spreadsheets."

To his relief, she laughed. "You know we worry about you—"

"I appreciate it. I just got a little carried away with some of our financial problems. Sometime I swear that we should just introduce our advertisers to National City Bank and skip the middleman. At least this month we did better than the interest we're . . ." Rick noticed Francine's expression. He placed a hand over his heart, beneath the tie he habitually wore. "I swear, out of sight, out of mind." She looked dubious.

"So, are you going to join the rest of us at the fireworks?"

"I really don't care for fireworks." She gave him that look again, and Rick didn't know a way to explain it without it sounding like an excuse. "But what the hell, sure, I'll make an appearance."

In the car, the conversation died. Francine tried to talk to him, but he couldn't bring himself to respond in more than monosyllables. His stomach knotted, tied around an ulcerous memory. His stomach crushed and churning as if it were a sky-blue Plymouth Duster wrapped around the base of a tractor trailer.

At least she's not going to Edgewater. . . .

If he closed his eyes, he could still see it, the inexplicable sight of the tractor trailer's cab, grille shooting down the wrong lane. The endless trailer defining the horizon, rolling across every lane to the left, threshing cars like a divine combine.

He never heard his mother's screams because of the truck's horn.

The truck's grille grew and grew, the Plymouth not driving but falling toward it.

Rick realized he was sweating, and he hoped that Francine didn't notice. He rolled down the window to breathe some fresh air. The sky was dark now, and he could hear the popping of distant fireworks. "Almost there," Francine said hopefully. "We won't miss all of it."

Rick grunted. All he could think of was the dog riding that grille—the chromed dog, leading the hunt for forty tons of bellowing metal.

The truck had almost reached the Plymouth before Dad turned the wheel. Horrified, Rick watched him turn it the wrong way, to the left. The Plymouth cleared the bellowing beast of the truck's cab, and raced directly into the path of the tumbling trailer.

The horn blew by like the cry of judgment as the Plymouth drove into a maelstrom. The trailer rolled over the hood of the Plymouth, throwing Rick into the footwell, slamming his head into the floor of the car. He saw the roof of the car smash inward, crushing the upper bodies of both his parents. When the sounds of tearing metal stopped, all Rick heard was the echoing of the fireworks at Edgewater.

A much louder, and nearer, sound brought Rick back to the present with a vengeance. With the wash of white, and the sound of a violent and immediate explosion, all Rick could think was: *One of those damn flying bombs hit the car.*

Even though he'd been wearing his seat belt, he was

thrown free of the car. It was bizarre, surreal, as if the car around him had simply vanished in a flash of white light. The car couldn't have been traveling too fast because Rick managed to hit with a splash—*splash?*—and roll to a stop at the side of the road with a stunning, but not injurious impact.

He was drenched within seconds, certainly before he had his mind collected enough to realize it was suddenly raining, and raining violently.

He pushed himself up to see a much different sky. It was a sky rolling with clouds that just hadn't been there a moment ago.

There was no sign of Francine, or her car.

CHAPTER 7

RICHARD

RICHARD knelt, placing flowers before a granite monument. The names on the stone were Charles and Catherine Brandon, beloved husband and beloved wife. The stone was a weathered gray everywhere except for the year under Catherine's last name. The carving was shiny and new, glistening like a fresh wound in the stone—despite being over two years old.

A cloying fog had descended, coloring everything beyond ten feet a feverish white. It muted the color of everything else that wasn't immediately before him, as if the world had aged and faded like the stone in front of him.

Richard stood and looked at his hands, thinking of himself as a fresh-cut wound in the rock of the world. The imagery faded before he could mold the idea into anything more precise. Richard let it dissolve into the blank fog in the back of his mind.

Behind him, a car horn blared. "You done yet?" a voice shouted up at him. The voice belonged to the guy delegated to give him a lift to the reading. The fog didn't do anything to mute the edges of his voice. "This place closes in—fuck—if my watch is right, five minutes ago."

Richard sighed and wondered why he'd agreed to a reading, today of all days. It wasn't as if he'd done any new work. He let that thought fade as well. That question opened up the question of why he should do anything, and he didn't have an answer to that one.

He picked up his slim briefcase and walked away from the grave. His head remained lowered, watching his feet for low headstones emerging from the fog. He stepped over a few, managing not to trip on any, and reached asphalt.

The car was only a few feet away, but it was only a shadow through gray haze. Richard wiped his forehead. It came away damp. Ugly weather all around—fog was supposed to be cool, but Richard felt as if he were in a steam bath. It was hard to decide if this was real fog or a misting drizzle the temperature of his own sweat.

He slipped into the passenger seat, feeling sticky and miserable.

"You come here every Fourth?" said the driver. Richard only knew the guy as "Fuzzy," and it was hard to decide if the nickname arose from appearance or his mental state.

"Yeah."

Fuzzy wore a strange hairstyle, a Mohawk of sorts, but instead of being spiked out like most punks, it trailed off into a ponytail that snaked down Fuzzy's back. That, combined with a bushy beard that jutted like a caricature of a Russian revolutionary, made Fuzzy appear a cross between a biker and a guru.

All the leather and jewelry Fuzzy wore weighted the image toward the biker side.

"Birthday or anniversary?" Fuzzy asked him. The transmission made ugly sounds as Fuzzy forced the car into motion. The car made Richard nervous because it was twenty years old—and because it was a Plymouth.

"What?" Richard forced himself to look out the window, at half-observed monuments gliding by within the fog.

"The day people choose to visit a grave, it usually means something. Birthdays, anniversaries—"

"Anniversary." Richard didn't elaborate. He had wheeled his mother here every July for twenty-three years. A constant reminder that Father had died, and they had survived. The past two years he had gone alone.

Somehow, in the act, there seemed some implicit criticism that Richard bore no visible scars from the accident.

Richard had never troubled his mother with the nonvisible scars.

"Sorry I was late," Fuzzy said to him. "If it wasn't for this car burning oil, I would've been able to—"

"Never mind. It's all right." Richard hadn't even noticed he'd been by the grave for a few hours. "Who told you where to find me?"

"Your friend Thomson, the guy who put together the reading."

The same guy who conned Richard into coming and reading his Quinque poems to a bar filled with students, young people who were probably more interested in scatological free verse from Fuzzy than romanticism published by a depressive English professor. They'd want rock and roll, not ballads, something more thorns than roses.

As if reading his mind, Fuzzy reached over and turned on the radio—a piece of equipment that was considerably newer than the rest of the car. Fuzzy found a station right in the midst of playing a new Jim Morrison single, all about Norse mythology and the end of the world. Despite the wintery imagery, the black mood of the song fit Richard as if it were written for him.

The reading was next to Case Western, where he taught, so it shouldn't have taken very long to get there. However, they became irrevocably caught in a traffic snarl on the way to University Circle. It took close to half an hour before the decrepit Plymouth made its way down the hill. In that time, daylight darkened into dusk, and streetlights ignited throwing halos around themselves.

At the bottom of the hill, blue-and-red lights swirled the fog with luminous pastels. The accident causing the tie-up wasn't visible until they were nearly on top of it. First the police cars and the fire engines appeared, as if fading into existence. Then, as the Plymouth inched past the scene, the wreck itself emerged, barely. It was a mass of twisted, steaming metal. The smoke and steam wrapped it in an even denser cloak than the rest of the world. It was impossible to discern exactly what kind of vehicles were involved, or how many.

Richard could not tear his eyes away, even when the Plymouth's open window let in the smell of smoke, burning fuel, hot metal, and the stomach-churning odor of melted rubber.

Everything involved had burned, the wreckage a black shadow in the fog. The shapes were surreal, the vehicles' frames had twisted, warped into near-organic forms towering over the police cars, three times the height of a man.

It looked like something . . .

For the briefest moment, Richard saw the metal wreckage resolve itself into a definite form. He saw a black steed emerging from the cloak of fog, only the front visible, its silvery forehoof about to descend onto a police car. Steam trailed from its nostrils, and its eyes glowed red.

Impossibly, Richard also saw a black rider, armored, raising a sword—

Richard shook his head, and the image disintegrated into its components. Silver forehoof became a rear bumper, steaming nostrils the smoking remains of an exhaust system, the red eyes, streetlight reflecting from shattered taillights.

There was nothing, however, that could account for the rider.

He had been staring at the wreck, unblinking, long enough for his eyes to water. His gaze was abruptly torn away to the blaring of the Plymouth's horn and the squeal of its brakes. The seat belt cut into him as inertia pulled his body toward the dash. Richard turned forward in time to see the rear brake lights of a minivan which seemed only a few feet in front of his face.

The taillight shattered with a soft crunch of metal. The Plymouth stopped moving and it felt as if his heart wanted to slam through his rib cage. He felt the impact jolting every part of his body, even though the collision couldn't have happened at more than two or three miles an hour.

"Shit," Fuzzy said. "Sorry, Prof—hey, what you doing?"

Richard was clawing the seat belt away. The sound of the traffic, the new crop of horns, even the fog, it was becoming too much. "Not far, I'll walk from here." He said it through clenched teeth.

He stumbled out of the car, and into the lane blocked off by the previous accident. He almost ran into a parked ambulance. He pushed away from it, and toward the side of the road, deeper into the fog.

In the fog, Richard managed to get lost fairly quickly. He knew the Case Western Campus itself, and University Circle—but his knowledge of the neighborhood didn't extend up into Little Italy. That was where he assumed he was wandering. He was somewhere around Murray Hill, but he had gotten off the main streets.

He was following a little one-way street. It was paved with red brick, bricks that alternately tried to slide his feet from under him or catch the toe of his shoe and pitch him forward. He had to walk in the street, because the sidewalks were used for illegal parking. Every few cars, he'd pass a little micro-gallery, paintings and ceramics invisible behind the condensation on the window. Of course, nothing was open, so there was nowhere to ask for directions.

At this point, Richard didn't much care. No matter if it made sense or not, the episode in the car had terrified him. He could still feel his heart shuddering in his chest, and the cloak of seeming fog didn't prevent cold shivers from shooting across his arms and back.

He needed to be by himself, despite his promises to Thomson. Thomson probably had good intentions in inviting him, both psychological and artistic. But Richard just wasn't ready for a public audience—not when a simple accident could . . .

Besides, his briefcase was still in Fuzzy's Plymouth. He doubted he could do a coherent reading from memory.

The little street opened up into an intersection that

Richard recognized. The Medical School was just ahead of him; he was going in the right direction. University Circle was just down the street, invisible through the fog—

Richard took a few steps, and the universe exploded.

The sound was a spike through his ears. A hot wet wind threw him back, and a searing white light blinded him. His back slammed into a dumpster with a hollow metallic sound. Rain, violent slicing rain, replaced the fog. Before his hearing and vision recovered, lightning shot out of a black sky, blowing through a building across the intersection from him. The thunder wanted to crack his ribs and shake the fillings loose from his teeth.

A wall of the building flew apart in a flameless explosion. In the space of two seconds, Richard saw lightning slam into the building five times. The last time, the lightning seemed to arrow up from the building and strike the sky in retaliation.

Then it was over. It was nearly half a minute before Richard began hearing thunder from farther away. Longer before he began hearing sirens. Longer still before he stood up to look at the Medical School below him.

At least, that's what Richard thought it was. However, the building that had been torn apart across the street . . .

Richard had never seen it before.

He turned his face toward the sky. Rain struck his face with a force that was almost painful. He had to close his eyes. "Rain?" he whispered, and his mouth filled with water.

A truck roared by him, blaring horns and sirens. He opened his eyes and stumbled back, slipping in the rain. The first in a long train of rescue vehicles and fire trucks shot down the street in front of him.

Richard felt dizzy and disoriented. He looked back up at the complex of buildings across the street from him. It was the Case Western Reserve University Campus. The signs said so, including the shattered sign the hook-and-ladder truck was driving over to reach the major site of the damage.

It was Case Western, but it *wasn't*. The buildings were all wrong.

He took a step across the street when he heard someone yell, "Dr. Brandon! Dr. Brandon, are you all right?"

Richard turned at the sound of his name. He had been working on his dissertation for years. This man, whom he'd never seen before, was addressing him by a title he had yet to earn.

CHAPTER 8

JULIA

JULIA stayed with her brother a long time. Sometimes she talked to him, babbled really. Most of the time she spent just trying to collect her thoughts. She didn't realize how much time she was spending with him until she heard a knock at the door.

The knock startled her, and for a moment she didn't react. It was out of habit. You didn't answer other people's doors for them. It took a moment for reason to catch up and for her to realize that the knock had to be for her.

She stood, cleared her throat, and said, "Come in."

The door opened, and a white-smocked man began backing into the room carrying a tray. Julia stepped around the bed and got the door for the man. "Thanks," he said as he turned around, bearing his tray. He walked around her and began deftly setting up a tray in front of Richard.

Julia watched him, and after a few minutes she asked, "Are you a nurse here?"

He shook his head. In the evening light from the window he looked like a teenager, almost cherubic. "Nah, just a volunteer. The real nurses have better things to do than watch people eat."

"You feed him?"

"Not really," he said. Once the tray was set up, he pulled the plastic wrap off everything, yanked a plastic spoon out of its wrapper, and placed it in Richard's right hand. "He does fairly well by himself, if he likes the food."

She glanced at Richard's face, which seemed as distant as ever. On the tray in front of him was a platter with mashed potatoes, mixed vegetables, and a Styrofoam bowl filled with beef stew. As she watched, the volunteer took Richard's hand, spooned some stew with it, and held it up to Richard's face.

Miraculously, Richard actually moved, as if he suddenly noticed the spoon in front of him. The volunteer let go of Richard's arm and slowly, mechanically, Richard began spooning food into his mouth, eating.

"My God," Julia whispered.

The young man stood, collecting discarded plastic. "You haven't visited before."

Julia shook her head no.

"Well, I'm Vernon," he held out his hand.

"Julia," she said, taking his hand. She kept watching Richard eat. "I'm Richard's sister," she said, feeling obligated to explain her presence here.

Thankfully, he didn't ask why she hadn't visited before. Instead, he noted that she was still staring at Richard. "It is neat, huh? He can feed himself, relieve himself, and he's got little if any impairment of motor function." He let go of her hand and looked at Richard, "Which makes you one of my favorite people here, right?"

Richard didn't react; he just kept on eating.

Julia shook her head. "I don't understand how that's possible."

"Well, it's not like he has some degenerative problem, like Parkinson's or Alzheimer's. None of the people here do. His problem isn't getting worse."

Julia watched him, "I don't see how he can still function."

"Like I said, his motor control's fine, he has all his voluntary motion. Dr. Kavcheck explained it to me that what's wrong is that communication between the pieces of his brain are broken. Things like reason and speech don't make it outside. The basic stuff—his reflexes, coordination, the stuff people do without thinking—all works fine."

She shook her head.

Vernon looked at his watch. "You probably should get going, visiting hours are almost over. If you got any questions, you should probably talk to the doctor."

Julia nodded, and scooped up her things. "When exactly are visiting hours?"

"Every Tuesday and Thursday, from one to eight. You can come any time you want, though, as long as you make an appointment with the Sisters."

Julia looked out the window at the rose-colored sky. "It's eight o'clock?"

Vernon nodded. "I heard you were in here, so I waited. Richard didn't mind, I'm sure."

"Thanks." Julia felt a little flustered, as if everyone knew what was happening but her. Right now she just wanted to rush home and bury her head under a pillow. She headed toward the door, realizing that Dr. Kavcheck was probably gone by now. She would have to talk to him later.

As she opened the door, Vernon mentioned, "Catherine came Sunday mornings, around ten. I'm certain he misses her."

She slipped out without saying anything more.

She had forgotten what day it was until dusk came on her drive home. Then it was hard to ignore the popping of fireworks, always flashing out of the corner of her eye, trying to distract her from the road. She was already as strung out as hell, and after a few really loud explosions startled her, she pulled the car to the side of the road and tried to calm herself.

July Fourth, of all the twisted ironies. The anniversary of the accident that had injured Richard. She grabbed her purse from the passenger seat before she realized that she had run out of Kleenex. She tossed it back in frustration. When she did, she noticed a yellowed notebook that had been sitting on the seat under her purse.

It was Richard's, the one he had drawn in. She must have grabbed it without realizing what she was doing. She sighed, wiping her eyes. It wasn't as if Richard would miss it. She would bring it back when she visited him this weekend.

It wasn't until that moment she realized that there had never been a question in her mind that she would make a Sunday appointment. After she had idled on the side of the road for about fifteen minutes, she felt collected enough to drive home.

The fireworks finally subsided.

Julia couldn't sleep when she got home.

She ended up lying on the couch, her mom's TV flickering a rerun of Joan Rivers on the *Tonight Show*. The sound was muted, and most of the other lights in the house were out. The phosphor light gave a blue washed-out appearance to the living room; piles of cardboard boxes cast ink-black shadows.

Julia's thoughts were never more than two minutes away from her mother, or Richard. She would try to distract her thoughts, mentally force herself to think of the subjects she was supposed to be taking this semester. She tried to review her last art history class in her head, but her thoughts kept drifting from Titian to Richard's scribbles.

She wanted to close her eyes and fall into an exhausted slumber, but the questions kept her awake. It had been bad enough when the thoughts that kept her awake were memories. Thinking about Mom—making faces as she sat on the living room floor grading papers, laughing politely at one of her six-year-old daughter's stupid elephant jokes, burning her one attempt at a Thanksgiving turkey—it was painful. But Julia could tell herself that it was normal. She had just lost a good chunk of her life. . . .

Staying awake, wondering what Mom had hidden from her, wasn't normal. Loss was one thing; she shouldn't have these confused feelings of guilt, anger and confusion as well. She didn't deserve it, and she couldn't help feeling that her mom didn't deserve it.

It wasn't right to lie here and wonder how many of the toys she had boxed upstairs were really hers, and how many used to be Richard's. Were there pictures anywhere . . . if there were, where had they gone?

Why didn't Mom tell her. . . ?

That was probably the easiest question to answer. By the time Julia would have been old enough to understand that she had an older brother, Mom would have fallen into one of her routines. She wouldn't have seen any reason to disrupt her daughter's life with the news. It would have been easier just not to deal with it. Just like she never dealt with Dad's death, never dealt with death, period.

Julia felt herself drifting into anger again, at the mess her mom left behind her. She sat up and walked into the kitchen and pulled a beer out of the fridge. She needed one.

She stood in front of the open refrigerator, holding the cold bottle of Miller to her forehead. The July heat wasn't helping her mood, and she was tempted to turn on the air-conditioning, and electric bills be damned.

She sighed and shut the refrigerator.

As she did, her gaze fell on the kitchen table while it was illuminated by a slice of the refrigerator's light. The kitchen table was half covered by boxes where she'd been packing her mom's dishes. The other half was the clear space where Julia ate. The clear half held a few dirty dishes and the remains of a bagel, her purse and keys, and Richard's notebook.

She felt overcome by curiosity. She'd been avoiding any thoughts about it, but now, looking at it, she decided that she wasn't going to get any sleep tonight anyway.

After opening the beer, she turned on the garish overhead lamp above the kitchen table and slid into the one clear chair. She took a swig from the bottle and opened her brother's notebook.

To her surprise, the first few pages of the notebook weren't the aggressive chiaroscuro dragons and monsters she had looked at in Richard's room. The notebook began with several blocky, handwritten pages, and for a moment Julia though that somehow Richard had managed to write something through his injury.

The surprise was short-lived.

Richard had dated the pages he had written on, and the dates were all before the accident. The notebook was older than Julia was. And somehow, the small handwritten dates gave a weight to the notebook. It was a relic, the only thing Julia could point to and say, *This was my brother's when he was well.*

She ran her hands across the yellowed page, thinking that her brother couldn't have been much older than ten or twelve when he had written this. At first she thought that it might be homework of his, never finished. Then she began to decipher the blocky juvenile handwriting, and found in it something very different.

"Everyone in Quinque knows," began the first page, *"that everything outside their land is nothing but dream. The truly wise know that Quinque itself is also a dream."*

CHAPTER 9

ROCKY

"DON'T panic," Rocky said to himself. "When people panic, they die."

Rain blasted through the remains of what should have been his apartment building. Water sluiced down his face and neck. The chill did nothing to ease the heat of his pulse, or the bite of adrenaline that tugged at his muscles.

The fuzz of alcohol faded from his body, leaving little behind except an inability to fully control his shivering. Lightning shot over his head, natural artillery fire that pressed Rocky's back to the granite blocks defining the Gothic door frame.

The flash illuminated something in the shadows of the ruined building. For a moment a pile of burned out wreckage took on the appearance of a red-eyed horse rearing out of a hole in the floor. It was only an instant's image. When the lightning dazzle faded from his eyes, Rocky could only see a pile of burned lumber, the eye simply some shiny debris.

Rocky walked over to the pile to reassure himself.

Nothing but broken timbers piled on the floor. On the linoleum remnants of the floor, a red object glistened in a puddle. He bent, allowing a new sluice of water down his neck and the back of his pants.

It was a toy, a small cartoonish figure, a dog or maybe a wolf. It was only an inch or so long, and lay on its side. The red plastic, shiny with water, made the toy appear brand new.

He picked it up and turned it over.

"Ugh—" Rocky dropped it when he saw the other side

of the plastic dog. The half that had been on the floor was a charred mass melted into something nearly unrecognizable. The dog was a casualty of the fire that had wrecked the building.

He stood up and walked out of the building, wondering what child had owned that dog.

I must have blacked out, really *blacked out.*

He stepped out of the building and rechecked the address. He wasn't mistaken. This had been his home at one point.

"How long ago?"

It was obvious from the condition of the building that it had been at least a few months. Possibly years. He'd taken a fall, maybe even been hit by lightning with the roaring flash that zapped him. He could have had a good part of his memory scrambled if—

Good Lord, don't let my head be scrambled. It's all I got.

"Face it, the drinking's caught up with you."

They should have fired him; suspension without pay was too light a sentence. Rocky rubbed his head, squeezing water fruitlessly out of his hair. Hell, maybe they *had* fired him, if there was a huge gap in his memory—

Rocky walked into the doorway of an intact, if run-down, building and fished his wallet out of his pocket. He didn't carry his badge or police ID there, but he had a lot of business-related cards in it, card keys to various departments, a law enforcement ID card, check card for the Credit Union. . . .

Rocky stopped rifling his wallet. Everything was still there, leaking water through his fingers. That wasn't the problem. The problem was that this was *exactly* the same wallet he had left the bar with. Everything down to the picture on his driver's license and the amount of cash he carried.

Rocky shoved everything back into his wallet and pulled out his keys. He stared at the keys in his hand.

There were keys to a building that he had just walked through the ruins of.

I'm wearing the same clothes, have the same wallet—same everything*—down to my cash.*

It couldn't be amnesia. Not unless he'd been wandering with the same clothes for long enough for his apartment to burn down.

Rocky felt his pulse racing and did some breathing exercises to calm himself. He pushed out into the rain and began walking down the street. He needed to think, but his thoughts made no sense. *Can I rule out a head injury? Can I rely on my memory of what I wore or carried in my pockets?*

"Can I rule out that I've gone nuts?"

After a few blocks, Rocky realized he was retracing his steps to the bar out of habit. After a few more, he decided he didn't care. He needed a drink. He reached the corner and received another disorienting blow.

His bar had been replaced by a liquor store. It was the same storefront, but instead of the brass bar and green curtains marking the windows, the windows were covered by rolling steel barricades. Instead of the green sign reading "Fagan's," above the door there was a generic urine-yellow sign announcing "Beer, Wine."

But it was the same granite scrollwork marking the top of the facade. The same, but somewhat dirtier and poorly maintained. Rocky walked up to the door and put his hand on the stone that marked the doorway. The stonework was plain, but recognizable despite the darkness and pouring rain.

Fagan's was gone.

He wasn't just disoriented or lost. The world had undergone some fundamental change. Rocky leaned against the metal gate locking off the door. The street was the same, but different, more run down. The cars were odd looking to him, with an almost European smallness to them. Even the streetlights had altered to a dirty yellow sodium. The color made everything look like the inside of a urinal.

"Time," Rocky whispered. "It'd take years for all this to happen. . . ."

But he was wearing the same clothes, carrying the same wallet, the same keys. How could he explain that—

There was a bus shelter up the street. Next to it he saw a newspaper machine. Rocky ran to it; one of his questions, at least, could be answered.

When he got to the front of the white, odd-shaped dispenser, he muttered, "What the fuck is *USA Today?*" Whatever it was, it was a dime cheaper than he remembered his own paper costing. He emptied quarters into the machine and grabbed a paper, retreating to the dry oasis of the bus shelter.

He sat down on the graffiti-swathed bench and opened the half-soaked paper and looked at the date.

July 4th, the same year he remembered.

Rocky read the paper, barely blinking. He tore through it, going from article to article in growing disbelief. He read, despite the headache bequeathed him by the small print and the sodium lights. When he was done, the rain had eased somewhat and the paper was a pile of damp shreds at his feet.

Either he had gone completely insane, or he was no longer in the world he remembered. Someone named Clinton was President. The guy Reagan had defeated in the '76 election was some sort of ambassador trying to negotiate some sort of peace in Eastern Europe, in the Balkans. There wasn't a Soviet Union, there was no invasion of Iran, and Iraq wasn't even our ally anymore. There was all sorts of news about computers that Rocky thought would only matter to the government agencies that could buy the things. . . .

Everything, every single story, was twisted. It couldn't be real.

Could it?

Rocky stood up, treading across the remains of the alien newspaper. The disorientation he felt now had nothing to do with intoxication. He looked out the glass of the shelter, through the rippling water. The world beyond looked distorted, unreal.

"What do I do now? If the world has changed, do I still exist in it?"

It was an insane question, but it was a question that gained weight because of the just-short-of-familiar landscape he'd been dropped into. How would he find himself, if he did exist in this twisted landscape?

He eventually found an open pizzeria with a pay phone inside. He'd passed a few phones on the street, but no booths, and no phone books at any of them. It was another surreal aspect of this world, to go along with the strange newspaper stories, and all the small Japanese cars on the streets.

The phone was wedged in the back of the greasy little place. It smelled like stale cheese back here, but there was a set of phone books for the Cleveland area. There was an unfamiliar logo on the white pages, "Ameritech" next to the familiar Ma Bell logo, and the phone itself was labeled "GTE."

Rocky barely noticed. It was already clear he was living in a *Twilight Zone* episode. He spilled four quarters on top of the phone, and spent the first two on numbers he knew.

By now he was convinced that any numbers *he* remembered would be useless. But he had to check them out. He tried the desk phone of the Morals Division at the Department—the number didn't exist. He tried Captain Gallagher's home phone, the man who'd suspended him, and got the voice of a high-strung teenager cussing him out and telling him how late it was, and no, there was no Gallagher there.

He raised the third quarter to the slot and realized he was out of places to call.

He finally opened the phone book. He held his breath until he found a listing for a Richard Brandon, a *Doctor* Brandon. However, it was the only listing of his name in the phone book. Rocky called the number.

It rang three times and then he heard a voice say, "You've reached the home of Richard Brandon—"

"Hell—" Rocky began, but he stopped cold, listening.

"I'm not home right now, please leave a message after the beep. . . ."

It was his own voice he was listening to.

Dr. Richard Brandon lived in Cleveland Heights, the opposite side of the city from Rocky. He had little hope of catching a bus this late on a holiday, and God only knew where the bus lines actually went in this twisted world, so Rocky used his last quarter to call a cab.

He only had fifty bucks on him, and he hoped that the price of the newspaper meant that things were cheaper here. He also hoped his folding money was still good. Both hopes were fulfilled, and a surreally white taxi—*Americab?* Rocky'd never heard of it—dropped him off in front of Dr. Brandon's apartment building, leaving him with more money than he expected, even after a tip.

Dr. Brandon lived in a residential neighborhood. Trees flanked the streets and shaded the brick facades of the apartments. It reminded Rocky of Lakewood, if Lakewood hadn't suffered the same fate as his little slice of Cleveland had. The streetlights here were white mercury.

The rain had receded to a more normal volume, and the trees seemed to absorb some of the storm's violence.

So, is this me?

He ran a hand over his head, squeezing water out of his hair. The weather seemed to have been even uglier in this part of town. The block across the street was blacked out, and branches had been scattered everywhere by the wind.

One car, an organically curved Ford, had a window smashed. Rocky was passing it when he noticed something.

No branches?

Storm-tossed leaves and branches were everywhere; the other cars parked on the street were covered with the crap. This Ford wasn't. The Ford was also parked directly in front of Brandon's address.

Rocky looked in the broken window and around the dash. It looked like someone had torn out the bottom of the dash and the steering column in something of a panic. Wires dangled everywhere. Rocky couldn't see what was rigged in the rat's nest down there, but it was obvious that someone had hot-wired the car and abandoned it.

If the wiring wasn't enough, cubed safety glass was scattered everywhere inside, except for the driver's seat. Someone had brushed the seat off.

"So what do I do? Call it in?" It seemed sort of pointless, considering everything else that was happening.

Rocky leaned out of the window, and stopped when he noticed something sticking out from under the driver's seat. He leaned back in and pulled the object out—

It was a phone book.

Rocky dropped it and leaned out to look at Dr. Brandon's building. "I have a weird feeling about this," he whispered.

He walked up to the front door, watching the shadows, looking for something. He didn't know what. In the lobby was a rank of mailboxes. Dr. Brandon's had been jimmied open. The door to the stairs was ajar and showed signs of having its lock forced.

Dr. Brandon lived in apartment four, up the stairs. Rocky flexed his hands and wished he had his gun with him.

Rocky slowly began climbing the stairs, feeling the full weight of the clothes drying on his body. He tried to step lightly, but he could hear his shoes squish on the treads.

When he reached the third landing, he wasn't surprised to see the door to apartment four hanging open a few inches. It had been forced. Rocky could see obvious splintering along the doorjamb, facing inside the room.

He inched toward the door, listening. He heard a muted television from the apartment across the hall, and the wind whipping the rain across the windows, but not much else. If there was anyone still in Dr. Brandon's apartment, they were being quiet about it.

He really wished he had a gun with him.

When he was next to the hinges, he began levering the door inside with his foot. That way most of his body had the wall for cover. The living room and the front hallway opened up in front of him. He saw a television and a stereo. Above a white couch was a poster hanging on the wall showing a black and white starscape in which Albert Einstein was playing craps.

There were books piled on the coffee table, a tumbled pile of magazines next to the couch, but nothing to indicate the place had been tossed, or robbed.

Rocky slipped through the door and into the living room. He had just stepped all the way in when he heard the door shut behind him. He spun around.

The man had been hiding behind the now-shut door. He leaned on the door with his left hand, and in his right he held a nine-millimeter pistol. He wore a leather jacket, jeans, and a pair of motorcycle boots.

"Dr. Brandon, I presume . . ." he began to say. His words tumbled to a stop.

The man had Rocky's face, he had long hair and a goatee, but it was still Rocky's face. Rocky slowly shook his head. He didn't know whether he was responding to the question itself, or to a reality that had just frayed beyond breaking.

"I don't fucking believe it," said the man with the gun.

CHAPTER 10

RICHIE

"I don't fucking believe it," Richie repeated, staring at a strung-out version of himself. He lowered the gun and openly stared. There was a shitload of differences between expecting to see another Richard Brandon and actually seeing yourself in another set of skin.

For a long time the only sound was the rumble of the storming night, and the television next door.

"Who are you?" the other man finally asked Richie.

Richie laughed. "It's nice to know that I've still kept my sense of humor."

"You're not Dr. Brandon. You broke in here."

"What are you, then? The police?"

The other looked at Richie a moment. There was a silent accusation in his expression, the kind of look cops always gave Richie.

"Fuck," Richie whispered as the other walked into the living room and collapsed on the couch under the Einstein poster.

Richie pocketed the gun and said, "So you *ain't* the doctor?"

The other shook his head. "No. I need a drink." He looked up at Richie and asked, "Where'd you come from?"

Richie decided that this guy might not appreciate the whole Rico scenario, so he just said, "East 119th."

"Been here a while?"

Richie nodded. "Just for the record, what's your name?"

"Richard Brandon."

Fine, my Delphic twin, just smack me with the obvious. "No 'doctor?' "

"No 'doctor.' "

Richie shook his head, "What a fucking coincidence. What a fucking-A coincidence. Christ." He paced back and forth in front of the couch. "And that ain't you mugging for the camera up on the mantel?"

The other leaned back and rubbed his temples. "What?"

"This!" Richie grabbed the picture from mantle above the too-shallow apartment fireplace. It was a gold frame with a family picture in it. Someone's family. Not Richie's.

But there he was, Richard Brandon, sitting in the midst of these alien people at a picnic table, cheesing for the camera. Richie squeezed until the glass cracked. "Who the fuck are these people?"

He tossed the picture onto the couch and started breathing, sucking in air, trying to calm himself. He'd been staring at that picture off and on ever since he'd jimmied the door to this place.

Richie sat down at the end of the coffee table. "Is that you?"

From behind him came the other's voice, like a tape recording of himself, not quite real. "No."

"Sure as hell ain't me. . . ." Richie shook his head. "And those people in the picture?"

"Damn it," the other said. "I don't know. I'm as much in the dark as you are."

Richie nodded and gripped the butt of the gun in his pocket. "Yeah, of course. Fucking twins." He looked at the other. The similarity wasn't exact. The other was clean-shaven and had what almost amounted to a crewcut. The other also looked a little beefier, a lot of muscle there, slowly going to fat.

The other also looked hungover.

"So much for lightning-induced amnesia," Richie said.

The other was staring at the picture Richie had tossed to him. Richie could almost see the tendons vibrate as he gripped the frame. If anything, the other seemed more disturbed by the picture than Richie had been.

"Fucking triplets," Richie said.

"What's going on?" the other said. There was a slight tremor in his voice and Richie felt for him.

If he's been through anything remotely as weird as I've been through . . . "I don't know, Richie. I wish I did."

"Don't call me Richie," the other said, dropping the picture on the table.

Richie shrugged. "Okay, *you* call me 'Richie.' What do I call you?"

There was a pause and Richie could see several possible responses play across the other's face. *If he says "sir," I'll pistol-whip the bastard.*

"Rocky," the other said. "Everyone calls me Rocky."

"Funny, you don't look Italian."

"Huh?"

Richie shook his head, laughing. "You know, Sylvester Stallone, *Rocky,* 'Yo, Adrian?' "

"Sylvester who?"

Richie choked off the laughter and looked at Rocky for long enough to realize that he wasn't kidding. "Where the hell are you from?"

"Not here," Rocky said.

Richie stared at the guy for a long moment, then he stood up and started pacing again. "Calm down, Richie," he muttered to himself. "Things are weirding out again. . . ."

He realized that his right hand had a death grip on the Beretta. He loosened his hold and withdrew his hand from his pocket.

After a while, Rocky said, "Neither are you, right?"

"Yes. No. I don't have a fucking clue." Richie turned to Rocky, "And I'd have to be a genius if I could give you an answer. A white flash, and the world changed."

"You've seen a newspaper?"

Richie was pacing violently now. "Of course I've seen a damn paper. The first thing I checked after someone changed the architecture. Christ, it's still July Fourth—but someone changed the cars, the buildings—"

"This history," Rocky whispered.

"—and listed me in the phone book as a fucking psychiatrist!"

"Maybe *Doctor* Brandon might have an explanation."

"And maybe he's wandering some other Cleveland wondering why all these Colombians are pissed at him." Richie sighed and said, "You're right about that drink." Richie got up and walked to the kitchen. *Could also use something to eat.*

Richie hadn't eaten since dinner, a few hours before the flash. It felt as if it had been much longer, both in body and in mind.

From the living room he heard Rocky say, "What's with the gun? You're going to question the doctor at gunpoint?"

Richie fished two cans of Foster's out of the fridge and yelled back, "You got a better idea? He may be responsible for what's happened to us." The fridge itself seemed to be devoid of much else, but Richie did find a little paper container of Chinese takeout.

He took the container and felt a little irrational fear. He remembered all the tales he'd read where the hero became trapped in some strange land for eating the wrong thing. Richie chucked a bit at the trepidation. Whatever had happened, he was pretty sure he hadn't entered the Underworld, or Fairyland.

Richie returned and tossed a can to Rocky. Rocky glanced at the can approvingly, then opened it. "You don't know he's responsible," Rocky told him.

"No, just another hell of a coincidence. Better safe than sorry, especially with all the weird shit going down. . . ." Richie drained a good part of the can, and was too keyed up to tell if the beer steadied him. He paced a little slower, though. "Damn, look at his bookshelves—"

On the wall, next to the TV, there were ranks of books. Richie read off random titles. "*Quantum Reality, Other*

Worlds, In Search of Schrödinger's Cat . . ." Richie took another pull from the can and walked over to the bookshelf.

"The search of Schrödinger's *what?*" Rocky said from the couch.

"It's a physics reference. You never heard of it?" Christ, it was eerie, so much of the shelf mirrored Richie's own reading back in high school.

"Uh-uh." Rocky was shaking his head. Richie felt odd. It was disturbing whenever the other missed one of his references,

Richie turned back to the shelf. "Well, it's sort of a riddle, like the tree falling in a forest." *Something the Sphinx might ask.* Richie's fingers traced along the spines, all creased in the paperbound volumes. Titles like *New Realities, The Mind of the Quantum.* "Anyway, the idea is that everything subatomic is a wave, a probability that only falls into place when someone observes the wave. So you lock a cat in a box with a little device that pumps out cyanide—"

"You got a dead cat," Rocky said. *He thinks like a cop.*

"Well, the device only goes off if a particle decays. And there is only a fifty-percent chance that it goes off before the box is opened."

"So?"

"So," Richie said, "according to the probability waves, the cat ain't alive or dead until someone opens up the lid and looks at it."

"Why's that?"

"The wave doesn't collapse until someone observes it."

"And the cat doesn't count?"

Richie opened his mouth and closed it. He found the idea disturbing, as if he suddenly identified with the cat. "Anyway, ain't all this kind of weird stuff for a psychologist to be reading?"

"Dr. Brandon's a psychologist?"

Richie nodded and trailed his finger down the shelf to the less credible-looking publications, *The Universe's I, The Worlds Inside Us, The Past Within*. . . .

"His sheepskin's in the den over there," Richie told him. "What the hell is this, past-life regression?"

"So what are we? Dead cats?"

Richie turned and looked at Rocky. He made the disturbing realization that he had trouble reading the expression on a face so like his own. Was Rocky saying things like that just to rattle him? "Fuck if I know." He looked at the lithograph hanging above the couch, Einstein shooting craps with the universe. "Half dead, maybe?"

"Funny," Rocky said.

Yeah, I've noticed we can't stop laughing. "How many of us you think there are?"

"At least three," Rocky said.

Richie was annoyed with his twin's simplistic logic. "Not even going to venture an opinion?"

Rocky shook his head. "You have some source of information I don't? How long you been here?"

"His apartment?" Richie shrugged and glanced at his watch. "An hour, about."

"Okay, let me think about this." Rocky leaned forward and pressed the can against his forehead. "What time is it?"

"Eleven forty-five." Richie looked around for a clock in the room, just to double-check. He saw the time displayed on an odd-looking VCR on top of the television. "Yeah, quarter to." He bent over to look at the TV and the VCR more closely.

"How long ago did this all happen?"

"The white flash and all?"

"Yeah."

"Ten thirty, maybe a little earlier?"

"Same as me. If there's others, they probably appeared at the same time."

Richie nodded, prodding the VCR. It looked damn clunky, the tape format seemed way too big. "Looks like some cheap piece of foreign—" Apparently one of the tiny buttons did more than it was labeled for, because the TV blared into life when Richie's hand brushed against it.

"*. . . Report from scene of the fire!*" some woman

yelled from a speaker right next to Richie. He stumbled back from it in surprise as a full-color picture of a burning building appeared on the screen.

"What the hell are you doing?" Rocky said, raising his voice over the noise.

"Accident," Richie said as he started manically searching for the off switch or the volume control.

"This was the scene earlier tonight at the Case Western Reserve University Campus, where a lab building erupted into flames."

"There you are," Richie said, as he found the volume control. "Who're these buttons for? Munchkins—"

"Shhh—"

"What?" Richie turned to see Rocky leaning forward in interest.

"Did you see it?" Rocky asked.

Richie turned to look at the screen. Some reporter standing in the rain in front of the fire trucks.

"—caused by multiple lightning hits, though both fire and police authorities say that the fire itself is under investigation. We have no word on any injuries due to the fire. Fortunately, the building was apparently empty for the holiday, though rescue workers are combing the building behind me—"

Richie turned to face Rocky, "What is it?"

"I saw something. . . ."

On the television the scene had changed again, "In a bizarre twist, a psychology professor, Dr. Richard Brandon, was admitted to Metro General under police custody shortly after the building behind me burst into flames."

On the screen in front of them was a picture of their face, Dr. Brandon's face, apparently from the university.

"The police have made it clear that Dr. Brandon is not suspected of any crime, nor does his admission have anything to do with the fire that's scarred the campus where he worked."

"Jesus Christ, what's going on?" Richie said.

"I don't know, but Dr. Brandon's at Metro General."

Richie nodded.

"Maybe we should pay him a visit?"

Richie nodded again. He turned off the TV just as it was saying, "This has been a special report."

Rocky headed for the door. Richie followed him, feeling an unearthly disconnection from what was going on, as if the entire world could wink out on him, just like he'd turned off the TV.

When they reached the door, he asked Rocky, "What did you see?"

Rocky shook his head. "Nothing."

Richie grabbed his shoulder. "Damn it, what did you see?"

Rocky looked at him, eyes red and staring. "A horseman. I saw a horseman in the flames." He shrugged out from Richie's hand and started down the stairs.

How much has the world changed? Richie asked himself as he followed his twin down the stairs.

CHAPTER 11

RICHARD

"DR. Brandon?" The man came toward Richard out of the rain.

Richard was still half blind and half deaf from the violent demise of the unknown building below him. He wasn't sure if he heard right. "Doctor?" he said, repeating the misapplied title, his own voice inaudible beneath the thunder still roaring in his ears.

"Thank God you weren't in there," said the concerned stranger. Richard still could not identify the man, even though he was far from average in appearance and was addressing him like an old acquaintance, at the very least one of his students. The man was black, over six feet tall, and extremely dark—so much darker than most Americans that Richard immediately thought of him as a foreign student, despite the complete lack of an accent.

The man placed a hand on Richard's shoulder. The motion opened the raincoat the man wore, allowing Richard to see a fresh cast on the man's right arm.

"I was half-convinced you might have still been in the tank there—" The man seemed to notice Richard looking at the cast. "Oh, yeah, that's the reason I didn't show up yesterday."

"Oh," Richard said, as if that explained everything.

Inside, Richard felt as if some vital portion of reality were draining away, as if he were an hourglass, and the world was the sand slipping through him. . . .

More fire trucks blared by. The building itself, the one claimed by the lightning, was beginning to toss flames out at the pounding rain. Fire rolled out of the windows on the ground floor. The firefighters were barely silhouettes at this distance. Part of the roof collapsed, its sound absorbed by sirens, rain and thunder.

"You thought *I* was in *there?*"

"Come on, Doc. Let's get you inside." The man tugged at his shoulder. Richard couldn't think of anything else he could do, so he followed.

They walked toward the campus, on the side of the street opposite the fire. *The explosion rattled me, that's all. In a moment I'll remember this guy.* Richard kept his head bowed against the rain, and kept the burning building in the corner of his vision as they passed the ranks of fire engines.

Richard turned to the man accompanying him and said, "Please forgive me, I'm somewhat rattled. But—"

"It's okay, Doc, I underst—"

"—who are you?" Richard finished.

The man stopped walking, the expression of concern deepening on his face. "Huh, Dr. Brandon? It's John, John Waters."

"John Waters." Richard slowly repeated the unfamiliar name. "Are you involved with the reading?"

"Reading?"

"Yes. There was an accident, and I—" He was interrupted by a shuddering explosion. The roar wasn't comparable to the lightning hit, but it was enough to force attention to it over the noise of the storm. Richard turned to face the building.

The entire right wall of the structure was collapsing in a rippling orange fire and a billow of red sparks. The sparks boiled and tossed in the air, defying the storm. The flames themselves shredded into a hundred ribbons as the remnants of the wall slammed into the parking lot next to the building. Smoke erupted, billowing with the sparks, as the wall seemed to melt into the damp asphalt. Firemen retreated from the collapse as another ball of fire erupted from the ground level, tearing itself to ribbons in the rain.

The smoke, sparks, and flames seemed to wrap themselves around a dark figure, as if a horseman were driving his steed out of the holocaust. Richard could almost hear the hooves clatter on the asphalt. For a moment he could see an equestrian shadow rip a hole in the night, and then the sight was swallowed by the rain.

"My God, did you see that?" Richard whispered.

John Waters tugged at his shoulder and said, "Inside, Doc, you'll feel better."

Richard allowed Waters to lead him to an unfamiliar building of Case Western. Richard wasn't sure if the building was unfamiliar because he'd never had cause to enter the Medical School, or if it was because something fundamental in the universe had altered.

Waters set him at a Formica table in a small cinder-block room where one entire wall was formed by vending machines. The remaining walls served as bulletin boards, flyers breeding beyond the edges of the small corkboard area designated for them.

As Waters went to a coffee machine, Richard could almost convince himself that nothing was wrong, that the subliminal strangeness was disorientation from the explosion.

He glanced up at a clock set higher than most of the flyers. It said the time was eleven oh-five. As he watched, the minute hand slammed into oh-six with an axlike thunk.

Waters set a cup of coffee in front of him. "You all right, Doc? Should we get you to a hospital?"

"I'm just a little lost." Richard wrapped his hands around the Styrofoam cup, letting the heat warm his rain-chilled hands. It took him a moment to realize what the cup was made out of. "Styrofoam?"

"Huh?" Waters sat down across the table from him, carefully removing another cup from the hand at the end of his cast.

"Styrofoam?" Richard repeated. "it's been banned for nearly ten years . . ."

"Doc?"

". . . during Carter's second term."

"Oh, fuck." There was a grave sound to Water's voice.

Richard looked up and saw Water's face go slack. It looked as if he had just told the man someone had died. It was the first indication from the man that he sensed the same wrongness that Richard did.

"Something's wrong here," Richard said.

"You were in the tank, weren't you? You went in alone and something went wrong?"

"What tank? What are you talking about?"

Waters took a deep breath. "What's your name?"

"Richard Brandon, you know—"

"What do you do for a living?"

"Right now? I teach undergraduate English here at Case." Richard did not like how uncertain his own voice sounded at the question. He rubbed his head, "You're one of my students, aren't you?"

"Sort of. Who's the President of the United States?"

"Paul Simon."

Waters shook his head. "Oh, God. You really did it to yourself this time."

"What?" Richard felt his hands burn, and he jumped up. He'd crushed the cup he was holding, spilling hot coffee across his side of the table. He sucked at the meat of his right hand, where the scalding was the worst.

Waters stood up. "Please, calm down, Dr. Brandon. You're disoriented right now. I think I know what happened to you, but it may be hard to listen to— Are you all right?"

Richard nodded, still sucking on his reddening hand.

"This may be hard for you, but what you remember right now isn't quite right."

Richard removed his hand. "What do you mean, 'Isn't quite right'?"

"I mean just that, I think you've rewritten your own past. Sit down, I know this isn't easy."

Richard nodded slowly and slipped into a seat that wasn't splattered by coffee.

"The Dr. Brandon I know, the man I work for, is not an English professor."

"He's not?" Richard said.

Waters shook his head and sat again. "I'm sorry, no, he isn't. He teaches psychology here. In the building that exploded."

Richard swallowed. Somehow the connection to the burning building made the claim seem much more plausible. "What's the 'tank' you keep referring to?"

"Sensory deprivation tank, in the basement of that building. Dr. Brandon was experimenting with it, as an aid to self-hypnosis. I was helping him, *you,* because it's not a good idea to use the tank without supervision. You were scheduled to go in last night, but I got involved in a three-car accident on Euclid." Waters waved his cast.

Richard remembered Waters' earlier comments about the tank. "And you think I went in anyway?"

Waters nodded. "I couldn't reach you after I got out of the hospital. You wouldn't answer the phone or your beeper. And you've been positively obsessive about these sessions lately, I didn't think you'd wait."

"So why I don't remember any of this?"

"What you were doing—and forgive me if I don't completely understand it, you weren't always forthcoming about it—was trying to perceive alternate realities."

"What?"

"Have you heard of past-life regression?"

Richard nodded.

"What you were doing was like that, but not quite. You use a lot of quantum metaphysics to justify what you were doing, but—" Waters took a deep breath and started over. "What you did was induce a hypnotic trance, and mentally take yourself back to a key event in your life, and alter that one thing, then you'd take yourself to the present to see what had changed."

"What are you saying?"

"Dr. Brandon was regularly living the lives of four different versions of himself. I think you're living one right now."

"You mean my entire life," Richard stood up, "my

entire existence is some fiction dreamed up by some dissatisfied psychologist!"

Waters stood up and placed his good hand on Richard's shoulder. "Dr. Brandon believed that those lives had an independent existence, real, not fictional."

Richard shrugged out from under Waters' hand and walked away from the table. "That is crazy! This whole situation is crazy!"

"Look, I understand that—"

"You *understand?* Is anyone telling you your life is a fantasy?"

"Do you want me to get you a newspaper?"

"What?" Richard turned around.

"A newspaper. Your life isn't the only thing that's different."

"Like what?"

"Name all the presidents since Johnson."

"Are you kidding?"

"No, name them."

Richard shook his head, the hourglass feeling was back. The uncertainty was numbing. "Okay, Johnson, Nixon, Agnew, Reagan, Carter, Dole, Simon."

Waters was shaking his head. "Johnson, Nixon, *Ford, Carter, Reagan, Bush, Clinton.*"

"Who the fuck is Clinton?"

"The President, Dr. Brandon. Bill Clinton is the President—" Waters was interrupted by a beeping. He pulled something out of his pocket. "Who's calling me now?"

Waters held up his hand and said, "Let me go to a pay phone and check this out. Stay here, okay?"

Richard nodded and leaned against the wall. All his strength left him. Thomson, his mother, the fog by the graveyard—could that all really be a delusion? Some manufactured past? Why would he inflict that life on himself, if he'd had a choice?

Richard felt the familiar tug of guilt. It was the same one he got whenever he resented his mother for the endless care she required. The same tug he got at her funeral, when he finally felt free to have his own life. It was the guilt that prevented him from doing anything of the kind.

Was all that, what he felt now, self-inflicted? What was he supposed to do? What was he supposed to think? What happened to his life if he opened up an almanac and found an unfamiliar list of presidents?

How long ago did his life diverge from Dr. Brandon's?

Waters returned after a short while. He wore an astonished expression, and he was shaking his head slowly. "My God," he said. "What the hell's going on here?"

Richard's chest tightened as he looked at Waters. In a few brief minutes the man's attitude had gone from concerned self-assurance to a state of apparent confusion approaching Richard's own.

"What's the matter?"

Waters rubbed the side of his face with his good hand. "That was a friend, a classmate. Told her to call if she heard any word about Dr. Brandon."

"Me?"

Waters looked into his eyes, as if looking for something. "I don't know anymore— I think we have to get to the Metro Health Center."

"We're right next to a hospital—"

Waters walked around to grab Richard's arm again. "No, that's where he is."

"*Who* is?"

"It's been on the TV. The news says the police brought Doctor Richard Brandon to the Metro Health Center shortly after the explosion."

"But I'm here—"

"Exactly."

CHAPTER 12

RICK

RICK decided, sometime after eleven, that he was undergoing the worst experience in his life since he'd quit the *Cleveland Press*. He kept telling himself that the white flash, the explosion, and his collision with the ground all represented some sort of automobile accident. But, from the questions the police asked him, it was beginning to look more and more as if that "accident" was something else entirely.

It might have been better if he had been seriously injured when he was thrown clear of Francine's car. If he *had* been thrown clear. Then he wouldn't have to deal with the police and their questions.

Then he wouldn't have to deal with his own questions.

"Let's go over this again." The man's name was Kavcheck. He'd seem pleasant enough if he weren't in charge of all the damn questions. Detective Kavcheck was tall, thin, and bald, and wore a jet-black mustache too large for his face. He'd been talking to Rick for hours, it seemed. Long enough for Rick's clothes to dry.

Rick sighed and rubbed the edge of his temple, along the edge of the gauze bandage the doctors had put there. It had been the only real damage. But, like all scalp wounds, it had leaked blood all over, spattering his shirt and tie, and making him seem much worse off than he was. Even the doctors had overreacted to it, all ten stitches worth. "How many times do we have to go over this?"

Kavcheck shrugged.

Rick sighed and stared out the window. The detective had borrowed a small waiting room on the ground floor, and Rick could see part of a storm-washed parking lot. The storm bothered him, and every time lightning flashed, he'd wince, but he couldn't take his eyes off of it.

"Francine was giving me a ride to the fireworks. There was a massive white flash, and I was thrown from the car. That's it; I don't know what's so difficult about that."

"But there's no car, Doc— Mr. Brandon."

That's the second or third time he's done that, started to call me "Doctor."

"I don't know why you can't find the accident—"

"If you could just remember the street where it happened?"

Rick shook his head and kept staring out the window, into the darkness. "I keep telling you, I wasn't paying attention. My mind was on something else—"

Kavcheck nodded and scribbled something in the notebook he carried. "Mind telling me what?"

Rick turned away from the window. "Huh?"

"What you were thinking about other than the road you were on."

"Yes, I do mind."

Kavcheck frowned. The expression was enhanced by his oversized mustache. "You may not appreciate this, but I *am* trying to help you."

"I don't see how my private thoughts have anything to do with it. I was thrown from an accident. I lost the car in the rain, and I wandered away lost until the ambulance picked me up. You're treating me as if I were some sort of criminal."

Kavcheck shook his head. "Forgive me if I am skeptical when you say you were in an accident with a car we cannot find, driven by a woman we can't even confirm exists—"

"What are you talking about? I gave you Francine's phone—"

"I'm not the only policeman in this town, Dr. Brandon. An officer checked out your story nearly an hour ago. The number you gave belongs to a Revco Drug Store in Cleveland Heights."

"I must have gotten the number wrong."

"There's no such woman, Dr. Brandon." Kavcheck stood up. "We've also checked a few other things. Like the address you gave for the *Observer*."

Rick felt a wave of nervousness. "Yes?"

"It's a historic site in Shaker, and the only thing in the basement is a pair of washing machines—"

"That's impossible."

"You want impossible? Look out the window again. Take a real good look."

Rick turned his head. Outside it was dark, and water sheeted across the window, the wind driving it sideways. The storm had let up for a while, but in the last fifteen minutes or so, it had regained some of its original ferocity.

"That storm has been on us for the past twelve hours, Dr. Brandon. There is no possible way you were going to any fireworks display within fifty miles of here."

"But it wasn't raining. . . ."

"So you say. The weather reports, as well as every other person in this town, say different." Kavcheck walked up and put his hand on Rick's shoulder. "You see, I think your private thoughts have a lot to do with what's going on. I think your private thoughts *are* what's going on."

Rick felt his chest tighten at the words. He had avoided thinking of how strange the world had felt since the accident. He had avoided thinking about the weather outside. Where had the rain come from? How could a clear, cloudless sky erupt into such violence within the space of a single thunderclap?

Outside, behind the twin cylindrical buildings across the street, the horizon erupted into strobing blue chains of rapid-fire lightning. The lightning was close enough that the sound was right on top of the light, like a nearby explosion. The sound shook the glass in the window frame.

"Are you saying I imagined—"

"I'm saying that nothing you've told me checks out

with reality, including the identification you provided to the hospital."

"W–wait a minute. What's the matter with my driver's license?"

Kavcheck shrugged. "The state of Ohio never issued anything with its peculiar format. The number on it doesn't exist."

Rick shook his head. "What are you trying to do to me?" He pulled out his wallet, stood up, and walked over to a table, then began dumping its contents. "Look, credit cards, Social Security card, draft card, press pass, all for Richard Brandon, me, okay? See, see, these can't all be fakes?"

Kavcheck sighed. "Ignoring the fact that there hasn't been a draft since the Seventies, and that Higbees doesn't exist any more, that Social Security number is wrong."

Rick stared at the pile. "How can it be *wrong*?"

"We've checked up on Richard Brandon's social security number, and that's not it."

Rick shook his head in disbelief. "You've been saying I've faked everything. If I'm not who I say I am, how can you possibly—"

"That the problem. You seem to be who you say you are. It's just that Richard Brandon *isn't*."

"What?"

"Sit down. The doctors advised against confronting you with this, but you don't seem on the verge of a psychotic break—and I want to know what you have to do with the fire."

"Fire? What fire?"

"Sit down." There was a hardness in Kavcheck's voice now that Rick didn't want to aggravate. He sat next to the table where he'd spilled the contents of his wallet. For some reason the waiting room felt too small.

"First," Kavcheck continued. "We only have one Richard Brandon in this city who matches your description—again, we've been checking. Your face is a perfect match to the picture the university gave us."

"University?"

"Case Western Reserve."

"Of course I've heard of it—"

"You work there, Dr. Brandon. The only part of your story we can confirm is the fact you *are* Richard Brandon. But Richard Brandon has nothing to do with newspapers—defunct, nonexistent, or otherwise. You're a professor. You teach psychology."

Rick turned away from Kavcheck to stare out the window again. "You're lying. Trying to confuse me." The words felt too thick in his throat, especially when he looked out at the storm that shouldn't have been there. "You're just trying to get me to admit something."

"Maybe I am, but that doesn't change facts. And the fact is your story is complete fantasy. Enough fantasy that the doctors here think you're delusional."

Rick turned his head a little so he could see Kavcheck again out of the corner of his eye. "And you don't?"

"For one thing, you're taking it much too calmly."

Rick turned the rest of the way to look at Kavcheck studying him. "Taking *what* too calmly?"

"Everything I just said. Psychotics usually take attacks on their worldview very personally."

"I thought I was supposed to be the psychiatrist here."

"Psychologist. And I said, 'for one thing.' There're two other things that make me think something more than a simple delusion is going on here."

"What two things?"

Kavcheck reached over and picked up some of the contents that Rick'd spilled from his wallet. He fanned them like a poker hand. "First off, you're weighed down with fake ID. All of it professional work crafted to support your story, but absolutely none of it usable. Even the format of the driver's license is wrong." He dropped all the cards back on the table except for the Higbees' credit card. "Who'd fake a credit card to a department store that no longer exists? And who the hell fakes credit cards in their own name?"

Rick wanted to say that they weren't fake, but he was too shaken. He had the same dry feeling in his gut now, looking at Kavcheck, that he always got when he looked at his teachers in school. It didn't matter who was right, how much work he did. He looked into their eyes and knew that Richard Brandon was irredeemably wrong, whatever he did.

Instead, he asked, "You said two things?"

Kavcheck nodded. "Due to some bizarre coincidence, at about the exact time you claim to've been involved in a phantom auto accident, there was an explosion at the building where you work."

"Explosion?"

"Witnesses claim that it was multiple lightning hits. The Psychology Building at Case Western Reserve no longer exists. They've only now brought the fire under control."

"Oh, God. Was anyone hurt?"

"Not that we know of. There were some reports that the University thought you might have been in that building."

There was a long stretch of silence before Rick said, "You don't care about the accident, do you? It's this fire you're investigating."

"The fire *happened,* Dr. Brandon."

"Stop calling me Doctor!" Rick stood up. "Am I being accused of anything? Unless you're arresting me, I think—"

Rick was interrupted by a uniformed policeman running into the waiting room. "I think you better get out here," the policeman told Kavcheck.

"What is it?" Kavcheck said.

The policeman opened his mouth, closed it, and shook his head. "You've got to see it to believe it."

Rick heard raised voices outside, in the corridor—disturbingly familiar voices. Kavcheck followed the policeman out, leaving Rick alone in the waiting room.

Rick gathered up the spilled contents of his wallet and pocketed them. It took him a few attempts because of the way his hands were shaking.

Stress and lack of sleep, he told himself. *There's nothing wrong with my mind.*

A flash of lightning pressed his shadow into the wall as if challenging the thought. The light had barely dimmed when the thunder rolled over the hospital, shaking the cheap-hotel pictures on the wall. He could feel the thunder through the carpet below him, almost as if it were a minor earthquake.

Rick turned to the window and saw that the reprieve from the storm was over. If anything, it was worse than it'd been when, when—

Whenever whatever had happened, happened.

Rick rubbed his head around the bandage on his temple. "What's happened to me?"

He followed Kavcheck out the door toward the raised voices. Another lightning strike followed him, strobing the parking lot, shaking the windows, and making the fluorescents above him flicker for a moment.

"—like you'd believe us." Someone was shouting down the hall. Rick couldn't see who it was. That end of the corridor terminated in a lobby facing the parking lot, and the mass of people were half around the corner from him. All Rick could see of the disturbance was the collective backs of a number of uniformed police and security guards. He could barely pick out Kavcheck's bald head.

"—if you aren't detaining Dr. Brandon for anything, we have a right to see him."

It was the same voice as the first, but different. The inflection had changed, was harder. Rick slowed his approach down the corridor.

"Hospital visiting hou—"

"So the police run this place now? I want to see the doctor in charge here."

Something about the voice made the scene distant. It sounded like his own voice heard down a tunnel.

"Please calm your companion down," said Kavcheck's voice. "Are you family?"

Rick was almost at the end of the corridor. He listened to the first familiar voice say, "I think we have to be. We're not here to foul up your investigation, but there's something else going on here. I think we all need to talk—us, you, and Dr. Brandon."

Rick stepped out into the lobby, not knowing what to expect.

What he did see stunned him into immobility. Two men who could have been his twins stood in front of a semicircle of policemen. Their attention was focused on Kavcheck, so Rick saw them before they saw him.

The one on the right was still chuckling. He dressed like a biker: leather jacket, chains, motorcycle boots, and ponytail. The one thing about him that didn't quite fit Rick's image of a biker was a goatee and mustache, which gave the man's face—his own face—a sinister cast.

The one on the left wore a blue shirt, and a crewcut a few millimeters short of baldness. He also seemed heavier, and had the mark of a nose broken a few times.

Rick cleared his throat.

Everyone turned in his direction. The move was so sudden that Rick almost expected the policemen to draw their weapons. The twins were looking right at him.

"I'm not a doctor," Rick said. "Of psychology or anything else."

"Oh, fuck," said the biker. "The bastard's another one of us."

Rick slowly approached the pair. The police parted for him, as if they were too stunned to do anything else. The lightning outside was growing more intense. "What do you mean?" Rick asked. "Another one of you?"

"Another misplaced Richard Brandon," said the one with the crewcut.

"Would someone explain to me what the fuck is going on here?" Kavcheck stepped forward, between Rick and the other two.

Rick rubbed his forehead. *My question exactly.*

"You know," said the biker, "Rocky and I were kind of hoping that the doctor might have the answer to that question."

Kavcheck looked around at the three of them. "Which one of you is Richard Brandon?"

"That's a trick question—" began the biker.

"*You* shut up," Kavcheck said.

"I'm afraid we're all named Richard Brandon," said the one that the biker called Rocky.

The doors to the lobby swung open, letting in the noise of the storm. Three people came in the door. A policeman in a drenched orange slicker scanned the room, and then made right for Kavcheck. The other two stopped in front of the doors looking around. One was a tall black man whose arm was in a cast.

The other man was a fourth Richard Brandon.

They started walking to the crowd, and the black man began talking. "Maybe you could help me. I heard that you had a Dr. Brandon here, I'm a student of . . ." The man stopped short the moment he saw Rick and the other two Richards.

"Good Lord," said the new Brandon.

Rick began noticing that the police and security guards had backed away from them, as if they had somehow become dangerous. Kavcheck was pulled away by the cop with the orange rain slicker. Four Richard Brandons were left standing in the center of the lobby, accompanied by the black man with the cast.

"You aren't the doctor either, right?" asked Rocky, the one with the crewcut.

The newly arrived Richard shook his head. Of the other three, he was the most similar to Rick. His hair was about the same length, and he was clean-shaven except for a razor-thin mustache. He wore a shirt and a threadbare tie, but his face looked even more threadbare for some reason. He was too thin, and his face looked positively cadaverous when the near-continuous lightning flashes highlighted the bones.

"Could your experiment have done this?" said the new Richard to his companion.

"What experiment?" Rick said in unison with the biker.

"I was the doctor's—" The black man said, "No, just no. This is impossible. This cannot be happening." Stressed, a Jamaican flavor crept into the man's voice.

"Experiment? What are you talking about?" Rocky repeated. He was rubbing his knuckles into the palm of his left hand.

The new Richard said, "Doctor Richard Brandon was doing experiments in an isolation tank at Case Western—"

"Fuck, that's where the building blew up," said the biker under his breath. Rocky muttered something similar.

"—this man, John, was his assistant. He was convinced I was the doctor."

"And the police were convinced I was," Rick said. There was something reassuring about that statement. It allowed him an identity separate from the mythical doctor that Kavcheck was trying to make of him.

"Then you're the man they were talking about on the news?" the new Richard said. "Dr. Brandon isn't here?"

Kavcheck rejoined them by saying, "No, he isn't."

They all turned toward him. John, the lab assistant, was still shaking his head.

"I just received word that they found a body in the wreckage at the Psychology Building."

Rick shuddered, feeling his stomach get kicked out from under him.

"Who?" asked John. Rick wondered if the three other Richards had the same gut-wrenching premonition he did.

Kavcheck confirmed it. "The body's been positively identified as a member of the faculty, a Doctor Richard Brandon." Kavcheck looked at all of them and waited for the news to sink in. Then he dropped the next bombshell. "I'm going to have to ask you to stay here while a few homicide guys come down here—"

"H–homicide?" Clearly, John was stunned.

"The fire didn't touch him," Kavcheck said. "He was murdered."

"How?" Rick asked.

"You don't want to know," Kavcheck said.

Rick stepped up and grabbed Kavcheck's shoulder and repeated, "How?"

Kavcheck turned to look at him, "Someone speared him through the lid of the tank. They haven't found, or even identified the weapon yet, but it punched through a steel lid, and through him, five times—" Kavcheck gestured the sign of the cross on himself, "Head, abdomen, heart, both lungs."

Rick let go of Kavcheck and slowly backed away.

The detective nodded at all four of them, and John. "Obviously, something strange is going on around here, and we're going to talk to every one of you until we find out what."

"You can't think any of us did—" the biker began.

"If you think I have anything close to an opinion on what's going on here, you're crazy," Kavcheck responded.

The word "crazy" had barely passed from Kavcheck's lips, when the loudest and closest explosion of lightning rocked the lobby. The light from outside the glass doors strobed, overwhelming the fluorescents in the high ceiling. The sound crashed across the floor in a tidal wave, washing everything away in a white rumble. It was a sound that could be felt in the skin, in the way the hair on Rick's arms trembled.

Wind blew in one of the doors, swinging it past the breaking point. The shattering glass was soundless under the wave of thunder shaking the building. Above them, the lights went out.

Then, suddenly, there was only the sound of wind, and rain. And outside the ruined door, the clatter of hooves on the pavement.

CHAPTER 13

JULIA

THE few pages of text she had kept her reading and rereading through the night. There wasn't a lot of writing, and it wasn't hard to read or understand, but Julia went through it very slowly, trying to find some glimpse of her brother's mind with the few words he had left behind him.

The one thing that came through the pages clear was a love of fantasy and mythology. The way some kids will develop a passion for dinosaurs or horses, Richard had poured his imagination into knights, gods, and demons.

He had written detailed descriptions of an imaginary place called Quinque, complete with maps and its own mythos. Most of the segment she was reading she considered a creation myth—

The Lord of Chaos was first, and for a long time he was all. The Lord dreamed, but dreams were poor company, so the Lord cut off a part of his chest to give birth to a child, Citas. In time Citas found the depths his father ruled to be barren, and he wished to create a world, a world that wasn't part of his father's dreams.

So Citas killed his father, cut out his stone heart to make the world, and cut out his organs to form his own brothers; Heros the warrior, Vitus the poet, Lucas the trickster, and Magus the sorcerer. Out of the blood of his father came the rivers and oceans, and all mortal life. To prevent his brothers from killing each other as he had done his father, Citas formed, from the limbs of Chaos, the five Artifacts that contained his father's power. Artifacts that could only be powered by the mortal spawn of Chaos' blood.

As long as the Artifacts existed, the gods tied to them could not perish. And it was Citas' wisdom that no God could touch or control any of the five. Citas cast the Artifacts to the barren parts of Midland, knowing that he and his brothers were safe from each other.

Until Vitus created mortal man.

Vitus gave man art, and poetry, the fruits of the field. Vitus was proud of man, and considered him a work of art. But Lucas was always ready to undercut his brother's pride. Lucas gave man knowledge, knowledge of fire, death, and murder. And man was wrapped in a chaos of blood, burning, and rape.

Vitus asked his brother Heros to help stop the senseless destruction, and Heros gave man tribes, and nations, and war. The blood, the burning, and the rape were now ordered and planned.

Vitus then asked his brother Magus to help, and Magus gave man the power of wizardry, of augury, and of divination. He collected the souls of dead men to populate his own kingdom.

Vitus then asked his oldest brother Citas to help, and Citas appeared to men and commanded them to stop.

Many stopped, but others did not, and others still resented the gods. Men retrieved the Artifacts and began to use them against the gods. The gods found their power trapped, and could only fight the usurpation of their power with the help of other men. . . .

The passage was rife with corrections and, from dates on the three pages it covered, told Julia it took Richard over two weeks before he was satisfied with it. Julia could almost imagine Richard lying on his bed, a dog-eared copy of *Bullfinch's Mythology* on one side of him, this notebook on the other. She could even smile a little at the lack of any women in his myths. School had just let out, and the whole endless summer lay ahead of him—

A summer that got cut drastically short, leaving this notebook as a last remnant of an intact mind.

Julia needed another beer. She got up and stretched; it was getting close to two in the morning. She should be getting to bed. Beyond the kitchen door, the muted television broadcast snow. The living room was lit as if from a flickering blue flame.

She yawned, fished another Miller out of the fridge, and sat back in front of her brother's notebook. It had fallen open to a drawing, but not one of the eerie smoky drawings made after the accident.

The drawing was a map, and it had been done very carefully. Richard must have been proud of it, because it had been drawn on thicker, unlined paper, and had been taped inside the notebook.

Julia drew her hand across the paper. It was decent acid-free stock that had taken the ink well and hadn't yellowed at all. She wondered if Richard had the same appreciation for paper that she had as a kid. His creativity, before the accident, seemed to fall more toward the literary than hers did. But she knew a few writers, and they had the same feeling, opening a ream of twenty pound bond, that she did when she splurged on an 11 by 17 pad of watercolor paper at Morse Graphic.

Somehow she knew he had felt the same way. There was something special about paper, and he had respected it. And no one would ever know if he would have followed that respect by becoming an artist, or a writer, or if he would let it die in the back of his head like most people seemed to do upon growing up.

"No," Julia whispered, thinking of the chiaroscuro drawings in the rest of the notebook. "It didn't die."

She drained more of her Miller and looked at the map. It had a familiar form, a coastline bisected by a knotted squiggle of a river. A native didn't even need to see the dotted outline of the city to recognize the Lake Erie coastline, and the Cuyahoga River. It wasn't until she read the lettering labeling the features on the map that she saw that wasn't what the map was of.

A small blocky outline enclosed the area around where the river emptied into the lake. The small outline was named Quinque, and enclosed an area confined to the east of the river. The river seemed to cut a patch just inside the western edge of the outline. Slightly south and east of Quinque was a blocky form called "The Fist of Chaos."

Across the river, to the west was the "Greythorn Woods," which covered much of the western part of the map. North of it were warnings, "Badlands," and "Here there be Elves."

Julia wondered what Richard had against Elves, and the west side in general. She wished she could ask him.

Most interesting was the way the river emerged, not from a set of tributaries, but from a stylized cave that Richie had labeled, "The Underworld."

There was one more section that seemed to be of a single piece. That was the description of the Thralls of Chaos. To Julia, despite the eerieness of the passage, it was the most hopeful section. The description of the Thralls matched one of the pictures that Richard had drawn after the accident. It gave Julia some hope that the person she had seen was still Richard.

She read about the Thralls again.

CHAPTER 14

Rocky

"GET away from the windows," Rocky yelled over the wind and rain. Something visceral seized his gut when the lights went out, pushing aside all thoughts of multiple selves and history gone wrong.

As a unit, all of them retreated from the front of the lobby. Next to him, he saw Richie reaching into his jacket. Rocky simultaneously wished for his own gun, and worried about the police cutting them to ribbons if one of them pulled a weapon.

The sound of metal-shod hooves was closing. *Horses? What the fuck is it about horsemen?*

The police didn't follow their lead. Someone had seen something outside, and about half of the cops were converging toward the front of the lobby. Most of the MetroHealth security guards were making for various exits to other parts of the hospital.

The bald detective, Kavcheck, stayed in the center of the lobby, next to the policeman in the rain slicker, trying to raise someone on a walkie-talkie.

The four Richards had made it behind an information desk when the front of the lobby exploded. Rocky had never seen an explosion like the one which blew in the entire glass facade of the lobby. A ball of electricity nestled itself into the center of a pair of revolving doors; Rocky could feel an ozone wind, as if it sucked the air from his lungs leaving only static in its wake.

Blue arcs leaped from the metal frames, through the cops, into the dead light fixtures. The fluorescent tubes above glowed briefly and exploded in a shower of glass and burning plastic. Rocky ducked behind the desk as the windows blew in.

Then it was gone, and the lobby was completely dark.

Rocky peeked above the edge of the desk. It was covered in broken glass and smoking hunks of plastic. "Shit," he whispered.

On the floor in front of the lobby entrance he could see four or five bodies. Only two were moving.

"Someone please say that was lightning," Richie said.

"It had to be lightning," answered Rick, the one with the bandaged head. In front of them, Kavcheck, a few other policemen, and the man with the cast, were moving toward the wounded who'd been too close to the window.

Rocky began to stand when the Richard who'd been last to arrive, spoke. "The horseman is coming." He said it flatly in a near monotone. Rocky heard it over the chaos of sound that filled the lobby, through the wind, thunder, rain, and the moans of the wounded. The dead statement filled Rocky with a fear he hadn't known since Central America.

Thralls here to correct a wrongness. . . .

Rocky shook his head. There was too much real to fear. He couldn't spare thoughts for fears he had created when he was a child.

"No." Richie stood next to Rocky. He was shaking his head, and his words carried eerie echoes of Rocky's own thoughts. "They don't exist." Richie was staring straight out the remains of the doors.

Rocky followed his gaze, unable to shake the anachronistic childhood fear. Outside, in the distance where the wind lashed a sidewise rain across the darkened parking lot he could see a ruddy glint, like an ember, or light reflecting from an unearthly eye.

"Trick of the light," Rocky said. Like the steed before, in the wreckage of his building, it had to be shadows. . . .

The unthinking fear brought back memories of dreams. Old dreams, dreams that he rarely thought of sober, dreams that had been created by an eleven-year-old Richard Brandon.

"Quinque?" whispered Rick. With that one word, Rocky knew that they all shared the same childhood dream, and that they all feared the same nightmare.

That one word sucked all the blood into a clotted mass in the core of Rocky's body. And, as if the word were a cue, the sound of galloping hooves dropped out of the wind.

The hooves became louder, and a horseman's shape cut itself out of the blowing rain. The mount was half again as large as any horse had a right to be, and it galloped in a manner that defied the laws of mass and inertia. Steam poured from its nostrils, and its eyes burned coal-red. In the darkness, its coat was the color of clotted blood.

Kavcheck was screaming something out at the rider, some sort of warning that was inaudible under the thundering pulse of the hoofbeats. The uninjured police were drawing weapons, and John—the man with the cast—was diving for cover.

"It's coming for me," said Richard. "The Thrall of Chaos—"

Rocky not only knew that he'd shared nightmares with these other Richards, but he also now believed that the thing in the parking lot could be what he thought it was. If so, he and the other Richards had to get the hell out of here.

He turned to yell at the others, but Rick was taking command already. "Move!" Rick said. "All of you, back this way!"

Rick led them, dragging a stunned Richard after him.

He ran toward one of the hallways off the lobby, one too narrow for the rider. As Rocky followed, reaching the edge of the lobby, he heard the screech of twisted metal, and a gunshot.

He looked behind them.

The rider had reached the doors. It swung a massive blade toward the policemen, slicing through the chromed remains of a revolving door. The cops were emptying their guns into it.

The rider wore a full suit of armor, the steel shot with blue rainbows where fires had tempered it. The seams, *all* the seams, bulged like metal veins, where they'd been welded shut. Twisted spikes and knives had been welded at random onto the armor, sometimes extending straight through limbs. The sword it wielded was an extension of its right arm, an arm whose hand had been lost beneath the welded additions.

All that, even the odd way the joints moved, could be explained.

But the rider's visor was open, exposing the void where the occupant's face should have been. The suit was empty—

Empty of everything but the spirit that swung that six-foot blade through the remains of the front door. As Rocky was watching, a policeman put a .38 slug straight through the thing's breastplate. For a moment, as the thing moved, he glimpsed a distant streetlight through the hole.

He had imagined such things when he was a child, out-riders between dreams and reality. Thralls that had served Chaos so long, hunting down everything unreal that trod upon the world, that their bodies had long ago crumbled to dust, leaving only the force of their duty to animate their armor. . . .

Rocky ripped his gaze away from the nightmare and ran after the other Richards, letting the gunfire merge into the thunder behind him. He tried to tell himself that it was a fantasy, and the thing in the lobby was something else, something sane.

Ahead of him Richie shouted, "That's no fucking nightmare chasing us. It can't be."

Rocky didn't argue. It was easier to dismiss when he wasn't looking at it.

The four Richards ran down the corridor. Glass crunched underfoot. Out of sight of the lobby, the hall was almost completely dark. The emergency lights had gone out. They ran past a single surviving spotlight, dangling from the wall. Facing the wall, it shed barely enough light to show that the other fixtures had exploded. An ozone reek clung to the air.

"Christ," Rocky muttered. God only knew what kind of surge that lightning strike—or whatever it was—put through the hospital's wiring.

"Where the hell are we going?" Richie yelled up ahead, at Rick, who was still leading them.

"Emergency entrance," Rick began. "Where I came in—"

He didn't get to finish his response. Another ball of electricity appeared, flooding the corridor with an evil static glow. It appeared from around a corner ahead of them, rolling across the ceiling. The buzzing sound was like a huge transformer taking enough amperage to melt. The smell was worse. Arcs shot from it to the walls and through the remaining light fixtures. One arc shot into a light switch, and crawled up the wall, following the wires inside. Wallpaper smoldered as the arc crawled across it.

The ball didn't fade so much as leak into the walls and disappear.

In the ball's final flare of light, Rocky saw another figure in welded armor. This one was different. Its faceplate wasn't open—it didn't have one. The Thrall faced them with a head covered by a flat expanse of blued steel.

Richie's gun fired.

Then everything was a mad scramble away from the armored figure. It was too dark to see anything clearly, especially after that dazzling burst of electricity. The darkness was made worse by air that made Rocky's eyes water. The air had a clingy static texture, as if he were trying to run blindly through the interior of a giant overheated television.

He felt, rather than saw, the others around him, and the armored Thrall was a pressure behind them, pushing them forward. Rocky could hear every move it made. Every joint bent with the sound of abused metal. Every step crunched glass into powder behind them.

"Stairs, take the stairs," one of them said, Rocky was

unsure who. They were approaching a lone beacon of light, a half-burned exit sign where an eye of white escaped from a hole where charred red plastic had melted. The sign dangled above a metal fire door.

"It can't climb very fast." It could have been the same Richard, could have been a different one.

Inside himself, Rocky transcended the panic of the moment, as the dash for the doorway took on a dream-like aspect. He felt outside himself, able to see the night-mare thing chasing behind them, as well as the door before them.

It had to be a nightmare, some bizarre dream. Those armor things, the Thralls, came from a world that only existed in the mind of a eleven-year-old. Quinque—and everything he associated with it—was a fantasy, an invention. It didn't exist.

Rocky slammed through the door, bruising his forearm on the crash bar. It was an emergency exit, and once it opened, the corridor filled with the sound of its alarm. Rocky burst into a concrete stairwell flooded with an intense yellow light.

The three others stumbled in after him, and—like Rocky—had run up half a flight before it sank in that something was badly wrong.

They stood in a stairwell in the Metro Health Building, that was undebatable. There were the whitewashed walls, and above them a charred fluorescent light fixture dangled from a wire whose insulation had turned to slag.

But everything was flooded with a dappled yellow light. It was blinding for a moment, but Rocky felt warmth on his face, and smelled a fresh breeze take away the transformer smell, and he knew it was—somehow—the sun.

"Fuck," Richie whispered.

"This can't be . . ." said Rick.

"Quinque," said Richard, barely audible.

Where the sloping ceiling above their heads should have continued, above the landing, bearing more charred light fixtures toward the second floor, the concrete faded into a mass of dots that tried to dance away from Rocky's eyes. The second flight continued up, away from the landing, and grew more substantial the further away from the landing it got.

On the landing itself, where a cinder-block wall should have faced them, there was *nothing*. The landing floor speckled into random noise that graduated from concrete into soil covered by brown-tinted grass. The walls to either side of the landing speckled into the gnarled trunks of two oaks. The ceiling above the landing simply turned to nothing, into air. Beyond the oak trunks, the only thing between them and the sky was a canopy of leaves that began five times above where the ceiling should have been. The sunlight filtered through those leaves, and into the stairwell.

There was an edge, but Rocky's eyes couldn't find it. Wherever his eyes focused, the scene firmed into nature or into concrete, and the floating motes of blurred pointillism migrated to the periphery of his vision.

The four of them stood, stunned, staring through the trees at a near-cloudless blue sky, until the fire door behind them exploded inward with the sound of tearing metal.

Rick shouted, "*Run!*"

Rocky ran for it. In the choice between two impossibilities, he'd take a garden over the metallic atrocity half a flight below him. He'd run up the stairs and was past the sentry oaks before he realized it. The only transitional feeling he had was a passage through a wall of uncertain air, as if for a moment he had been trying to breathe an Impressionist painting.

He stumbled over a root and fell against the tree to the right. One of the other Richards bumped into him, and they both fell to the ground. Rocky turned his head to see the last of them dive out of the stairwell.

Less than a half-step behind was the Thrall. It was the first time Rocky had gotten a good look at the thing. The armor was superficially medieval-looking, but it had the burnished look of steel that had been burned and welded together. Thick plates covered everything, including the face. The plates were covered with thousands of barbed hooks. The hooks were every size, and colored from black to an oxidized red. Each finger of the reaching gauntlet was tipped with one of those back-curving spikes, each barbed like a harpoon. Merely being brushed by that hand could cost someone a pound of flesh.

As if in response to the dive of the last Richard, the bizarre pointillism that marked the edge of the portal spiraled to the stairwell like a swarm of surrealist insects. He looked at the Thrall through a tornado of glass beads, whose vortex seemed to be the extended arm. The vortex narrowed to a horizontal funnel, throat spinning around the arm, the bell pushing the Metro Health stairwell off toward infinity.

A shriek of torn metal ripped through the air as the funnel collapsed into itself, and the Thrall's twitching gauntlet fell to the ground between the two oaks. The wrist fell facing Rocky.

The gauntlet was empty, but even so, it twitched like a newly severed limb.

CHAPTER 15

RICHIE

THE world had gone nuts. One moment Richie had been running up fire stairs in the hospital, the next he was stumbling through someone's sculpture garden. Sun made his eyes water.

"Fucking insane," Richie said. He whipped around, looking for the pile of junk metal that was following them moments before and trying to figure out how the hell he'd ended up here.

He—and the three other Richards—were in the center of a walled garden, surrounded by exotic plants, flagstone pathways, statuary, and marble fountains. The garden radiated out from around the two oaks that they had passed between. The oaks were ancient, millennial. Their roots and branches had intertwined, making them one entity.

Richie didn't see any doorway. There wasn't even a space that could hint at a way back to the hospital. All that remained of the thing that had chased them here was the twitching metal gauntlet.

Richie tightened his grip on the Beretta.

As a kid he imagined a place like this, a garden surrounded by a palace as old as the Acropolis and as large as the Pentagon. Richie kept turning, looking at the surrounding garden, "Fuck, fuck, fuck—"

It was hard to believe that he hadn't just gone insane.

It was the great garden, almost as he had imagined it. But it was going to shit. The grass was brown, many other plants along the flagstones were yellowed and dying. Weeds choked the flagstones, and fountains were empty but for a scum of brown algae.

Even the great sacred oaks, the axle of the world, were touched by death. The topmost branches were bone-white and naked.

"No," Richie shook his head. He didn't care what the hell had been chasing them; he wasn't about to believe in Quinque. He didn't care what he thought he remembered. . . .

The whole situation pissed him off, the anger growing when he saw that no one was reacting. The entire world had just gone completely insane, and all these imperfect copies of him could do was stand blankly and stare. The most recent addition, the one with the faggy hairline mustache, looked as if he were tripping. The one with the head wound was staring at the hooked gauntlet that'd almost torn open his shoulder, and Rocky was looking at him as if measuring Richie for a police lineup.

"Fuck this," Richie said, leveling the gun at the Richard with the head wound.

"What are you doing?" he said.

Richie gritted his teeth and stared into this Richard's shocked expression. This was the asshole that he had come to the hospital to see, the one who'd begun shouting orders as soon as all hell broke lose. Richie was pissed at this guy, if for nothing else, for leading them into never-never-land.

He took a step forward, and Richie said through a clenched jaw, "You better freeze, Fearless Leader, unless you plan to take a bullet." Richie noticed Rocky moving toward him as well. *"No one fucking moves!"* Richie ordered, taking a few steps to close the gap between him and Fearless Leader.

"Now," Richie said to him, "I don't know who the fuck you are, or where the hell we are. Frankly, I don't give a shit." He looked at his watch. It read one thirty-eight. Richie looked at it long enough for the second hand to pass the twelve. "What I do know is you got six minutes to get me back home."

"Stop it," said the last Richard, the guy with the faggy mustache. It was only the third time Richie had heard him speak since an animated suit of armor carved its way into the lobby. "Stop it," he repeated. "We're all lost here."

"Someone knows what the fuck is going on here!" As Richie pressed the gun against Fearless Leader's chin, his imperfect twin winced slightly. "I didn't let Rico get away with fucking with me. You think I'm going to let you people? I'm through with the games, and if I don't get some quick answers, I'm turning someone's skull into brain salad—"

"Stop this, Richie," said Fearless Leader. "You don't know what you're doing."

Richie's hand shook. "Five minutes."

Despite his bravado, he didn't want to see what would happen if he spattered Fearless Leader's head over the lawn. This garden was supposed to be a sacred reflection of the world, and spilling blood here was supposed to have evil consequences. An evil here would be revisited on Quinque a hundred-thousandfold.

It was an insane fear. Richie told himself that it was all bullshit. He rationalized his trepidation as a subconscious reaction to never having killed anyone before.

Whatever the hell was going on, the bastard in front of him was part of it, and someone had better send him back. "You got until one forty-five, don't waste time."

The other Richards surrounded him now, Rocky to his left, the remaining one behind him.

Rocky looked from Richie to Fearless Leader, and back again. "Calm down, Richie. Take a few breaths, *think*."

"*Calm?*" Richie almost giggled. "Give me one good reason to be calm." Next to the gun, he felt sweat leaking down the inside of his palm. "Come on," Richie coaxed.

"What do you want me to say?" Fearless Leader asked. "That I did all this, that it's my fault. I'm as lost as you are. Before you showed up, bringing your Thrall—"

"Not my fucking Thrall," Richie growled.

"—the police had already insisted that my entire life didn't exist, my paper, my job." Fearless Leader glared at him. "If he was right, what the hell can you do to me?"

"*Fuck!*" Richie's grip tightened on the gun, and he almost fired.

"Richie!" Rocky said. "This ain't going to fix anything. It won't tell us what's going on, it won't get us back where we're supposed to be. Put the gun down."

Richie stared into Fearless Leader's eyes. He was hoping for some sign of deception, some sign that this version of himself knew what was going on. He didn't see it. "You got four minutes to convince me not to shoot you," he backed off a bit. He could see the relief in Fearless Leader's eyes.

"We're all stuck in this together," he said. "The only lead we have on what's going on, and how it happened, is each other. Take any one of us away from this before we know what is happening and we've cut our chances of getting out of this by a fourth."

"Put down the gun, Richie," Rocky repeated. He reached out and gently placed a hand on his wrist. Richie tensed, then he sighed. The clone brigade was right, at least as far as the fact that blowing people away wasn't going to do any good. He let Rocky lower his arm, but pulled away before the other could take the gun.

Richie backed away quickly; he didn't like the idea of the others jumping him. It seemed all too likely at the moment, and he wouldn't blame them too much. Everything had put him too much on edge.

"Are you all right?" Rocky asked Fearless Leader.

"Stupid question," Richie muttered in disgust and backed between the oaks. The gauntlet still lay there. It had stopped moving. "This is crazy," he said to himself. "You all know that this is completely nuts." His voice was low enough that no one appeared to hear him.

Rocky talked to Fearless Leader while he none-too-subtly edged between him and Richie. *Definite cop,* Richie thought as Rocky talked to Fearless, keeping his gaze locked on Richie, "Sorry about this, ah—"

"Call me Rick," Fearless Leader said. Richie could almost tell the voices apart now.

Rick kept talking, "You're Rocky, right? He's Richie, and . . ."

Fearless Leader—Rick—faced the last of them. Rick seemed to have recovered his composure after having a gun shoved in his face, but the final Richard still seemed to be in shock over what happened. It took a moment before he realized that a response was being asked from him.

"Richard," he said hollowly. "Just Richard." His expression seemed to say, *You are all mad.*

That probably wasn't too far from the truth.

"Richie," Rick called over toward him. "I understand that you've just been through a lot of stress—"

"Fuck you," Richie snarled, continuing to back away from everyone. He almost raised his gun again. "I don't know any of you bastards, and for all I know you're all in on—"

Richie stopped talking. He was now on the other side of the oaks, staring at everyone between the two trunks. His foot had just stepped in something.

"Would you take it easy?" Rocky said softly.

I want to know who died and put Rick in charge, Richie wanted to say, but the breath dried in his throat as he heard liquid resistance under his heel. His boot had sunk in damp sod, and he could smell something, a briny smell laced with something like iron. He didn't want to look down.

"Put the damn gun away, Richie," Rocky said. His voice became harsher. "Don't force me to do something we'll both regret."

Rocky was coming toward him with a cop swagger, but Richie couldn't say anything. He was trying to look down, toward his feet, but something had frozen his neck muscles. Like a dream, his brain screamed at him to move, to face whatever it was, but his muscles remained frozen in place.

"Don't fuck with me," Richie whispered through his teeth. It was more a plea than the oath it usually was. He could smell a hint of smoke now, as well.

"I'm not fucking with you," Rocky said, oblivious to whatever sat by Richie's feet. *Maybe it isn't anything,* Richie thought, *but if it isn't, why can't I look at it?*

Rocky stepped through the paired oaks, repeating himself, "None of us are fucking with you. But you're acting like a cheap little punk. One more incident, and I'll *treat* you like a cheap little punk. Now put the gun away—" Rocky stopped talking. His gaze had drifted away from Richie, down towards Richie's right foot.

That broke his paralysis, and Richie turned to face what he had trod upon.

"Oh, holy God," Rocky whispered.

Behind the oaks a circle of blood-tinted brine had spread in a circle across the grass, killing it. Richie's foot stood on the edge of the circle, sinking into the ground. In the center of the circle lay a body, naked except for a pair of blood-covered swimming briefs. Vast wounds had been torn in the body, leaving gaping, red-lipped wounds to drain into the ground.

The face was the worst, a blow had cleaved through the center of the skull, splitting the head nearly in half. Despite the mutilation twisting what remained of the body's features, enough was left to be recognizable, much as Richie wished it wasn't.

Somehow, Doctor Richard Brandon had joined their little cabal.

CHAPTER 16

RICHARD

RICHARD had fallen sick into a nightmare. He saw the body and recalled everything John Waters had told him, about Dr. Brandon, about the sensory deprivation tank, about four other Richards. . . .

He stared at the body, at the blood that still oozed from its fresh wounds. He watched the grass wither underneath it, as if the doctor's death had killed part of the garden.

He didn't listen to the others as they argued around him. He was too stunned; the world had been drop-kicked out from under him. He had seen a Thrall, had been ripped from the halls of the hospital, it was just too easy to believe where he was. . . .

And Richard *believed*.

He suspected none of the others did, even though they had the same childhood dreams. He could see that in their faces, hear it in their voices. Twinned familiarity and denial. Richard had no denial within him. He had been scribe to this place ever since he could write. The others might have forgotten how real Quinque was, but for Richard, the poet, that was impossible.

Ever since the armored Thralls had herded them to this place, Richard had been nearly struck dumb. The enormity of actually being present, walking on the soil of his dreams, was too much for him to absorb at once.

The body's appearance slammed into him like a hammer. If he had seen it anywhere else, he could have turned away, denied what it was. Seeing it *here*—

"Are you all right?" Rick was shaking his shoulder, turning him from the corpse.

Richard shook his head. Too much, too fast. Too much to deal with. "No," he whispered. "Nothing's all right."

"You have to pull yourself together," Rick said. He looked in Richie's direction. "We're all frayed enough. We have to calm down and deal with it."

"Calm?" Richie spat the word. He had edged around the other side of the corpse. Waving the gun at it he said, "How the fuck can I be calm with that—"

"What's that?" Rocky spun around, away from the corpse. His whole manner seemed to take on an attitude of alertness that Richie and Rick seemed slower to pick up on. Richard turned in that direction as well.

Through the sickly foliage Richard could hear the sound of booted feet. The footsteps were quick, but in time with each other. A half-dozen men, maybe more, marching in sync toward them. In moments the sound seemed to surround them.

"No, this crap ain't happening . . ." Richie moaned. Richard wished he could agree with him.

Richard looked for the approaching marchers, but the hedges, though threadbare, surrounded the field, only allowing the garden walls to be seen beyond them.

"Where are they?" Rocky said as he slowly turned in place.

Richard knew, and he suspected Rocky did as well. The four of them were surrounded.

As if in response to Richard's thoughts, a dozen armored figures stepped through the surrounding hedges. They appeared as one, completely surrounding them, as if they suddenly materialized as one. They all wore leather armor reinforced with layered rings of metal, bullet-shaped helmets, and all but one carried a pike. The last one, the captain, wore an elaborate plumed helmet with an equally elaborate nose guard in the form of a dragon, and a sword as a sign of rank.

The captain emerged into the clearing, stared at them, and the corpse. His face was ashen as he looked at the body. "None of you move."

The guards around them glared from under the shade of their helmets. Richard felt no impulse to move. Rocky stayed in his ready stance, but Richard could see the confidence drain from his expression.

Richie moved. He brought the gun up toward the captain, whether to shoot him or merely to threaten, Richard was never sure. As soon as his arm moved, the pole ends of three pikes slammed into him, one batting down his arm, one slamming into his abdomen, the last slamming into his kidneys.

The sound was like a car slamming into some small animal. The gun dropped from Richie's fingers, and he buckled under the impact, falling in a fetal position at the edge of the dampness spreading from the corpse. Richard almost doubled over in sympathy.

The three guards who'd made quick work of Richie hovered over him, looking toward the captain. The captain, still ashen-faced, shook his head. "No, alive." It was almost a whisper. The guards nodded, and Richard felt that he had just come within moments of seeing a fatal rain of blows upon his twin.

The captain walked over and picked up Richie's gun. Richie was still curled up on the ground, unmoving.

Rick began to say, "Sir, I'm sure if we can talk to—"

The captain's face turned into a twisted mask as he bellowed, "*Say nothing!* By all the gods, I would have you dead if a sacrifice on sacred ground would not serve your master's purpose."

Rick froze, and no one else spoke.

"All of you, over there!" The captain pointed toward the edge of the clearing, toward the fountain and away from the body. Everyone moved in that direction except Richie. The guards had to kick him a few times to get him moving.

The captain said no more except to bellow orders to his troops or his prisoners. If any of the Richards threatened to talk, the raised butt of a pike would silence them. Richard had to support Richie as they were escorted out of the garden. Richie's bloody mouth leaked on a jacket that was still soaked from rain.

The four of them were ushered to the edge of the garden by most of the captain's guard. A few stayed behind with the body, for what purpose Richard didn't know.

By the entrance to the garden, the guards pushed them past a courtyard honoring the gods. Facing inward, from the courtyard's perimeter, the five gods of Quinque stood in stone effigy, towering over Richards and their captors.

They were only in their presence briefly, but Richard got a general impression, an impression buttressed by his memories of Quinque.

Toward the gate, was the seated figure of Citas, head crowned by a plain circlet, his hand extending from marble robes to offer a benediction—or to entreat an audience to kneel. Next was Vitus, robed, with a wise, smiling face, raising a goblet, as if leading a toast. Then Heros, a sword raised above his head, armor of a style that didn't conform to a specific time or place. Then Lucas, the only other smiling figure, arms crossed, head tossed at a sarcastic angle, seeming to laugh at the observer.

The last statue was that of Magus. His hooded cloak shadowed his face from view, staff raised as if about to strike the watcher down. Richard had only a glimpse, but there was something wrong with the statue. The marble itself had taken on a sinister cast, darker than the other statues. Light green veins wept from the stone, becoming black near the base, and every plant within five yards of that statue was dead.

Richie whispered so that only Richard could hear him. "So what the fuck's all this, the Pantheon?"

Richard tensed, but apparently the guards didn't hear him.

As they passed, Richard felt he could smell the corpse's odor of blood-tainted brine around the statue of Magus.

The guards tossed them unceremoniously into a room near the garden wall. Their prison seemed to be one of expediency rather than design. The doors of the place were a pair of oak doors, each one covered in elaborately carved vines, large enough to admit a Volkswagen, heavy enough to withstand a collision with one.

The four of them were led into the room, and the doors slammed behind them. Richie immediately went back to the doors and started a futile effort to open them again.

The room was stone, dominated by a huge fireplace. Somehow, the scale of the hearth made the rest of the room seem cozy, even though the room was at least fifteen yards across. The only illumination was from a pair of small circular windows impossibly high on the wall. The windows were like eyes to the hearth's mouth.

All the available walls were covered by wooden shelves, most of which were laden with books and scrolls. The smell of paper and mildew overpowered any more subtle odors.

Richie cursed and kicked the door while the others milled around. Rocky finally said, "Now what."

Rick said, "I think we should sit down and try to figure out what's happened to us."

"Fucking genius," Richie muttered from behind him. "We've been imprisoned by the local Gestapo, that's what." He sounded disgusted.

However, in a few moments the room filled with the sound of wood scraping stone as the others grabbed chairs. Richard sank into a chair by the door, allowing fatigue to finally sink in. Richie remained contrary, standing though his efforts with the door had proved futile.

The four of them faced each other, the dim light seeming to highlight their differences rather than their similarities.

Richie, who remained standing, arms folded, seemed more a part of the shadows, while Rocky seemed to be cast in a bas-relief to emphasize his physique. Rick sat next to the cold hearth, across from Richard, and his eyes seemed to capture what light came from the windows and hold it burning inside him.

"Sarcasm aside," Rick said, "this is the first chance we've all had to compare notes on what's happened to us.

And I think we should start with the experiments 'Doctor' Brandon was supposed to be doing." He looked at Richard.

"I think we should start with trying to get the fuck out of here," Richie said. "We're prisoners, in case you hadn't noticed."

Rick looked up at him and said, "I have noticed. I'll bow to you if you can think of an escape plan that won't get any of us killed. The door's impossible, we can't fit through the windows, and I don't think we can dig through the stone walls or overpower a heavily armed guard—"

Richie looked pensive, but he didn't say anything. He just wiped the back of his hand across a still-bleeding lip.

Rick nodded, "So at least we can do something constructive," he turned to face Richard again. "The late Dr. Brandon's experiments?"

Richard sucked in a breath. His instincts lay with Richie; he had a bad feeling about being captured like this. But he looked at the other three and decided to go along with Rick's logic. "The man I came to the hospital with. His name was—is—John Waters. He was a graduate student, assisting Dr. Brandon."

Richard repeated what Waters had told him. Even though it had only been a few hours ago, it felt much longer. When he finished, Richie said, "That explains the doc's weird book collection."

Richard wondered if Dr. Brandon dreamed of Quinque.

"You've been to Dr. Brandon's home?" Rick asked Richie. The question had a note of command in it.

Rocky responded. "That's how me and him met." He began going over his own experiences in Dr. Brandon's world.

Richard rubbed his temple. Hearing the same voice, over and over was giving him a headache. Having his clothes slowly drying on his body wasn't helping. He felt he was half of the mildew smell in the room.

After listening to Rocky for a while, Rick said, "We should go over our personal histories."

Richie said, "Who died and put you in charge?"

"Someone has to pose some constructive suggestions."

"And that's you?"

"Yes, it's him," Rocky said. "You're getting on my nerves, Richie."

"Trust a fucking cop."

"And what the fuck are you?"

"Stop it," Rick said. "Both of you!"

There was a pause for a moment before Rocky said, "Look, if there has to be a spokesman for the group, I'm behind you. If only to make him shut up."

"Fuck both of you," Richie said.

"What do you think of electing this guy leader?" Rocky looked at Richard and hooked a thumb at Rick. Richie glared at all of them from the corner of the room. Richard rubbed his temples and nodded, not really paying attention.

Rocky looked at him a little oddly, then turned around. "You got the floor, Boss," he said.

Richie snorted.

CHAPTER 17

Rick

RICK was high on his own adrenaline. It wasn't the fact that the four of them had come close to being slaughtered by an armored nightmare, or that they all seemed to have slipped sideways through at least two realities, or that some medieval guardsmen had taken them prisoner, or even that he had seen what was almost his own body, hacked to pieces—though that was all part of it. What excited Rick was the fact that he was managing to hold together a situation that was just this side of complete chaos.

When Rocky offered him the mantle of leader, it didn't surprise him. It was self-evident that the four needed a spokesman. Just as it was self-evident that they needed to discover what was happening in order to have any hope of finding a way back.

First, though, they needed to find out about each other. Discovery of their differences might lead to clues to why everything had happened and, perhaps, how to reverse it. And he wanted to know about these "alternate realities" that Richard's Mr. Waters had talked about.

"In one sense we're the same person," Rick told the others. "However strange that might seem. At some point, we stopped living the same lives." He tried not to think, *at some point your lives went wrong*, but it was hard not to. Richie was sarcastic and abrasive, Rocky seemed dull and wrathful, and Richard seemed meek and submissive to the point where he almost wasn't there at all.

However, Rick knew his own opinions were biased, and he took that into account. He coaxed the lives out of the other Richards by beginning with his own to give some baseline for comparison.

He told them about his work, his education, and the family that'd adopted him. When he reached the point when his parents died, the accident that had killed them, he could see in everyone's eyes that he had reached a common trauma. All of them had lived through that accident. All of them had seen that truck tumbling into the wrong lane—

In the subsequent tales, the other three confirmed that. Up until July Fourth, 1970, they had all experienced the same life. Like Rick, all had come out of the accident in a coma. Each remembered dreaming of Quinque during those weeks of unconsciousness. But each awoke to a different world.

Rocky's father had survived the accident, and—according to Rocky—promptly crawled inside a bottle. Rocky joined the army to get away from his lone parent, serving in "one of Reagan's dirty little wars" in Central America. He joined the Cleveland police force right out of the army.

Richard's father died in the accident, and his mother died from it, eventually. According to him, he had always been a teacher or a student, and still was both. He was a writer, and he'd written poetry about this place, Quinque.

Richie apparently had gone through a number of foster families after the death of his parents. According to him, he'd spent the first half of his life getting screwed by the world, and spent the rest screwing back. He almost seemed proud as he described several stints in prison.

After a long time going back and forth, questioning the others about their lives, Richard interrupted him.

"Name the presidents since Johnson," Richard said.

"What?" Rick asked.

Silence drifted down on the candlelit chamber. Everyone stared at Richard, who seemed to shrink a little under the attention. He cleared his throat and said, "Waters asked me to name the presidents since Johnson."

"Yeah," Rocky said. "Who the hell is Bill Clinton anyway?"

Rick shrugged and said, "Johnson, Nixon, Reagan, Bush, Dole . . ."

"Now that's a depressing lineup," Richie interrupted. "I take it they didn't shoot the bastard?"

Rick looked at him, feeling a wave of surrealism. "Shoot what bastard?"

"Nixon, who else? He barricaded himself in the White House, and they had to take him out—" Richie looked at everyone and sighed. "Alternate fucking universe, yeah, right. Johnson, Nixon, Ford, Rockefeller, Anderson, Kennedy, Mondale, Reagan, Perot."

"Good God," Richard said. "How many is that?"

"Too many, but Ford doesn't really count. He resigned because of Nixon's little war. He was only in office a week. Theoretically, I think Haig was in charge for a little while, but that wasn't official."

"Nixon was impeached," Richard said. "Johnson, Nixon, Agnew, Reagan, Carter, Dole, Simon."

Rocky shook his head. "Unbelievable. Nixon was assassinated. Johnson, Nixon, Ford, Reagan, Bush."

"And?" Richie said.

"That's it. Reagan served four terms."

"He's kidding. Someone tell me he's kidding," Richie said.

Rocky shook his head. "There was a suspension of elections in the eighties."

"Holy fuck," Richie said. There was silence after that. The darkness seemed to press in against the twin shafts of light coming from the windows, pushing all the light into the center of the chamber. The light seemed suspended, ephemeral as a soap bubble. For a moment Rick felt as if any one of them could say something that would make that bubble of light burst, plunging them into a dark void.

"I don't get it," Rocky said.

"What don't you get?" Rick asked.

"According to Richard here, Mr. Waters said that Dr. Brandon was hypnotically going back and changing a single key event in his life. Our lives, right?"

Rick nodded, "It seems pretty likely that it was the accident."

"Whatever it was," Rocky said. "If this doctor was reliving one event, over and over—how the hell can an auto accident in Cleveland affect Nixon's presidency? Can someone explain that to me?"

Richie was scanning the spines on the bookshelf next to him. Richard rocked forward in his chair and shook his head. "I don't know how to explain it. Perhaps we, in our differences, affect the world more than we know."

Rick shook his head. "It seems so arbitrary."

"Does it?" Richard asked.

Richie slid a book off the shelf and began leafing through it, holding it toward the light. "Face it, we know jack about cause and effect," he said, flipping carefully through thick pages. Rick was impressed at the care Richie showed in handling the thick tome. "History's a bloody chaotic mess. Someone breaking wind in the streets of Boston could lead to the assassination of an Arab Prince—or vice versa." Rick could see the glint of colored inks and gold leaf when Richie turned the page. "The way a teacher arranges desks in a class could determine who's our next president. It's all random."

Rocky said, "I don't want to think that way."

"Then you don't like reality. Me, I got another really interesting question, if you boys can handle it."

"What?" Rick asked.

Richie hooked a stool with his foot and dragged it into the center of the room, directly under the light from one window. He placed the open book on it. Open, the book was nearly too large to balance on the stool, and he held it steady with his hands. The book glowed in the sun as if it were under a spotlight.

Richie knelt so he leaned over the top of the book without obscuring the light. The manuscript was hand drawn, and heavily illuminated. A quarter of a whole page was taken up by medieval illustration of a battle, cavalry charging up a fortified hill, driving back an army of distorted humanoid creatures.

The text was verse, the lettering highly stylized. The part illustrated by the battle scene was entitled, *The Battle of Echelle.*

It was Rocky who said, "I don't get it."

"It's in English," Richard said. "Reasonably modern English—no archaisms, no Chauceresque spellings."

Richie nodded. "And I want someone to explain that to me. . ."

Richard bent over the illuminated text and began reading. At first his voice was only a mumble, but in the space of a stanza it took on an almost stentorian deepness that seemed to resonate throughout the chamber.

"*. . . The wood, the hill, and the land*
The sky, the wind, and the air
All dark with the blood of man
rank with darkness, death, despair
A thousand came and fought here
A thousand men to charge Echelle
A thousand faced the evil slaughter
A thousand corpses on the road to hell.
The evil host broke not that day
And supped that night on human hearts . . ."

"I wrote this—" Richard whispered. Richard raised his head from the manuscript. "I wrote this. In high school. The battle for the fort of Echelle, the orcs, the cavalry charges—everything. . ."

"But that book looks five hundred years old," Rocky said.

"My point," Richie said. "We didn't have modern English five hundred years ago. Certainly not modern English spelling."

Richard looked up at Rick. It was unpleasant to see an expression of fear in a face that was essentially his own. Rick could feel that fear himself, a darkness creeping in from the dark corners of the room.

Rocky voiced Rick's fear. "This isn't real. It *can't* be."

Rick went to the shelves and started confirming that all

the books in the library, however old they seemed, were written in fairly modern English. His browsing was interrupted when the doors were finally thrust open. The captain, their captor, was now flanked by nearly ten guardsmen, all bearing short pikes and axes. They were better dressed than the ones in the garden, each in mail and bearing a tunic with an elaborate coat of arms on their breast, their caps of metal and leather.

They looked no less sinister than the previous batch.

The captain addressed them. "His Majesty will see you."

The Richards were taken to an octagonal meeting room, where a trio of men stood before a table strewn with papers and not a few maps. The men spoke among themselves, ignoring the guards and their prisoners.

Rick tried to pick out "His Majesty" from among the three, trying to rekindle dim memories of the Quinque of his childhood. There wasn't anything particularly regal about any of the men, and none wore a convenient crown. The one on the left had a deeply wrinkled face and gray hair that faded to salt-and-pepper when it reached his beard. Rick thought of him as king first, because he was the most senior of the three.

The middle one was younger, and had jet-black hair and beard that he wore in a style reminiscent of Richie's. Rick had an impulse to distrust the man; there was a dishonest cast to his face, and he had a politician's smile.

The youngest man was on the right—no more than twenty years old, if that. He was blond, and his beard was little more than a suggestion.

It took the trio a moment to finish their discussion, something about the collapse of the border to the east. The gray-haired one was talking about the loss of ten thousand swords within a fortnight.

Rick shuddered when he realized that they were talking about the loss of men.

The blond one raised his hand and turned toward them.

"Ah, Claedon, you've returned with our visitors." There was an unsubtle irony in his voice.

The captain bowed his head, "Your Majesty." Claedon stepped aside so all four Richards stood facing the young man.

Once the young man was indicated as king, Rick saw it as obvious, despite the man's youth. The man bore himself with the arrogance of royalty, and everyone else seemed to offer him a subtle deference—even, Rick noticed, Richard the poet.

"Emissaries from the shadows that plague us?"

"Sir—" Rick began.

The young man held up a hand, silencing him. "Please, we are not finished talking. You are in our domain." The young man circled the table to walk back and forth in front of them, like an officer inspecting his troops. "We are Alveron the Second, defender of Quinque. Do not interrupt us again."

That was a mistake, Rick chided himself. *This is royalty, dream or not. Speak only when spoken to.*

Alveron turned around and faced his two companions across the table. "Your opinions, General?"

The gray-haired one snorted. "You know my feelings about these 'shadows.' Especially now. Whatever good such otherworldly things bring us, the door is then opened to much greater ill. Every ripple in the aether makes us more vulnerable."

"Yes," nodded Alveron. "But about our guests?"

Rick felt as if they were all being toyed with, as if all the decisions had been made before they'd come here.

The general answered his sovereign. "They are dressed as foreigners, and this is no time to trust foreigners. They trespass in the most sacred places, and leave the corpse of one of their own in their wake. Kill them and be done."

Rick felt his heart sink.

"Uncle?" Alveron said, turning toward the younger of the two.

The man steepled his fingers and seemed to look right at Rick as he spoke. "In the village where I was a lad, midwives would kill identical siblings because they only had one soul between them."

"Hey—" Richie started. Rocky grabbed his arm. Rick grabbed the other. Rick did not like the way this was going, but the guards outnumbered them. Any provocation at this point would probably be suicidal.

Alveron turned to face Richie. "We did say not to interrupt." He shook his head. "No matter, really. Our General is correct, as usual. You are foreign. You trespass. Why are you here?"

Rick steeled himself. He hoped he'd be able to explain something he didn't really understand. "It was an accident," he said. "We didn't intend—"

Alveron sighed and shook his head. "We need not know what you did not intend. We wish to know how you serve the Adversary."

Adversary. The word chilled Rick, though he did not know why. *This place is at war,* came the slow realization. *They are at war and they think we're the enemy.* This was worse than it seemed—

"We don't serve the Adversary," Rick said. *Please, listen.*

"Ah," Alveron said, turning around and walking back around the table to the General and his uncle. "So you know the mind of our Adversary, then?"

"That's not what I said," Rick said.

"Swift move, Fearless Leader," Richie whispered, shrugging out of his grasp.

Alveron nodded. "So, you four are here to fight the Adversary?"

"Ah—" Rick began.

"Say, 'yes,' you shithead," Richie said, low enough that Rick hoped no one else heard.

"If I may, Your Majesty?" said Alveron's uncle.

"We always welcome your council, Uncle."

"Perhaps Sir Claedon will show us the weapon again." He held out his hand to the captain. The captain darted forward and handed the gun to him.

Rick didn't know what he expected the man's reaction to be. Presumably these people didn't know firearms.

The man took the gun from Richie, holding it nominally by the grip. "Fine metal," he said. He slowly tilted the end toward the ceiling. Rick noticed his grip shift, finding the trigger. "A tube encased in metal. Presumably it fires something, like a small crossbow?"

The man carefully handed the gun, butt-first, to the general. "You are the military man, my friend. Tell me your opinion."

The general took it, and held it with even more respect. "I smell fire here. Something has burned in this device, and the pipe is enclosed completely of metal. No arrows, milord. There is no track for the shaft of the bolt, nor space for fletching. This is more akin to some fey cannon."

"Otherworldly, indeed." Alveron's uncle folded his arms and looked more the politician. "We seem to have three alternatives, do we not? One, they were drawn here by the gods to support us. Two, they were sent here by the Adversary to fight us. Three, they are mere random flotsam, drawn by the crumbling of the aether around us."

"I vote for random," Richie said.

The man chuckled. "I am a pragmatist, not a mystic who sees patterns in the splatter of mud on the flagstones."

Alveron stroked his spotty beard as he stared off somewhere to Rick's right. It was pretty obvious that other things were weighing on his mind. "We would wish some straightforward advice, Uncle. We wish to dispose of this matter."

His uncle bowed. "Mine is a simple reasoning—"

Alveron sighed, as if he were bored with everything here, or simply irritated by it. "Then you shall keep it simple, and brief. This has already taken too much of our time away from the war."

"Simple and brief, Your Majesty. We know it is by the will of the Adversary that the barriers between us and a host of shadow worlds crumble. So, it is more than likely that the Adversary brought them here for his own ends."

Alveron nodded. "General?"

The general ceased his examination of the nine-millimeter automatic. "I've always preached caution to the Crown. Now more so than ever. You remember that I was against bringing these strangers into your presence."

"We know your concerns, and we trust our officers to protect us." Alveron waved at the Richards. "Enough of this diversion. We have a nation to defend, and this has little bearing on our concerns. Have our guests separated and housed individually to await questioning at our pleasure."

The captain bowed, "It will be done, Your Majesty."

Alveron, his uncle, and his general walked away as if nothing much had happened. Rick had the sick feeling that the "housing" that Alveron referred to would be anything but pleasant.

More guards marched in, past the exiting nobles, until each of them had a three-guard escort.

"May the gods look after you," the captain said, making it sound like a curse. "Take them away," he told the guards.

CHAPTER 18

JULIA

THE phone woke Julia up.

She pushed herself up from the kitchen table, blinking at the morning light streaming through the kitchen window. The kitchen phone was an old tanklike Western Electric model. It had a bell rather than an electronic beep, and the sound felt as if it drove a spike through Julia's skull.

She stood and grabbed the receiver, knocking over a few empty bottles from the table in her scramble to shut the thing up. She leaned against the kitchen wall and said a weary, "Hello."

"Julia Brandon?" said a voice on the other end of the line. It was slightly familiar, but not enough to cut through the sleep clouding her brain. At least it was for her. One of the more depressing things about living in the old house was how many telemarketers kept calling for Mom.

"Speaking," she said. She stretched and could hear her neck popping. Her back ached from the way she'd fallen asleep, and the beers she had last night were a pressure right behind her sinuses. She needed a shower badly. All in all, she felt horrible.

"It's Lawrence Kavcheck—"

Julia woke up further. "Oh, hello. What can I do for you?" She straightened up, almost unconsciously. She felt an irrational fear that the doctor had called her to chastise her for taking Richard's notebook. It was a silly thought, more silly because the tone in Dr. Kavcheck's voice told her that this call was something more serious.

"I'm sorry to call you at this time of the morning—"

Julia felt the floor lurch. Whenever it began with an apology, the news was bad. That was how she knew her mother had died, the policeman had begun apologizing to her.

"Miss Brandon? Are you there?" There was worry in the doctor's voice, and Julia realized she had just missed what he had to say.

"Could you say that again?" Julia repeated. Why was she so terrified of what might happen to her brother? She had only met him yesterday. . . .

"I said, we checked your brother into the Cleveland Clinic. He developed a partial hemiplegia last night, but it doesn't seem life-threatening yet."

Julia was fully awake now. "What? Doctor? What's a hemiplegia? What's wrong?"

The doctor sucked in a breath. "Your brother has probably suffered a stroke. Hemiplegia is a paralysis of one side of the body, and your brother has lost the use of his left hand and a partial loss in the left leg—"

"Oh, my God—"

"There's a good chance he'll recover, if it's a stroke. There are drugs that we didn't have during his first one. Most of the affected area of the brain may not be permanently damaged, so it'll recover."

Julia nodded until it sank in that she was talking on the phone. "I understand," she said, feeling like a liar. "But he seemed all right yesterday—I mean not all right, but—Christ, I don't know what I mean."

"I'm sorry to tell you this, I don't want to give you any additional burdens. But I thought you'd want to know as soon as possible."

"You're right, I just wish . . ." *Just wish my brother was all right, really all right.* She changed the subject, "Can I come and see him?"

"Hmmm. He's going to be having examinations through most of today—"

"A few minutes, I won't get in the way."

"I'm sure I can manage to bring you up to see him.

Why don't you come to my office at the Clinic, about three. That's right before I'm scheduled to go down and see him at brain imaging."

"I'll be there, thank you."

"No problem. I'm sorry I had to wake you like this."

"Don't be, I'm fine."

"Good-bye," he said. The receiver clicked.

Julia held the receiver until the line began beeping at her. She hung it up slowly, feeling about as far from all right as she could be without suffering from a stroke herself. She felt as if she were going through her mother's death again, in slow motion.

She ran her fingers through her hair and looked at the little digital clock on the microwave. It was nine in the morning. She wondered how she was going to get through the next six hours.

She went to the Cleveland Clinic at three, and as Dr. Kavcheck promised, she saw Richard. It wasn't easy for her. They had laid Richard out flat on a cart, and his motionlessness made it difficult for Julia to tell that anything had changed from yesterday. She watched as they fitted a mask to his face, needlessly immobilizing his head.

While she stood with Dr. Kavcheck in a room that looked like a NASA control room, Richard was behind a vast sheet of glass, alone in a stark white room dominated by a giant piece of equipment that looked to Julia like nothing more than a huge industrial clothes dryer.

Richard's cart rolled forward until his head slid into the dryer's aperture. Eventually, the screens in the control room began to display multicolored blotches. Julia knew that the images were pictures of the activity in Richie's brain.

To Julia, the pictures resembled nothing so much as a topographic map of some alien planet. Which was probably close to the truth.

The pictures, mostly fiery digital washes of white, yellow, and red, had an unexpected effect on Dr.

Kavcheck. She had expected him to point somewhere on the screen and say, "That's the site of the stroke." But his first reaction was to turn to one of the technicians and said, "You people haven't been fooling with the settings on this thing, have you?"

The technician shook his head. He was looking at the image himself, "A bit more active than you expected, isn't it?"

Julia looked at the orange-white splotches and turned to the doctor, "What's the matter?"

"I'm not sure, I've never seen anything like this."

Julia turned to see Richard, lying still with his head immersed in the machine. He looked like a decapitated corpse. Dr. Kavcheck must have noticed her shudder, because he placed a hand on her shoulder.

CHAPTER 19

RICHIE

"FUCK all you bastards!" Richie yelled at the guards, at the walls, at his three fellow prisoners. It didn't do any good. Why the hell had he listened to those other losers at all? He should have blown away Fearless Leader Rick when he had the chance.

The guards' reaction to his cursing was the butt end of a pike to the side of his head. The impact stunned him and dropped him to his knees. Two other guards half-dragged, half-carried him away. By the time he had recovered his senses, he was away from the royal part of the building. The architecture was rougher, less mannered and decorative.

He was still spitting blood and holding on to his kidneys for dear life when the guards dragged him through a utilitarian stone corridor that seemed the epitome of a dungeon to Richie.

It was nowhere near the dungeon.

They entered a long passage and, at the first intersection, Richie's guards turned right, dragging him away from the other Richards. "Hey," Richie said. "What are you doing?"

The guard ahead of him answered him with another blow to the kidneys. Richie didn't ask any more questions.

They took him through a massive door made of planks as wide as Richard was, studded with nails the size of his fist, and led him down a spiral staircase. The air in the stairwell was heavy and fetid, and Richie's world became delimited by a sphere of torchlight; a breadth of curving stone wall, a few steps, and a cylindrical pillar of stone to his right. Rats scurried away from the fringes of the light.

It took an age to descend to the bottom of those stairs. The walls degenerated the farther down they went, becoming slick with moisture and white with mineral deposits. All the while, the air became weighted with moisture and the smell of decay. The humid smell made Richie's damp skin and clothes feel as if they were rotting off his body.

When they reached the bottom, rats escaped the light in an undulating wave, as if a brown carpet were being withdrawn from the light.

The guard pulled him along a floor covered with straw that rot had rendered into little more than black slime. Heavy chains, ocher with rust, hung from staples set in the walls. Some dangled manacles while others followed the wall threaded through heavy iron rings.

They unlocked another massive door, and Richie saw his first prisoner. "Oh, fuck,"

At first, Richie thought he was looking at a corpse. Its skin was drawn tight, and it had collapsed in a heap on the floor. Maggots had gotten to it, squirming in the torch light.

However, as the light passed it, Richie heard it moan, and heard the chain rattle slightly.

"Oh, fuck," Richie repeated. Suddenly it didn't matter that he was outnumbered by three armed guards. He just had to get the hell out of there. He yanked his arm away from the one guard who was still holding him. His arm came free easily, the guard hadn't expected the sudden move.

Richie took a stumbling lurch backward, his feet sliding on the rotting straw. The shadows sprang away, growing across the stone walls as the guard with the torch moved toward him.

Richie turned and ran back toward the door. The trailing guard reached for him, but Richie managed to dodge around him. Richie's feet slipped, and his shoulder slammed into the rock wall, releasing a choking cloud of niter. He pushed away from the wall—

Something slammed into the back of his head. His eyes watered, and his vision blurred, but his momentum carried him another step and a half. Then it hit him again, and he was sliding into the ground without remembering the fall.

He spat out a mouthful of straw. The pain seemed to dig claws in behind his eyes. Through his blurred vision, the shadows shrank toward him.

Then a boot slammed into his abdomen. He spat out more straw, as well as most of the contents of his stomach. A fist, or the butt of another pike, found the side of his head, then it was an indivisible rain of blows up and down his body.

Pain brought him back to reality, or at least consciousness.

His body was one big bruise. Moving anything fired an ache that brought tears to his eyes. It took several minutes before he was able to open his eyes and turn away from the floor.

"Fuck," Richie said. His lips cracked when he spoke, and he tasted blood.

At least he could see his prison. The guards had left a torch burning outside the door. The light filtering through the tiny barred window was enough to see by.

He apparently rated a little better than the gentleman with the maggots. This place was an individual cell, about the size of a large closet. The door was about five feet away from the spot on the floor where they had dumped him, filling the yard or so between the walls. The largest dimension was the room's height, which vaulted a grand ten feet above him.

No bed, no furniture, just the slime-eaten straw.

Richie slowly sat up, having some thoughts about examining the lock on the door. When he sat upright, a rattle informed him that he was chained to an iron ring in the floor.

"God," he whispered in a hoarse voice. "This makes Lucasville look like a Hilton—"

He broke off, seized by a fit of coughing that burned his chest. When he was done, his chest hurt, making him think that the guards had cracked a few ribs.

In the distance, through the door, Richie heard someone begin moaning. After a few minutes another voice began yelling, "Shut up and die, you gutless, crazy bastard!"

English again. It made no sense to Richie. This whole place made no sense. Nothing made sense except the guards, and they just acted like cops anywhere.

At least they left him his belt. He could hang himself if he could figure out how.

He examined his wrists. The guards had manacled them tightly, iron to the bare skin. From the feel of them, the metal was already abrading his flesh away. It was too easy to picture the flesh torn away, layer by layer, then the infection would start, then the maggots—

There had to be a way out of these things.

Each manacle was made of two semicircular pieces, the semicircle terminating in a flat tongue perpendicular to the surface. Each tongue had a hole in it. Slapped over his wrist, the tongues of metal mated, the holes lining up with each other. Through one hole, a link of the chain held the manacles together. The other hole was filled by a hammered metal rivet the size of his thumb.

Richie wanted a keyhole, some mechanism that he could pick. They hadn't given him that luxury. It was fiendish, simple, and cheap. No keys, or locks, and in the unlikely event that they wished to free someone, all the guard would need is a chisel.

Handcuffs he could get out of, given time. These things, probably not.

The chain passed from one manacle to the other, though a giant iron ring set into the floor. There was just enough chain for him to stand upright. There was no possible way for him to reach the door. Standing was painful, so he slid back to sit on the ground.

If this was a dream, or a hallucination, this was the time

to wake up. Instead he closed his eyes and fell into a tainted slumber.

Richie dreamed of one of the nightmare riders that had chased them in the hospital, blue steel armor and demonic steed. He stood on some precipice, fog cloaking all the world except what was immediately before him. The rider was between him and where he needed to go, so he tried to run past it. The horse reared, and a spiked hand struck him down. Before he was overcome, he saw his destination.

A shadow stood on an outcrop of rock above his destination, a shadow bearing a staff, a shadow like Magus' statue in the sacred garden. The shadow was somehow worse than the Thrall. Richie, for once, feared for his soul.

The staff lowered with a flash of white light and a deafening thunderclap—

He awoke, expecting the world to have shifted again. It hadn't.

He had no measure of how long he had been asleep. It could have been minutes or hours. The torchlight through the door seemed no dimmer, but his eyes had spent hours adjusting to darkness.

Thirst and hunger joined the other pains plaguing him, which made Richie realize that his captors had made no move to feed him, or give him water. It was a terrible thought, but Richie began to believe they'd just meant to toss him here and forget about him. Who would care if some stranger croaked in the palace dungeon?

He tried not to think like that. But, as time passed, it became harder and harder not to. They didn't even give him a pot to piss in. All he had were the clothes on his back, which stubbornly refused to dry in this place's sick atmosphere. He checked his pockets and found them empty. They'd taken everything; loose change, wallet, keys, pens—they hadn't even left him his watch so he'd know how long he'd been trapped here.

Just like cops. All they left him were his clothes—and his belt.

His belt . . .

To go along with his biker attire, its buckle was a brushed stainless-steel death's head. Seeing it gave Richie some inspiration.

He examined the rivets holding the manacles to his wrists. The metal had to be softer than iron to be hammered cold like that. That meant that the rivets were probably softer than steel.

He took off his belt, and used the buckle to gouge at the head of one of the rivets on the left manacle.

The buckle made a definite scratch. The line was almost silvery against the gray metal rivet and the rusted iron manacle.

He went at the rivet with a sense of purpose, scraping the hammered head away scratch by scratch. As he worked, he noticed that he had gained an audience. A large, sleek rat had somehow reached the window of the door. It sat on its haunches, almost like a squirrel, bigger than one. It cast a shadow over his work, but his eyes were so adjusted to gloom that it didn't bother him.

"Greets, rat," Richie said.

The rat was still, intent on his movement.

"If you want a corpse to gnaw on, you're a little early," Richie chuckled to himself and continued to worry away the head of the rivet. Just saying the word gnaw brought home how hungry he was. "If I don't get out of here soon, you might be the one on the menu, rat."

It was distressing the way the idea didn't immediately turn his stomach. He glanced up and saw the rat still there, unimpressed.

It took hours to scrape away the head of the rivet manacling his left hand. By the time he was done, his fingers were blistered and bloody, and the repetitive movements shot cramps up his right arm all the way through his abused back.

However, he had exposed all the iron there was to

expose. The rivet was confined to an even circle of gray metal piercing the iron. Richie dropped his belt and tried to pull the halves of the manacle apart. But his right hand was little more than a bloody claw. His fingers refused to bend, and they couldn't find purchase on the iron.

"Fuck," Richie whispered. "What bullshit . . ."

A chittering sound came from the door. Richie looked up at his rodent audience. He had almost forgotten about the rat as he worked, and looking at it now, he found himself growing angry. It was as if the ugly little thing was laughing at him.

"What? This is funny?"

Richie stared at the chittering rat and balled his left hand into a fist. He slammed the manacle into the wall. The impact sent a painful shock though his wrist, but the rat shut up.

He slammed the manacle into the wall again. A few weak orange sparks leaped from the collision. He grunted. The shock felt as if he'd slammed a dagger into his shoulder.

However, the manacle loosened. Richie looked at it and could see a gap where the halves had begun to part. He smiled and looked up at the rat. "You're on borrowed time."

Richie slowly stood upright. Every joint in his body protested the move, as if the moisture down here had begun to rust his insides as bad as his restraints.

Once he was standing, he placed his feet on either side of the ring on the floor, on top of the chain. Then he began pulling his left arm. The chain was taut once his wrist reached the level of his hip, and his shoulder and elbow began to ache.

He squatted so he could fold his arm upward. He shifted his feet to give the chain more slack on the right side so he could support his wrist with his right hand. He pulled the left side of the chain taut with both hands while he was squatting.

The rat chittered again.

Laugh while you can, you disease-bearing vermin.

Richie pushed up with his legs, fighting the chain. He watched the top of the manacle, and saw the gap widen. He smiled grimly and felt the muscles vibrate in his legs. After a few long minutes his whole body was soaked with sweat.

He stopped for a moment, and let his back collapse against the wall. *I can do this. I am going to do this. I am going to do this and kill that fucking rat.*

After a rest, he pulled up with his legs again. The chain came taut with a jerk that felt as if it dislocated something in his wrist. After the jerk, the metal clattered to the ground and his back slammed into the wall, knocking the breath out of him and firing the pain in his ribs.

It took a few coppery breaths for him to realize his wrist was free.

He looked up and, predictably, the rat was gone from its perch on the window. He stepped off the chain and pulled it though the ring in the floor. As he hoped, the ring was big enough to allow the two halves of the manacle through it. He didn't have to go through all that with the manacle on his right wrist.

He would have to eventually, though. Escaping with six feet of iron chain attached to his right hand would be awkward—and noisy. Right now though, it was enough that his freedom of movement had increased by an order of magnitude.

He paced around, dragging the chain, trying to walk the pains out of his legs. As he did, he heard a chittering coming from the rear of the cell. He turned to see a rat squatting by the iron ring.

"Okay, you fucker, time to die." Richie lifted a boot to crush it—

"Tsk, don't do that," came a voice from behind him.

Richie spun around, overbalanced, and felt his back slam into the wall again. "Who the fuck?"

There was nothing to account for the voice. But a rat was back in the window. "You don't even know it's the right rodent."

The voice was definitely coming from in front of him. From the door or beyond. "Who's there? Show yourself."

"Who?" The word was accompanied by an odious chittering. "The master of appearances and illusion. The monarch of trickery and deception. The arch-lord of change." The rat jumped from the window.

The rat didn't fall when it jumped. Instead, its shadow unfolded in front of Richie, blooming like a dark flower. In less than a second a humanoid form stood in front of Richie. A humanoid form that was carrying Richie's gun.

"Nor," it said, "am I hiding."

CHAPTER 20

RICHARD

THEY had condemned him to hell, and there was nothing he could do about it. This land that had made its home in his dreams, in his poetry—this land that Richard still felt as if he had, in some sense, created—this Quinque had dismissed him without so much as a thought. Richard felt it as a betrayal.

He had not fought his imprisonment, how could he? For a long time, this land had been all he had. Losing that was losing everything. He'd been led away, a stunned, empty shell.

How could this place be so alien to his expectations?

Imprisonment here went against everything he'd ever written about this place. Quinque was supposed to be a place of honor and hope—

In his poetry, he had missed the smell of rotting straw and the moaning of demented prisoners. Even the air was subverted by the setting, becoming heavy, humid, and slimy.

Richard sat, staring at the door to his cell, trying to understand. The best he could conclude was that if Quinque was common to all of them, to each Richard, perhaps they each bore a slightly different part of it among them. Richard could believe that Richie had dreamed this dungeon. That made him wonder from whose mind came the Adversary Alveron had referred to. . . .

He sat for a long time, wrapped in his thoughts, long enough for the chains he sat on to cut into and bruise his thighs. He didn't move, seeing little point to it, even to remove the discomfort. Richard felt he would be dead soon in any event.

He tried to force his thoughts along more constructive paths, but that took mental energy that his imprisonment had sapped from him. All the questions about how he had come here, and how Quinque itself could exist, all of them sank into the black pointlessness that flooded his mind. Even thinking about his companions, the other Richard Brandons, couldn't help him struggle against the blackness—

They would have fought their captivity and, in that fighting, were probably already dead. After a few hours in that cell, had someone offered him a way to speed oblivion, he probably would have taken it.

He stared, long past seeing the door to his cell. Fatigue swallowed his awareness as blackness engulfed his thoughts. Sitting upright, and watching the door, he fell asleep without knowing he did so.

He dreamed of falling from a precipice. There was no true sky above him, only a boiling maelstrom of black and gray. Silhouetted against that background, a human figure bore a staff.

Below him, the ground was dissolving into the same black maelstrom.

Richard woke with a start. There was a damp cloth on his forehead, and he jerked away from it. Someone was in the cell with him.

"You needn't be afraid, my son." The man sat on a stool next to where Richard was chained. He'd been mopping Richard's brow.

"Who are you?" Richard asked.

The man smiled. "Friend," he told him. "You shouldn't despair so easily."

Richard stared at the man incredulously. It was impossible to determine age or race from his face, which was of an androgynous handsomeness. His smile was simple and unforced.

"Who are you? What are you doing here?"

The man reached into a leather pouch next to him and removed a loaf of bread. He broke it in half and offered one half to Richard. "Isn't aid enough for the moment? Why not just take bread with me for now?"

Richard stared at the man. He was familiar, somehow. He had seen this man's face before, or had written of him.

He was very hungry, but he was still too stunned and afraid of this sudden visitor to reach for the bread. The man shook his head and left his hand outstretched. "Are you so worried about poison? Not long ago you would have welcomed someone plunging a knife into your breast." He leaned over and rested a half-loaf in Richard's lap. "Or perhaps you worry about my supplies. Do not fret, my friend, I have more than I or you would ever use." The man took a bite out of his loaf.

Slowly, encumbered by the chains, Richard gathered the half-loaf from his lap. To his surprise, the bread was warm, as if it had just recently seen an oven. The broken end was steaming in the dank air. Then Richard smelled the bread. It was a breeze of cleanliness, washing away all the oppressive odors of the cell around them.

Richard took a tentative bite.

Within a minute he had consumed the whole delicious thing. He not only felt the fatigue drawn out of his body, but he felt the shadows clouding his brain withdraw enough for him to think clearly.

"There now," his visitor laughed. "Things can always be improved on a full stomach."

"Vitus," Richard named him.

Vitus laughed. "Indeed. Though I prefer 'Dancer of the Field.' I would offer you wine, my friend. But you are in more need of water." He extended a wineskin from out of his pouch. Richard took it, and, true to his word, it was filled with fresh spring water.

Richard found it hard to drink, since he simultaneously couldn't help thinking that he was sitting in the presence of one of Quinque's five deities.

When he put down the skin, he found himself unable to

speak. What does one say to a god? Somehow, direct address seemed inappropriate.

Vitus reached down and retrieved the skin, which seemed no more empty than when he'd handed it to Richard. He unstopped it and drank his fill, and now it seemed to be dispensing wine.

He finished, wiped his mouth with the back of his hand, and said, "Come now. Feel free to speak, friend. I am *your* guest right now."

"Ah, sir, why are you here?"

Vitus laughed. " 'Sir' says he." He shook his head. "Dispense with that, friend. Earth crusts my nails and my feet are stained with wine. Only a peasant, I." Vitus laughed again. After a moment he stopped, shaking his head. "But, indeed, there is a purpose to my being here. So attend my words carefully, friend."

Vitus leaned over Richard. "You have a purpose here. For an age there's been a balance in the world, and that balance has been upset. You and your fellows are set here to right it."

"How?"

"The Adversary has one of the five Artifacts, Magus' Staff. You shall retrieve the other four before facing the Adversary."

"Why us?"

"Because there can be no others. The existing order cannot hold, you must bring a new one."

Richard shook his head, "I, all of us, we want to go home."

Vitus laughed. It wasn't an unkind laugh, but it still disturbed Richard. "You do not realize what you ask. Your home is part of the unbalanced order. If you are to go home, or have a home to go to, you must gather the Artifacts and face the Adversary."

Richard stared, not fully understanding. He knew of the Artifacts, of course; he had written of them. There were five of them, created when the world was made: the Staff, the Horn, the Ring, the Sword, and the Cirque. That was one of the first details of Quinque he had created, or the first detail that had been imparted to him, it was hard to be sure.

The world had been made when the Lord of Chaos had been destroyed, and Midland had been formed from the stone that was the Lord's heart, and the gods of Quinque had been formed from his head and limbs. The power of the Lord of Chaos had been divided and trapped in those five Artifacts.

At least that's what Richard remembered from what he'd written about it, decades ago.

Vitus smiled. "Do not fret. You will understand what I am telling you, eventually." He nodded and placed a hand on Richard's forehead. "For now, though, sleep. Do not worry about the chains on your wrists. Worry more for the chains you cannot see."

"But . . ."

"Shhh," Vitus hushed him. "Sleep now. You will wake in time."

And Richard slept.

CHAPTER 21

ROCKY

WHEN Rocky finally slept, he dreamed of menacing shadows and the world dissolving away. The shock of cold water in his face brought him to sputtering consciousness. He had only a moment to hope that everything that had happened was a drunken nightmare.

But when he opened his eyes, he was still in the hole where Alveron's guards had chained him.

"The time for rest is over." The gruff voice came from above him.

Rocky blinked water out of his eyes. Standing before him was a tall armored figure that, at first, Rocky thought was one of the palace guards who had escorted him down here.

"Awake," the man said. As he spoke, he casually tossed a bucket to the side of the room. His manner reminded Rocky of his drill sergeant.

Rocky shook his head, "I'm awake, damn it."

Rocky heard scraping metal echo off the stone walls but didn't realize that his visitor had unsheathed a sword until the blade was between them.

"Who are you?" Rocky asked, straightening up, his back to the wall. The figure was backlit, and even with eyes adjusted to the gloom, Rocky had difficulty discerning any detail in his visitor.

The armored figure pointed a sword at the ground in front of Rocky. "Stand."

"If you're here to kill—"

"*Stand.*" The voice was firm and undeniable. Rocky pushed himself upright, against the chains on his wrist.

As soon as Rocky had reached his feet, the sword came down. The whistle of cleft air rang in Rocky's ears as the wind of the blade's passage brushed his face. The sword struck the ground between his feet, blossoming in cherry sparks.

Metal clattered at Rocky's feet. His back straightened as all the resistance on his manacles was removed. On the ground, to either side of the sword's blade, lay the remnants of the iron ring that had held Rocky's chains to the ground. The ring had been sliced in half, as had the chain that'd passed through it.

Rocky's visitor withdrew the sword from the groove it had made in the stone floor. As he sheathed it, Rocky realized that the armor he wore bore little resemblance to the mail worn by the guards who'd imprisoned him here.

"Who are you?" Rocky repeated. Even as Rocky spoke the words, he knew. He knew and could not believe what he knew. One part of his mind told him that he faced Heros, Quinque's god of war. The other part of his mind refused to accept that he stood before a manifestation from his bloody-minded adolescent fantasies.

"I am your patron, Richard Brandon," came Heros' answer. "Your destiny, and your fate, lies not in this cell."

Rocky did not like the talk of fate. He would almost prefer being left to rot in this cell. He didn't like his visitor. Even so, he found himself asking, "Where does it lie?"

The armored figure stepped forward and placed his hands on Rocky's shoulders. The gauntlets were cold through Rocky's thin shirt, and their grip was unbreakable. A smell clung to the armor, a bitter, smoky smell—the same smell that would persist for weeks around a napalmed Sandanista village. The smell of a battlefield. The smell of burning death.

"It lies with the Adversary, and on the hilt of a sword forged out of Chaos." Rocky could almost hear the clash of swords underlying the words. "To end your exile, to gain the escape you seek, a balance must be struck. You must face the Adversary, and you must commit everything toward facing him, with no counting of the cost."

The shadows drew away from them, and Rocky could not tear his gaze away from Heros' eyes. There was a slight red glow to them, the brightest part of Heros' face. His skin was tinted red, blood red, dark enough to be just short of black.

Staring into those eyes, Rocky felt the rush of battle. The coppery taste of fear, the surge of adrenaline, the too-sharp vision. The feeling of seeing the truck ahead of him evaporate from a mortar hit; of seeing the man next to him collapse with a bloody pit for a chest; of stepping on something in the woods, and hearing a click.

All the questions fell from his lips unspoken. All his internal denials withered under the assault. He knew he didn't gaze upon the eyes of a man.

"You will join your fellows, you shall all gather the five Artifacts, and you will take the Sword." Then Rocky's shoulders were released. He stumbled back, falling when the wall he expected was not there to meet him.

The world had changed again.

Under him, the floor of his cell had changed to damp sod. Its ceiling had disappeared, replaced by a sky heavy with stars. There had been no movement, no great flashes of disorientation. He was just, suddenly, somewhere else.

Rocky got to his feet. "What . . . ?"

There was no one to ask. Heros had gone. The change had the surreal abruptness of a dream. Rocky stood, alone on a hillside damp with dew, encircled by silent ranks of trees. A soft wind brushed against him, carrying the scent of pine. The chains that had bound him were gone.

He turned around, looking for Heros. He sensed something—not seen or heard, but a gravity he felt in his gut—that quickly dissipated. As the sense of weight left the clearing, Rocky heard the crickets begin to sing again. Other night creatures joined the crickets until it was hard to believe in the unnatural silence that this place had greeted him with.

"A magic sword? Someone has got to be pulling my leg." Rocky whispered the words, as if afraid of being overheard.

Rocky walked, despite fatigue and hunger, because he couldn't stand still in the clearing where he'd been left. He headed downhill, because he figured downhill was water, and if he followed water, eventually he would find some sign of civilization.

He wondered where the other Richards were. He wondered where *he* was. The woods around him could be anywhere, to look around he could be wandering around the Metroparks in Cleveland. The thought again gave him some hope that it had all been an alcoholic fantasy.

But after the impression Heros had made upon him, he didn't really believe it. Around him, Quinque made too good an argument for its own existence, and Rocky was at heart a pragmatist. However much he didn't want to believe that he was trapped in this place, he would take the evidence of his senses at face value.

That made it easy to believe that what Heros had said was true, that his route home, and out of this exile, lay with him finding a legendary sword. And, if that's what it took . . .

Eventually, as the stars began to surrender to the coming dawn, he came across the sign of civilization he was hoping for. He stumbled across an old overgrown road. He followed it down into a mist-shrouded valley, toward the dawn. Eventually, he came to a stone bridge set into the western side of the valley.

On the other side of the valley, high on the bluff overlooking the gray mist, stood a walled city. He knew the turrets of Quinque the moment he saw them, a twisted amalgam of medieval and Renaissance architecture. Now that he was within sight of the city walls, he wasn't so sure he wanted to be here.

The bridge was cloaked in a fog that made scale and distance hard to measure. As he approached, the span seemed wider than he expected, and he could see hints of darkened sandstone arches. While the architecture seemed vaguely Roman, something about it nagged at him, an anachronistic familiarity.

The fog was lifting. As he stepped out onto the bridge, the first brush of sunlight touched the towers on the bluffs of the opposite shore. The veil parted enough for him to see that the bridge ahead of him led east, toward the river—

Then, abruptly, stopped.

The bridge marched across seven sandstone arches until it met the banks of the river, then it stopped, as if it had never been quite finished. Rocky stopped walking. He stood there in the center of the roadbed, watching as the morning breeze swept away more of the mist shrouding the anomalous bridge.

Vines spilled over what appeared to be iron guardrails—which seemed an extravagance. Ahead of him, about midway into the existing span, a vine-draped fence crossed the width of the bridge, a central portion hanging open.

As sunlight began to spill across the bridge, Rocky saw a figure standing on the end of the bridge, as if he had started walking across and had stopped just prior to plummeting to his death. Recognition came slowly, because the figure faced the river and because Rocky wasn't expecting him.

After a moment Richie zipped up his fly and turned toward Rocky with a jingle of chains that was audible even with the distance of the bridge separating them. He called to Rocky, "Did you just have the weirdest fucking night of your life, or what?"

"I guess you could call it that," Rocky said, catching his breath.

Richie walked toward the vine-draped gate. "So, recognize an old friend?"

Rocky stared. "I can't not recognize you—"

Richie chuckled. "Not *me.*" He kept walking, started kicking gravel away from the roadbed. "The *bridge.*"

Rocky knew then that the feeling of anachronistic

familiarity wasn't going to go away. The bridge felt familiar, because it *was* familiar.

"*What?*" Rocky whispered, kicking away some of the gravel under his own feet. He knelt down and muttered, "Asphalt," as if the word confirmed what he'd felt in his gut ever since seeing the span terminate before reaching the river.

"Rocky, I'd like to reintroduce you to the Superior Viaduct."

Rocky shook his head.

"Trust me. Peel away the vines from that fence down the way and you'll find a chain-link fence. Rusty, but still got the "No Trespassing" signs. From the vines, I'd say this had been here a while."

"But—" Rocky tried to object, but he couldn't. He knew the bridge well enough. He had seen it hundreds of times. It was familiar to anyone who had ever ventured to the Flats of the west side of Cleveland. And the century-old structure was unique out of dozens of bridges in the valley of the Cuyahoga, because its Roman arches had not led past the water's edge since 1918.

CHAPTER 22

RICK

A sourceless white light woke Rick from an uneasy slumber. It hurt his eyes. He blinked, but the light erased the rest of his cell, reducing the universe to him and the light.

"Richard Brandon," spoke a voice as sourceless and omnipresent as the light.

"Yes?" Rick said. His own voice was hoarse and cracked.

"You are my vassal, Richard Brandon. You are to do as I bid."

Rick tried to look up toward where he thought the voice might be coming from, but the light prevented him. His eyes watered as he struggled to his feet.

"Who are you?" Rick asked.

"I am lord of my world and this one, monarch of the gods, father to the world. You are charged with a task, Richard Brandon."

Rick swallowed. This was getting too Old Testament on him, and he didn't like the idea of being anyone's vassal. Especially not a disembodied voice. "Show yourself," Rick said. "If you're some sort of divinity, prove—"

"Do not test me!" The voice beat him down with the force of a blow. The light turned orange and burning. Rick could feel sweat breaking out on his skin, as if he stood too close to a furnace. "You have earned no right to question."

The shackles fell away from his wrists. The clatter as they fell to the dungeon floor was barely audible. An ominous rumble filled the air. Rick felt panic tear at him when he realized that his feet no longer touched the ground. He was falling upward, into the light. He should have struck a wall, but he kept falling past the point of any walls.

"The Adversary must be faced. You and three others are the ones who can face him. To free yourself and this world the Artifacts must be gathered, and you shall gather them. To free yourself and this world the Adversary must be faced, and you shall face him. You will bear my Cirque upon your brow when the fragments of Chaos are brought together."

Rick wanted to shout, to question, to say *something*. But he was paralyzed by fear and awe. He could feel the light rushing by him. Despite the fact that there was no wind, and he couldn't open his eyes more than a slit, his inner ear kept telling him he was falling—turning what should have been above into below. The voice surrounded him, shaking him. He felt the words in his stomach, in his teeth, behind his eyes.

With the voice came a feeling of destiny that sank deep into the core of his being.

"You will do this because I command you. I give you two warnings. One of you shall betray the others. And only one of you shall face the Adversary."

Rick managed to force some words out into the light surrounding him. "Betray . . . who?"

"The betrayer is named Richard Brandon. The one to face the Adversary is named Richard Brandon."

With that, Rick stopped falling. The light faded around him, leaving his dazzled eyes blind to what seemed total darkness. He lay on the ground, with no real sense of how he had come in contact with it. He clutched his hands into fists, and came away with handfuls of grass. Crickets began singing around him, and slowly his eyes adjusted to the absence of light, revealing a sky full of stars above him.

God help me, I'm no Moses, Rick thought. *I don't even think I make a decent Frodo.*

He wandered through the trees for hours, or what seemed like hours. His clothes smelled of rot and mildew.

A mist still hung over everything, increasing the feeling that he would never be dry again. He was hungry to the point of dizziness, and he felt as if he were stumbling around in circles.

However, as dawn began to break above him, he found an ill-used road. It gave him some sense of direction. Without thinking too much about it, he headed east, toward the dawn.

Shortly after, he smelled a nearby campfire.

Rick was suddenly aware that he had no idea where he was, and if strangers would represent friend or foe. He'd already been imprisoned once, and from the talk of Alveron and his court, there was a war on as well. People tended to kill strangers in wartime.

But he needed food, water, and a sense of where he was. He had to confront other people sooner or later. Now was probably better than later. Around him, shadows were beginning to color themselves in the morning light as the mist lifted. Black began to show hints of brown and green.

Cautiously he edged down the road, and he could see signs of a clearing past the lightening trees. As the trees thinned, he saw a campfire, and a single figure on the ground next to it.

He approached the sleeping form cautiously, and by the time he reached the side of the fire he was barely surprised when he discovered that the form sleeping by the fire was Richard, the English professor. He bent over his twin and wondered if that was how he looked when he slept. Richard's expression seemed too sad, too lost.

Rick squatted down and shook Richard's shoulder. Richard muttered something that sounded like, "Vitus?" before he came fully awake. He blinked a few times and looked at Rick for a moment.

Then he looked around the clearing, as if he hadn't seen it before. "Where are the others?" he asked, finally.

Rick shook his head. "I don't know."

"I think they'll be here soon." Richard sat up, looking into the fire.

"Why? Do you know what's going on?"

Richard looked at him and said, "We're here for a reason. We're supposed to be together." He turned back to the fire. "You had a visitor, didn't you?"

"You?"

He nodded.

Rick thought back to the clearing in the garden, the quintet of statues. Citas, the Monarch of Gods, Father to the World, had been the throned statue, the one with the crown. Now he thought of the others, Vitus, Heros, Lucas . . . Magus?

He squatted next to the fire and said, "You realize that this is insane."

It wasn't long before a too familiar voice called to them. "Will you look at that. We just start down the yellow brick road, and there's Scarecrow and the Tin Man."

They both turned around to look back toward the road, and there were Rocky and Richie. Rocky stared at the campfire as if he couldn't quite believe that the two of them were there. Rick realized he was probably staring at the two latecomers with a similar expression.

Richie walked up and sat by the fire, slowly. In the dawn light, he looked as if he'd been slammed face-first into a wall. When it came down to it, Rick wouldn't have been surprised if he had.

Rocky shook his head. "I don't like this." He walked around and sat down opposite Richie, peeled off his shoes and socks, and began massaging his bare feet. Rick had the uncomfortable feeling that Rocky's socks did not start out black. Thinking about that made his own feet itch.

They all needed new clothes, or at least a chance to wash what they had on. Rick was glad all he was smelling was the campfire at the moment.

Rocky switched feet and said, "I don't like the feeling that I'm being jerked around."

Richie chuckled. "Look at any mythos, that's what gods do. They're the jerkers, you're the jerkee."

Rick massaged the knuckles of his right hand. "So we *all* had some 'divine' visitation?"

The response was a series of nods from around the fire, Rocky's the most hesitant. Richie said, "Guess the only one who didn't was old Doc Brandon."

Rick saw Richard wince, and he felt a bit queasy himself thinking about the dead body. He forced himself to think of other things.

He was a businessman, a manager. What he did was lead people to act as a team. The four of them needed to act as a team. "So," Rick continued, "who visited all of you? Citas grabbed me with a white light out of the Old Testament."

Rocky shook his head. "Heros. No light. It was just . . . His presence is difficult to describe."

Rick turned to Richie. "What about you?"

Richie shrugged. "This guy comes into my cell, calls himself the master of illusion, and walks me out of the place telling me that there's a ring with my name on it."

"Lucas," Richard muttered.

"Yeah, how'd you know?"

"We all *know,*" Richard said. "We all have this place in our bones." He turned to Rick and said, "My visitation was by Vitus, the lord of farming and the arts. He charged me to take the Horn."

"How fucking original," Richie said. "The gods send us out on a quest. This was getting old before Odysseus was born."

Rick looked at Richie and thought of the warning he'd received. One of them would betray the others, and only one would reach the Adversary. . . .

After a moment Richie said, "Enough of this quest crap, tell them about the bridge, Rocky."

"What bridge?" Rick asked.

Rocky told him.

CHAPTER 23

JULIA

SISTER Magdalene led Julia up to Richard's empty room. On the way upstairs she expressed sympathy for Julia, and expressed confidence that Richard would pull through well enough to come home. Julia found herself touched by the realization that by "home," she meant Devereux House.

Why not? Richard's probably lived here longer than she's worked here.

For all the secrecy, Julia supposed that Mom had done well by her brother. As she opened the door to Richard's room, Sister Magdalene said, "I know some of what you're going through. My uncle suffered a stroke when he was only forty-five."

"Oh," Julia said. "I'm sorry." For some reason that surprised her. She had never pictured nuns with family. She felt silly. She also felt odd because she had only met Richard two days ago.

Sister Magdalene shook her head and smiled. "Don't be. He has a limp and a slight lisp, but he's lived twenty-five years since. Uncle Sean is as active as he ever was—Richard will make it through too."

Julia wished she could muster that kind of faith. Or at least make sense of all the emotions she was having at the moment. For the life of her, she didn't know if she should be more shaken because all this was happening to her brother, or less so because Richard was a total stranger to her.

Everything she felt seemed inappropriate for the situation.

Julia walked into the room and tossed a traveling bag

on the bed. She zipped it open and then stopped, feeling frozen and at a loss. She turned to Sister Magdalene and said, "I have no idea what to pack. I'm afraid you'd know better than I would."

"Oh, yes, of course. This has to be difficult for you." She went to the dresser-nightstand and began sliding open the drawers and picking up items and handing them to Julia. "How long did the doctor say he would be at the clinic?"

"At least a week."

Sister Magdalene nodded and handed her a small leather bag. Julia was surprised to see that it was a shaving kit. It was even monogrammed; the initials were "C.B." Julia slipped it into the suitcase with the bizarre double realization that someone had to shave her brother every day, and that the shaving kit must have belonged to her father. Richard was all she had left of Mom and Dad. She could feel tears welling up, but she didn't stop packing.

A sadistic part of her mind kept saying that she shouldn't be here. She had work to do, untying the knots Mom left behind her, selling the house, paying the creditors, packing up everything. Focusing on Richard wasn't going to do anyone any good. Not even Richard was going to notice.

It was the same evil part of her mind that accused her of being a hypocrite, that she was only doing this because she thought she was supposed to.

If Mom had just told me, at least I'd know what I felt. . . .

Julia felt a swell of anger at her Mom. She turned away from Sister Magdalene, as if the resulting guilt shone through her face. Julia walked to the bookshelf and started running her hand across the spines. In motion the shaking didn't show.

"Which of these should I pack?" Julia hated the sound of her own voice. She was certain that it sounded as if she were on the verge of a breakdown.

"Oh, you read to him, too? That's nice." She hated the

way that sounded. There was nothing nasty or sarcastic in Sister Magdalene's voice, but Julia might have felt better if there had been. There seemed to be a willful ignorance, everyone here acting as if Richard hadn't been Mom's dirty little secret.

No one here acted as if Julia hadn't seen her brother once in the past quarter century. Even though it hadn't been Julia's fault, the fact that everyone seemed to ignore it paradoxically drew her to dwell on it, and the guilt she felt over it.

"I don't know what to pack," she repeated. To her own ears she sounded as if she were harping.

Sister Magdalene walked up next to her and looked at the bookshelf. "I would take something that you enjoy reading."

Julia's hand rested on one of the spines. It was a popular science book about quantum mechanics. "Is that what Mom did?" she asked. "I didn't know she liked this stuff." The philosophy Julia understood. That had always fascinated Mom. Julia understood the fantasy, too. Richard had obviously enjoyed the stuff before the accident.

"I asked her about it once," Sister Magdalene said.

"What did she say?"

"She voiced a logical argument that it would take a Jesuit to untangle. It was a while ago, I only remember the broad outlines of it. She said that, 'The precepts of quantum physics support the view of the German Idealists, that the world is created by our own perceptions of it.' Or something along those lines."

Julia nodded. Now she could understand the books, they were of the same order as the philosophy. She nodded, "That's Mom. She taught graduate philosophy. She tied her students into knots with arguments like that—"

"That isn't all," Sister Magdalene said.

"Oh?"

"She said that Richard might actually be perceiving a different reality than we did, something created through whatever perceptions he had." She walked up next to

Julia, looking at the spines of the books. "It is a comforting thought, believing that Richard still has a world beyond this one."

Julia looked at her, "Do you believe that?"

"Please, Miss Brandon. Of course I do. Perhaps not what your mother believed, but I don't find it unlikely that Richard's soul might have a life fuller than that expressed in his body."

"I wish I could believe that," Julia said.

"What's important, right now," Sister Magdalene said, "is what Richard believes." She began handing her yellowed copies of C. S. Lewis.

Julia left with a packed suitcase, a few dog-eared paperbacks, and two more of Richard's old notebooks. When she got into her car, she leafed through one of them.

It was an old composition book with a cardboard cover of mottled black. In the white space for name and subject, Richard had penned his name and the word "Quinque" in a child's deliberate calligraphy.

Unlike the first notebook, this one was filled. Every page was penned with careful notes. Julia rested the book on the steering wheel and read a few pages at random.

The first page she looked at was a glossary, complete with pronunciation guide. There she saw that Quinque was pronounced "(kwin'kwe)" and was a reference to the five human gods. Quinque was the name of the capital city and the kingdom it ruled. She also saw that "fay" was a noun and "fey" was an adjective, thought they were pronounced the same way.

Apparently a fay can be fey but not vice versa.

On another page she found descriptions of the Artifacts she'd read about in Quinque's creation myth. The Sword of Heros apparently conveyed infallibility in battle, and the wielder could not be slain in combat. The Horn of Vitus was a nexus of life and creativity, and he who held it was immortal. The Staff of Magus gave the wielder control over all that was fey—definitely not *fay*—and magical. The Ring of Lucas controlled illusion, deception, and knowledge. And the Cirque of Citas gave the wearer the power of command.

Julia grinned slightly, wondering if the young Richard knew about the symbolism he was playing with. The smile was short-lived when she thought about Richard now, as opposed to the boy who wrote this notebook a quarter century ago.

She closed the notebook and laid it on the seat next to her. She started the car, turned on the radio to distract herself, and began the drive down to the Clinic—and her brother.

CHAPTER 24

RICHIE

RICHIE watched the other bogus copies of himself try to deal with the new information. They had trouble handling it, except for Rocky, who didn't seem imaginative enough to find it disturbing.

"Things are leaking in here from our world," Rick said.

Worlds, you arrogant shit, Richie thought.

After a long hesitation, Richard the poet added, "I am worried."

"Well, hurrah," Richie said, "at least someone is having a sane reaction to all this twisted bullshit—"

Richard shook his head as he stared into the fire, almost as if he were denying Richie's accusations of sanity. "We've all known Quinque since we were children." It was a flat statement of fact. Richie disliked the automatic assumption, even if it were true in his case, but no one objected to the assertion and Richard continued. "This isn't the same Quinque, is it? Has anyone here dreamed of an Adversary, a war, or this ruler, Alveron?"

No one spoke.

"Something is wrong here," Richard finished. It was one of the longest speeches Richie had ever heard him make.

Richie didn't know whether to laugh or scream. "Come on, people, listen to me. We're in never-never land, of *course* something is wrong here." The whole situation was twisted. At this point Richie would rather be home dealing with Rico and pissed Colombians. Worse, he didn't want to give this world the option of being real. That would mean that everything that had happened in his cell was real, and he wasn't ready to accept that.

However, everyone just looked at him quietly, as if he were the one who'd gone nuts. Richie stared back, "Are we just going to accept all this?"

Rick looked at him, "Do you have a better suggestion?"

"Aside from all the metaphysical bullshit, getting something to eat comes to mind."

For once Rick agreed with him. "Richie's right. We have a host of practical concerns, and food tops the list. We aren't that far from the city gates—"

"Christ on a stick, man," Richie said. "You aren't seriously thinking of going back there after the way we were trounced?"

Rocky said, "It's the closest source of food, clothing, and shelter. It's more of a risk for us to go into the wilderness unprepared."

"And," Rick said, "there's little chance that concern about us has passed beyond the palace walls yet." Rick stood up and began kicking dirt over the fire, as if everything had been decided.

Fearless effing leader, Richie thought. "Maybe I should point out the fact that we stand out like the quadruplet day parade? Not to mention we're dressed to attract attention." Richie could still remember Alveron's uncle saying, *"In the village where I was a lad, midwives would kill identical siblings because they only had one soul between them."* The memory chilled Richie like little else he had experienced since his world had gone insane. He stood up to face Rick. "I don't know where you've been living your life, but the one thing I know is when the hell you're pushing your luck too far."

Rocky stood. "Look, Richie. Sometimes you have to take a risk—"

"Why the fuck are you on his side?" Richie asked disgustedly, waving in Rick's direction. "I'd think a cop'd know better than to risk getting rousted by the local gendarmes."

"I think," Rick said, "he realizes that, beyond the essentials of food and water, we need to be unified."

"I didn't ask you—"

"He's right," Rocky said.

"Sheesh," Richie responded. He turned to look down at Richard, who was still sitting on the ground. "What about you? What do you think?"

Richard looked surprised at being asked his opinion.

"I think," he said, "that we will be in equal peril wherever we choose to go."

Fucking philosopher.

"That's it, then," Rick said. "Let's go."

The guy takes the control thing seriously, Richie thought, as they started down the valley, toward the river.

Richie went with the others without complaining about how much his body hurt. He still felt the feet of the guards in the small of his back. As he walked at the rear of the quartet, it felt as if he were being kicked again with every step.

Rick kept glancing over his shoulder, giving him looks that Richie didn't like. Richie was starting to think that if these guys were alternate versions of himself, somewhere along the line he'd gotten shafted—

Not that I'd change places with any of my balls-up alter egos. Richard the professor was a weak sister who looked like he drifted with whatever prevailing wind caught him. Rick was one of those cocksure assholes with a grand belief in his own superiority, and Rocky was a goddamn cop.

And, of course, everyone else was willing to follow Rick-the-leader. Richie was ticked that no one else seemed to give a shit about his point of view on anything.

As if Rick were somehow the expert on what had happened to them.

Hell, if anyone had it on the ball about this place, it was the effing professor. At least Richard wasn't obnoxious about throwing his weight around.

The terrain didn't want to cooperate with them. Their

ever-loving destination was almost constantly visible through the trees to their east, but every time the road seemed to close toward it, it would hook left or right just before the ground fell down into the river valley.

When there was a good view into the valley, Richie could see docks and small boats anchored by the eastern shore. The western shore, where they were stuck, seemed undeveloped for the most part. Richie was lost enough that he couldn't really tell how much the terrain actually mapped on to the Cuyahoga Valley, but the one thing that was clearly different was the dearth of bridges.

Every time they approached a bluff overlooking the river, they would search for a crossing. Too many times they were disappointed. Between the curves of the river and the curves the road made, a trek that should have been less than a mile, seemed to stretch interminably. Their progress wasn't helped by the fact that the road had a habit of disappearing out from under them, its dirt track vanishing into the undergrowth.

Of course, as soon as Richie began to feel they had made some progress down the coast, it started to rain.

There was a conspiracy to prevent him from ever feeling dry again. Richie was beginning to feel as if he'd need a spatula to take off his T-shirt.

Within minutes after the rain began, the path they followed turned into a muddy river. "Hold it," Rick said over the rain. "We aren't going to get far in this mess."

Slap me in the face with the obvious, Richie thought.

"I think I saw a building," Rocky said, "about a hundred yards back, down the hill."

"Christ," Richie muttered, "You could have said something back then." No one seemed to hear him, and Richie didn't really give a shit anymore. He was battered, hungry, and thirsty, and his feet felt like hermetically sealed fungus.

They slogged back to where Rocky had seen his building, and it was as bad as Richie had imagined. It lay down at the bottom of a slick, rain-drenched slope, and the rain was getting worse.

The scramble down was a nightmare. It was a barely controlled fall, broken at intervals when Richie could grab hold of a sapling. His hands were raw and sticky with sap, even through his gloves.

Somehow he made it to the bottom still standing. He stood, ankle-deep in mud and dead leaves, and breathed. His ribs hurt, his back hurt, his feet hurt, rain poured down his back, and he had to breathe through his mouth because the half of his nose that wasn't clogged with blood was now heavy with mucus.

Fuck it, dreams don't work like this.

He felt a hand on his shoulder, and he almost jumped out of his skin. It was Richard. "Are you all right?"

Richie nodded. "I just need a minute."

Ahead of them, Rick and Rocky were already going over the small blocky stone building. The place had little to recommend it but a roof.

Rocky called back to them, "It's empty."

Richie didn't want to move, but Richard led him up to the small structure. *Fuck, it isn't even a real building.*

It was little more than three walls and a roof. The walls were rough unmortared stone, the roof seemed little more than a few rough-hewn planks. At the rear of the building seemed to be a pile of debris around the base of a broken stone pillar. Two long benches lined the side walls, little more than logs cleaved in half. Richard led him to one.

There was a small pit for a fire, and Rocky was already fiddling at it. "What is this place?" Richie muttered to himself. It made him uneasy.

When Richie sat, he felt every bruise wrapping his body. He must have moaned, because Richard asked, "Are you sure you're all right?"

"Come on, I'm doing as well as any of you guys. The way things look, I *am* you guys."

"Yeah," he said. "But you're the only one of us that was beaten to a pulp."

"I guess you got me there."

Richard touched the collar of his jacket and said, "Maybe I should look at—"

Richie grabbed his hand and said, "No."

He said it sharp and loud enough for the other two to stare at him from across the dead firepit. Richie shook his head, "No, not right now." With everyone still looking at him, Richie said, "What *is* this place?"

Rick answered him. "It appears to be some sort of shrine." He was standing at the rear of the structure. Richie saw that what he had taken to be a broken pillar was actually a crude statue. The debris at its base now seemed offerings of some sort.

Rick bent over and said, "There's a loaf of bread here that still seems edible."

"Is swiping food from a local god a good idea?" Richie asked, though he could feel his stomach moving just at the suggestion of food.

Rick handed the brown slab of bread to Rocky, who hadn't managed to do anything with the fire. He said something that Richie couldn't hear over the rain pouring outside.

"What?"

Rocky raised his voice and said, "Four to one that we know the God in question, right? Besides, I'm hungry."

Rocky broke the bread with an audible snap, and Richie felt an unwanted flashback to Doc Brandon's apartment, where he last had fears of eating the wrong thing. . . .

Richie took his piece when it was passed to him. It felt suspiciously like a block of Styrofoam. In order to eat it, he had to suck on a corner long enough to soften it, and its taste was somewhere between moss and sawdust.

For a long time, no one spoke. Outside, the rain became the fourth wall of the building, blocking the entrance like a solid wall of rippling slate. Richie kept thinking, over and over, that he was well and truly fucked.

Gods. That's all I need to be thinking about right now. How the hell can you accept anything said by someone calling himself "Monarch of Trickery and Deception?"

The Rat Master hadn't decided to make his life easy.

His visitor had told him that the Ring held his only

escape from this place, and that one of the four would face the Adversary.

"Bullshit," he'd said. "This is all an effing hallucination."

Lucas had laughed at Richie. "Shall I agree with you? This all is a phantasm, an unreality in which you are entrapped."

Lucas had never left the shadows, and the shadows had reached out to engulf Richie. The cell had become a boiling void, and a whirling maelstrom had opened beneath Richie. He had fallen, dangling from a single manacle. The drop had almost popped his shoulder from his socket.

"A dream, Richard Brandon," Lucas had said from above him as if Richie was an insect over a campfire. "Whose dream can it be? Perhaps it is mine. Perhaps you are the phantasm, and I can drop you into the nonexistence from which you came."

Richie had stared into the vortex and the doubt had leeched out of him. He didn't want to die.

"Perhaps it is reality, in which case you look at your own death. Then again, you could be right. It *is* your dream. And you will descend forever, never waking. . . ."

The chain had jerked. "Shall we find out?"

Richie had screamed when the chain let go. He had screamed all three feet into the surface of the road. For hours after that, he had thought the wind was laughing at him.

It wasn't until much later that he had slipped a hand into his pocket and discovered that he now carried his gun, with no memory of how it had been returned to him.

He had to admit that if this was some sort of hallucination, it was the heaviest, baddest trip he had ever taken. He didn't like having his own doubts thrown back at him.

If the world couldn't prove to him that it wasn't a dream, how could he prove that *he* was real?

As the rain pounded above, his hand drifted to his pocket, and the gun. He had almost blown it when Richard tried to take his jacket. He didn't want to let on.

He knew Rick or the cop would try and take the gun as soon as they knew he had it back.

From the looks of things, Richie thought it was the only edge he had.

CHAPTER 25

RICHARD

RICHARD sat next to Richie and felt a knot of worry in his gut. Richie looked as if he were trying not to wince every time he took a breath.

Richie stared out at the rain. Richard placed a hand on his shoulder. Richie winced and turned toward him.

"I really think you should let someone look at your injuries."

Richie folded his arms as if he were defending himself, "Look, I'm all right—"

"No, you aren't," Richard said. "You should let me do what I can."

Richie sighed. "Okay, what the fuck."

Richard smiled weakly and undid what was left of his tie, the cleanest piece of cloth he had. He walked to the front and held his arm, with the tie, out in the downpour.

He wrung it out a few times, then he returned and reached out for Richie's chin. Richie shrank back. "What the fuck're you doing?"

Richard sighed. "I'm washing the mud out of your wounds. Or do you want an infection where they've never heard of an antibiotic?"

Richie gave him a lopsided smile with his busted lip. "Oh."

He grabbed Richie's chin and began washing out the worst of it with his wreck of a tie. He hoped he was doing more good than harm, especially when some of the abrasions under the hairline began weeping new blood.

It was like washing a mirror, handling a version of his own face like that. Time and again, his gaze locked on

Richie's eyes and he knew that Richie was staring at his own face, perhaps with similar thoughts.

Richard worked around behind Richie. When they were no longer staring at each other, Richie asked, "Do you think this is really happening?"

"Yes." Richard said, gently wiping dirt off a wide abrasion that descended from Richie's right ear down to where the leather collar of his jacket protected his neck.

"Then how do you explain it? How come English, how come this battle with the ultimate evil and a divine quest—"

"A situation that was ancient before the birth of Odysseus," Richard finished for him.

"Not my exact words, but yeah—ouch." Richie winced as Richard pulled the collar of his jacket.

"Sorry," Richard said. "Probably you should take that off for a minute."

Richie grunted. He was quiet for a long while before he said, "To be honest, I think the jacket's what's holding me together." Richard noticed that he was looking at Rocky and Rick as he said it. The other two weren't paying attention to them at the moment; they were wrapped in their own discssion. Probably about the best approach to the city.

"You really should take it off," Richard said.

Richie muttered something, but he unzipped. Richard tried to help him take the jacket off, but Richie pulled away sharply. "I'll do it," he insisted.

"Gods, do I stink," he heard Richie mutter. Richard noticed how careful he was, placing the jacket in his lap.

Must have some sentimental value, Richard thought.

Without the jacket, Richie was left wearing an abused sleeveless T-shirt. It was spattered with dirt and dried blood, and it was damp enough to be semitransparent in places. Richard could see the purple-red of Richie's bruises through the material.

Richie stripped the shirt off gingerly. Watching him wince, Richard asked, "Think you've got any broken ribs?"

Richie grunted. "Don't think so. Had a few busted ribs once, I think I could tell." He tossed the shirt on the floor of the shrine.

Bruises ringed his torso, mapping livid continents across his otherwise pale back. There were dozens of places where his skin had broken, but not nearly as many as there would have been if it weren't for the jacket. Richard could trace one place under his shoulder blade where the bruises took the shape of the sole of a boot. That bruise was dotted with dime-sized spots where the boot had been studded.

Richie looked over his shoulder at Richard and said, "Answer my effing question, would you?"

"How I explain it? What if Quinque is the real world, and the places we come from is—are—the fantasy?"

"You've got to be joking. That makes no sense."

"Doesn't it?" Richard knelt and began washing the blood off of Richie's back. "None of us can quite agree on what the real world *is*. We all come from *different* real worlds. And none the same as the Doctor's world . . ."

"Yeah, but that whole many-worlds thing can be explained with quantum mechanics. This place can't. You can't get there from here."

"This place is different, Richie. It operates on different laws. What if this place is the hub of reality? 'Midland, the real world from which all worlds, above and below, come;' I wrote that phrase."

"Bullshit," Richie said, but his heart didn't seem in it.

"How would we know the difference if we were the fantasy, drawn here by this place's magic?"

Richie stood up abruptly. "Fuck that noise, professor." He turned around, pointing at him. A flush bled across his face and the unbruised part of his chest. "I ain't no one's fucking dream. You got that?"

He shrugged on his jacket and turned away from him, to stare out at the rain.

Richard sighed and tossed his tie next to Richie's T-shirt.

"So, Rick?" Richie asked, still facing the rain.

"Yes?" Rick said. His tone had a slightly condescending note, as if he were interrupted doing something more important than anything Richie could possibly say.

Richie didn't seem to notice. "I wanted to ask you what your take on all this is."

"What do you mean?" Rick said.

"I mean, is this really happening?"

"Does it matter?" Rick asked. "This is the only point of reference we have. . . ."

Richard saw Rocky nod slightly.

"Yeah," Richie said. He waved generally in Richard's direction. "The prof has the wonderful theory that this world may have created *us*."

"The reverse might also be possible," Rick said. "Perhaps we, or maybe even the late Dr. Brandon, *created* this place."

Richie turned around to face him. "Say what?"

"We are evidence that there are multiple parallel realities, what Dr. Brandon was studying. We all shared the idea of Quinque; he must have as well. What if his experiment somehow created a real Quinque out of whatever quantum probabilities he was manipulating to, in some sense, become us?"

Richie took a step backward.

"Think about it for a moment," Rick said. "Five gods, and if you include Dr. Brandon, there are five Richard Brandons."

Everyone looked at Rick, and Richard felt slightly uncomfortable, as if Rick were blaspheming.

"So the prof says we're a dream," Richie finally said. "And you say we're the *gods?*"

"It makes as much sense as anything else that has happened," Rick said.

Richard didn't like the thought, because his mind kept returning to the corpse in the garden, and the crumbling statue of Magus.

"Rocky?" Richard asked.

"Don't ask me to venture an opinion," Rocky said. "It's difficult enough dealing with things as they happen."

Richard rubbed his hands together. He didn't like the sense that they were drifting here. "What are we going to do?" he said.

Everyone turned toward him. They all looked surprised that he'd said anything.

Rick said, "We're going into town—as soon as the rain stops—and try to get some food and lodging."

Richard shook his head. "That's not what I mean."

"You mean the Quest B.S." Richie said.

Richard nodded. That question had been hanging in his gut since this morning. He knew that no good ever came from talking to the Gods of Quinque, who were as arbitrary and petty as any other pantheon man had invented. He also knew that defying them usually led to disaster.

"Good question," Richie said. "Boss?"

Rick looked thoughtful. "We all want to get back home. I don't know about any of you, but I have a newspaper that might go under without me—" Richie snorted. Rick went on, "Anyway, if we take that as our priority, is there anyone here whose visitor did *not* say this 'quest' would end our exile here?"

Rick waited for a long time; no one contradicted him.

"There," he said. "So far that is the only lead we have. We can't very well ignore it."

"Yeah, right," Richie said, as if it were nothing more than he expected. "Am I the only one who remembers where the Artifacts actually are, and how suicidal that'd be?"

"If the gods are behind us—" Richard began to say.

"They would have been behind Doc Brandon, too, right?" Richie asked. Richard fell silent, thinking of the corpse again.

"The dumbest religious mistake anyone ever made was the belief that the gods were on their side," Richie concluded.

The rain slackened off in the afternoon, and the quartet of Richards headed south along the coastline to find a crossing. They came in view of a bridge—one that actually crossed the water—after following the coast along another oxbow.

The bridge was a massive construction, connecting opposite sides of the river valley, nearly a mile long. Massive pillars flanked the central span of the bridge, bearing winged carvings that would have seemed Assyrian if Richard wasn't already familiar with the origin of the bridge.

"Holy fuck," Richie said, "another one."

They kept approaching the roadway, as if seeing the Lorain-Carnegie Bridge wasn't unexpected.

Something was wrong here. Richard could feel it, even if he couldn't put the wrongness into words. Quinque was its own reality. It had its own validity. If something from his world—Richard's world—had invaded to this extent, it represented a serious breakdown. . . .

More disturbing was the fact that the same reasoning could carry over to the Richards' presence here.

The closer they got to the bridge, the older it seemed, and the more it tried to appear an integral part of the landscape. It was a mission that it never quite achieved; its construction was an anachronism.

Where are the Thralls? Richard thought. It was their job to prevent dreams and reality from mixing—or dream mixing with dream. Richard didn't like the idea that the Thralls had something better to worry about than a vaguely Assyrian pile of iron and concrete.

The people of Quinque didn't seem to have any qualms about the bridge. Carts and horses had queued up to cross, not a huge number—minuscule given the scale of the bridge—but easily more humanity than they'd seen ever since arriving.

They emeged on the cobbled surface of the main road about two hundred yards from the bridge itself.

Richie stared after the queue waiting to cross. "Okay, Fearless Leader, now what? From the looks of it, the natives have put up a customs house on our bridge. And we don't look any less alike than we did this morning."

"That, at least, shouldn't be a problem if we go across

one at a time," Rocky said. He pointed next to the carts, "We can mix in with the pedestrians. They're probably more interested in what's in those wagons."

They followed Rocky's suggestion and merged with the peasant horde that accompanied the wagons. They spaced themselves far enough apart so it was unlikely that any guard would spy them all at once.

Rocky was right, in that the officials holding up traffic seemed more interested in searching the vehicles than anything else. Even the people with whom they merged seemed to have little attention to spare for them. The pedestrians had all the appearance of refugees fleeing a war zone. They wore ragged clothes and carried heavy bundles. Women dragged oddly silent children after them, and most showed little inclination to talk.

What conversations Richard overheard were of evil things taking over the landscape, of the Adversary's armies to the East, and how the land itself seemed to be becoming more uncertain.

The Richards' clothes didn't stand out as much as Richard had thought they would. They blended in with the others, ragged, dirty, and torn. Rocky, Rick, Richie—and finally—Richard were passed through to form a shuffling line across the right side of the bridge.

CHAPTER 26

ROCKY

DEAL with things as they come up, Rocky thought. Any other attitude was inviting insanity. He didn't want to dwell too long on the bridge, and what it was doing here. So Rocky kept his eyes on the guards. And, once past the guards, he watched the northern horizon, and the city.

For a walled city, Quinque was huge. Buildings crowded together and climbed three, four, and five stories. The horizon was dotted by cylindrical towers that climbed as high as fifteen stories. Statuary topped buildings, presiding over city squares.

The city overspilled its central walls to crowd against the eastern bank of the river. Buildings followed twisted roads down to where the bridge met the eastern bluffs of the river valley.

Behind the city walls, Rocky could see the palace, a webwork of towers and walls that lorded over all the smaller structures from a point overlooking the bluffs down to the river.

The smell of wood smoke and animals greeted him on the opposite shore. He walked away from the aisle of refugees and waited for the others to catch up. The scene was too reminiscent of the roads he drove down in Nicaragua. There the aisles of displaced population were so ubiquitous that their absence was a sign of trouble—snipers, impending attack. . . .

The others collected around him, loitering, watching the passage of people down the road toward the town. When Richie showed up, he said, "Where the hell do they think they're going?"

Rocky looked at the passing faces, dirty and empty of most expression. "Away from whatever's out there."

Richie looked around, at the sparse collection of buildings that flanked the road. "Well? We're here. Now what?"

"We find food and lodging," Rick said.

Richie stared after the file of refugees. "I don't want to burst your bubble, but assuming that there's any left to be had, I don't think they'll take American Express."

Above them, the sky was threatening rain again. Gray clouds hung low over the road to the city, the dim light turned the buildings' plaster walls gray to match. Projecting timbers—projecting rafters to entire Tudor frameworks—had been darkened by rain, and appeared black. Everything smelled cold and earthy, mud, smoke, and horseshit.

What was he doing here? He'd done his time in Central America.

Maybe it's my turn to be a refugee—

Richie's shouting interrupted his thoughts.

"The fuck you are! You touch anything of mine and I'll pound my face off that swelled head of yours."

"Wha—" Rocky turned back to the others. Rick was grimacing, sitting down in the mud by the side of the road. Richie was hovering over him, his fist raised. Richard grasped his arm, holding him back, looking ineffectual.

"Stop it!" Richard was shouting, Rocky could almost swear the man was crying. "Stop it. Stop it!"

Rocky stepped between Richie and Rick. He held up a hand in front of Richie's chest. "What in the hell is going on here. Christ, did someone call recess?"

"It's all right," Rick said. "I slipped." He slowly levered himself out of the mud.

"Bastard is lucky I *didn't* slug him," Richie said.

"What happened?" Rocky repeated.

Richard let go of Richie's arm. He spoke fast, gesturing as if he was unsure what to do with his hands. "Rick just started going over how we could go about paying for food and a room and how we could barter for what we needed if we found someone willing to trade and what we had that we could barter with—"

Richie interrupted, raising his fist. "Fearless Leader wants to sell my jacket."

"—*please,*" Richard whispered.

"Curb this shit," Rocky told Richie, "before *I* slug you."

Rick backed away from both of them. He started to brush off his pants, but only succeeded in smearing more mud. "All I was doing, Richie, was going over everything we had among us that we could trade with."

"Stunning coincidence," Richie said, backing away from Rocky. "My jacket and my boots top the list."

Rocky sighed. "And what if that's the only way we can get some decent food—not to mention decent clothes for the rest of us?"

Richie stared at him. "I don't like suddenly becoming community property."

"Rick's just going over options," Rocky said. "We're begging the question of whether someone will even be willing to barter for room and board."

"Christ, I just don't want people selling my shit for me."

"Look," Rick said, "If the subject comes up, you'll be doing the bartering, okay?"

Richie stared past Rocky, at Rick, and nodded slowly.

Next to him, Rocky could hear Richard exhale. Rocky could feel tension lift from the group. Unfortunately, it didn't dissipate completely.

Far from completely.

Quinque was a large city. As they walked, the line of refugees blended into the native population. About a mile toward the city wall, it was impossible to make out any line, as such. The refugees were individuals again, slipping into a tightening webwork of streets.

Once across the bridge, it wasn't possible to restrict access to the outer city, war or not. Rocky didn't see any checkpoints after the bridge, or even any city guards. He supposed that all the guards were concentrated around the walls to the inner city, those that weren't involved in the war itself.

Eventually, winding paths gave way to a grid, and buildings packed closely enough to merge. The road they were on was a main thoroughfare, but Rocky suspected that once they turned off it, they would be lost.

No one seemed to pay much attention to them, however unusual they appeared. The roads were crowded with people. Vendors called out to pedestrians. Horse-drawn carts crowded each other on the street. People carried parcels here and there in an almost deliberate chaos. Beggars called to affluent looking passersby.

Not one beggar called to them.

Finding an inn wasn't a problem. Finding an inn with room, that was something else. Every place they stopped was filled beyond capacity, so the question of payment never came up. They walked the streets for hours as the afternoon darkened. It became a repeating pattern. They'd pass a sign swinging in the wind, they'd walk in, and the man behind the bar would tell them, "I canna help you."

If it weren't for the obvious overcrowding at each place they visited, Rocky would have thought that their appearance had something to do with it. However, even if the patrons would stare at them as they left, for the most part they were too caught up in their own lives to spare four newcomers any mind.

The last place they came to was near the wall to the inner city. They had run out of the main road, and were following the city wall east. However, it was starting to look as if they were going to be reduced to a choice between trying to get through the gate in the city wall, or descending into a twisted maze of alleys.

The sign above the door was like all the others, no writing, just a heraldic design. In this case it was a garish painting of a head mounted on a pike. It had pointed ears.

They all looked at each other, and Rick shrugged. He walked inside, taking a step down into a dark, windowless space. The city had done its best to numb Rocky's nose, but the smell of roasting meat awakened it and set his mouth watering. As they walked in, he placed a hand on Rick's shoulder, he was about to say that they should barter for the meal, even if a room wasn't available—

He never got the chance.

A flagon full of dark liquid sailed by his right ear to shatter against the door frame.

"Perhaps it's not the best time to ask about lodgings," Richie said.

Tables and chairs had upended on the sawdust-covered floor. Three men were beating on someone. Their victim was curled into a fetal position on the floor. One of the three was trying to hold off a short bearded man who was trying to thrash the trio with a club at least as large as he was.

"This is quite enough!" Rocky pushed his way past Richard and Rick. Adrenaline was surging through him, and the fight pulled him forward. He acted before he had made any conscious decisions.

Only one of the trio of attackers looked in his direction, and then only for a moment. The arrogance of that one dismissive glance infuriated Rocky. That and the paralysis of the patrons who had retreated to the walls.

He bent over and picked up the remains of a chair leg, which had a thick dowel emerging from its side. Held by the dowel, it made a half-assed tonfa.

To his surprise, he heard a jingle of chain next to him. He glanced over and saw Richie slowly unwinding a chain that had been wrapped around his waist. He was grinning.

Rocky gritted his teeth and, holding his improvised club, descended on the trio.

His arm descended, backhanding the face of one of the attackers. The impact sounded like someone slamming a door on a melon. The attacker jerked backward, face spraying red, and Rocky felt the man's blood splash his forearm.

He carried the motion over to straight-arm his makeshift tonfa into the right kidney of a second attacker.

That one folded over Rocky's arm, and Rocky took a half step and turn that tumbled that guy on top of the man with the bloodied face.

The third one, who was holding off the short man with the beard, tried to back away. Richie swung his chain at his feet, making the man tumble backward. That gave the bearded man a chance to clout the side of the man's head.

The fight was over by the time Rick and Richard reached Rocky's side.

The little man shuffled around the perimeter, kicking the fallen attackers. "Hell this is. Whole city's gone to shit. You are militia, making this your business?"

"No, not militia. Do we look like militia?"

Rocky tossed the club away, and turned to help the victim. Richard was ahead of him. Richard had led, or followed, the victim to the end of the bar and was now tending to the battered figure.

At least someone's taking care of that.

"No," said the short, bearded figure, "not militia you look like."

Rocky turned back to the little man with the club, and began to notice oddities about him, oddities that marked this person as something other than a man. His skin was too ruddy, almost crimson. The skin was craggy rather than wrinkled, and as thick as leather. His irises were red as well, and had retinas that reflected the firelight. None of these oddities considered individually was enough to mark him as nonhuman, but somehow, when the impression was taken as a whole, collectively they marked him as something else.

Richie walked to Rocky's side and patted him on the shoulder and said, "Used to be, though. Old habits are hard to break, ain't they?"

The little man, who seemed to be the innkeeper, stepped on the chest of one of the attackers who was still moaning. "No moves, you wretch, or my club will find new lodgings in your backside—" He looked up at Rocky. "Militia or not, you have indebted me." He sighed.

"Further indebted I would be, if you would help in disposing of these unwelcome ones?"

Rocky looked at Richie, who shrugged.

He grabbed the shoulders of the man whose face he'd pulped. Richie grabbed the man the innkeeper had coshed in the head. The innkeep himself grabbed hold of the collar of the man whose chest he trod upon. With Rick helping, the three thugs were dragged out the door into the street, under a haze of misting rain.

Once his burden was out of his domain, the little man returned inside the inn, followed by Rick. Rocky was about to do likewise, when he noticed Richie fumbling about one of the unconscious men.

"What the hell are you doing?"

Richie looked at him with an expression of astonishment. "What the hell do you think I'm doing?"

It was Rocky's turn to feel incredulous. "You're robbing these guys?" He looked around. The streets were as crowded as ever, despite the misting rain. Passersby glanced at Richie and the trio of unconscious men, but only briefly. None looked disturbed, or even particularly interested, in what was going on. Even so, Rocky was shocked by Richie's sheer brazenness. "How can you—"

"Christ," Richie muttered as he stripped the belt off of the second man. "Like this is worse than beating these guys to a pulp? Why do you think I jumped in with you. None of our fucking business, but if we're involved, we might as well get something out of it, right?"

Richie snatched up a pouch that jingled. His face broke into a grin. Rocky shook his head, unsure of exactly what to do. He couldn't very well tell Richie to give the stuff back. In the end, Rocky simply watched over Richie, in case someone did object to his brazen thievery.

No one did.

When Rocky returned to the inn, Rick was engaged in a conversation with the innkeep.

"This war leaves us no law anymore," the dwarfish innkeep was saying. "No courtesy my guests have. Before they would take their battles out of the common room. Today they drag their war into my house. Wretches all."

"Sir—" Rick said.

"Torin, lad, that is my name."

"Torin, then, we—that is, the four of us—were looking for a room. . . ."

"Aye," Torin said. "If I say I am in debt to you for ending this fay-induced violence, then my guests you are. The just-vacant room I have is yours, along with any belongings those wretches left behind them. That and meals for two more days I reckon. They paid—little else recommending them."

"Thank you, sir." Rick said. He smiled as he turned to Rocky.

"What was that about 'fay-induced violence?' " Rocky asked.

"He's referring to the elf," Rick said.

"What elf?" Rocky asked.

CHAPTER 27

RICK

RICK led Rocky and the short innkeeper to where Richard was caring for the elf. He knew by the intake of breath when Rocky realized that the person Richard was tending was female, as well as nonhuman.

Rick knew what Rocky felt, doing this to another man was bad enough, but this was pure barbarism.

Her clothes were torn and spattered with blood, and her face had been bruised so badly that Rick couldn't form a picture of what she would look like in normal circumstances. The eye that wasn't swollen shut had a silver iris. Not gray, but a metallic, glittering silver, which had an oval pupil.

It was an evil replay of every rape story, every domestic violence story, that he had ever printed. It was the kind of story that made him glad he wasn't a reporter, so he never got close enough to what was happening to feel any of it. He had worked hard on his precious objectivity—

What had been the point?

Richard was washing away watery blood, and occasionally she would wince from his touch. Whenever she did, Richard would mutter a reassurance, "Don't worry, we're here to help."

The most disturbing response he got from her was when she said, "Why help your enemy?"

Richard kept working. He kept tending to the woman, washing too-thin blood from too-pale skin. Her bones seemed so long and thin that Rick had been worried that Richard would find a compound fracture, or worse, as he worked.

He and Rocky watched for a few moments before Torin, the innkeep, interrupted.

"And what are you doing?" Torin asked Richard.

"Patching up her wounds—"

"Ach, why not you go and minister to your own countrymen?" He made a disgusted snort, as he leaned over Richard. "The fay I'd toss out with the rest of them. Like as not I'd cheer them on if they did their business civilized, outside my rooms—"

Richard turned and looked at the dwarf sharply.

"Gods," Torin muttered looking across at Rocky and Rick, "you must all be brothers." He walked around Richard and started cleaning debris from the floor. "I make no mind if you're intent on aiding her, but I'd take kindly if you'd remove the fay to your own room. I am trying to clean here." He turned and spoke quietly to the people who still lined the walls. "Off with you all. If my housekeeping is such a spectacle, I will charge a crown to each man who wishes to see it. Lunch shall be delayed, if that fact has yet to penetrate those heads of yours."

Torin bent to his task, and the crowd began dispersing. Some walked outside, some climbed the stairs to where Torin presumably kept his rooms.

"Pardon," Rick said to Torin.

Torin let out a cavernous sigh. "Am I to regret my generosity? What? Speak quickly before I lose more money and use your bill to compensate for it."

"Just where exactly is our room?"

Torin slapped his forehead and shook his head. "Ach. Top of the stairs, end of the hall. Please hie there with that damned elf, would you?"

There was a surprised sound from Richie, who apparently had just entered on the end of Torin's monologue. "What damned elf?"

Rick shook his head sadly and looked down at the "damned elf." "You better come with us," he said to her.

She shook her head. "I shall, but it is not better for me, as your aid shows you do not know what is better for you." She held out her hand, and Rick helped her to her feet. Her grip was surprisingly strong. "My name is Daenan. You don't want me to thank you."

Rick nodded, not knowing how else to react.

Rick was still feeling some satisfaction with himself as a manager as they reached the threshold of their room. He had managed to talk a bar fight into a roof over their heads. Even with the elf as an added responsibility, he felt that he'd done well.

When he reached the room that Torin had bequeathed them, he almost changed his mind.

"Ugh," Richie said as he stepped across the threshold.

"Obviously maid service is not included," Rocky said.

Rick silently agreed. If it were not for the dearth of lodging in the outer city, he might have had trouble considering Torin's bequest a favor.

The three prior occupants had left the room in a state reminiscent of a compost heap. The place was thick with the smell of their garbage. Bones and crusts littered the floor, feeding a small insect civilization. The bedding amounted to a framework covered with straw. At least it had the texture of straw. The color, and the smell, was of something less wholesome.

Peels of some ancient fruit crunched under Rick's feet as he stepped into the room. For the first time, he noticed the burden Richie was carrying. As he watched, Richie shook his head and looked for a place to set down his load.

"I've seen homeless junkies with better hygiene," Richie said as he tipped over a table by the window. Debris slid off, onto the floor.

"Was that necessary?" Rick asked. "What is all that?"

"What?" Richie looked down at the floor, "Are you worried about the mess?" Richie put his bundle on the cleared table. "While you were haggling and treating the injured, I was collecting some local coloring."

Rick leaned over and saw a short tunic, spattered with some blood, a chain-mail shirt, a collection of knives, two swords with scabbards, belts—

"You stripped them naked," Rick said.

Rocky shook his head. "He left them with the local equivalent of underwear—"

Rocky looked as nonplussed as Rick felt. Rick wasn't comfortable with Richie's theft, he was even more uncomfortable with the thought that someone so close to himself could take such things in stride. Was the moral line inside so thin?

Richard kept him from having to answer. "Could someone open a window and let some fresh air in here?" He stood in the doorway, supporting Daenan. Now that Richard had cleaned off most of the blood, the normal shape of her face was discernible, if puffy and swollen.

Rocky turned to loose the shutters on the window.

"Go help Richard," Rick told Richie, glad for the sudden change in subject.

"All right, all right," Richie said.

Rick turned to look at Rocky. He stood by the window, clutching the sill with whitened knuckles. There was no glass in the way, so cool outside air blew past him into the room. His breathing was quick and shaky.

Rick put a hand on his shoulder, "Are you all right."

Rocky nodded, "Just . . . if I'd known."

"Known what?"

Rocky shut his eyes. "That they were attacking a woman."

Rick looked back to where Richard and Richie were cleaning what they could of the bed so they could lay Daenan down on it. "I know what you mean," Rick said.

"No, you don't," Rocky said. "You have no idea."

He kept clutching the sill, sucking in Quinque's excuse for fresh air. Rick lowered his hand because he didn't like the feeling of tension in Rocky's back.

"They suspended me from the force," Rocky whispered. "I was drunk, off duty, and walked into a domestic dispute. Put five shots into a man armed with a frying pan." Rocky turned to face Rick, and looked at him with a fury that was barely contained. "They might have pressed criminal charges, if his wife hadn't died from the blows he inflicted." Rocky shook his head. "Those bastards don't know how lucky they are."

Rick nodded, because nothing he could say would be an adequate response. How could he even mention how he felt about it, when he had spent his professional life in a retreat from involvement in anything. Leadership as a refuge from human contact.

He left Rocky at the window and helped Richie with the evil job of cleaning the bed.

It was filthy work. Things were alive in the straw, and there were parts that had turned into black slime. Fortunately, the rear window looked out on a deserted alley, so they had a place to toss all the garbage.

Once Daenan was on a bed that was now little more than a framework, and the rest of the room had achieved some semblance of order, Rocky returned to something approaching normalcy.

He ran his hands across his crew cut and set his face in an impassive expression, then asked Daenan, "So what is it we broke up down there?"

Richard looked up at him. He was seated at the head of the bed, as if guarding her. "Can't you give her some time to rest before—"

Daenan shook her head and removed a compress that Richard had been holding next to her face. "Your concern is misplaced. Let your brother ask his questions."

Richie looked around. "Look, if this is going to take a while, I'm going down and seeing this place's excuse for food."

Rick looked at him and felt pangs in the pit of his own stomach. "Bring something up for the rest of us."

"Yeah, right." Richie's tone said he didn't care for running errands, but at least he didn't make another argument of it. Every time Rick found himself sparring with Richie, he thought of the words Citas—or someone—had given him, "One of you will betray the others."

Rocky ran a hand through his hair again. "Get something for me to drink. Something strong."

Daenan looked up at Rocky, and Rick had trouble reading her expression. It wasn't just the bruising, which was horribly vivid against her pale skin.

He saw something in those odd silver eyes. Her gaze saw everything with complete disinterest. Rick thought that he could see the stare of a sociopath in Daenan's eyes.

"Why were those men attacking you?" Rocky asked her.

"You are a human soldier," she said. "You should know the purposelessness of human violence."

Rick could see a shift in Rocky's expression, as if Daenan had scored a hit.

"I'm asking what started the fight," Rocky asked.

"They carry their war here. All things fey are their enemy."

Rocky sighed and walked back to the window. "So is that who they're at war with? Elves?"

Daenan laughed humorously. "You are at war with all things magic, because you have lost control of your gods."

"Do not include me with those men."

"You are included with everything."

Rick looked at Daenan. She still lay there, frail and bruised. He was starting to get the impression that the frailness was an illusion, and that there was more strength within her than within any of the Richards.

Rocky glared at her. "You insist that we are your enemy?"

"I do no insisting."

"They attacked you."

"Yes," she said.

"Describe what happened."

"Is it necessary to put her through this?" Richard asked.

Rick rested a staying arm on Richard's shoulder. "We need to know what is happening here," he said.

"I doubt I'm distressing the lady," Rocky added. He walked up to the edge of the bed and looked down. "Am I?"

"I do not think any human can distress me."

Rick thought of her three attackers. He was beginning

to think that the beating she received was much more severe than her appearance attested to.

"What happened?" Rocky asked.

"I walked on the street outside. One man dragged me inside. They insisted I give an oath to Alveron."

"I assume you did not?"

"Oaths are sacred."

That phrase awoke a dim memory in Rick, memories he had been only dimly aware of before. This world he was trapped in had been constantly assaulting him with feelings of familiarity, faint and strong. It had come to the point where even elements wholly new to his imagination contained the seeds of déjà vu.

Oaths are sacred.

Rick could see the same recognition in Rocky's face, and Richard's.

He'd had the same dreams of Quinque as a child as had his brothers. Now he remembered how powerful those dreams were. How important they had been. What little he had enjoyed that was honorable or praiseworthy, especially after the accident had taken his parents, had been walled off in those dreams.

The elves here were not mortal. They carried none of the emotional or moral weight that man did for his mortality. Their universe was not ordered along human dualities of life and death, good and evil. Theirs was a universe ordered by oaths, honor, and ultimate personal sovereignty.

All of this came as an instantaneous impression, a sudden gestalt pulled from his mind by Daenan's words.

What came first? This place, or my memories of it?

"I understand," Rocky said. From his expression, he *did* understand.

"They attacked you because you would not pledge fealty to their kind," Rick said.

"This is so," she said.

"Why didn't you defend yourself?" Rocky asked finally.

"How can you ask—" Richard began.

Rocky held up his hand. "Please, Professor. You're the one who wrote epics about this place. I can assume that you wrote more than enough about Daenan's kind."

"Yes, but—"

"From what little I remember about the fairy races, those delicate limbs hold the strength to throttle small herd animals. But none of those men had a mark on them before I stepped in. Why didn't you defend yourself?"

"You assume that I am worth defending."

Rocky looked at Rick.

"Why, Daenan?" Richard asked. "Why let them . . ."

"Perhaps I gain a bit of my honor by accepting their judgment. They would have stopped in time."

"Not until you were . . ." Rocky began.

Daenan smiled. There was something alien in it, as if the expression had been learned. "You were about to say 'dead.' "

Rocky nodded.

"I can no more choose to die than you can choose not to. Even were this body taken to Chaos himself and merged therein, I would still be." Daenan's artificial smile vanished. "Much as I would wish otherwise."

"You *want* to die?" Rick asked incredulously.

"It is my dishonor to not wish to exist outside this world."

Rocky shook his head. "I think you better explain that."

"My people see this world as a prison, they would see it consume itself and free them from the material."

"Material what?" Rocky asked.

"The material everything. They seek the end of all things not themselves."

Rocky looked over at Rick and Richard. From their expressions, this was a new wrinkle to all of them. Rick certainly didn't remember such a self-destructive streak in the Quinque he imagined.

"Is that why there's a war? Why humans fight the elves?"

Daenan looked into Rocky's face, then Richard's, then Rick's. Her expression was impassive, but the sense was that she was looking for something. She leaned back and closed her eyes, as if she'd found what she had been seeking. "The humans fight the Adversary, because he will bring change. The fay aid him for their own purposes, not the Adversary's. The Adversary will allow the world to end, no matter his wishes."

"What—" Rocky began.

"I shall rest now," Daenan said, eyes closed. That effectively ended the questioning.

CHAPTER 28

JULIA

"I don't understand why you can't just tell me how he's doing," Julia said. She was embarrassed at the edge of desperation that had crept into her voice. It was an ugly reminder of how she had acted when she heard about Mom.

Dr. Kavcheck nodded. "I understand your frustration," he said in a tone of voice that managed to sound soothing without being condescending. She was glad for that, at least. She already had experienced enough condescending sympathy in the past few weeks to last her for the rest of her life. And the disheartening fact was, he probably *did* understand, and probably better than she did.

They were talking in his office at the Clinic, which was neater than his office at Devereux House, but windowless and smaller. Half the room was taken up by Dr. Kavcheck's fairly modest desk. The fluorescent lights seemed to emphasize the closeness of the whitewashed walls, making her feel claustrophobic.

"Is he going to die?" Julia asked him.

"I can't answer you." He steepled his fingers. "I don't know."

"How can you not know?" Julia heard the stridency in her own voice, and felt her face get hot. She turned her gaze down into her lap. "I'm sorry, that was unkind."

"No, it's fair," the doctor said in his unflappable voice. "The truth is I work in a field of medicine that is still just on this side of what deserves to be called a science. Most of neurology is a diagnostic art. Even with all the tools for testing, measuring, and imaging the brain, nine tenths of what I do is observe the history, take note of the symptoms, and define what the problem is—and if we're very lucky, there's a treatment."

Julia looked up and saw him shaking his head somewhat wistfully. "We can describe what happens with an incredible precision; rarely do we understand why, or even how what happens happens."

"So what is happening to my brother?"

"Symptomatically, he's had a stroke, localized damage to a specific part of the brain—"

"So you know what—"

Dr. Kavcheck held up his hand. "*But* your brother's tests, and there've been a lot of them, are not consistent with the diagnosis. There's no sign of a blood clot, or hemorrhage, or any of the normal indications of the sort of damage associated with a stroke. In fact, the tests can't find the remnants of his prior stroke."

"How could that happen?"

"You've come up against my wall of ignorance. It is as if certain localized sections of Richard's brain have decided that they don't want to work any more."

"Could someone have mixed up the tests?"

He shook his head. "You were even there when we took his PET scan. The fact is, your brother is afflicted by something rare and undocumented. It could be some sort of toxin, an exotic virus, some genetic disorder. . . ." He sighed. "I'm sorry to say that your brother's history, having the massive head trauma he suffered, might have colored all his subsequent diagnoses."

"What do you mean?"

"This is the first time he's been tested with modern imaging equipment. The first chance we've had to directly see any physical damage to his brain. Organic damage does not seem as severe as his obvious deficits show it has to be."

"You're confusing me. Are you saying he doesn't have brain damage?"

"No. I'm saying that, despite our best efforts, we know much less about what is wrong than we thought we did."

* * *

Julia went to Richard's room and sat with him a while. It was odd looking at him; in a strange way she felt closer to Mom when she looked at him. Maybe that explained how she could get so emotionally caught up with someone who was so unresponsive.

Richard's room was semiprivate, the other bed empty at the moment. A TV hung facing the bed, muted but showing the image of some sitcom or other. Richard, facing forward on the pillows, gave the impression of intently watching the program, and in that gaze, Julia could see some of the unpleasant slackness on the side of his face, sign of the almost-a-stroke.

She had started reading some of the books she had brought, but endurance and interest trailed off. She was amazed that her mother had been able to sustain herself through one book, much less the library she had stacked in Richard's room.

"What are you thinking?" she whispered to him. "Was Mom right, and are you somewhere better, somewhere you aren't bothered by a pesky little sister?"

She looked up at the clock. She still had thirty minutes left before visiting hours were over. She didn't feel right leaving before then, so she pulled out something else to read. Not a novel this time, but one of her brother's old notebooks.

She read a long section about the mortals who had come to grief by bearing the Gods' Artifacts.

She read about the cruel joke of Heros' Sword, giving omnipotence in battle, but giving no wisdom when it was carried by an incompetent general. Every battle he joined was an unqualified success, strewing the land with the dead of the enemy, but his orders to the whole army were fatal and flawed, allowing them to swarm past the flanks of the general's invincible company, and sack his homeland.

She read about the healing vital force of Vitus' Horn, and how it was sequestered near the heart of the living world, allowing the mortal land to live forever.

She read about the commanding force of Citas' Cirque, and how it allowed a despotic king to command even the trees to make way for him. She read about the lad who took the king's throne because he wore the Ring of Lucas, which made the wearer master of deception and illusion, allowing the lad to see through the kings' supernatural command, while giving him the ability to creep up and seize the Cirque hidden by his own power over illusion. The lad ruled for a time, before he wandered off, insane, because the Ring made him immune to even the necessary illusions that everyone uses to deceive themselves.

Julia was about to read the fragment about Magus' Staff, but that was when an orderly came in to tell her visiting hours were over.

She closed the yellow notebook, sighed, and kissed her brother on the forehead. "Sweet dreams," she whispered.

As she left, she wondered if those dreams were about the land he had written so much about. Behind her, Richard continued to stare passively at the muted television.

CHAPTER 29

RICHIE

RICHIE returned to their room carrying a wooden platter full of the local home cooking. When he entered, he was struck by the absurdity of the scene. The elf, whom he had mentally labeled the Bystander, was unconscious on the bed, looking like a defaced marble effigy. Around her, the trio of Richards stood debating. The professor sat at the head of the bed, looking nervous and stroking his thin mustache. Rocky had planted himself next to the open window, opposite the bed, arms folded as if in judgment. Rick paced at the foot of the bed, gesturing as he spoke, giving an air of desperate animation to his speech.

The evening sunset was all the light there was. Streaming through the window, it illuminated the figures while leaving the rest of the room in dusky shadow. The effect had the eerie impact of a Rembrandt painting, but a Rembrandt painting by some surreal-punk artist. All of them still wore the ragged clothes they'd started with, shirts and slacks stained by rain, sweat, mud, and shit.

Their appearance made their apparent earnestness all the more laughable to Richie.

He didn't interrupt the conversation, but slipped quietly next to the table, set down his platter, and watched them, gnawing on a piece of bread.

"What we want," Rick said, "is a way to back out of this dream we've fallen into—"

"Is it a dream?" Richard asked, the expression on his face slightly hopeful, as if there was some expectation that he might receive an answer to the question.

"—a return to the place we've come from."

"No argument there," Rocky said, "but how the hell is this supposed to get anyone home?"

Rick kept gesturing. To Richie, it was an absurd sort of posturing for an audience of three. "All of us were told, weren't we, that the way out of our exile was to collect these Artifacts and face the Adversary."

"That's more or less what was said," Rocky agreed.

"There," Rick said, as if he had proved something.

"But?" Richie asked, prompting Rocky. Rick turned as if he had just realized that the other was here. It galled Richie that Fearless Leader seemed quite willing to attain some major decision without him present.

As Richie had expected, Rocky had reservations. "I don't like going into a potentially dangerous situation. There is a war out there, one with fairly uncertain boundaries. I don't like doing this on the strength of what might be a collective delusion."

"I do not believe it was a delusion," Richard said. "We all saw this place before. It is connected to us. Perhaps we have a purpose here—"

"You vote for this quest B.S.?" Richie asked.

"What else should we do?" Richard asked.

What else indeed?

"The bridges," Rocky said, "the terrain—there has to be some physical connection between this world and . . ."

Into the pause, Rick inserted, "Whose world? Mine? Yours? His?" He waved at Richard. "I have a job, a business to return to. These 'visitations' are the closest things I've seen or heard of that might give a way back to the way things were."

Richie shrugged. "Me, I could care less who the president is as long as I can get back to real food and real beds."

"So do you think we should go on Rick's quest?" Rocky asked.

Richie found the sudden possessive amusing, as if it had all been Fearless Leader's idea. He wondered if the four gods in question would appreciate the thought. "Quoth the prof, 'What the fuck else have we got?'" He rattled the platter. "By the way, in case you haven't noticed, I got food."

That managed to end the debate for a while.

In a number of ways, lodging in the inn was worse than the dungeon. Four people had to sleep on the floor. In an odd example of mass gallantry, or unease, no one wished to share the bed with Daenan. That gave Richie less room to move. And the odor of his nearby roommates was distinctly foul, the dank mildew smell of the dungeon was almost comforting by comparison. It was also much colder. The shutters could blind the glassless window, but they couldn't completely shut out the night wind. Lastly, things less wholesome than Sir Rat were making him itch.

If his belly hadn't been full, it would have been a pretty good definition of misery.

Richie's mind wandered. He thought of the others, and how wrong they seemed. Richard, the professor, seemed alien to him, barely there, as if life itself upstaged him. Rocky, solid to the point of petrifaction. Rick, with all the charm of a dictatorial social worker.

How the hell did all of them get from point A to point B? He could see little of himself in any of them, and when he did see something of himself, in a gesture, or an expression, it was as if they were somehow mocking him.

Richie cracked his eyes open and looked at Rick. He was asleep, leaning against the opposite wall. Richie was starting to loathe him. He had all the boundless confidence of someone who had never gotten his dick caught in the wringer. A Daedalus too sure of his own competence to conceive that Icarus might fall.

It took a moment to realize, looking at the blue-gray shadows across Rick's face, that the shutters on the window were open.

No wonder it's so damn cold in here.

Richie carefully got up to close the shutters. As he did, he realized that he must have slept without realizing it. It was much later than he thought it was, and everyone else was sprawled sleeping on the floor. As he carefully stepped over Richard, he saw the empty bed.

"Where the hell is the elf?" he whispered, taking another step to the window.

No one stirred in the shadowy room as he looked around. The bed was empty, the door was closed, barred from this side, and with Rocky asleep, leaning against it. The table, and the loot from the assholes he'd rolled, was still undisturbed.

There was only one place the elf could have gone.

He took another step and leaned out the window. The clouds had receded, and a full moon washed the alley below in cool bluish light. There was no sign of anyone.

"What the . . . ?" he whispered.

Above him he heard something clatter on the clay tiles of the roof. A shadow cut across the moonlight shining from above him. Richie clutched at the butt of his gun and whipped around to look up.

She stood on the roof of the inn, silhouetted by the moon, ghostly, the moonlight a nimbus around her.

"What the hell are you doing up there?"

"Watching the end of things," Daenan said. She looked impassively toward the horizon. "You have brought death with you." Her voice was flat and affectless, as if she were phonetically reading the words of a language she didn't understand.

Richie just stared up at her. He saw a cold perfection there. Her skin was so pale that it seemed to repel the shadows in front of her, her hair a nameless color between blonde and red. She didn't look at him as she spoke, she kept staring at the horizon.

"What end?" Richie asked.

"*The* end. This is a mortal land, formed by mortal gods. It will die."

"Okay, right." Richie didn't like the way she said that. "I get you—"

"No, you don't." A coldness crept into her voice, the antithesis of emotion. As if her voice were the voice of a corpse. "I am exiled from my people because I do not wish this world to die. You present the means of its death."

"Hey, lady, I don't know what the fuck you're talking about—"

She turned to face him, and the words dried in his throat. Her stare was so intense and frightening that Richie slowly began to withdraw the gun from his pocket.

"If your death would not destroy what I wish to save, I would slay you all now. You know neither what you are, or what you do." She extended a finger toward him. "Abandon this quest, accept the world given you. Do not uncreate what is."

Richie's gun was nearly out of his pocket, but Daenan took a step back from the edge of the roof and, in a moment, she was gone.

"Fuck," Richie whispered.

He stood at the window waiting for some more sign of Daenan, but she didn't reappear, and the only sound to greet him from out of the night was a distant howling of a dog or wolf.

Richie felt very nervous about that howling.

In the morning, no one heard the news with good grace. Richard took Daenan's escape personally, as if they had somehow been remiss in giving aid. Rocky saw it as some sort of failure in personal security. Rick acted as if Richie's report of Daenan's words were somehow directed at him, personally.

Richie spent his time worrying about those howls he'd heard during the night.

The four of them divided what they could of the items Richie had lifted from Daenan's attackers. Rick and Rocky got swords out of the deal, and Rocky got a chain-mail shirt that didn't look very comfortable. Richie got a knife, and a linen shirt to go under his jacket, replacing his late unlamented T-shirt.

And Rick wonders why I went ballistic when he wanted to sell my leather, Richie thought. *I'm the only person who's dressed for this crap.*

Rick counted through the money Richie had liberated and declared, "There's enough here, I think, to get us some decent clothes, and maybe supplies for traveling."

"So we're going through with this, even after last night?" Rocky asked.

Rick nodded, "Even if the woman was in her right mind—and with the roof-traipsing I'm not willing to grant that—it doesn't change the fact that this is the only hint we've gotten of how to get our own lives back." Rick slapped the pile of coins on the table. "We're going."

No one raised any objections. Even Richie, who was feeling uneasy about this now, was constitutionally attracted to action rather than inaction. So, instead, he raised the question, "Which pilgrimage first, then?"

Rick paused and Rocky filled the silence, "The Sword. If we intend to wade into this, we could use the god of war on our side."

"Makes sense to me," Richie said.

Rick nodded. "It makes geographic sense, too, if my memory of this place isn't too distorted."

Richie remembered, too. The realm that held the Sword wasn't quite in this world. One had to follow the river south and find the red mists that were a sign that the barrier between the worlds had thinned. That was written in one of the notebooks he had lost sometime after the second foster family. Those destined to find the Sword would cross the red mists when they traveled downriver.

All they had to do was follow the river, not a difficult task, until Heros, or something, parted the red mists and let you find the Underworld.

The four of them collected what they had and left the inn. As Rick predicted, the coins from Daenan's attackers supplied three of them with clothes—Richie refused to replace his leather, boots, or jeans, all of which seemed more appropriate than the tunics the others bought.

Everything else went into packs, food, and bedrolls.

After that, there was little else but to leave the city, start downriver, and hope something would lead them to the Sword.

CHAPTER 30

RICHARD

RICHARD wondered if he would write the same way if he ever made it back home. His colleagues had always treated everything he wrote as archaic and somewhat silly, when they'd deigned to pay attention to it at all. Now, two days down the coast of a transplanted Cuyahoga, Richard wondered if he could ever write anything so light and optimistic again.

It wasn't just how the world had greeted him, or the plodding endless hike along the banks, or the constant desire for a real bed. Mostly it was simple fear.

In the night he heard the hounds; both nights they seemed closer. Sometimes, he looked across the river and imagined a shadowy rider on the opposite bank, astride a mount with coal-red eyes.

The idea of the Thralls was a constant pressure on the back of his mind so intense that he wondered that the others could act normally with that threat out there. They were empty of everything but purpose, merciless, relentless. The four of them did not belong here, and the Thralls would close upon them eventually.

Two days south, and another night approaching, and Rick's enthusiasm seemed undimmed.

"Come on, I see the remains of a path here. We have daylight left," Rick said, driving them ever forward.

Richard followed, since there was nothing else he could do.

Rick had found the remains of what was left of a path. Rounded stones sank flush with the sod, slick, moss-covered, and nearly invisible for the undergrowth. The path led away from the river, and eventually, up a rise. Rick stopped at the top of the rise. Rocky stopped next to him and shook his head. "I don't like abandoned buildings."

Richard reached the top of the rise and saw what Rocky was talking about. Once, there had been a small village here. Richard could see the outlines of buildings written in stones scattered around the field. The stones that mapped the long-vanished town were as moss-covered and clogged by underbrush as the path.

"Whatever this place was," Richard said, "it has been like this for years. Over a century, maybe."

"Well, that makes me feel better," Richie said. "Let's get a move on." He started down toward the stones of the ghost village. His boots crunched through the undergrowth, and Richard heard his chain jingling—

That was the *only* thing he heard. He looked up and around. "Birds," Richard whispered.

"What?" Rocky asked, turning to him. "What birds?"

"No birds," Richard said. He looked at the trees that grew in isolated clumps at the borders of the dead village. They seemed wrong to him, too vivid a green, too twisted a trunk. This place felt unnatural. "Something is wrong with this place."

Richie was down by the closest foundation. He kicked a stone and looked back up at them.

Rick glanced up and seemed to notice the odd quiet. Unease appeared to seep into him as he said, "Let's get across this place as quickly as possible."

Richie shouted up at them, "So, you all going to stand up there gawking?"

They followed him, leaving the bounds of the village within a few minutes.

That didn't take them outside the bounds of the unnatural influence. Richard was beginning to have worries about who this place might belong to.

The little folk was their most common name, what he'd called them in his notebooks. He had written of them, or at least of their acts. They could be blamed for the disappearance of things ranging from cooking pots, to infants, to lost travelers.

Unlike Daenan's race, these fay cousins of hers were mischievous to the point of cruelty. Amusement was of the highest value to them. When he wrote about them, Richard had thought of them as evil, supernatural children.

He was hoping now that they had some redeeming features he had overlooked.

From ahead of them Richie interrupted Richard's thoughts. "Hey, guys, I think you'd better come see this."

The three of them walked up to Richie. He had stopped in the middle of the field they were crossing. Richard looked at the ground where Richie was staring. He shuddered.

In front of them, a circle almost fifteen feet in diameter had been eaten into the grass. Odd white mushrooms guarded the perimeter, while the interior was tarlike black earth. The mushrooms were larger than Richard's fist, their gray caps taking the aspect of tiny cowled men looking into the circle.

"This is some sort of sign, isn't it?" Richie asked. Richard heard an uncharacteristic note of fear in his companion's voice.

Richard nodded.

"What sort of sign?" Rocky asked.

Richard looked up and started turning around. Things had changed. An unbroken line of trees surrounded the field now, a perfect circle of wood and intertwined branches close-packed enough that Richard couldn't see beyond gnarled bark.

"They've marked their territory," Richard said.

"Oh, wonderful," Richie remarked.

Richard saw movement in the grass around them. The grass was ankle-high, and it undulated as if the ground beneath it moved.

Richard heard the slide of metal. He turned to see both Rocky and Rick holding their swords out at the field, at the moving grass around them.

The grass waved in spirals and rings, as if dancing in

linked circles around them. The wind began carrying sounds, like faraway laughter, a song too faint to make out the words.

The grass seemed to be a moving pattern of spokes and circles now, the rotating humps becoming more and more complex.

"Fuck this," Richie said. He pulled a gun from his pocket and pointed it at the closest ring. "Show yourselv—"

Before anyone could show surprise at his sudden production of a firearm, Richie's words were stopped by a sound like tearing canvas. Everyone turned to face him, where the sound had come from.

Richie was wide-eyed, staring at his feet, or where his feet should have been. From all appearances, he now stood in a hole that brought the ground up to his knees. Richard could only see grass around his legs, which was now rippling like a pond.

Richard and Rocky started reaching for him at the same time. The tearing canvas sounded again, and Richard saw Richie jerk into the ground all the way up to his chest.

"Shit, get me out of here!" Richie yelled at them. "I can feel them pulling my legs!"

The laughter got louder.

Richard and Rocky got hold of Richie's wrist as the canvas sound ripped through the ground under him. Richie was yanked under, his hand tore free from their grip and sank under the grass.

Richard fell to his knees, feeling the ground. But it was only sod and dirt, no sign of where Richie had gone.

Rocky struck at the dancing grass. His sword severed one of the closest circles. The laughter stopped with a high, hysterical screech, and the accompanying song died on an eerie flute note. The grass fell still around them, and around the spot where Rocky's sword sank into the ground, the grass had withered black and died.

"They don't like iron," Richard whispered.

"Yeah," Rocky agreed. "Would someone please tell me that it was this easy."

Silence covered the field like a shroud. The light had faded to match the feeling.

"Richie?" Richard called out. His voice died in the air, flat and echoless.

"I don't like this," Rick said, turning around as if to spy where Richie had gone. But he wasn't there.

Rocky slowly withdrew his sword from the ground. Rick placed a hand on his arm. "That may not be a good idea."

Rocky looked down at his sword, whose point was still lodged in the sod at his feet.

"The iron," Rick said. "It may be keeping them away."

Richard got to his feet and looked around the field. Nothing moved. There wasn't even a wind. There was no sign of Richie.

"Where'd he go?" Rocky asked.

"These little folk don't live wholly in this world." Richard said. "All of Fairy lives partway in another world, these more so than most. They've taken Richie there."

They stood there, fixed, as the sky continued to darken.

"How do we—" Rocky began. He was interrupted by a sound, the first external sound to penetrate the silence cloaking the field. The sound was of howling dogs and distant hoofbeats. As he listened, Richard could feel them getting closer.

"If that's what I think it is," Rocky said, "everything has just become much worse." He looked at Rick, then he turned to face Richard. "All things considered, we don't have a great chance against one of those things, but it will be a lot better if my sword isn't stuck in the ground."

"We can't be sure that's a Thrall out there," Rick said.

Rocky nodded. "It's less than fifty yards to the trees. By the time we see it, it will already be on us."

Rick looked at Richard, and Richard nodded. "There's also the chance that the little ones might fight it with us," Richard said.

"From the looks of things," Rick said, "if Rocky pulls that sword, we won't be here to meet it."

"Not necessarily a bad thing," Richard said.

The hoofbeats were much closer now.

Rick finally nodded. "Pull the sword, Rocky."

Rocky lifted the tip of his sword out of the sod. The reaction wasn't immediate, but within a second or two a babbling sound overwhelmed the sound of hoofbeats. Richard couldn't perceive individual voices, but he could perceive a mood—

Anger.

No songs or laughter this time, and when the grass moved, it wasn't in complex circular and spiral patterns. The grass waved toward them from the tree line, like breakers heading in from the ocean. Rocky raised his sword.

When the lead wave was within a dozen feet of him, a gray line shot from the ground to wrap around his upper arms. The motion was nearly too fast to see. One instant, Rocky had his arms raised to stab the ground again, the next his forearms were bound in silky webbing.

He kept the sword moving down, but more silken lines shot out of the ground, a dozen or more, wrapping the sword and pulling it away.

Rick cut at the line binding Rocky's arms. His sword severed the line, but the ends animated, like they were part of a living thing. Both severed ends extended and wrapped themselves around the blade of Rick's sword.

Richard took a step toward them, and a gray thread shot out of the grass, binding his ankle. The touch was like silk, but pulling on it was like trying to stretch a steel cable. As he watched, his foot was pulled into the ground, the grass rippling around his ankle.

He grabbed his calf, more in reflex then in hope of pulling his foot free. More lines shot from the grass around him, coiling about his arms and legs like something alive.

He looked up to see Rocky and Rick. Rocky had sunk to his elbows in the sod. Rick was bent over him, bound to him by silken threads. Richard heard the familiar tearing sound, and Rocky was sucked under, pulling Rick's arms after him, up to the shoulders.

Rick's face hit the sod and he struggled to rotate his head and spit grass out of his mouth. Richard heard the laughter again. Rick grimaced as a flowering of silk billowed around him, dragging him under the grass.

Richard felt the world jerk, and suddenly he was waist-deep in the ground. He looked down at the laughing grass as the ground reached up to smother him.

Darkness sucked him in, an impenetrable blackness that gave him no air, no sound, no sense of up or down. The only concrete sensation he felt was the accelerating beat of his heart. Panic crashed over him in waves, each wave a step blacker, toward the darkness around him.

Hours could have been minutes, or only seconds. His brain, panicked and sick for air, began filling the void with its own sensations—

Richard could smell hot metal, gasoline, and exhaust fumes. His ears filled with the crackling of a fire, the sound of sirens, and in the distance, fireworks. He could feel the vinyl of a seat pressing against his backside, pinning him to the ground. And before he lost consciousness completely, he could feel the blood seeping into the carpet underneath his too-small hand.

Richard gasped for air so violently that the spasm woke him. For moments he only gasped, paying no attention to his surroundings. Air was all his body was concerned with. It took a few moments to realize that the dizziness gripping him was not solely due to near-suffocation.

He was hanging upside down.

As far as Richard could tell, they were all there. All of them webbed to the wall of this cavern—if that's what this was. It didn't look natural. Circular formations predominated in the rock, and stalagmites and stalactites jutted out of the walls and at odd angles, not just the floor and the ceiling. In fact, the terms floor and ceiling didn't seem to apply here.

The native population didn't help. It took a few seconds for Richard to recognize the little folk themselves, because his brain stubbornly refused to accept them, or what they were doing. What they were, were tiny humanoid creatures ranging in size from one to six inches in height.

What they were doing was walking across every available surface, up down and sideways, as if gravity didn't exist. Though, as thoroughly as Richard was pinned, he couldn't really tell where gravity was, even though he still felt as if he were hanging upside down.

"Is everyone here?" Richard assumed the voice was Rick's. He coughed something of a reply as the others assented.

Meanwhile the minuscule horde crowded around them. They babbled among themselves, but the sound was much too faint for Richard to make out any individual voice.

"*Silence!*" The horde ceased babbling, though Richard heard a few snickers and a cough. The one who called the group to attention stood on one of the oddly placed stalagmites, that from Richard's point of view jutted from the wall to his right. That perch put the speaker front and center, looking at the four of them webbed to the wall.

His size made it easy for Richard to imagine him as standing on a mountain far far away, when he couldn't have been more than four yards from any of them.

"*Silence!*" the little man repeated, stilling the coughs, but not the snickers. He was a stooped creature, a hump on his back subtracting nearly an inch from a height that could have been four inches. He had ears that pointed up above his head, and he wore a cloak that seemed to have been made from a skinned rat, complete with head and tail.

"The brutes regain what sense they have!" he called to the multitude. "And we must extract a toll for their passage upon our land."

A selection of the multitude that congregated around Richard's feet seemed to find this uproariously funny.

Someone in the crowd called out, "The second joint of their fingers! So we can play dice." The suggestion brought a smattering of applause.

"A pound of flesh apiece!"

"A spectacle."

"A fight to the death!"

The crowd's voices mingled until the individual voices were indistinguishable. The one on the stalagmite raised his arms. *"Silence!"*

The little hunchback turned to the four of them, "Who is your leader?"

"I am," Rick said. No one contradicted him.

"Then you speak, no one else. One word from anyone but you and your lives are forfeit."

They don't want us consulting with each other, Richard thought. *They'll offer something, some evil choice that feeds their twisted humor.*

"They understand," Rick said.

Richard hoped Richie did. He also hoped Rick understood exactly how untrustworthy these imps could be, even for imps that kept their promises.

"We need to extract service for passage," he chuckled. "My people have called for several things, but I will settle for one." He held up a crooked finger, "You each leave us a limb for our larder. We'll even let you choose which one." Then he smiled in a way to warp his face out of proportion. "Or, you all have an opportunity to duel our champion in a fight to the death."

That's it, Richard thought. Whoever their champion was, Richard doubted he was under six inches tall. Unfortunately, it was the only acceptable choice.

"I'll grant you one of your requests on one condition," Rick said.

There was a chorus of boos from the horde.

"Oh, the brute wishes to make a deal." The hunchback sat cross-legged on his stalagmite. "This I must hear."

"You grant us safe passage through this realm of yours under the hill, all the way to our destination," Rick said.

The hunchback rubbed his chin, as if in thought. "It depends which of these choices you are offering."

"If you grant us that passage, we will fight your champion."

The hunchback clapped his hands. "Perfect. It is done!" He stood and shouted, "To arms!"

The silken bonds holding Richard yanked him through the wall and into the darkness again.

CHAPTER 31

Rocky

THE ground vomited him onto the black earth of the Fairy circle. To his right he heard Richie spitting and cursing, yelling at Rick, "What the hell are you thinking!" To his left he could hear the tearing sound of the little creatures shoving a fourth body through the ground.

However, the sound that occupied him most was the sound of hoofbeats close by, in front of him. Rocky scrambled to his feet and yelled, "Get to the tree line behind us, *now!*"

Rocky squinted in the darkness, looking for the swords that he and Rick had abandoned here.

Someone, Richie or Richard, said, "What?"

Rocky stepped in that direction, grabbed a shoulder and lifted. "Move!" he shouted.

It was too dark, and they were way too open. He heard the rest of them running for the woods behind them, but the hoofbeats were nearly on top of them. Rocky was certain that he could see part of the woods ahead of them moving. At this distance it was nothing more than a piece of shadow.

The shadow reared, and Rocky saw the red of its mount's eyes. *Thank God there's only one of them,* Rocky thought.

He ran along the perimeter of the earthen circle, trying to locate his sword. They had no chance against this thing unarmed. Precious little chance they had with a sword.

The Thrall made a sound, an eerie battle cry, the sound of a violent wind passing through metal cracked and shot with holes. To Rocky it sounded like a battlefield long after the battle was over.

"Get out of there!" someone yelled at him.

Rocky glanced behind him and saw the Thrall, unmistakable now. The armored figure blotted out half the sky. Its weapon was raised, a sword, or part of its arm. The thing was nearly upon him, and he barely had a second to react.

Rocky dodged to the left, out from in front of the charging Thrall, and away from the side with the weapon. His eyes were on the attacker, so by the time he felt something catch his feet, it was too late for him to avoid a fall. He turned the stumble into a dive at the ground just as the Thrall thundered past.

Rocky felt the breeze as it passed him. The wind burned on his neck and carried the smell of hot metal. He hit the ground and felt it vibrate with the thing's passage.

Rocky looked past him and saw that his legs were tangled with Rick's fiber-wrapped sword. He reached for it as the Thrall reared to cut him down.

He saw the strobe flash of the gunshot a split second before he heard it. The sound echoed endlessly as the right rear leg of the Thrall's mount collapsed in a spasm of shadowy ichor.

"*Yeeesss, mama!*" Richie shouted from near the tree line.

Rocky scrambled to his feet. The demonic mount was keening, a sound no horse would ever make, a sound that sucked marrow out of Rocky's bones, a sound that shook his soul like a dried pea in a rattle.

The Thrall showed no pain or disorientation from its fall. It pushed its mount off of its armored leg, tearing more pieces free of the animal without any concern for its thrashing.

Rocky backed up, holding Rick's too-small sword up to defend himself. The Thrall was hampered enough by the wounded beast for Rocky to put ten or fifteen yards between them before the Thrall was completely upright. It was the first time Rocky had gotten a good look at the thing.

It wasn't one he'd seen before. It still had the welded

seams and the heat-burnished metal, but its decorations were different. No hooks or blades. This one was wrapped in an endless spiked chain welded to its armor. The armor itself seemed older. Holes dotted it, revealing emptiness inside, dents caving in part of its chest and helm.

It pushed aside the still trembling horse-thing with its weapon arm. The beast stopped trembling, and smoke rose from where its weapon had cleaved.

Rocky kept backing away as the Thrall advanced. Its movement was slowed by its right leg. The beast had fallen on that leg, and the armor had bent into immobility.

Rocky smiled grimly. He could outrun the thing now. He backed away, pacing it, keeping its attention. He looked beyond it, at where he thought the others were. He could only spare a glance at the shadows, enough to see movement, not enough to tell who was moving or what they were doing.

That glance was almost a disaster. The Thrall's walk was impaired, but it moved faster than a human being, and its reach was much greater than Rocky's. It sensed Rocky's momentary distraction, and swung its blade at him. Rocky reflexively dodged in response to the Thrall's movement, bringing Rick's sword up to guard.

The impact drew sparks, and Rocky had to stumble backward to keep from losing his grip on the sword. The collision broke a notch out of Rocky's blade.

Rocky was no longer grinning. He had to stop this thing somehow, he couldn't back away from it forever. His sword wouldn't last.

It swung again, but now Rocky's attention was completely focused. He could avoid the blow. The Thrall was relentless, throwing the sword up and down in heavy arcs that no human arm could maintain. The rhythm of the attacks was almost hypnotic. Rocky's attention was on the Thrall's hand and wrist, seeing where the rest of the sword would go.

It did have an obvious weakness which he saw after the first three cuts. There was no way the Thrall could change the grip on its weapon. Its right gauntlet was welded in an overhand swing, and surrounding the hilt, the gauntlet, and the lower part of the blade, was a chain wrapped around it and welded in place.

Rocky saw what might have been his only opening, and he took it.

He waited for the Thrall's mechanistic upswing, and ducked forward, bearing his sword two-handed. For a moment the Thrall's sword was descending directly at Rocky's head. Then Rocky's momentum had hurled him past the Thrall to his right, while his backhand strike with the sword hit right where he was aiming, the bottom of the Thrall's wrist.

Rocky could smell the sparks, and he could feel hot flecks of metal hit his cheeks. The impact tore the sword out of his hands, as if it were chained to the yoke of a panicked ox. That didn't much matter, since the impact broke the sword in half.

The stinging pain in his wrists didn't slow him. He took a stumbling step forward and ran back for the circle, away from the Thrall. He stopped his dash when he passed someone in the darkness.

The whistling sound of wind through metal increased in volume.

Rocky turned to see Rick next to him. Rick was carrying Rocky's sword. Rocky reached over to ask Rick for the weapon, but he never had the chance. The Thrall had been on his heels all the way back, and it was swinging. Its sword was unsteady, but Rocky's desperate cut at its wrist seemed to have had little if any effect.

Rick had no choice but to block with the sword. And the way Rick held it, Rocky was certain that the Thrall's blow would tear the sword out of Rick's hands.

Its sword descended, not toward Rick, but toward Rocky. Even as he tried to scramble out of the way, Rocky was certain that it was death hurtling toward him. The whistling reached its zenith as Rick interposed the sword. Rick swung the blade like a bat at the Thrall's weapon, and the clangor of the impact was deafening.

Sparks flowered not only from the blades this time, but from the Thrall's wrist.

This time it was the Thrall's sword that was torn away, complete with its gauntlet. Rocky's blow had weakened that joint enough for Rick's frenzied swing to tear the hand free of its arm.

Rick fell away from the Thrall, dropping the sword. The Thrall's arm continued its follow-through, the sword swinging free and chaotic from the chains welding it to the armor. A smell like molten iron came from the hollow of the Thrall's wrist.

At the end of its swung, it started to take a clumsy step forward. Another gunshot hammered through the darkness. This time the crack of the shot was right on top of the muzzle flash. Rocky barely had time to curse the uselessness of shooting at an empty suit of armor, when he saw the Thrall toppling to the left.

Its good leg, the left one, now had a paired set of twisted holes at the joint of its knee. It might not be enough to destroy the joint, but it was enough to topple it. Rocky didn't wait to find out how permanently disabling Richie's shot was. He ran up and grabbed the sword from where Rick had dropped it.

The armor had fallen facedown on the ground, and Rocky brought the sword down on the back of its left knee, twice, rapidly. He was barely in time. The Thrall's arms were still good, and it was pushing itself upright as the second blow severed its leg from the knee down.

Rocky saw wisps of steam rise from the open hollows of the armor.

It pushed itself around so it faced him. It couldn't stand, but it had torn the sword free from its chains, and was swinging it, gauntlet included, with its left hand.

For once, avoiding the blow was easy. The Thrall couldn't grip the weapon properly, and it couldn't maneuver its body for the follow-through. It was rooted to the spot. Rocky dodged behind it and brought the sword down on its left shoulder.

It tried to turn to bring its clumsy sword up to defend

itself. It didn't make it. The Thrall had lost all its advantages in speed and reach. Rocky's sword hit the joint while its arm was moving. Its shoulder could not take the stress, and a weld popped in a shower of sparks, releasing wisps of hot metal steam.

Its sword reached for him, the Thrall turning at the waist to aim for him. Rocky darted around to its right, away from the sword.

He brought his weapon down on it again, and again, and again. . . .

"I think you killed it," Richie said, after a while.

Rocky looked down at what was left of the Thrall. It was almost fully dismembered now. Rocky had hacked the helmet and both arms from the torso. Its sword lay on the ground, still with the armor's right gauntlet clutching the hilt. The spiked chain that had wrapped it was spiraled over the armor. The chain was broken in several places. Steam no longer rose from the hollows of the armor, and the armor itself had stopped moving.

The attack had left his own sword battered until it was slightly less useful than a lead pipe. From the dents and nicks in the metal, it was probably now more dangerous to him in combat than any opponent would be. He tossed it on the pile of debris, and, obligingly, three inches of its length broke off.

Rocky looked up from it. The others were there, Richie, Richard, Rick, standing around him.

"You did it," Rick said.

Rocky nodded, feeling the strength drain from his legs. He started to collapse next to the Thrall. Richard ran up to him and caught him before he fell completely to the ground.

"Are you all right?" Richard asked.

Rocky could feel his arms shake from fatigue. He became aware of dull aches around his chest and right arm, aches that were the center of a warm wetness that was spreading under his clothes.

"No," Rocky said. "I'm not all right."

Rocky leaned his head back as Richard helped peel the

chain mail off his wounded chest. He heard Richard cursing, so he knew he didn't want to look down there, not yet. He let the fatigue wash over him, as the adrenaline boiled away.

Rocky smiled, not because he'd won, but because he was still alive. It was the same feeling that he'd had in Nicaragua, a spiritual high that he had almost forgotten about back in the world. Coming that close to losing everything, and surviving, made everything that much sweeter. Even the air smelled better. He clutched at the grass, just because he liked the way it felt between his fingers.

The sky began to lighten. The sight was disorienting, as if someone had ripped six hours of the night away. He smiled as stars began winking out.

"It's not as bad as it looks," Richard said. "It got a glancing blow off of you, but the armor did its job."

Rocky nodded and looked down. Richard had bared his chest and the side under his right arm was a mass of bruising surrounding a nasty looking diagonal slash that went from his armpit to his lowest rib. The wound was jagged and ugly. Rocky knew that the reason for that was that the sword hadn't fully penetrated the mail he wore. If it had, the cut would have been much neater, much deeper, and probably would have killed him in less than fifteen seconds.

"Can you move your arm?"

Rocky lifted up his arm and shuddered at the pain as he pulled it through its range of motion.

Richie shook his head. "The good news is you seem to have a full range of motion, so the muscle isn't severely torn, or severed. The bad news, I can see on your face."

Rocky nodded, wiping the sweat off his brow with his left hand. "I'll have to be left-handed for the time being. I've felt worse."

Richard nodded as he tore strips to bind Rocky's chest and shoulder. Fortunately, some of the supplies they had purchased in the city included a primitive first aid kit.

As Richard bound him up, Rocky asked, "How'd

it happen that you're our medic, my dear English professor?"

Richard shook his head. "Caring for someone became something of a necessity for me. I had to take care of Mother."

That was such an alien thought for someone who wore his face, and his name, that it took a while for it to sink in. "You said something about that," Rocky said. "When we were talking back at the palace."

Richard nodded. "The accident. Father died, Mother had severe head injuries, much more severe than mine." Richard kept working. "She kept telling me that she'd get better, all the time I was a child. But instead of getting better, her voice kept slurring, she stopped walking, and in the end I was taking care of everything for her. By then I didn't know if she even saw me. She died two years ago, a massive stroke in the wounded part of her brain."

Rocky just sat there staring past Richard, at the grass. "I'm sorry."

"Why should you be sorry?"

"You don't know how many times I wished my mother had been the one to survive that crash. Did you ever know your father, really?"

Richard looked thoughtful for a moment, "A face, a voice . . ."

A fist, Rocky thought. Rocky placed a hand on the tightened bandages. "Are you finished?"

Richard nodded, his face was still lost in thought, not looking directly at Rocky.

Because he had been a police officer, Rocky had thought Richie was his opposite in their little group. Now he began to reconsider. Here was a version of him that had spent a lifetime dedicated to keeping one person alive, where he had spent a large portion of his training how to kill people.

Rocky rose with some difficulty; he had to grab Richard's shoulder to steady himself. Richard stumbled slightly, but helped support him. Once he stood, he saw what had been occupying Rick and Richie.

Standing in the middle of the circle was a familiar hunchbacked figure. The tiny gnome did not look pleased. ". . . all I promised you was free passage. And that is generous, since any fool knows that a Thrall cannot die and therefore your win is suspect."

"Why, you crooked little bastard—" Richie started. He was waving the gun around, just like when Rocky had first met him. For once his worry wasn't who Richie was about to shoot, he was wondering how the hell he got the gun back from the palace guard who had confiscated it.

Rick held up an arm to restrain Richie and said, in a voice calmer than Rocky expected, "Your promise was free passage through your realm under the hill. Not here on the surface of the world. We have done no ill to you or your people." Rick waved in the direction of the dismantled Thrall's armor. "Do you make a habit of breaking promises to those who grant you such a boon."

The gnome king turned his back on them and grunted. "You insult me, sir. Why should I grant you anything after such an accusation?"

Rocky walked up to the edge of the circle and looked down upon the tiny, hunchbacked figure. "Why's this victory suspect?"

The gnome king whirled around, rippling his ratskin cape. "Those things aren't mortal creatures. The spirits trapped within such armor can only be freed by the hand of Chaos itself—"

"What about Chaos' children?" Rocky said quietly.

The hunchback king stared at him, and his too-large ears flattened against his skull like those of an angry cat. "What is it you are saying, warrior?"

"I'm saying that I'm doing the will of the Lord of Battle, that the Thrall is dead as far as such a thing can die, and that you'd best keep your promises to our leader here."

Rocky saw an expression of uncertainty cross the gnome king's face. He must have been certain that he'd been sending them to their deaths at the hands of his "Champion."

Richard spoke, "The king's acts don't surprise me. These beings are known for preferring to lose anything in preference to losing a wager."

The gnome king snarled. "That is just typical bigotry."

"Is it?" Richard said. "You're giving up all you have because you don't wish to lose a bet."

"What? I lose nothing."

Rocky noticed Richard smile slightly. Richard said, "This was not the only Thrall. The land is thick with them."

"Do I care about the ravages of mortal lands?" the gnome king asked, but his voice was uncertain.

Rocky saw where this was leading. He spoke up. "They are ravagers of everything not entirely of one world." He waved a hand to encompass the clearing and the land beyond. "Their presence would make it inconvenient for you to walk abroad in this land you're so fond of protecting."

"You do not frighten me," the gnome king said. However, his ears were now completely flattened against his skull, and he was whirling around so quickly to face the speakers that Rocky was amazed he didn't fall over.

"Obviously it does not," Richard said. "Since when the Lord of Battle himself sends an emissary to deliver you from these creatures, you spurn him and his party. You are brave to insult a god."

The gnome king stood in silence for a moment, looking at Richard with a glare of pure hatred. Then he clapped his hands and said, "But of course I am willing to help a divine emissary on his mission. This I do as a gesture of goodwill, even though you did not fight the Thrall to the death—since such a thing, as everyone knows—cannot truly die. You shall have passage under the hill, as you request."

CHAPTER 32

RICK

THE hunchbacked gnome walked to the edge of the circle, to station himself at Rick's feet, as if acknowledging Rick's authority. "I shall lead you to where you are supposed to go. Where is your destination?"

"The realm where the Sword of Heros is imprisoned," Rick said.

"Then that is where we shall travel," The gnome king whirled around and spread his arms. *"Let the earth receive its children!"*

In response to his words, the black soil within the circle fell away. The ground inside spiraled down in an earthen whirlpool, sinking beyond any limit that Rick could see. Hearing Richard gasp, Rick stepped up, next to the gnome king, so he could lean over and see what Richard saw.

Rick gasped as well.

It was a tunnel, a circular bore that somehow never quite lost its walls to shadow. An earthen stairway descended in a helical path along the walls, down, and down, and down. . . .

Somehow, his eyes knew that this spiral staircase, hugging the walls as it did, should have steadily decreased the diameter of the hole, halving its diameter within the first hundred feet, after it had spiraled twice. That was not what he saw. What he saw was a constant diameter all the way down, the walls all perpendicular to the ground he stood on, the stair spiraling down dozens of times to a vanishing point.

"Come," spoke the gnome king. "Stay with me or lose my protection."

The gnome stepped down, leading the way under the hill.

The physical distortions did not cease with the spiral. Somehow the gnome king trod upon the stairway as well as any of them, despite risers that were taller than he was. Somehow, the manner in which he walked convinced Rick's eyes that he was as tall as any of them, but seen from a much greater distance.

"Good lord," Rick heard Richard mutter above and behind him. Rick turned around to see what was the matter. Richard was still helping Rocky, to the extent of carrying his share of the group's provisions. Right now Richard had turned to look behind them, and up.

Rick saw the source of his distress immediately. To all appearances, the five of them had yet to make a complete circuit around the edge of the hole, but already the sky was invisible.

"Come," came the distant voice of the gnome king. "Do not fear, time and distance here are not what you conceive. It is why you struck such a bargain with me, is it not?"

"Keep moving," Rick exhorted the rest of the party. The gnome king was right. It was why he had asked passage through this realm. His memories of this land seemed to be improving with every hour he was exposed to it. He recalled the special nature of the land under the hill, how an hour spent here could be a week upon the Earth, and how ten yards traveled here, could be a league upon the surface.

With every step he could see and feel space twisting. The steps he walked upon tilted away from the wall of the pit, and toward the endless hole they descended into. The steps tilted, but Rick's sense of balance told him he still stood upright. He felt as if he stood upright even when the steps buried themselves in the wall and he walked along a helical path set into the walls of the hole—which was no longer a hole, but a massive tube that extended an infinity before and behind him.

"I wonder what the speed of light is down here," Richie

said. His voice echoed with odd, atonal harmonics. "Hell, I wonder if Relativity works here. . . ."

For some reason, Richie's anachronistic reference disturbed Rick more than a lot of the other wiseass comments.

Rick fell back and grabbed Richie's shoulder.

"What, man?"

"Keep moving," Rick said, "and tell me where the damn gun came from."

Richie sighed. "When Sir Rat—Lucas—busted me out, he gave it back to me. How he got it, you'd have to ask him."

"Why did you keep it secret?" Rick hissed.

"It's mine, and I didn't want you nationalizing it for the greater good. I'm keeping it, and the five remaining bullets, got that?"

Rick looked into Richie's face and thought about his own visitor, Citas, and the grave pronouncement that one of them would betray the others. What better betrayer than a criminal punk whose patron was the deity of deception and trickery?

Rick slowly let Richie go. He didn't know yet exactly what he was going to do about this.

The tunnel eventually became the odd caverns which showed no fixed floor or ceiling. The irregular walls all pointed conical mineral fingers toward the center of the chamber. When Rick saw the first cavern, he felt as if they were descending into the throat of a gigantic stone lamprey.

Once they entered the caves, the tunnels immediately became complex, branching, and irregular. They still walked the clockwise spiral, showing no preference for the direction of gravity. Whenever the caves branched, the gnome led them down the right-hand path.

Rick began to think that where they arrived had more to do with how they spiraled, deasil or widdershins, than the direction they chose to walk. He had the feeling that if he now tried to backtrack their route, traveling their spiral route backward, that he would end up someplace other than the surface.

As they walked, Rick didn't see any of the gnome king's subjects, but he could not evade the feeling that their procession was being watched by multitudes that sat just outside his field of vision.

After a time, Richard said, "I smell water."

It took a moment for Rick to sense what Richard did. The smell was sharp enough to cut through the dormant air of the cavern, and it was not long before a cool breeze accompanied the smell.

Another spiral around a cavern that no longer bore resemblance to a cylinder and wisps of ruby fog began leaking through the stone teeth of the cave. Staring past the gnome king, Rick no longer saw an endless cave disappearing into infinity. The cave, instead, faded away into a red mist a bare fifty yards away.

The gnome king stopped walking. He turned to face them. When the four of them had gathered in front of him he spoke:

"Forget not this boon. Every traveler that passes through our land shall depart with some of it. You have taken this from us, and we do not forget."

"Where have you taken us?" he asked the gnome king.

"You are at the edge of the Underworld where the Sword is held. Beyond, you will find a boat and the river. I presume your gods will provide you with what you need."

The gnome king walked straight back the way they had come, passing between Rocky and Richard. Rick turned to follow the king's progress, a question on his lips. . . .

The question went unasked because behind the four of them was a solid wall of rock. There was no sign of the gnome king or the land under the hill.

Rick led the others out into the red mist to see where it was they had been taken.

CHAPTER 33

JULIA

THE next time she visited Richard, Julia brought more of his old notebooks. Somehow, reading them gave her more of a sense of connecting with him, even if the Richard she was connecting with was the child he was a quarter of a century ago.

The TV was still on, muted, showing CNN this time. Richard watched it as passively as he had watched the sitcoms, as he had watched out the window of his room at Devereux House.

Julia wondered if he missed the view.

She kissed him on the brow and talked to him a little before she took out one of the notebooks.

"Well, Bro," she said, "life goes on. I *finally* got my financial aid to stop hemorrhaging after I withdrew from all my classes, so I'll be going back to school after all. . . ."

She looked into his face. "You'd be out of school by now, wouldn't you? Somehow you don't seem the perpetual student type. You'd be *doing* something with your life—not like your sister, who'll be getting a doctorate in something artsy and useless." Julia sighed. "Married and with at least one kid, I bet."

She shook her head and muttered, "Listen to me."

Julia picked up one of the notebooks she'd brought and leafed through it for something that resembled a narrative passage. "You need to learn something about organization. I don't know how you ever found anything in them."

Her eyes caught on a passage describing more about the iconic Artifacts that Richard had woven nearly everywhere into his fictional world. Julia grinned a little and said, "Why break a streak?"

There were five little vignettes about the current guardians of the Artifacts, and the places where they were kept. None were kept in the mortal land of Quinque itself; all were placed on a world slightly offset from the mortal plane. They were so placed that only those men meant to bear the Artifacts could reach them.

The guardians of the Sword of Heros were the immortal beings that inhabited the land of the dead. The Sword was carried into the Underworld by the spirit of its last wielder, who walked into a lake of molten rock and allowed the stone to envelop the Sword. The passage was accompanied by a vaguely Arthurian drawing of an arm holding a sword upright. Julia could see hints of the person who made the scribbled drawings in the last of the notebooks.

The guardian of the Ring of Lucas was Lucian, the singular being that was the wyrm in the heart of Chaos, the immortal creature that held the last of Chaos' soul. The great serpent hoarded its wisdom, and the ring, inside the great rock known as the Fist of Chaos. A sketch of a serpentine dragon accompanied the passage.

The guardian of the Horn of Vitus was the mortal soul of the world-tree, accompanied by the dryads that lived in her wood. The sketch of that was a tree with a vaguely humanoid face.

The guardians of the Cirque of Citas were the highest of the elves, who kept it way up on a mountain in their own fey realm. They would only pass it to someone who would free them from the physical chains of the mortal world. The sketch here was a bleak snowscape haunted by tall forms that had a vaguely evil cast. There was a hint of a very far horizon.

Julia was amazed at the quality of the pictures. She had to keep reminding herself that it was a kid less than half her age who drew this stuff. The lines were crude, but there was enough of a sense of drama and composition there that the crudeness could have been taken as deliberate.

She turned the page to look at the guardians of the Staff of Magus. The picture there was only a swirling void.

Julia looked at the picture for a long time before she read the accompanying text. The image was purely abstract, but she found in the scribbled black shadows a disturbing familiarity. In the blackness was the same person who had drawn the pictures after the accident. It was the same use of line and shadow, the density of the near-random lines defining swirling figures with no set boundaries. . . .

The Staff of Magus was banished beyond reality itself, in a place outside of the remains of Chaos' dreams. Nothing could reach it except a being with the power to create or destroy the world.

Julia stopped reading and looked back at the swirling picture. In it she could see the darkness Richard had fallen into, a swirling black space from which he couldn't communicate. Somewhere he probably couldn't even hear her. There was a hole inside her brother, and everything she could do or say would fall into that swirling void and disappear without a trace.

Julia closed the notebook and wiped her eyes.

She gave Richard the effort of a false smile and said, "That's enough of that."

She congratulated herself for not breaking down.

CHAPTER 34

RICHIE

RICHIE cursed the unreality of this place. Everyone else seemed to accept it, and Richie felt as if he was rapidly losing any choice in the matter. They stepped out of what was a cave, or what seemed to be a cave, that was instantly swallowed by the omnipresent red mist. Within a few steps, it was as if the cave no longer existed.

The mist cut all four of them off from everything more than a dozen yards away. Rick led them toward the sound of water, and eventually, from out of the mists, emerged a lone boat floating on the surface of a river black as ink.

The boat was ebon as well, long and narrow, the bow curling up into a figurehead of vaguely skeletal appearance. Richie expected to see Charon himself manning the boat, but it was empty, tied to a slimy black piling that could have been made of wood, or some evil black mineral.

"Come on," Rick said, with little trace of hesitation. Lack of sleep, Rocky's injuries, none of that seemed to matter. Richie himself felt almost asleep on his feet.

Rick boarded the boat with no apparent thought of the cost, even *sans* boatman. Richie stood by and watched as Rick helped the injured Rocky into the long craft. Rocky had more right to preach some caution than anyone else, but other than a few stoic grunts, he said nothing.

"Richie?" Richard said. He had stopped next to Richie.

Richie turned to look at him. Even this close, most of the detail of his face was lost to the mist. Richard's profile gave the impression of a backgroundless sepia-tone picture from a century ago. "You know," Richie said, turning to look at the boat, "at first I thought Rocky was the one I really wasn't going to like."

"Oh."

Richie heard a depressive note in Richard's voice and said, "I ain't talking about you."

"You don't have to explain."

Rick had turned to face them, and Richie could see the impatience in his expression. *Get on with it,* his look—rapidly becoming an indignant stare—said.

Richie said, "Prof, if my opinion matters, I think you're the only one of us that turned out halfway decent."

"No, Richie," he said. "I'm probably more screwed up than any of you."

"I don't know about that." Richie met Rick's gaze and whispered, "Der Führer over there seems to be loosening his own screws as he goes along."

"You're being unfair."

"Am I?" He continued to whisper, afraid of Rick hearing him even though the mist seemed to suck up sound like cotton batting. It was an uncharacteristic feeling for Richie. He usually had no problem offending people, bursting their bubbles. If he had told off so many people who took the state's money to pretend to be his parents, why did he feel uneasy talking about a version of himself?

Richie continued in a low voice. "He's in the boat. That's a decision risking our lives without even asking us about it. I like to choose my own Scylla and my own Charybdis. Much less my own Styx."

"We need a leader," Richard said.

"Is everything all right up there?" Rick shouted from the boat. There was a hint of irritation in the voice as he called up the shoreline at them.

Richie grunted in disgust. He turned to look at Richard. "Someone forgot to enlighten me about that particular detail. I fail to see the necessity."

Richard reached out and squeezed his shoulder, "That's all right, I think we need you, too."

"Thanks for the vote of confidence."

Richie walked over and climbed into the back of the ebon longboat.

When Richard got in, Rocky pulled the rope free from its mooring and Rick took a pole from the floor of the boat and pushed them into the darkling river.

The boat slid into surprisingly calm waters, and Richie had a brief thought that maybe there *were* gods on their side.

Richie had a long time to ponder who exactly had left the boat for them, and whether they were on the Richards' side. He almost wished he was poling the craft, so he didn't have to think about it.

He didn't know how long they poled the boat toward what should have been south. The mists never lifted, nor did the lighting ever change from a dim twilight. Despite the enormity of the situation, Richie eventually found the presence of mind to fall into an exhausted slumber.

Eventually someone woke him for a turn at poling the craft down the dark waters. Richie took the job in what he thought was good grace, which meant he didn't bitch about it.

Eventually he was the lone consciousness in the boat, the three others in their own exhausted slumber. It wasn't long before his hands felt raw and his arms and back ached from the effort of keeping the boat moving, but by then there was no one awake to bitch to.

They had passed into lands obscure and lonely, an area of Quinque that his adolescent dreams had only brushed upon. It was on his watch that he saw the first signs of their arrival in the Underworld.

As the shadows began to loom over either shore, Richie had no idea what to expect. And all he could have expected would not have been what he actually saw.

Silvery objects began bumping the sides of the boat. It took Richie a while before he realized what they were. Dead fish, floating on the surface in the hundreds, in the thousands. Richie slowly stopped poling the craft as he lost the bottom of the river.

An oily chemical smell began adding a rancid flavor to the omnipresent mist. Rainbows shimmered on the water they floated on. Eventually, the shadows began to resolve, not just on the horizon, but all around them.

Richie prodded his nearest companion, Rocky, with the side of his boot. Rocky grumbled a little and slowly opened his eyes. Richie looked down and said, "I think we're here."

Rocky gradually pushed himself up in the boat to look around at what Richie was staring at. They were slowly going forward on a current that was the reverse of the current that had been in Quinque. The river itself had become infinitely fouler.

The Cuyahoga as the Styx. Here is a river that could burn.

Rocky woke the others as Richie stared at the landscape they passed. He was paralyzed by the hellish visions they passed. Chimneys belched flame around them, more than had ever bordered the real Cuyahoga. Evil blocky shadows crowded the water, lit inside by ruddy lights.

"My God," Richie whispered as they passed under a drawbridge. It was a skeletal railroad trestle, frozen ocher in the act of levering over the inky water. Everything inside Richie shriveled as he saw, hanging from the girders above, distorted bodies dangling from chains.

The skeletal remains appeared to have been dead a long time. But as they passed below the bridge, Richie caught a glint of a coppery eye staring at them.

It was like the world he remembered, but enough unlike it to be more alien than the streets of Quinque. Quinque had, at the very least, given him dreams to prepare. What surrounded him was no dream he'd ever had.

The redness of the mist was lit by chimneys belching fire, by bonfires that roared in the distance, by the red eyes of warning lights that glowed in sunless twilight, and by dusky sodium arcs trying to burn their way through sulfur-smelling air that was as thick and opaque as gauze.

The buildings around them made Richie think that both

CEI and LTV Steel had gone malignant and had metastisized the entire shoreline.

"Could we have found another Cleveland?" Richard asked. There was an almost metaphysical unease in the tone of Richard's question.

No one answered him.

They began sliding beneath another twisted interpretation of the Lorain-Carnegie Bridge, where the art deco sculpturing was now dark and demonic.

"They're watching us," Rocky said.

"Who?" Richie asked, his attention moving from the bridge to the shoreline.

"I don't know," Rocky said.

Richie followed Rocky's gaze, seeing nothing but twisted shadows among buildings that were little more than orderly wreckage, piles of bricks and twisted ocher girders.

Richie thought, *We are in deep shit.* He said, "I can't see anyone."

In fact, the bodies dangling over the river were the only signs that this place wasn't entirely abandoned. He could still see them receding behind the boat, and he also could catch sight of other dangling bodies, from girders, telephone poles, smokestacks. . . .

But, except for a cloud of black avian forms silently circling low in the sky, there was no movement anywhere.

The boat spent another ten minutes floating down the dead river while everyone talked in low tones. There was something malignant about the stillness here and it seemed to keep everyone from raising their voices. What they talked about was where to land, and where to look for Heros' Sword.

They had no clear sense of where to look; the hellish city around them marched off into the mists as far as they could see. Richie wouldn't have been surprised if the mutant factories and blind-eyed warehouses went on forever, or at least for an area equal to that of the Cleveland he knew.

He got the sense that now—that they were here—if

they persisted for long on this river, they would eventually return to their starting point. It was a sense renewed when they passed a scissored iron drawbridge, frozen in place, hung with bodies.

Rick was scanned the shoreline. "We have a job to do here. At some point we will have to put ashore."

Like we have a choice now, Richie thought. He was beginning to dislike Rick more than ever.

"Are they hiding it?" Rocky wondered aloud in a voice that was little more than a whisper.

"Perhaps there," Richard said, pointing.

Richard pointed east of them, where the skyline should have been. There was something there, casting a silhouette about where Richie would expect one. However, the mist was thick there, and Richie couldn't be sure if he saw a building where the Terminal Tower should be, or a vertical pillar of rock. In either case, the shadow seemed to glow from cracks in its surface, and appeared to vent steam into the surrounding mist.

"Tower City," Richie muttered. His thoughts drifted to the multimillion dollar renovation the Tower had undergone in his Cleveland, the conversion from a glorified train station into a mall. Richie wondered what kind of underground renovations this place had experienced.

"It is the most prominent place I can see," Rick said. "From the tales, I suspect that what guardians there are have no need to hide the Sword. This entire place is hidden."

Richie didn't bring up the subject of returning from here. He already had a nasty suspicion that Heros had opened the door to let them in, and might not open it again to let them out. At least not until Rocky had the Sword in his hand.

Richie tried to be mad at himself for taking this insanity seriously. But, for some reason, the place around him was terribly convincing—perhaps because he had no idea what to expect now. The déjà vu that he associated with all things Quinque had left him.

They put ashore in sight of the base of the ersatz

Tower. In this twisted place, it was a spire of rock. If it had been fashioned by hands, human or otherwise, it had been a very rough job that still left it and its visible neighbors looking like an abused mountain.

Holes in its base faced them, venting steam, and sitting on a plain of rock that had oozed from them. The cavernous openings bore some resemblance to the openings that fed the trains into Tower City, but not much. From inside those holes, Richie saw a ruddy glow through the mist that he didn't find encouraging.

CHAPTER 35

RICHARD

THEY tied the boat to a jagged spit of iron that hung over the dead river. The others made decisions on what was best to take with them, but it was merely a delay of the inevitable. Richard stared at the holes in the wall of rock, passages into the underworld, and felt their pull. The longer he stared, the less regular they seemed, the more the resemblance to the passages under downtown Cleveland seemed to leech away.

Eventually the other Richards filed by him. He was following them in before he realized he had started moving.

It took about fifteen minutes to reach the cave mouths from the river. The footing along the way was slick and treacherous; the once molten rock never condescended to give them certain footing. Here and there, on the way, twisted fingers of iron would pierce the surface, jutting out over the Richards' heads. The ancient girders sometimes would bend into near-organic forms, as if they walked within the rib cage of some long-dead beast.

Richard was at a loss to explain the superficial similarities to the topography of his home. It was as if someone used the pigments of hell to paint an impressionistic portrait of where he had lived all his life.

The likeness was only apparent at a remove. This close, this place resembled nothing he had ever seen before. Still, it gave him pause to consider the origins of this place, to wonder how it was related to him, and the others. It was as if he walked though a landscape that he might have written, but never had.

The caves were huge, leading to vast spaces beyond.

The mist was thicker here, fed by steam venting from the caves, reducing visibility that much more. The mists rolled along the top of the cave, an endless cloud above their heads, lit from within by a red glow, like the mist hid molten rock within it.

"This is a fucking nightmare," Richie said.

Rick nodded, staring into one of the caverns. "Yes, but this is the first bit of terrain that coincides with my memories of where the Sword should be."

That was true, Richard remembered his childhood notebooks describing the Sword's prison as a cavern in the Underworld. But Richard wondered if that was a rationalization, wondered if Rick felt the same tidal pull toward these caves that he did. Rocky seemed to, or if nothing else, he was decisive about which entrance to use.

"This way," he said, pointing toward one of the larger cave mouths. Looking at his chain shirt spotted by flecks of blood, and at the empty sheath on his belt, Richard realized how ill-prepared they were for this. The only protection they had was Richie's gun, and Richie had a hand in the pocket where he kept it.

Richard was unarmed with anything except the stolen knife that Richie had given him. He didn't draw the knife. He wouldn't know what to do with a weapon.

He stayed back during the descent. When they entered the maw of the cave, it enfolded them with arms of twisted rock. It was easy to imagine that, beyond the haze, the walls were biological in origin. The haze pulsed red, almost as if it were a beating heart.

Rocky led them down, through the divisions in the vast chambers, always down. He led them through air that became nearly thick and heavy enough to be a solid barrier. The light became ever more inconstant and surreal, severing continuity from moment to moment, until Richard could only perceive their progress as a series of frozen tableaux captured in a pulse of ruddy light.

When the light faded to darkness, it seemed that the shadows around them still moved within the darkness.

No one spoke. Their progress slowed as Richard watched the others look for signs of the creatures that seemed to move in the shadow. Richard didn't know what he was looking for in the pulsing light. . . .

Richard saw it for a long time before he understood what it meant.

"By all that is holy," he whispered.

It wasn't the light that was inconstant. It was the shadow. *Their* shadow. Richard could see nothing of their semblance, but in time to some distant pulse, their forms interrupted the light, dimmed it enough to darken the passage. In that darkness, Richard could see them almost as a thickening within the air, a heat shimmer writing an outline of a body, a body that was twisted and deformed.

The shapes that Richard almost saw were disturbing beyond his comprehension. His brain could not create an image to accompany the outline, it refused to, but he still found the barest glimpses making him sick with disgust and fear.

He froze in place, and Rick said, "What's the matter?"

"Can't you see them?" Richard whispered, his voice cracking. "They're all around us."

"What?" Rocky asked. In each pulse of the light he had swung to face a new direction, searching for a threat that had already swarmed around him.

"Thick spots in the air," Richard said, giving the best description he could of the horror surrounding them. "Thick spots casting shadows."

Richie was the next one to notice. "Holy shit." He drew his gun, but its barrel pointed at the ground as if he wasn't quite sure what to shoot at.

The periods of light increased in frequency, but decreased in magnitude. Richard felt his own heart quicken to match the pace. In the shadows, the things were almost visible. Thankfully they were cloaked in darkness then; Richard didn't think he could take an unobstructed view of them.

With every pulse of the light, the things seemed to press in on the Richards, forcing them toward the center of the tunnel. Rick and Rocky also saw them, even though, to the eye, they were little more than an ominous trick of the light.

As Richard backed toward the rest of his companions, he could feel their effect on other senses. They were hot, every pulse of the light was followed by a wash of air in the darkness, a breath from a forge, carrying the scent of hot iron. They advanced with a very quiet chittering sound, like rusty nails scraping across a slate roof.

The four Richards had fallen into a tight circle, facing outward toward barely seen enmity. The few flashes of light were now very brief and very rapid. Richard felt Rocky turn in a full circle behind him, and raise his arm.

"I am here for the Sword of Heros," Rocky said to the darkness.

The darkness responded.

The last of the light disappeared.

CHAPTER 36

ROCKY

ROCKY heard Richard yell something about thick spots in the air, and suddenly the darkness in the tunnel started to have a texture, as if the shadows surrounding them were a living creature. The next few minutes took on the inevitability of a dream. It felt more dreamlike here than in any setting he'd experienced in Quinque.

Paradoxically, it may have been because, of all the places Rocky had seen in Quinque, he had never dreamed of this place.

The shadows closed on him and the others in the pulsing light. Shifting forms in the darkness weren't the only changes he saw when the light went away. In the dark the character of the tunnel changed. In the ruddy light the walls around them were near-organic forms molded from molten rock. In the darkness the walls seemed artificial, constructed of concrete and iron, the organic feel only granted by once-living things that had been set into the wall.

When the light faded, Rocky could see the faces in the rock wall, calling for release, reaching for him. He wanted to scream as his heart tried to ram through his chest.

As if in a reverie, he felt himself raise his arm and call into the hostile darkness.

"I am here for the Sword of Heros."

It felt as if he *had* to say those words, as if his presence here had been scripted. As though caught in a dream, he was compelled to say them, and as he would in a dream he did so without thought of the consequences.

The consequences were immediate. The darkness claimed the tunnel fully, and Rocky felt it rush him. The darkness broke over him, smelling of blood and hot iron, tearing a corrupt hole in the world around him.

Rocky heard Rick say, panicked, "Stay together, everyone stay together."

His voice sounded muffled, distant, as if Rick's mouth, or Rocky's ears, had filled with the near-solid dark. Rocky couldn't see Rick anymore, all the light had gone.

He hadn't moved, he hadn't taken a step, but he knew he'd been separated from the others. Even in total blackness, he could sense that they were no longer next to him. He held up his arms defensively, though he didn't know how that could defend him against something that seemed to be made of light and air.

The air was thick, his heart was racing, he felt as if he might be drowning. Something sounded near him, a noise like someone sharpening a knife, or slowly drawing the lid off of a tomb.

It took Rocky a moment to realize that the sound was modulated, that he was listening to a whispery voice, as if someone were trying to talk through a speaker that had completely blown.

"What do you mean, Richard Brandon?" was what the voice said.

Rocky spun around to see if he could place the speaker, but he couldn't. Even with his eyes adjusting to the gloom, he couldn't make out anything more than twisted shadows layered across more shadows. The voice seemed to come from everywhere at once.

"What do you want, Richard Brandon?"

He stopped spinning. The act of motion stole any anchor he had in a world that was suddenly without a point of reference. "I want the Sword!" he called into the darkness.

The response came from several directions at once, though it was all the same voice.

"We husband pain—"

"—ours and the world's—"

"—why give you our pain—"

"—when we can provide you with your own?"

The bastards had beaten him. He felt it in his gut, an agony of despair. No matter what he did, where he went, the bastards would beat him down. He was surrounded by enemies that he couldn't even touch, whether it was his father, or sneaking away from a failed war in Nicaragua, or just the endless plodding fight against a tide of corruption that was eating the city away—

Even as his emotions swirled into a depression blacker than the darkness around him, he knew that the emotions weren't wholly his own. Somehow these things were pulling his mind down.

It wasn't fair, the guardians should *fight* him. That's what he was *for*.

"What do you want, Richard Brandon?"

I want to fight something and finally win.

I want to do to my father what I did to the idiot with the frying pan.

I want this to end.

"I want the Sword." It was a whisper he forced out between his teeth.

"He wants the Sword," the voice echoed, as if it were finally acknowledging what Rocky had been saying. The scraping in the darkness seemed to be something laughing at him.

Rocky wanted to strike something, but there was nothing. . . .

The shadows began falling away, the world lightening around him. The dim shapes—the misshapen things that seemed to be made of darkness and a thickening of the air—receded to the periphery of his vision.

The others were gone, or he had wandered into another chamber in the darkness. The impression of things imprisoned within the walls was now much more than an impression. All around him, faces tried to emerge from the stone, contorted beyond the limits of human expression. They reached for him, hands twisted into claws or fists.

Rocky wanted to believe them to be sculptures, but his

gut shriveled as he noted the way the muscles drew in on all of them. He had seen the way the bodies of people burned alive tried to curl up in the same way. It was a posture that seemed to epitomize agony.

The ruddy light brightened around him, and the air between him and the wall became unstable and wavy.

"He wants the Sword," the voice repeated.

Rocky glanced down and saw why the cavern was brightening. Beneath his feet the floor cracked, revealing a river of molten rock beneath the stone. He stood on a black crust that seemed paper-thin, floating on the magma. The heat reached him as he watched, a searing pain up his leg. The air itself was hot enough to burn flesh.

He tried to move, but his boots were fused to the rock. He grasped his right calf. The searing washed his arms as well. He could smell the rancid odor of his own hair vaporizing.

"Let me through!" It was an agonized cry as well as a command.

"Why not join us here? Your monument will be more enduring. . . ."

Cracks appeared in the slab of rock he stood upon; he could see the magma glow through the cracks. He felt the heat wash his face, and he imagined what it was like for the prisoners in the walls here, to be wrapped in molten rock so quickly that the flesh turns to solid ash—

"Let me through," he repeated. This time it was nothing more than a hoarse whisper. He could feel the hair burning off his face, and the heat was a brand across his arms and legs, a pain that seemed to strip flesh from bone and leave his limbs locked and immobile.

He couldn't get his leg free, and the rock supporting him began sinking. He saw steam rising from his boot, and the pain was making his gut spasm. His vision was darkening, his mind only able to focus on the agony in his limbs. When glowing rock the consistency of toothpaste oozed from the cracks toward the sole of his boot, Rocky stared at it, unable to recognize what it was.

Sweat stung his eyes, and the remote, inconsequential

sting brought part of his mind back. He redoubled his struggles, and a thought came to him.

They aren't talking.

They'd stopped talking ever since he'd spoken the second time—

"Let," Rocky said, though lips that blistered and bled. "Me." The oozing rock reached the sole of his boot, and the leather erupted into flames that danced as high as his shin. "Through." Rocky fell forward—

—toppling onto cold, damp stone.

"Wha?" It wasn't a question so much as a surprised exhalation. He realized that his lips no longer burned or bled, he no longer suffered from burns on his arms and legs, and he no longer smelled the reek of roasted hair.

He pushed himself upright. They were putting him through some sort of test. He had passed this part of it, and he had little doubt that a failure would have been fatal.

It's the repetition. I have to keep focused enough, whatever it is they do, to state something three times.

Could the next one be worse than the last?

"Richard Brandon, oh, Richard Brandon."

God, no.

Instinctively he felt for his sword, but it was long gone, one with the Thrall. As he felt for it, he realized that his hands were much too small.

The feelings rushed over him like a wave, uncontrollable. He couldn't speak, mustn't speak, or he'd find him. He was drunk, he could hear it in his voice, and that voice was as bad as he had ever sounded. If he didn't say anything, if he didn't move out of the shadows, maybe, maybe—

Rocky pressed himself against the wall of the cavern, trying to make himself as small as possible so his father wouldn't see what he was doing.

"Richard, oh, Richard Brandon."

The voice was coming closer, and the small Richard Brandon could smell the liquor on his father's breath, hear it in the heavy fall of his steps, and in the evil slur of his words.

If I get through this, I'll never drink again.

The thought, the reflexive promise, managed to filter through to the front of his mind. The small voice of Richard Brandon tried to think, *No, Dad's the one who drinks*—but Rocky was there, too, and Rocky knew better. Rocky knew that what he fought wasn't his father, no matter what his gut, his ears, and his nose told him.

Rocky clenched his fists and felt a kernel of hate for the beings who would use *this* against him. Very, very low he whispered, "Give me the Sword."

"There you are, you nasty little *shit*." No preamble, his father was just suddenly there, reaching for him. Worse, it was Dad right after the accident, the stitches carving a purple road map across a face too swollen to appear human. His father grabbed him by the neck. His fingers were too long, and his grip was too strong for Rocky to escape.

Rocky had to close his eyes before he could speak, otherwise he found himself staring at his father's scarred face. "Give me—" he began to say, choking the words out.

Before he got the complete sentence out, a liquor bottle slammed into the side of his head. It didn't shatter like they did in the movies. It slammed into his skull with a hollow thump, like a baseball bat.

Rocky fell to the floor of the cavern, stunned. It felt as if his jaw were broken, and he could feel the bruise appearing on his throat. "Not even a scratch, not a fucking scratch," his father was screaming down at him.

Rocky was frozen on the ground, staring at the puddle where blood leaked out of his mouth. Just as he'd done a hundred times before, he went limp and waited for his father to kill him, half-wishing he would.

"They had to peel off my goddamn face! And you, not a fucking scratch I can see." Rocky heard a pause that meant his father was taking a swig from the bottle he carried. "Your mother is killed, and I'm left having to *support* a worthless little shit like you."

Rocky's brain recovered some thought. *I got through this. I survived him. He didn't manage to kill me.*

His tongue found the unfinished statement. "—the Sword."

"Shut the fuck up." Rocky felt his father's foot slam into his stomach. He knew the exact tenor of his voice. Any push now would send his father ballistic. He had always been terrified of provoking his father when he was like this. It seemed all too likely that it would end with his father killing him.

Rocky managed to choke back the terror and say, "Give."

His father descended on him with an inarticulate scream, raining blows on his torso.

"Me." The word, a simple pronoun, infuriated his father. Rocky felt a fist break ribs, slam into a kidney, shatter a collarbone. It was as if he had fallen into some sort of machine. His mind wanted to pull back, withdraw completely, but he managed to draw the breath to speak.

"The." The word sprayed out of his mouth in a shower of bloody spit. It felt as if he were drowning, choking on his own blood.

"Sword." Rocky finished, closing his eyes.

Rocky fell through a brief dreamless eternity. He didn't know whether he was alive or dead, nor did he care. For a shining instant he was stripped of identity, of ego. For a moment he could see the whole terrible unity. For a moment he *knew*.

It didn't last. Senses washed over his awareness, erasing understanding before he had become fully aware that he had it. All that was left was a sense of loss. He could feel the memory, there, tangible, and slipping away as he grasped it.

As he struggled up from the ground, he had little sense of the thing, other than it was something he did not want to know. Suspect, perhaps. He could live with suspicions. He didn't want to deal with certainty. . . .

I don't even know what I'm thinking about.

Rocky shook his head and pushed himself to his feet. He was himself, and the landscape had changed again. It had returned to the aspect that had greeted them when they descended into this place. Ruddy light, mist, and caverns that seemed oddly between something that was fashioned by hand, and something that had grown out of the molten heat of the mountain. He saw no sign of the others.

One end of the tunnel was brighter than the other, so that was the way he walked. He crossed the threshold into a large chamber, almost spherical, a bubble in the earth. Light shone from cracks in the rock, making the surface seem blacker than it was. The bottom of the chamber was flat and cold, as if molten rock had surged in the chamber and cooled, finding its level a quarter of the way up the sphere.

The surface of this floor was smooth black glass, except in the center, where the rock swirled upward in a spike, the size and shape of a human arm. From the top of the arm of rock Rocky could see the shine of metal, reflecting back to him a red eye of light.

"Good Lord," Rocky muttered. He remembered the agonized faces imprisoned in the rock. The owner of this arm had plunged into a lake of fire and molten rock, and had kept his arm raised against the heat, bearing the Sword.

He walked toward the Sword of Heros. It was plainer than he expected. A simple unadorned blade emerging from a rocky embrace. It was plain yet somehow not plain. There was something about the way it caught the light. A gravity in the reflection that couldn't be seen in the thing itself. In some immeasurable way, Rocky felt as if the simple iconic Sword parted the world around it, cutting into the reality around Rocky only enough to show a form that Rocky could understand and perceive.

Looking at it, Rocky had the feeling that it was a physical metaphor for something else, something he wouldn't quite understand, even if he knew what it was.

"You believe you have won?" The whispery voice wasn't finished with him.

He kept edging toward the Sword, searching against the walls for the speaker. There was something about this room, or the light, or the presence of the Sword, that made them easier to see. These fay creatures distorted the light around them, but backlit by the cracks in the rock he could begin to see their form as a distortion of light and shadow. It was like trying to see a solid glass sculpture immersed in turbulent water.

They were not things that were pleasant to view, even so dimly. He couldn't form a complete image in his mind of what these things were, he could only perceive one incongruous detail after another. Their bones were twisted, gnarled and lumpy like the limbs of an old tree. They wore devices that, barely seen, could have been jewelry, armor, or surgical implants. Rocky saw shadows that could have been knives—or claws; cloth bindings—or shreds of skin; capes—or demonic wings.

He felt that, by seeing them this well, he had somehow come closer to wherever it was they lived. Rocky didn't like that thought at all.

"You believe you have won?" the voice repeated. "The last man to hold it believed he had won."

Rocky was next to the arm of rock. Unlike the Arthurian sword in the stone, in this case the hilt was buried in a black stone fist. There was no way to remove it without shattering the rock.

He was about to make another threefold demand, but apparently that part of the game was over. As he watched, the stone hand opened, releasing the hilt.

"Know, Richard Brandon, when you take that offering, you doom yourself and the world."

Rocky stopped reaching for the Sword. He turned to face the audience, which had become painfully close to visibility. He tore his gaze away from them, and back to the deceptively simple Sword, now free for the taking, guard balanced on the edge of an open stone hand. "You are lying. The gods sent us to fight the Adversary. We're here to save this place."

"You do not know why you are here."

"Bullshit."

"Take the Sword. We shall not stop you."

"Why? If you think I will end the world with this, why let me take it at all?"

"Pain is all this world leaves us, the only sensation we can savor."

Rocky stared at the unadorned hilt of the sword, because he felt the speaker was now fully visible behind him. "I understand—"

"No," the voice was there, alien in its monochromatic intensity. He could feel the breath of the words, hot and ferric on the back of his neck. "We despair because even the edge of that sensation dulls over time."

Then the speaker was gone. They were all gone. Rocky was alone, in the chamber with the Sword of Heros.

For the longest time he could not bring himself to move.

CHAPTER 37

RICK

DARKNESS washed over them, and Rick could sense a sudden upsurge of panic. He fought to retain control.

"*Everyone stay together!*" he yelled at the others. After all this, he was afraid of separating the group, afraid of what might happen out of sight.

"Richie?" he called into the darkness. He was uncomfortably aware of shadows moving around him. He could sense them even in the darkness. And despite the fact that nothing touched him, he had the feeling of being surrounded by others. . . .

"Yo! Here, man." Unmistakably Richie's voice, from about where Rick expected it to be. "I ain't moving."

"Richard?" Rick called next. There was an eerie quality to calling his name out like that, as if he were simultaneously lost and part of the search party to find himself.

"I'm here."

"Rocky?" Rick called next.

No answer.

"Rocky?" he called out again, and Richie and Richard joined him. But no answer came. The shadows watched impassively.

"Rocky?" Again no answer.

He heard Richie mutter, "Fuck."

Where did he disappear to? He had been standing next to them less than thirty seconds ago. Rick had the sense that Rocky hadn't wandered off. The shadows—or the things inside the shadows—had taken him.

Rick held out his arm and felt back to where he had heard Richard's voice. He felt a shoulder wince under his touch. That reassured Rick. He didn't feel that the things in the shadows around him would wince at his touch.

"Richard?" Rick asked.

"Yes," came a whispered reply.

Rick called out, "Richie, feel for my hand." His call was more a warning. Richie had a gun and he didn't want to startle him.

When they had all groped into contact with each other, Rick called out at the beings surrounding them. "What have you done with our companion?"

Silence.

"Return him immediately," Rick commanded. He tried to sound authoritative, and just managed to keep the fear out of his voice.

A scraping sound echoed through the cavern. The sound could have been the lid of a tomb opening, but to Rick, it sounded like one prolonged word. "Wait."

The three of them stood in darkened silence for a while. Then, when Rick was about to call another challenge to these things, the shadows drained away, and the area down the corridor from them began to lighten.

Rocky was easy to find after that. He was at the common terminus of all the tunnels, where a train platform would be if this were truly some twisted analog of downtown Cleveland.

Rick was the first in the domed chamber, and he stopped when he saw Rocky, and what Rocky was looking at. What Rocky stood before was a sculpted arm, as if the Statue of Liberty had been buried up to her crown, leaving only the forearm free of the rocky floor.

Only, instead of a torch, this arm bore a sword.

The Sword.

Rocky stared at the arm, and for a moment Rick thought he was in some sort of trance. Rocky broke the impression by looking up at him. "This is it," Rocky said needlessly, "what we came for."

"Then grab it," Richie said, coming into the room behind Rick. "Grab it so we can get the fuck out of here."

"They want me to take it," Rocky said.

Richie stood by the edge of the room, staring at Rocky as if he couldn't quite understand why that was a problem. Rick couldn't quite understand it himself. Rocky was just standing there, in front of the Sword. That was why they were *here*.

"What's the problem here?" Rick asked him. He stepped up next to Rocky, keeping alert for another resurgence of the darkness. "This is what we are here for, correct?"

Rocky nodded, staring at the unornamented weapon, not at Rick. Rick looked at the Sword and felt an odd twinge. It was disturbing to look at.

Most things had at the least an impression of mass. In this thing, Rick seemed to feel an absence of mass, as if it weren't really there. It was almost a hologram, or an illusion, but more so. With an illusion, there was still a *there* there. The feeling that Rick had was that he was looking at a Sword-shaped absence, a hole in reality. . . .

He dismissed the feeling, because nothing he saw could account for it. What he saw was a simple blade of gray metal, with a hilt and a guard of the same material.

He could feel Rocky's tenseness.

"What is the problem?" Rick asked.

"The beings here," Rocky said. "They spoke to me." He did not move his gaze from the Sword.

"What did they say?" Rick asked.

"Can we get a move on?" Richie muttered from near the entrance.

Rick repeated the question.

"They said that if I took the Sword, I would doom myself and the world."

Rick understood his reluctance now. He was about to ask what they had said, exactly, when something totally unexpected happened.

Richie pushed Rick aside, muttering some scatological comment, reached over and snatched the blade's hilt. He had lifted it out of the stone grasp before either Rocky or Rick could react.

"What are you doing?" Rick shouted. The unexpectedness of the move infuriated him. That wasn't what was supposed to happen. They all had their own Artifacts, for someone else to handle them smacked of blasphemy, or—somehow worse—implied that there was less control over what was going on.

Rick trembled, suddenly realizing how much he was relying on fate and destiny, and simultaneously realizing that Richie was its antithesis. Rick realized in that moment that Richie was disruption personified.

Rick now knew—*knew*—that it was Riche who would betray them. Richie was his Judas, his Loki. In that moment Rick hated his twin.

"To hell with this debate," Richie said. "We're here to grab a Sword. Now we got one. Now do I carry it, or do you?" Richie held the Sword before him, point upward, toward Rocky.

Rick grabbed Richie's arm. His hand was shaking, and the vibration was transmitted all the way to the point of the Sword. The strength of his grip surprised him, and even through the leather jacket, it must have surprised Richie as well.

"What do you think you are doing?" Anger kept Rick's teeth clenched, so the words came out in a hoarse whisper. Richie turned to stare at him as if he spoke a foreign language. "It was offered to *him*."

Richie's stare made Rick want to throttle him. "Look, man, I do not want to hang out here long enough for the shadows to return. We're supposed to get the Sword and get out, not to debate whatever line of bullshit these things—"

"Shut up!" Rick yelled at him. "Don't you understand? It was offered to Rocky. *Rocky!*"

Richard's voice came from behind him. "Maybe you should calm—"

"Calm?" Rick sucked an intake of breath. "How—" His words were choked off by his anger. He looked into Richie's eyes and took a deep breath. If they were following a fated path, then Richie himself was part of the journey. Like the rest of them, playing his role. When he could speak again, he said, "You cannot play games with this kind of power, Richie. There is one person who is supposed to bear that Sword."

"In case you haven't noticed," Richie said, "we're all the same person."

Rick felt the fury try to return, but he controlled it this time. He had to retain control. "No, we are *not*." Rick released Richie's arm. "There are rules," he said quietly.

Richie said, "Huh? Rules?"

Rick ignored him and stepped away. He had to keep control. He knew that there were rules, there *had* to be rules. He could just barely see patterns swimming in the darkness. He could see himself and Richie as opposing poles on the magnet. Order and anarchy.

His God had told him that there would be one to face the Adversary, and one who would betray them all. One deceiver, one savior. He knew who they were, who they *had* to be.

"Give Rocky the Sword," Rick said. He felt the tone of confidence, of authority, return to his voice. That was good. It meant he was back in control, which meant that he was back in control of their Quest, back in control of their destiny.

He turned around and saw all three of them looking at him, a triad around the arm extending up out of the floor. "Go on," he said. "Whatever our hosts here have said, it doesn't make sense to vacillate now that the Sword is out of its resting place."

Richie extended the Sword toward Rocky, point upward and canted so his offer led with the hilt of the weapon.

Rocky gave Rick a look, as if considering his options, and then, very slowly, reached for the hilt of the Sword.

The others were intent on the transfer of the Sword. Rick was far enough away that the event didn't occupy the whole of his attention, so he was the first to see the walls fade away. He gasped.

In a moment, the others joined him.

The stone of the walls was the first to fade from view, turning into the heat-shimmer forms that had been all Rick had ever seen of the natives. For a flickering moment all that was visible was the iron skeleton of this damned mountain, twisted metal in shapes arcane and sinister. The metal structure showed the tunnels, the mountainous skyline above them, to be as much artifice as the damned factories lining the river.

Then even the iron ghosts faded from view, and a cool wind buffeted them from a slate-gray sky. The wind smelled of the river, not of molten iron. They stood on a rocky bluff upon an extended oxbow of the river. If Rick's sense of direction still served him, they were on the same shore on which the gnome king had left them.

From the rocky ground at their feet emerged a stony arm that, now without the Sword, appeared to be making an appeal to heaven. As the wind picked up, cracks appeared in the blackened stone skin. Flakes fell off the palm, uncovering an interior of compacted ash. The wind took up the ash, whipping it into a fine cloud. The arm crumbled, shedding ash into the air. For a few brief moments a finer structure of muscle and bone were visible in the packed ash, but that, too, disintegrated. In less than a minute, all that was left of the Sword's previous bearer was a layer of gray ash on the rock.

"I guess our friends took their ball and went home," Richie said.

No sign was left, not the Underworld, not the boat. From appearances, they had just walked through something that was little more than a shared hallucination.

Perhaps that could explain the look of the place. The resemblance to the industrial Flats of Cleveland. Rick didn't feel comfortable with that conclusion. He needed to accept the reality of this place, of all the places they traveled to here. Dismissing any part as a phantasm inevitably led to intolerable conclusions.

As far as Rick was concerned, they were four separate and distinct individuals, from four separate and distinct worlds, and they had all come to a place that was, itself, separate and distinct. Rick could believe that the five of them—them plus the late Doctor Brandon—had somehow created this place, but it was a physical creation. Not a dream, not a phantasm. How could anything in a dream have any importance whatsoever?

Rick knew what they did was important, was real. He was also certain that he would ensure that they did things right. Rick looked at Richie, who was scanning the now-normal horizon and muttering, and for an instant felt as if the only illusionary thing here was the sense that he was in control of the situation.

CHAPTER 38

JULIA

JULIA returned to the Clinic, as she had every afternoon since her brother was admitted. But this time was different. Something had happened to Richard. It took her several panicked minutes before she was finally redirected to Intensive Care.

She was on her way down, and Dr. Kavcheck intercepted her in the hallway. "Julia," he said, putting a hand on her shoulder.

She turned to him and started to say something, but the words were mangled in her throat. Eventually she managed, "What happened? I need to see him."

He nodded and said, "Let me buy you a cup of coffee before that. I think you need to compose yourself a little."

"But—"

"Come on," he said, leading her down a different hall. She shook her head, but was too dazed to really object. "What happened?" she asked again.

Dr. Kavcheck waited until they had reached a room filled with vending machines before he confirmed her second-worst fear. "He's had another pseudo-stroke. This one was worse than the first. He had to be put on a respirator."

"Oh, God." She stared into the Formica surface of the table. She could almost see the black void eating out the inside of her brother. She could picture a reflection of it swirling just under the surface of the table.

"There's some good news, though," he said. "We were able to take him off the respirator this morning."

Julia looked up from the table. "Then he might get better?" she asked.

Dr. Kavcheck looked grave. "Before last night I would have said he had a good chance. But I think you should prepare yourself for the worst. Whatever is happening, we don't have a means to control it."

"But, but . . ." Julia sputtered. Eventually she said lamely, "He's the only family I have left." As if that made a difference. There was a despicable cruelty to all of this, finding a brother, however crippled, only to lose him.

How could she bear going through all this again? She had just buried her *mother*.

"Julia?" he asked, touching the back of her hand. She could feel her own hand tremble under the pressure of his fingers, and she pulled away from him. "I'm all right," she said. "I don't have a choice. I *have* to be all right."

When she had collected herself, Dr. Kavcheck led her down to see Richard. She was convinced that she had prepared herself for the worst, but when she saw Richard, it was all she could do to keep from breaking down.

Before, Richard had looked normal, as if he had just been distracted, oblivious to the world around him. Now there was something obviously wrong. The muscles of his face were slack; to Julia, it gave his face a grotesquely alien expression. He lay on the bed, unable to sit or hold up his neck like he had before.

He looked like a corpse.

Before, he had something of a stoic dignity in his unresponsiveness. Whatever evil had struck his brain had taken even that from him.

It was hard to keep up the pretense of believing that Richard had at least some internal life. She looked into his eyes and could only see a black, swirling void. She felt as if something were destroying him, piece by piece.

On the way home, Julia bought a pair of six-packs. When she entered the house, she dropped onto the couch, put the six-packs on a cardboard box in front of her. She pulled out a can and methodically began to get herself drunk.

When she began to feel slightly light-headed, she got

up and went up to her room. She hadn't unpacked much aside from her clothes. Her art supplies were still where she had stowed them when she had returned home. She hadn't touched them since her mother died.

She pulled out one of the four boxes, the red one that used to be a tackle box, and opened it. She took out her watercolors, and a few brushes.

She returned to the kitchen with those in one hand, and an oversized pad of watercolor paper in the other. She scattered boxes to clear the table, and set up her paints.

Once she retrieved the beer from the living room, she went to work.

The picture began as an oversaturated black spot in the center of the paper, and it swirled black tendrils out from there. A swirling vortex of black and gray emerged, engulfing the white of the page, as Julia tried to exorcise the image. It was an empty darkness, but still it seemed to have a form, a twisted, evil texture that seemed to be the antithesis of all thought or reason.

She painted the abyss, entropy personified. She only added one element of color to contrast with the blacks and the grays. Two patches of red that could have been the eyes of the abyss, looking into her.

When she finished the picture, at four in the morning, she could finally go to bed.

CHAPTER 39

RICHARD

THEY were beyond the apparent edge of the gnome king's domain, at least judging by the character of the trees and the presence of birds—predominantly crows. There were still signs of ancient human habitation, all of it overgrown and nearly buried.

Everyone was drained and on the verge of exhaustion. The four of them abandoned the bluff and made camp amid the old foundation of a long-vanished farmhouse. The foundation was little more than a low stone wall. The only shelter it offered was an old tree that had grown huge and whose roots buckled half the eastern wall.

Richard collapsed at the base of the tree. Rocky slowly levered himself down, wincing. Richie didn't look much better as he sat on a flat spot on the low mossy stone.

Rick stood, though he must have felt as tired as Richard did.

Richard couldn't help feeling that something was badly wrong, and it was an ugly feeling since he couldn't identify exactly what was causing it.

"God," Richie said, "it feels good just to be sitting down."

Rocky grunted an assent.

"You should sit down," Richard said to Rick.

Rick looked at Richard with a gaze that made him feel uneasy. He stared for a moment, then he nodded. He didn't sit. "We need to decide on how we proceed next—"

"*Jesus*—" Richie sighed, "we've done enough for one night—"

"Several nights," Rocky said.

"Let's just give it a rest till morning."

Rick shook his head. "A *rest?*" His voice sounded strained, as if he were about to start yelling. But his face smoothed out again. "Yes, of course. I'll gather some firewood. . . ."

With that, Rick walked off. Richie stared after him, his face an unreadable mixture of emotions. He looked for so long that Richard began to worry.

"Are you all right?" Richard asked him.

"The bastard's going nuts," Richie whispered.

"What?" Richard asked.

Instead of responding, Richie turned to Rocky and said, "I think our leader might be losing it."

Rocky stared at Richie a moment. "Losing what?"

"His marbles," Richie said.

"That's a little extreme," Richard said.

Richie shook his head disdainfully.

"Come on, you two," Richie said. "You saw him go off in the tunnels. He ain't stable."

"Please," Richard responded. "There's some concern about the person bearing the Artifacts—"

Richie stared back. "You *know* why he went off." He turned his gaze from one to the other. "Control, people. He's developing some internal vision of how this all's supposed to go, and if anything fucks with that, he loses it."

"So you should bear the Sword?" Rocky asked.

"Fuck no! I got the willies when I touched it. But for some reason he doesn't want me near the Artifacts, any of them."

Richard could see the fabric of their group tearing as he watched. It was an awful sensation, seeing it and having no idea how to fix it. "You're being paranoid—"

"Yeah, right. Paranoid." He gave Richard a withering look, then he turned his attention to Rocky. "What about you?"

"What do you think I'm supposed to do?"

"Look, man. You got the Almighty Sword, that ought to count for something, right?" Richie said. "If you say something, Rick can't say jack."

Rocky sat there, looking at Richie. There was a note of disgust in his voice as he asked, "You want me to take over by force?"

"I wouldn't put it quite that way—" Richie began.

"If force of arms was all that mattered," Rocky told him. "You still have the gun."

Richie looked at both of them, as if he disbelieved how they were behaving. Richard felt he had to say something in his own defense. "I don't think your perceptions are quite fair. We're all under stress here, but the way we've proceeded seems to have worked—"

"Look," Richie said, "At the very least, let's get the Ring next."

"Your Artifact," Rocky pointed out.

"Damn straight," Richie replied, "There should be some balance here. Right?"

Richie and Rocky stared at each other, and Richard finally felt he was able to smooth things out. "I remember the legends I—we—wrote. The mountain where the Ring rests is not far from here. The others will require a river crossing. There is some sense to it."

"The Fist of Chaos," Rocky said, naming the outcrop where the Ring was held.

Richard nodded. Eventually Rocky did also. By the time Rick returned with the firewood, they had a destination to offer. He looked uneasy at the suggestion, but Richard eventually convinced him that it was the most accessible destination to tackle next.

The ragged band of Richards slept on the bare ground, around a small fire. It took a long time for Richard to sleep. He couldn't help trying to piece together what they were doing, why they all were here. It had seemed clear; the gods of this place had pointed out a direction for them to leave their so-called exile from their own worlds. But first Daenan, and then the creatures confronting Rocky—

More was happening than just the four of them trying to leave this place. Rick certainly seemed to act as if he'd developed definite ideas of how things were supposed to proceed. Richard had few such preconceptions, despite all Vitus' talk of balances upset. All the certainty he had ever had had been on paper. His life had always been withdrawn, uncertain. He envied the assurance the others seemed to have, Rick, Rocky, even Richie.

For all he had written about this place, he had problems forming opinions, much less voicing them. All he really had was a deep sense of disillusionment. If anything, the charge from the gods relieved him of the duty of thinking about what he was doing. . . .

After going through the effort to find and retrieve the Sword, Richard began to wonder.

In his preadolescent myth world of Quinque, the Artifacts were foci of the power that had created this world, even the chaotic dream worlds that swirled about it. They were the fragments of primordial chaos—Chaos—which bent the world in ways the gods couldn't interfere with. When they were scattered, none were left wholly in the world, and none were guarded by the mortals who could bear them.

They had not been together since the death of Chaos and the creation of the world. They were gathering four, the fifth was carried by the Adversary.

The divine command to face the Adversary was tantamount to bringing all five Artifacts together again. Thinking about the warnings given to Richie and Rocky, he began wondering if such a gathering would be benign.

It was a long time before he slept.

The trek to the prominence known as the Fist of Chaos wasn't difficult. It was simple to establish that their memories were one on the matter, and the position of the rock, on a great bluff overlooking both river and lake, made it easy to discern on the horizon as soon as they had traveled a quarter of the way there.

The journey did not bother Richard half as much as the guardian that was supposed to make his home in the rock. The presence of Lucian there prevented anyone from settling within the shadow of the rock.

Memories of this place, a jumble of mythology from Bullfinch and Tolkien, were vivid enough to displace Richard's memories of the real world. All that day, he scanned the skies for signs of the black-winged guardian.

The sun set behind them, and their shadows preceded them to the rock. From this angle, it was easy to see the "thumb," a diagonal shaft of rock on the western face that thrust up at a forty-five degree angle, forming the base of a shadowed depression that marked the curl of the stone "fingers."

The depression was about two or three hundred feet up the side of the rock, and was deep in shadow even with the setting sun shining directly in.

They reached the edge of the rock as evening fell. It was definitely an *edge*. As its name implied, the rock looked as if a stone giant had thrust its arm up from underground to expose its fist as far as the joint on the base of its thumb. No foothills, just the red stone of the rock itself, towering over them.

The fact that it sat upon a nearly treeless bluff made it tower even more. From its base, they could just see some of the taller towers of Quinque reaching above the rolling green woodlands that surrounded the city.

"We'll make camp here," Rick said, indicating a spot at the base of the rock. "We'll go up in the morning."

Rocky was turning around, looking at the view the bluff provided. They could see miles in every direction, and in every direction, animal bones littered the landscape, cracked, broken, rose-colored in the sunset light.

"I don't know if it is a good idea to camp this close to the thing that lives here," Rocky said.

"Lucian," Richard said, feeling that respect demanded its name. The great wyrm, ancient, singular, timeless, as deathless as the elves. Lucian was hatched from the birth of the world, and may have been a fragment of Chaos himself. Lucian. The Wyrm. The Dragon.

"How do we intend to get the Ring?" Richie asked, still looking up at the cave two hundred feet above them.

"Once we're rested, we climb up there, find out where the Ring is . . ."

"All four of us?" Richie asked Rick. "Like last time?"

"We have to stay together," Rick answered.

"And the guardian?" Richie asked.

"We have the Sword," Rick said, looking toward Rocky. Rocky still stared at the bones littering the horizon. Eventually, he nodded.

Richard looked at the littered landscape. *Let's not have to use it,* he thought.

CHAPTER 40

RICHIE

RICHIE'S thoughts upon hearing Rick's plan to go after the Ring was *Arrogant SOB. An arrogant SOB who doesn't know the first thing about B&E.*

Sleeping up there, in this imposing rock, was an immortal creature that could have any dozen of them for lunch, a creature that had yet to notice them. Primary goal: keep the thing not noticing you.

Richie said nothing about it, because it was obvious, to him at least, that Der Führer was nuts and intent on getting everyone here killed.

The fact that Rick said that they'd go in *en masse,* and said it with a straight face, made Richie feel a little less guilty about the fact that once he was free and clear with the almighty Ring, he was going to split from this little band and try to get home. Sir Rat had said that the Ring held his escape. Let someone else face the goddamned Adversary.

There was nothing to keep him here after he'd snagged the Ring. Nothing that said he'd need to be one of Rick's little storm troopers any longer than necessary.

As they made camp, he kept looking up the face of the rock, staring at the shadowed depression two hundred feet up the side. The moment Richie had seen it, he'd known that was where he was supposed to go.

It was an uncharacteristic feeling for him. He could almost understand where Rick had been coming from when he had spoken of "rules."

Which didn't make their fearless leader any less nuts.

He was beginning to perceive how a man could climb

the face. It didn't appear too difficult to follow the edge of the "thumb" upward. Its ledge was never more than forty-five degrees, and it didn't appear to narrow to less than a yard in width. Doable.

He stayed quiet as they laid out the campsite, and when it came to deciding watches, Richie took the second one.

After two hours of uneasy sleep, Rocky woke Richie up for his watch. Richie opened his eyes, expecting to see the laughing shadowed form from his dreams. For a moment, he did, then his eyes focused and he saw that it was just another malformed Richard Brandon. "It's your turn," Rocky said.

Rocky had his hand on the Sword, and for a moment Richie thought that Rocky knew what he'd been planning. Again, a moment passed and Richie saw that Rocky just meant that it was time for his turn at watch.

Richie pushed himself up and stood next to Rocky. Rocky's expression looked more sour than usual.

"What's the problem?" Richie asked.

Rocky shook his head, "I don't think it's something you would appreciate."

He turned away.

Richie shrugged; he had other things on his mind. He walked over to the stubby rock that'd been Rocky's seat for the past two hours and sat facing the low fire and the rest of the group. He kept his eyes on Rocky as the soldier tried to sleep. He wasn't going to move until he was sure everyone was out cold.

The night was dark and moonless, and the fire was too weak to erase much of the overwhelming starscape above them. That starscape demarked the Fist. They weren't close enough for the fire to light the side of the massive rock, but they were close enough for the mass of the Fist to bisect the sky above Richie. Half the sky was spattered with stars, the rest was a matte darkness, blacker than the spaces between the stars.

The night beyond the camp was silent. Here the only sounds Richie was aware of were those immediately within the camp. The breath of his sleeping companions, the pop of wood in the small fire, the rustle when someone turned in his sleep.

From beyond, Richie heard nothing, not even wind. It was as if there were a character in the air that damped noise down to nothing a few feet from its source.

Richie suspected the explanation was that everything living, even singing insects, avoided this rock and the thing inside it. The thought was disturbing enough that Richie almost abandoned his plan.

Almost.

A forest of doubt grew in Richie's mind, but still, as soon as he was sure Rocky was asleep, he slipped away, outside the small glowing circle that marked the domain of their little campfire. Quietly, he jogged to the edge of the Fist, and felt along for the base of its thumb.

His eyes had yet to fully adjust to the new darkness outside the range of the campfire. *Should have spent that time looking away from it. Live and learn. Wish I had a MagLite.*

Despite the dark, the ledge he looked for was easy enough to find. The "thumb" marked a massive discontinuity in the rock, a fissure that sprouted a two-yard-wide ridge ninety degrees from the surface of the rock. The ridge tilted away from Richie, going up.

He didn't hesitate when he found the ridge. He felt for a handhold and pulled himself up. It wasn't difficult. The slope was shallow enough that he could probably move along without handholds, relying on friction to hold him in place. Richie didn't try. His eyes were adjusted enough now that he could see all the way to the ground; the campfire already seemed tiny below him.

He inched forward on his stomach, his belt buckle digging into his groin, his boots making scraping sounds below him, and his leather jacket sliding on the stone. The progress was monotonous. He would grope ahead with his hands until he found a handhold. Then, pulling up with his arms and pushing with his legs, he'd inch up a foot or two. Then, holding himself to his handhold, his feet would grope for a rest that could support his weight. When his feet found purchase, he'd repeat the process.

His movement was so touch-oriented that he almost didn't need to see where he was going. Sight was so vestigial to what he was doing that he almost climbed past his destination.

He'd inched to the top edge of the cave wall before he looked to his right and realized that he had made it. He was climbing next to the center of the Fist, the dark hole the fingers curled around.

He pushed himself back down a few feet and rolled to his right, into the space, to give him enough distance from the edge to feel safe in standing.

The roll dropped him a yard into the darkness. In the split second of free fall, Richie felt an exquisite sense of panic, as if he had pushed himself off the wrong edge.

Then he struck the relatively flat floor of the cave. The drop had been because he'd rolled from the high end of a ledge that kept angling upward when the cave beyond kept the same level.

Richie pushed himself up and looked around. His eyes were nearly adjusted to the darkness. Even so, he could barely see the ceiling above him, like a gigantic gothic arch. The space was huge, the walls only rough huddled shapes in the shadows.

Ahead, away from the entrance, Richie saw the cave lighten. It was a soft glow that drew him. . . .

"*Motherfucker,*" Richie whispered. He had taken a few steps, and one of those rough shapes had resolved itself. It was a VW minibus, just like the one they'd left for Rico.

Richie took another step and saw it wasn't quite like that one. This one was rusted out under the psychedelic paint, and it rested on rims that squatted in detritus that could have once been tires. Richie placed a hand on it, and felt metal, cold and hollow.

The minibus had Ohio plates.

"*Motherfucker,*" Richie whispered again. He was close enough to see the rest of the near wall. The entrance resembled an auto graveyard, a graveyard of cars that were over twenty-five years old, VW Beetles, Mustangs, Econoline vans, Saabs, Datsuns, Plymouths, the glittering grille of a Mack truck peeking from out of the wreckage.

Richie turned away. *Coincidence, maybe,* he thought, *or all this really is happening in my head. My subconscious dredging memories in the form of vehicles. . . .*

What bothered Richie was he had never remembered the microbus until now. The Mack truck bearing down on his dad's Plymouth. That he remembered. The grille falling toward them like a chrome-plated avalanche, that he remembered. Until now he had forgotten one of the cars that huge trailer had ground beneath it.

A psychedelic VW minibus had been crushed while little Richie Brandon had watched from the back seat of a doomed Plymouth. Richie could even remember the driver, joint clenched in his teeth, panicking. . . .

It was Duke.

It couldn't be Duke—couldn't have been Duke—if Duke had been alive when that Mack truck had threshed part of Deadman's Curve, he'd have been three or four years old at best. He couldn't have been driving the microbus that Richie remembered.

Futz of a memory circuit, Richie thought. *Christ, he's even smoking the same joint he was when I left him with—*

Richie swallowed a couple of times. The memory of the accident was starting to seem clearer and more definite than his memories of Duke, Rico, and the rest of his real life. He had to push all the memories away, or lose what he had to hang on to.

If his life was a hallucination, what was the fucking point?

Richie drew his gun. Solid reminder that there was a real world beyond the psychotic fantasy drama around him. Never mind that the wall of cars from the late Sixties-early Seventies were just as solid, and bigger.

Richie walked toward the glow. It came from the rear of the entrance chamber. As he did, he passed more debris from a world this wasn't supposed to be. Mailboxes, street signs, bus shelters that were made of green corrugated metal rather than glass, old console RCA televisions with built-in record players, benches, and things that Richie couldn't make out for intervening gloom.

Somewhere, in here, is a way back. Richie thought. It was like the sham Flats that was just some distorted reflection of the world he knew. These were real objects from the real world. That's what he told himself. . . .

Real objects from the real world. Real as he was. Real as the gun was. Plymouth, microbus, Mack truck, those were all coincidental. Whatever his dreads, if he had the time, he could go back to the Plymouth and prove that it wasn't his dad's car.

Hell, he just had to look at it. His dad's car had been mulched under that Mack truck's—a *different* Mack truck—trailer. This one had been nearly intact. Like he remembered it.

Richie shied away from those thoughts and pressed forward.

He reached the end of the chamber, which was only the opening into a much larger chamber. The antechamber was big, but the space beyond was huge enough to defy comprehension. It was difficult to credit it as being wholly within the rock Richie had climbed inside.

The walls exploded away in every direction, above, below, and to the side. The floor fell away so dramatically that a bridge had to carry the path to a rise a hundred yards away, where the ground again reached the level where Richie stood.

Below him, and the bridge, the floor was lost in darkness. Across, on the subterranean hillside, light came from torches spaced too far apart. The hillside before him was dotted with statues, obelisks, and other forms of stone and bronze. In a few places Richie saw architectural forms that were too small to immediately suggest a function—until he realized that he looked upon a graveyard.

Richie had been walking toward the hillside, keeping to the shadows on the side of the bridge, and the realization gave him pause. He stopped and stared at what lay before him. It was a huge graveyard, shrouded in eternal darkness within the stone grasp of the Fist of Chaos.

Richie began to realize that the knot in his stomach was fear, real gut-wrenching, spiritual fear that only gripped his soul in his dreams. He could feel Lucas laughing at him, in true divine fashion, god of a people who knew they were playthings.

He didn't believe in omens, but if they ever were valid, they would be in the crazy place he found himself. Seeing the naked hillside, cloaked with graves, Richie became convinced that before the night was over, someone would die, and there was nothing he could do about it.

He slowly resumed walking in the face of that fear. That was the one defining characteristic of Richie's life. He never backed down, never stopped moving.

Pride of place on the subterranean hillside was given to a Gothic structure that Richie was just now resolving from the darkness behind it. It was made of black stone that camouflaged it in the darkness, and the light from the few torches didn't quite reach it. It was a squat cylindrical tower that lorded it over the entire landscape. Richie squatted by the end of the bridge, in his last bit of shadowy cover, and stared up at the building.

He recognized the place.

Lakeview Cemetery in Cleveland was lorded over by the same Gothic structure, a tower that represented its largest tomb. Towering over him, over acres of anonymous gravesites, was a monument erected to memorialize James A. Garfield, the twentieth president of the United States.

All Richie could think about was that Garfield had been shot, and that couldn't be a good sign.

When he reached the other side of the bridge, and first trod upon the anachronistic hillside, he heard a dimly familiar voice say, "*Stop.*" Richie turned around, facing the voice, pulling the gun out of his pocket.

It was Daenan, the elf.

Seeing her here was as disorienting as seeing all the

physical apocrypha of normal twentieth century Cleveland. She stepped out from the shadows near an obelisk that more likely marked the death of a Rockefeller than some barbarian hero. She was pale as ever, and now the paleness was cold, harsh. "Go now," she said, "before your death further upsets the land."

Richie took a step forward. "Fuck that noise. What the hell do you think you're doing here?"

Daenan stepped lithely to interpose herself between him and the Garfield Monument. She pointed a finger at him, "If you gather the Ring, both you and the world shall die."

Déjà vu, sister. Didn't I hear this from Rocky?

"Look, Daenan, I ain't going around ending people's worlds. I'm here for the only ticket home anyone here's offered me. You ain't going to stop me."

"Listen to me, Richard Brandon," she said. Her voice had lost none of the almost hypnotic monotone quality, but had taken on an insistent stentorian tone that was the first measure of emotion he had ever heard from her. Her voice filled the chamber around them, echoing in the darkened caverns.

"I am exiled because I do not wish this world to end. My fellows see release from chains of matter where there exists only oblivion. Every step you take brings you closer to a rebirth of Chaos. I cannot let that happen; the Adversary is preferable to the destruction my people would wreak."

"Look—"

"Silence!" For once, Richie saw anger twist Daenan's features. She walked toward him slowly. Her face didn't flush as he'd expected, but as her eyes narrowed, they seemed to begin to glow. "Of all of you, you are the worst. You have no idea what you are, and you behave as if your actions have no effect. You ignore the evidence around you—and you would deny the existence of this place as casually as stepping on an anthill."

Richie just stared at her.

"Go. Leave this place."

"All I want is to go home—"

"Can't you see anything? *Your home is gone.* Chaos' palsied dreams disintegrated with the first of your deaths!"

Richie backed away from her. She kept approaching him, her face twisted, and her eyes glowing, a personification of all the Furies looming over him. "I don't believe you!"

"Abandon this search of yours," she shrieked at him. "With each of your deaths more of the world is lost. . . ."

Richie was shaking before this apparition. His gut was turning to water. He raised the gun between him and the transformed Daenan and said, "Get out of my way."

"You give me no choice," she said, and reached for him with a spectral hand that'd twisted into something like a talon.

Richie fired. The gun's report echoed through the chamber, the muzzle flash illuminating the necropolis for a split second, only long enough to carve the stark white monuments into his retinas. Daenan's head snapped back as the bullet impacted her face.

Richie stood there, gun in front of him, shaking. His eyes slowly readjusted to the darkness, and he saw that Daenan's body refused to fall to the ground.

A sound filled the chamber. A repetitive, pulsing sound that took long moments for Richie to recognize as laughter.

Daenan slowly raised her head to face him again. It was her laughter. Impressed in her forehead was a too-perfect round hole. Richie gaped. It was as if he had fired into a mannequin.

"You are a *fool,*" she said as her hands shot up, grabbing his gun hand. His gun fell as a flash of agony told him that his wrist might have been broken.

He was pulled with a force that wrenched the arm from his socket with a pain that made him forget his wrist. His feet left the ground, and his back slammed into a monument twenty feet away. He lay there stunned, the right side of his body trembling with the wreckage of his arm.

Guess you just got the fuck-up award, he thought as Daenan walked toward him.

Her voice had returned to its emotionless monotone. "An interesting weapon, but futile against an immortal creature. Only the Sword has such a power."

She bent over and gripped his neck. "I give you a choice now, Richard Brandon. Leave this place, or die."

Every rational sense inside him told him to give in and meekly depart. Rocky had the Sword, and could lay the bitch open with it. But something inside him acted quicker than thought.

"Fuck you," Richie said.

The hand tightened on his neck like a vise. Richie began to hear his pulse in his ears, and he tried to reach up with his left arm and pry away her hand, but it was like a metal band around his throat.

His vision began to darken. Too quickly, in fact. A great shadow draped itself around him and Daenan. Richie could not see its source, but Daenan could, and she raised her head to face it.

"This is not the agreement."

It was a voice unlike any Richie had ever heard. The words were loud, but so low in frequency that they were nearly inaudible. He felt the words in his chest, his teeth, and in the stone pressing into his back. The words rumbled, almost purred, but the purr was of a cat the size of a 747.

"He cannot be allowed to—"

"Cease, elf. I gave you leave to convince, not to kill. Not one of them."

Daenan was shaking her head. "You cannot give him the Artifact, Old One. You, of all, know what it will mean."

"You presume?" The resonance of his voice threatened to shake the cavern apart. ***"I, the last remnant of Chaos' soul, can you say what I do?"***

"They cannot be brought together. Everything will end."

"Everything dies. Everything ends."

"You know this," Daenan said. "*You know this.* And you would give him the Ring?"

Daenan refused to release the grip on his throat and his world became a black ocean, the surf the crash of his own pulse in his ears.

"You defend a corrupt creation."

"I defend my own existence."

"You do so by denying him his?" Even the rumbling, omnipresent voice seemed far away. He couldn't make his left arm move anymore. At least the pains in his right arm seemed to be fading.

"You know nothing, deathless one. Your path ends the world as surely as mine, and leaves nothing in its place. Begone."

Daenan's response was the merest faraway mumble.

"You do not know who they are, BEGONE!" The voice's command was barely audible, and it was the last thing he was aware of before his world slipped into complete blackness.

CHAPTER 41

ROCKY

"KNOW, Richard Brandon, when you take that offering, you doom yourself and the world."

Rocky awoke in the darkness, with the echo of those words in his ears. The fire had guttered out, leaving the immediate world a dark monochrome. A pressure had awoken him, as if something deep inside him were trying to force itself out.

Rocky sat up and touched the hilt of the Sword, and felt a sharpness to the knowledge within him. It was as if the blade were part of him—

Rocky stood unsteadily, he still felt all the ravages of the last fight. His chest ached with every breath. But the pain—in his chest, in his arms, everywhere—was fading under a wash of adrenaline. He turned around and scanned a horizon dark with trees.

Something was coming, he felt it. It was as if the Sword was a part of him now, a part of his mind. It saw more than he did, and now that part of his mind seemed to be thinking thoughts he only had dim access to, accessing the situation, marking the place to make a stand.

"Rick, Richie, Richard!" he called to the others. *"Wake up!"*

He had unsheathed the Sword in front of him. He still saw no threat. But through the Artifact, he could feel it. The air itself was resonant with oncoming menace.

He held the Sword in front of him, in a defensive posture. He knew nothing of swordplay, but the thing seemed to guide his motion.

"What is it?" he heard Rick ask from behind him.

"Back to the rock, all of you."

The blade was perfectly visible in the darkness, even though it didn't glow or change its aspect. It hung before him as gray and featureless as ever, exactly the same as it had been in the chamber before him, its appearance a constant. Shadows couldn't mar its plain surface, as if it reflected a light that wasn't there, a light eternal and unchanging. Rocky could feel the power there, and it was becoming a part of him.

Or, more disturbing, he could feel himself becoming a part of it.

"What's going on?" Richard said.

"Move it, all of you," Rocky said, "You don't have time."

"Where's Richie?" one of them asked.

Rocky didn't know. He did know—had known without being aware of it—how many of them there were. He could feel the others' presence near him, just as he could now feel the presence of a massed shadowy force in the surrounding woods. He knew they were there before he could feel their hoofbeats trembling the ground beneath his feet.

"Move," he shouted, putting all the authority he could into his voice, all the desperation of an impending battle. *"Richie's gone, move! The enemy is coming."*

He heard movement behind him, and sensed the others scrambling to shelter. As they did, he stared out at the woods and whispered, "There. . . ."

It was a red star moving through the trees. Then another. Then a multitude. Red motes that drifted, almost leisurely, near invisible. But they were not stars.

They were eyes.

The hoofbeats were now audible, a vibration, a low rumble that was steadily increasing in volume.

Someone called from back at the rock, a question, "How many?"

Rocky knew the answer as the question was asked, but he couldn't bring himself to voice it.

All of them.

The Thralls of Chaos, the defenders of dreams and reality, all of them had been loosed to converge on them. Even as he prepared to meet the charge, the awareness lent by the Sword was telling him what that meant.

Everything beyond Quinque was a Dream of Chaos, all the reality that was not this place was protected by these things. If all the Thralls had been loosed upon Quinque itself, that meant one thing—

There was nothing out there left to protect.

The sound of crashing metal and snapping wood reached him. The Thralls were a blackness infecting the woods, enveloping it like an evil fog, demonic canines leading mounted soldiers that were no more than empty metal. The sound of the onrushing horde was crushing, inexorable, steadily increasing in volume.

The horde announced themselves with a horn, an endless wail. Then they were through the tree line, and in seconds they were upon him.

A last attempt to save their world.

Rocky didn't know if the thought was his or the Sword's as the eruption of the fight fused the synergy of himself and Sword into one inseparable organism.

The Sword's preternatural appearance seemed somehow enhanced as he raised it to fend off the lead attacker, a demonic hound. The Sword was perfectly visible in the darkness, giving off no light, but somehow it felt more *there* than the creature attacking him. A swing separated the hound's head from its shoulders as easily as if the only resistance were air.

After that, Rocky could not cease moving the Sword. It drove into the enemy as if it were the only solid thing here, and all else, Rocky included, was mere shadow. Like a sound from outside the dreamer that intruded into the dream, the Sword seemed more real than the world that contained it.

The advance of the Thralls brought with them a change

in the character of the air, heavier, metallic, hotter. Rocky felt swamped in an invisible cascade of blood.

Rocky met the advance, and the Thralls swirled around him like a whirlpool. Thralls fell upon him, and the blade met the armor and clove it with a scream of torn metal, and the smell of superheated iron. Smoke rose from the holes in empty armor, as if the spirit imprisoned within were escaping.

The sound was crushing, a steel band around his temples. The clash of iron, the growl of unnatural beasts, and above all of it the horn blaring with the advance. The sound was like a cascade of machinery crushing everything in its wake.

Threshing cars like a divine combine.

The Sword clove into the Thralls, and their blows could not fell him. The fusion of the battle drew part of the Sword into him. Their weapons seemed so much shadow cast upon Rocky's flesh.

The Sword was omnipotence solidified; nothing in this reality could alter it or change its course. Rocky shared that power as he waded through the stampede of otherworldly flesh and metal.

Rocky smelled the sparks, heard animal screams, and tasted the ferric tang of his own blood.

Smoke. Metal tearing. Screams. The taste of blood in his mouth. The car collapsing around him—

It's still happening, the accident never stopped. . . .

The battle was over.

Rocky stood in the midst of a field of twisted armor. He had won. He had lost. The Sword had kept him alive and omnipotent during the battle, but Rocky could feel its influence ebbing. As the Sword withdrew from him, it took a small apart of him along with it. What was left of him began leaking into the ground through a dozen wounds.

He slipped to his knees in the midst of the carnage. *Christ almighty, what's left? Everything is a fraud, twenty-five years as fictional as this place.*

He looked at the fallen Thralls. Armored wreckage littered the landscape around him. The black smoking limbs of animals lay everywhere scattered. Empty Thralls lay everywhere, their armor torn open, deprived of whatever animate spirit they once contained. The smell of overheated metal cloaked the scene in a haze.

Rocky thought, as his vision began to blur, *Nothing left out there now, precious little in here.* He slipped to the ground.

"Good God," someone said from above him. He felt tentative hands trying to put pressure on the worst of the bleeding. He opened his eyes and saw Richard with a painful expression on his face. Rocky tried to say something to strip the worry from his comrade's face, but all he could do was cough up a mouthful of blood.

"Please, don't move. I can—"

Can what? That's the central irony of the Sword. No wielder can lose a battle, or fall in combat—but afterward. . . .

Rick walked into Rocky's field of vision, "Can you help him?"

"We have to stop the bleeding," Richard said, maneuvering around Rocky.

Rocky felt his consciousness slipping. He knew that he was bleeding inside, and that there was nothing they could do that would keep him alive. That didn't bother him. He knew that it wasn't them that mattered so much now.

With a last expenditure of energy he reached for Rick.

Rick leaned over him and Rocky managed to whisper, "Don't kill the Adversary." His voice was choked with blood, and barely audible.

"What?" Rick said, looking into his face as if he didn't understand.

"Don't—" He erupted into a coughing fit that racked his chest with agony at a dozen points. He had to turn his head to avoid choking on the froth coming from his own lungs.

Even so, when the pain in his chest eased, he finished, "—kill the Adversary."

As Rocky closed his eyes, allowing the darkness to claim him, the last thing he saw was the light of understanding in Rick's eyes.

CHAPTER 42

RICK

RICK was locked, staring into Rocky's eyes as they closed, holding Rocky's hand, paralyzed.

"Help me," Richard was saying. "He's going into shock."

Rick stared at Rocky, through him. Rick could see the animation leak from his face, as if it were not just his blood spreading beneath them, but his soul.

Richard had managed to pull off the armor, and Rocky was much worse off than Rick had imagined. His chest and abdomen looked as if he'd been gored by some wild animal. A hole in his chest was frothing blood, and a fractured rib glinted through the gore.

"We have to do something—" Richard was staring at Rocky, his words were almost a sob.

Richard looked into Rocky's ashen, masklike face. Rick could see that Rocky's wheezing attempt to breathe had stopped.

Rocky had stopped.

Richard stared into Rocky's face for a long time. In Rick's thoughts swam the last things Rocky had said to him, "Richie's gone," and "Kill the Adversary."

If there had been any doubt in Rick's mind about the path destiny had laid out, those words had erased it.

"This is not supposed to happen," Richard whispered.

Rick stood and Richard repeated, "This should not have happened." He turned to Rick and said, "You should have helped me."

"What could I have done?"

Anger seemed an alien expression on Richard's face.

"Something," he spat at him. He turned back to Rocky's body and repeated, "This was not supposed to happen."

No? Rick wondered. *One of us will face the Adversary. That means three of us will not. That is fate.*

"Look at me, Richard," Rick said. He stepped over and grabbed him by the shoulder.

Richard turned to glare at him.

"I can't lose you now," Rick said, trying to put all the persuasive force he could muster into his voice. "This is more than just us now. . . ."

"What? We're trying to get home—"

"Look at this—" Rick waved at the scattered remains around them. The flesh and metal was livid in the predawn light, visceral and unholy. "We're in a war here. Didn't you hear what Rocky said?"

Richard looked at him intently, as if searching for something in his face. "What are you talking about?"

"I'm talking about destiny. We're here to save this world from the Adversary."

"Are you sure you heard—"

Rick stepped up and grabbed Richard's shoulders. "You and I are all that are left, and there are two remaining Artifacts."

"But Richie—"

"Richie has abandoned us for his own purpose. He's our Judas."

Richard shook his head as if he couldn't quite understand what Rick was saying. That was all right, there would be time for him to understand, as long as he did what Rick said.

There were two Artifacts left, the Horn and the Cirque. The Horn was marginally closer to them, across the river in the Graythorn Woods. Rick decided that was the logical next step, since he didn't know how long he could rely on Richard.

Rick bent down next to Rocky and picked up the Sword. Richard stared at him as if he were performing some unmentionable desecration of the corpse. Rick thought of the way he had felt when Richie had touched the Sword.

"The Artifacts must be borne to the Adversary," Rick said. "To our fight."

Richard looked from him, to Rocky's body, and back to him. His face flushed. "*God.* Don't you feel anything?"

"Of course I—"

Richard balled his hands until they shook. "He's *dead!* Doesn't that affect you? Another you, *another us,* was just torn to pieces in front of you."

"I regret the loss. But we have to move on." Rick turned and walked back to the trampled remains of their campsite. There was little left worth saving.

"That's it then? We just leave him? Just leave the Ring we came here for?"

The constant hammer of questions grated on Rick. He was supposed to be the one in authority here. He was certain that Richard didn't see their destiny as clearly as he did.

Rick turned around and faced Richard. "The Ring is Richie's, and Richie has abandoned us with it—"

"You don't know that. He could come back."

Rick shook his head. "Believe what you wish, but I know him as our betrayer. If you wish to stay here, bury Rocky, say some words over him, wait for the one who's abandoned us, go ahead, I will not stop you." He stepped up to Richard and rested a finger on his chest. "But you will do so alone."

Rick started walking away.

"Wait, you can't just leave—"

I spent years of my life in a cramped little office, trying to make a difference around me. All my life I've lived in a world that was, at best, indifferent to my existence. I have been handed a direction that will let me affect the world, a destiny, importance. I've been offered a chance to become an indispensable part of the history of this world. I've been offered the mantle of savior.

I can no more stop walking toward that than I can stop my heart from beating.

The sky had lightened and sunlight brushed the trees he walked toward. The sunlight painted the forest in livid golds, reds, and yellows. At first Rick thought that it was the dawn light that was colored, but it took only a moment to realize that the trees themselves had turned color.

A forest that had been a vibrant summer green yesterday, had now erupted into autumn. It wasn't just the trees nearby. From this high bluff, he could see miles of rolling woodland, all of it turned color. The seasons had changed overnight. Also, and somewhat more strange, from this overlook, he could see many more stands of deadwood, naked white areas, like the skeleton of the forest. Seeing that, Rick thought that he felt an increased chill in the air.

He had made it halfway to the tree line when, behind him, he heard Richard say, "Wait for me."

Rick smiled.

CHAPTER 43

JULIA

RICHARD kept getting worse. They had to put him back on a respirator, and most of the time he wasn't even conscious—if he ever had been conscious. Julia still visited, but the visits turned brief. They seemed too much like waiting for him to die.

She returned to doing what she was supposed to do: untangling all the loose ends of Mom's life. Boxes went to storage, to a few friends, and to the Salvation Army depending on their contents. Gradually, her phone calls to Mom's creditors, and to her banks, began to make sense. Real estate agents began bringing people around to look at the house.

Julia went through it all with a feeling of numb resignation. As if Mom wouldn't really be buried until all the technical crap had been dealt with systematically.

She filled the voids in her day by painting. Her brother's images haunted her, and she filled pages and pages with her own watercolor demons. She painted forms that seemed to be no more than coalesced smoke. Horsemen, dragons, twisted humanoid forms that seemed to blame the viewer for their own insubstantiality.

The pictures started as interpretations of what Richard drew, but they slowly became her own. The red eyes bled into the images until her paintings were no longer monochrome, but livid with reds and yellows, as if closing on the flame that generated the smoke of the first pictures.

They became a watercolor vision of hell, twisting flames and molten forms bent over in agony. . . .

The pictures were so unlike her that it seemed as

though someone else were painting them, and somehow the act of painting was drawing that other self out of her. Drawing it out into the picture, so it wouldn't hurt her anymore.

Wherever the images came from, however disturbing, she felt better for each one she finished. She could understand why Richard had drawn when he was still able. Illustrating the image, drawing the inner demon, was a way of putting it outside of yourself, removing it. Julia never felt that more than when she was painting the flames she felt inside her.

It was when she was packing away the last of Mom's things that she found the pictures. They were in a battered little jewelry box buried in a bedroom closet. She'd only opened it because she was checking everything to decide whether it should go to the Salvation Army, or the trash.

She expected earrings, tennis bracelets, and other knick-knacks, but instead found a folded sheet of paper tied with a blue ribbon. Seeing that, her next thought was that she had found a cache of love letters, though she thought blue an odd color for that.

She sat on the bare mattress. The bedding and frame were long gone. The mattress and box spring were the only furniture left in Mom's bedroom other than the empty bureau. Both were still there because they were too large to move by herself, and she'd been putting off getting someone to help her. The task still felt too personal to invite anyone to.

Seated, she pulled out the little package, and could immediately tell that it wasn't a set of love letters. It was too stiff, and the contents were the wrong proportion.

She untied the ribbon and unfolded the sheet of paper. A stack of thirty or forty photographs spilled into her lap.

So there they are, she thought.

Looking at them, color portraits of her father and her brother, she felt a surreal disconnection from the world the pictures showed. She saw her father pushing a two- or three-year-old Richard in a swing, and it was like looking into an alternate universe. The sense was enhanced by seeing how much her father looked like Richard now. In the picture, he was about Richard's age.

Julia sat a long time, shuffling through the family pictures in the nearly empty bedroom.

For the first time she saw Richard as a normal human being, reacting to things, smiling, laughing, crying. There were Halloween pictures of him dressed in a cardboard suit of armor. Pictures of him at Geauga Lake, Cedar Point, or some other amusement park, carrying a stuffed panda almost as big as he was. There were pictures of him wrestling with her father. By Richard's apparent age it had been taken shortly before the accident. In it she could see a shadow of the man he could have grown into.

In that picture she saw an intensity to Richard's expression, a sense of drive that was absent from the broken man he was now, a drive that would have dominated the man if he hadn't been stricken. She saw everything that could have been in that one picture.

She had to blink back a few tears as she gathered the photographs and put them away. She wasn't ready to look at them all yet.

As she wrapped them back in the paper—which turned out to be Richard's birth certificate—the phone rang. The noise startled her, and the pictures slipped out of her hand. They scattered on the floor, fragments of a broken past.

The phone rang again. The sound filled Julia with dread. For a few long moments she couldn't make herself move.

On the third ring, she ran down to the kitchen.

She caught it on the fourth.

"Hello," she could hear the tension in her own voice stretched to the point of breaking.

"Julia, it's Dr. Kavcheck—"

On hearing that voice, every emotion within her broke free, and she started to cry.

CHAPTER 44

RICHIE

SLUMBER was a drugged stupor. Richie was feverish, and his perceptions were of a nearly hallucinatory quality. At times he saw the cave and its underground necropolis; other times he saw a window.

Perhaps he merely remembered a window.

Through the window he thought he could see buildings, real buildings, a skyline he could almost touch. In the background he could sometimes hear a female voice, never saying anything that made sense.

He would try to hold on to it, keep it in focus. It would always be lost before the unseen speaker said anything he could understand.

A wind blew across him, bringing a scent of something sweet and organic. He opened his eyes and blinked a few times, trying to place where he was.

He lay on a couch in a large cylindrical chamber with marble floors and a ceiling far above. The space was wrapped in gloom that was little affected by candles spaced around the couch where he was draped.

The statue was gone from the center of the building, so it was the murals that told Richie where he was; scenes of a Civil War hero who had an abbreviated presidency.

Garfield's Monument, Christ, why this creepy old place?

Richie pushed himself upright and felt the sudden presence of something else in the huge chamber with him. The sense of mass was overwhelming.

Something scraped against the marble, and Richie turned

to face it. A shadow loomed out of the darkness, moving, undulating like a serpent.

"My visitor," the shadow said. The voice was unmistakable, a subsonic rumble that somehow formed comprehensible words.

"Light for my guest!" The shadow unrolled itself upward, and a column of flame engulfed the ceiling. The jet of ruddy, smokeless fire lasted less than a second, but it engulfed an iron framework suspended from the ceiling.

The light persisted, coming from a forest of torches set in the framework above. Richie lowered his gaze from the ceiling. As he did, he felt the words within his chest, **"You face Lucian."**

Lucian's head towered above him, looking down, a lean form both serpentine and birdlike. It was supported on a neck thicker than Richie's body that snaked into a body the size of a tractor trailer. Lucian's skin was black and shimmered like an oil slick with his rippling muscles. Forearms longer than Richie's whole body rested on the floor in front of the couch. A finger the size of Richie's forearm tapped a tapered matte-black talon on the marble floor.

"Who are you?" the dragon asked.

For a long time Richie was speechless. Lucian was beyond all the impossibilities he had seen up to now. Beyond in scale, beyond in presence. His body seemed endless, black serpentine coils wrapping the interior of the misplaced monument.

The head descended to regard him. Lucian's eyes were as black as his skin, and reflected Richie's face perfectly. ***"Who are you?"*** At this distance, the words made Richie feel as if he were the diaphragm of a speaker with the bass tuned way below the audible point. Every one of Lucian's consonants felt as if it tried to vibrate a kidney loose.

"My name's Richie."

The massive head cocked to the side. ***"Ah, you know something."*** It withdrew somewhat as he added, ***"Is that who you are? A name? A label?"***

Richie looked up at the dragon and felt a wave of frustration. It was a suicidal impulse, but he yelled up at Lucian, "What the hell do you want for an answer? Some sort of Zen koan? A meaningless little tautology? A spiritual little adjective? You want me to manufacture titles like a demented hobbit? Fuck that." Richie stared up at the dragon and said, "The name is Richie, Richie Brandon. And who that *is* is none of your goddamn business."

He was still hurt, and the breath he expended on the tirade left him dizzy and made his throat hurt. He reached out to hold himself upright with his right hand, but a warning twinge in his shoulder and wrist made him switch to his left.

He braced himself for the consequences of his burst of bravado. Instead, the chamber echoed was a rhythmic rumble that Richie only belatedly realized was laughter. If possible, Richie would have backed away from Lucian, but it was all he could do at the moment to keep himself from collapsing back on the couch.

"Good, you still retain an identity."

Richie sucked in a breath. "Still retain . . . What are you talking about?"

"If I grant you what you seek, what shall you do?"

Richie felt a dizziness, and he rubbed his temple gingerly with his right hand. Amazingly, his arm seemed to work, despite the abuse it had received at Daenan's hands.

"If I grant you what you seek, what shall you do?"

The voice rolled over him and through the great space.

Richie thought of his arm, and decided that Lucian was monopolizing all the questions. "What happened?" Richie felt his neck. It was intact, but he felt swelling and the tenderness of a deep bruise. "How long was I unconscious?"

"You were injured. I treated you."

"Fuck." Richie tried to stand, but a wave of vertigo forced him down again. For some reason he suddenly remembered the window, and the skyline beyond.

"If I grant you what you seek, what shall you do?"

Again with the same question. Richie looked up at Lucian. The dragon seemed to fill the room opposite him. "I want to go home. That's all I ever wanted."

"Do you know what that home is?"

"Damn it, of course I do. . . ." Something about the question tore at Richie. He didn't want to think about the fact that his memory of before his parents' accident was clearer than the years since. He didn't want to think of remembering that Parma pothead, Duke, driving a familiar psychedelic VW minibus into the wreckage that had killed his parents. He didn't want to think about what Daenan said, that his home wasn't there anymore.

Is that why the cars are here? Are my parents buried here—

He couldn't remember where they were buried, and that scared him.

He'd been wandering around this land half-convinced that it was some sort of hallucination. But if that was so, where were the boundaries of the hallucination? If he suffered a paranoid-schizophrenic fantasy from the inside, why would his personality, his memory, his sense of self, be any less delusional than the world around him?

"No," Richie said. "I know who I am."

"Do you know what you are? What you and the other Richards are?"

He pushed himself off of the couch and got unsteadily to his feet. His vision throbbed. His hands shook. He looked desperately around the chamber, but wasn't quite sure what he was looking for.

His eyes focused on a pedestal squatting where the statue of President Garfield used to be, should have been, *was* in the world Richie thought of as real. The squat pillar hadn't been there the first time he looked, or he hadn't seen it. On the pedestal was the gun, the Beretta that he had liberated from Rico's safe. Something real—

As real as the VW minibus rusting at the entrance to this cave.

Richie walked forward. His approach was automatic, as if he had never awakened from his drugged dreams. He reached for the gun and picked it up. Its weight felt solid in his hand, as clear as the feel of sweat rolling between his shoulder blades, as obvious as the chiaroscuro vision of Lucian before him.

He could feel the barriers between real and unreal crumbling within him.

"What's happened to me?" Richie whispered, staring at the gun. He raised his gaze to face Lucian. "How do I get home?" The words came out as a plea where before they would have been a command, or a threat. Richie was exhausted. He wanted this to end.

"This world is. Despite your denials, this world is. Your world also is. Both are fragments of what was once whole. The Artifacts you all seek are reflections of that fragmented unity."

Richie nodded his head, as a reflex, not because he understood the booming words. "Daenan said—"

The dragon laughed.

"She is but a splinter of a shattered world. No more solid than a Thrall. A shadow." The dragon's neck snaked down toward Richie, bringing the massive face down to his eye level. When Lucian spoke, Richie could feel his hair flutter in the wind from the dragon's hot dry breath. ***"You are important, because you and your twins are the most solid remnants of the true world. If you all die, as she seems to wish, the world will continue to fragment endlessly, become shadows of shadows without the depth to submerge a grain of sand. If the first of you should die, there will be naught left but void."***

The speech shook Richie. He felt the strength of it drawing matter from his bones. "But what about you?"

"I am a memory with its own memory. I may be the most solid shadow in this shadowland, but I know what I am."

Richie opened his mouth, and closed it. He had already shaken himself with the possibility that this world might in fact be more real than he was willing to admit. But now Lucian seemed to be asserting the opposite.

"Is this real," Richie waved the gun at the tomb around them, and by extension, at the whole outside world, "or isn't it?"

"Real is a term neither objective nor absolute. You are more real than I. The whole is more real than the sum of its parts. When you came here, the world you left behind became less than a shadow. It is now only left in your memories and how they affect this place. It is no longer real."

"Damn it!" Richie yelled in frustration. "I've had it up to here with the Transcendental Philosophy."

Lucian withdrew. Without the dragon's mass in front of him, Richie felt as if he would pitch forward. The massive head was shaking from side to side, almost sadly. Lucian's voice lowered, the bass rumble completely lost to Richie's ears, felt only in the pit of his stomach.

"You do not wish to understand."

Richie felt as if he had offended Lucian, and that was a bad idea on just about every conceivable level. Why couldn't he control his temper? "Look, I'm sorry. This has all got me strung out. This ain't my place. And someone who's supposed to be a god around here told me that this Ring is my only ticket out of this nightmare."

Lucian stayed immobile, impassive. His shadowed, serpentine form towered above him. Richie felt the rage and frustration boiling inside him; his nerves were ragged with stress and disorientation. He forced himself to contain it. The hand with the gun shook; sweat stung his eyes. Richie clamped his face in a rickety smile and spread his arms.

"Okay, you're the boss here. Tell me what you want."

"What I want?"

Richie nodded. "Give me my ticket out of here and you got whatever you want."

"The Ring?"

Richie nodded vigorously.

"What about the others?"

The question caught Richie off guard for a moment. It led to another ugly thought. "Shit, Daenan, she didn't—"

Lucian shook his head. ***"She's yet to do harm to any others."***

Richie snorted. "Guess I was just lucky."

"What about the others?"

Richard sighed. He wanted a fast ticket out of here, but he didn't know if he wanted to do that while there were three others left behind. He had always been a loner, and he thought like a loner, but did that mean he could drop a trio of brothers like that? Fearless Leader could take a flying leap, but the professor acted as if he actually gave a shit about him. . . .

"I guess I'll go down and join them. Help them get home, too." He'd need to know what happened to Richard, their misplaced English professor, before he went home.

"Look down before you."

Richie did as Lucian asked. On the pedestal before him, where the gun had rested, lay a small metallic ring. It was barely as thick as a wedding band, and it gave Richie the same bizarre feeling of thereness that the Sword had. It also showed the same strange optical property of appearing perfectly and evenly lit even when sitting in the shadows on top of the pillar.

Richie knew it was the Ring, and he knew also that it had always been there in front of him. He had the strange feeling that it was the only thing that was here, that the monument around them, the underground necropolis, himself, Lucian were all merely projections of the Ring.

"You may take it."

Richie nodded, but he didn't move. He continued to stare at it. "But?"

"The Ring is master of illusion and deception. It can wrap you in false appearances. But it can also withdraw all deceptions, even those within yourself. Know yourself well, Richie Brandon, and hang on to what you are in the face of it."

Richie's throat was dry. He wiped his neck with one hand, checked the safety on the gun, and slipped it into a pocket. Slowly, he reached for the Ring.

"What I want."

Richie looked up at the dragon, pausing in mid-reach.

Here's the catch. "Yeah," Richie said, "I did make that promise." He waited for Lucian.

"You have been in slumber for five days. Your companions have left on the remainder of their search."

"Shit."

"Do not follow them. Go to the city. Go there and wait for them to come. Wait for them all. Then bring the Artifacts together, along with yourselves and the world."

Richie stood, still paused in mid-grasp.

"Is that it?" he asked.

Again, in that bass rumble that Richie only heard in his stomach, Lucian said, ***"You do not wish to understand."***

"Okay, fine, agreed." Richie reached out and scooped up the Ring. "Now why don't you . . . ?"

Richie never finished, because there was no longer anyone to talk to. He was standing on the ledge outside the cave, as if he'd never gone inside. Bright sunlight nearly blinded him, and when he looked behind him, the cave only seemed to go back ten feet. Apparently Lucian had dismissed him.

If it ever happened at all.

Richie felt the pulse beat in his neck as he looked down at his hand. He slowly unclenched it. There, sitting on his palm, was the Ring.

The descent was easier than the ascent, despite a lingering wooziness. The way down was broader and shallower in daylight than it had seemed during the night. It gave him an opportunity to give attention to the ground below, and the wreckage visible there.

Something had happened. Twisted black shapes littered the ground in front of the Rock, enigmatic and unmoving. As he descended, a few shapes took on the form of inhuman bodies; black forms, shapes vaguely equine and canine, shrunken with decay, shrouded in clouds of carrion insects. No birds, no higher forms of life came to feed on the dead flesh, only the insects.

Richie saw humanoid forms as well; empty shells devoid of even insect life. He recognized the armor as belonging to the Thralls of Chaos. The same welds, the same bizarre attachments to the plates that formed them. . . .

Nemesis no more, they were now only inert piles of empty metal.

He was nearly to the ground before he recognized Rocky. The gorge rose in his throat when he realized the significance of a tarry insect-cloaked pile of chain mail. Thralls did not wear chain mail.

Richie ran to the site, as if there were something he could do. However, all there was to do was witness the mortified flesh of someone who might have been his brother.

Richie had seen death before, but never before as such a stark dissolution. Always he'd seen death in a situation where the fact of violence, or disease, pushed away other considerations. He had never seen decay.

He looked at Rocky, the soft parts collapsing as if the flesh itself were dissolving away, and the smell hit him. He turned around, dropped to his knees, and tried to vomit. Nothing came but the sour taste of bile.

He crawled away from the body thinking that it could just as well be him collapsing under a blanket of flies. In some sense, some very important sense, it *was* him.

Richie gained his feet and stumbled away from the wreckage of the battle. He walked in a daze. But he walked northwest, toward the city.

He had yet to put the Ring on his finger.

CHAPTER 45

RICHARD

RICHARD withdrew, wordlessly following Rick's lead. Rick had insisted on taking all the supplies that had survived, immediately leaving the rock to head west, across the river, toward the Greythorn Woods.

The objections were too difficult to maintain in the face of Rick's obssessions. In a twisted way, Rick was all Richard had left connecting him with the real world, and he wasn't strong eough to let him leave. Richard didn't think he could manage to remain sane if he were alone here.

Richard tried to talk to him, but Rick seemed impervious to words. When Richard pushed too closely against Rick's plans, Rick threatened to abandon him.

So Richard went along meekly.

They had, under Rick's urging, force marched west toward the sunset, the river, and the wildwood beyond it. Every step, Richard felt more and more as if his identity were draining away, leaking like sand from a broken hourglass. More and more it seemed that this place, this Quinque, was *wrong*. There was something fundamentally alienating about it, an evil shallowness that sucked reality away without becoming any more real, an infinite coldness that drained the heat from its surroundings without feeling the warmth.

Rick, bearing the Sword, seemed to personify the dread Richard now felt. Rick strode through the woods ahead of Richard, and he now seemed to be more *there* than his surroundings, almost as if, once things passed from Rick's awareness, they ceased to exist.

That was part of Richard's fear. If Rick no longer perceived him, he might slowly fade away into nothing. Richard knew the fears he felt and the feelings gripping him were close to insane, but he didn't have the strength to talk himself out of them.

Near dusk, he collapsed from exhaustion and dreamed nightmares of a dead city where every corpse wore his face. Richard didn't remember waking up.

He was slow to come to full consciousness.

When he did, he was lying on a bed of straw that moved and rocked beneath him. He was surrounded by the sounds of tramping feet, hooves, and creaking wood. At first he thought that they'd finally been claimed by the Thralls, Thralls that would return them to their point of origin rather than destroy them out of hand.

No, Richard remembered, all the Thralls were destroyed. Those immortal things were no more. They no longer protected the barriers between Chaos' dreams. Those dreams themselves might no longer exist in any form that mattered.

He raised his hands and rubbed his temples. The air was thick with the smell of horse, and straw, and sweat. He could make out the creak of the wheels below him, a repetitive wooden sound.

He felt sunlight on his arms, and he opened his eyes slowly, expecting to be dazzled by the light. It wasn't as bad as he expected. He lay under the open air, but above him the brightness was mollified by a spread canopy of trees that draped dappled shadows over him. Even so, he could barely squint, and for a few moments all he could see clearly was a scatter of abstract blue forms surrounded by dead black shadow, as if he were watching the fragments of a cerulean mirror tumble into a void.

"How's your strength?" someone asked him, someone in the cart with him. Richard turned his head and opened his eyes again. A figure leaned toward him from the opposite side of the cart. "Are you all right?"

"I am awake." As far as Richard felt, that was the extent of his improvement. "Where are we?"

"We're traveling with the Royal Hospitalers, rendering aid to Agathon's army."

Richard pushed himself upright, and felt a wave of dizziness, but not as bad as he had expected. "What? We're going to the *war!*"

"The war's come to us. There's no point on the compass that doesn't lead to a front." Rick frowned. "The knights have said the Adversary's all but won."

Richard looked around at the people surrounding them. They were knights, wearing the colors and signs of Vitus rather than Heros. Other carts followed the road they were on, some bore from two to half a dozen men, bandaged and bloody. Most were yet empty.

"Where are we going?"

"The Massacre of Greythorn Woods, they've named it already. That's the destination, but the Hospitalers render aid along the way, which is how we, and these others, come to be here." He waved at the few carts that bore wounded.

"Greythorn?" Richard repeated.

Rick smiled. It was a grin almost alien to Richard. "An arrangement with destiny. We'll find what we search for there."

Richard's collapse had been from hunger and heat exhaustion. Even though he was recovering, the knights still treated him like one of the wounded.

It didn't last long. There were only a small number of Hospitalers and they only had a finite amount of aid to render. Soon they reached the edge of the battle. Richard stumbled out of the cart without being told to.

It was bad.

It wasn't that he saw an overwhelming amount of wounded, not at first. The woods were too dense around the path to permit them to see more than a few. But he could hear, and he could smell.

He heard moaning and calling from the woods around

him, and worse, the sound of flies. The woods were rank with the smell of men's flesh, their bowels, and their gangrene.

At first, Richard walked next to the Hospitalers, and saw no more than those who'd fallen within reach of the side of the road. But when he looked into the woods, and stared at any segment for longer than a few seconds, some abstract collection of shadows would resolve into a body. More often than not, one that didn't move.

Their convoy of carts stopped, and one of the King's Knights pulled up next to Rick and Richard. He dismounted with the rest of his companions. "You may now repay others for the aid you have received," he said to them. "We are too few, and too many need our aid."

Rick nodded, "Whatever we can do to help."

Richard still felt unsteady on his feet, so it took several long moments before some faded sign of recognition washed over him. It was the bald head and too-large mustache that marked him.

"Good." The Knight's expression was set and grim as he surveyed the area. Eventually he pointed in a more-or-less northerly direction. "You'll take the center aisle that way. You will have one of us to either side of you." He opened a pouch at his side and took out a handful of scarlet ribbons. "When you find someone alive, take him back to the cart. If he is dead, tie a ribbon about him so the others can see he is beyond help."

Rick took the ribbons, as Richard stared at the knight who bore too-much the semblance of Detective Kavcheck.

Other Hospitalers were calling orders and arranging a search pattern. Their Kavcheck-Knight gave them a small bow and said, "Life go with you," and hurried to his own post.

"Let's go," Rick said. He gave no sign of noticing the enormity of the knight's appearance.

Richard wanted to say something, draw attention to it. But what could he say that didn't sound like rank insanity. Of course if the knight really was Kavcheck, Rick would've noticed, wouldn't he?

Richard stumbled after Rick as he led him north into the woods.

There were three bodies immediately north of the path. Rick made a show of stopping by each of them, making sure that they merited a ribbon.

Richard was overwhelmed. He stared at the victims and wished desperately that he could render some sort of help. But for most it was too obvious that there was little that could be done.

The first victim Rick stopped by had been split up the groin and had died holding his intestines inside. The second had taken an arrow in the chest and had drowned when his lungs filled with his own blood. The third had lost an arm and had bled to death. As he stopped by each one, Rick would stand over the body, then watch the woods around him.

Richard could hear the Hospitalers moving around in the woods, though by the time he had helped Rick tie the third ribbon, about a hundred yards from the path, he had lost sight of them. He could hear a few shouts and yells from wounded, as if they wanted to reassure him that there *were* living left in these woods.

They went another hundred yards in, Rick pulling him along. The sounds of the Hospitalers were growing fainter now. They moved more slowly, and seemed to be finding more of the living than Rick was.

He took Rick's shoulder and said, "Wait. We shouldn't rush through. We could miss someone."

Rick stopped, but he didn't look at Richard. He stared into the woods beyond them, peering through the trees. "That way," he said.

"What? He told us to stay north, other people are going to be searching in that—"

Rick's hand shot out, grabbing his wrist. A handful of crimson ribbons fell out of his hand, scattering on the leaves. "Don't forget why we're here."

It was the same tone of voice he had used when Richie had touched the Sword. This time, his voice carried less restraint.

"But—" The one word was all the challenge that Richard could muster under Rick's eviscerating stare. Helping the Hospitalers had merely been a means to an end with him. Rick carried no compassion, or even acknowledgment, of the wounded in the woods around him.

Richie had been right, Rick was dangerous—

"Come. This way," Rick said, pulling him along. Richard followed, wishing for the strength to pull away.

It didn't come.

Rick didn't let them stop, even when Richard saw a body through the trees. Now that they were out of the Hospitalers' sight, Rick had abandoned his pretense of charity. Certain of where he was going, he tolerated no delay.

"Where are you rushing to?" Richard asked in frustration.

"Toward the Horn and its guardians." Rick's voice was colored by a frightening impatience. Richard didn't ask him any more questions.

The woods darkened around them as they progressed. The trees surrounded them, cutting off the world more than ten feet in any direction. Losing sight of the wounded did not allow the victims to disappear. Their moans still filled the air, becoming sourceless and eerie.

Mist clogged the woods where the sunlight didn't quite reach. It carried the sour smell of the battle's aftermath, as if the woods itself had been wounded and left to fester. Soon the mist had draped everything around them in a gray shroud.

Richard wanted to ask Rick how he knew where he was going, but he didn't have the courage. Rick seemed to have absorbed all of Richard's lost faith in this world. Richard would not be surprised if Rick had told him that he had struck out at random and trusted to fate to bring them and the Horn together.

That would not have been quite as unexpected as what did happen.

They were walking through the spectral wilderness when something from out the mists called to them.

"Dr. Brandon," the voice was weak and carried a slight Jamaican flavor to it.

Rick frowned, but Richard recognized the voice as soon as he heard it. Rick stopped moving.

There was a cough from in front of them and to the right.

"Who is there?" Rick called back.

"Over here." There was a cough and a muttered, "Shit."

Rick placed a hand on the hilt of the Sword and edged in the direction the voice came from. The voice issued from a stand of trees that seemed thicker than most, a place where the mist seemed to become almost opaque.

"Over here," the strained voice continued.

Richard had to place a hand on Rick's shoulder to keep from being separated from him. The mist had become nearly too thick to see through. Rick shuddered at the possibility of the voice belonging to who he thought it did.

Then the mist broke, almost completely. It was as if they walked through a wall and into another forest entirely. The mist had faded to mere wisps, and the trees had pushed back to give space to a small clearing.

On the ground in that clearing, leaning against a log, a tall black man had collapsed in a pool of his own blood. His clothing was anachronistic, and he held a blood-stained plaster cast to a gaping hole in his belly.

Rick stopped short, looked at John Waters, and said, "What are you doing here?"

"The doctor was right, wasn't he, man?" Pain had deepened the foreign flavor of John's voice.

"The last time I saw you," Richard said, "you were in the lobby of the MetroHealth building."

"And Armageddon riding in the doorway, I know that, man." He coughed again and Richard knelt down by him. He shook his head weakly, his voice losing much of its projection. "No, don't bother any with that. You can't hold my life in any better. . . ."

Rick was shaking. "What the hell are you doing here? This is Quinque—*It's ours.*"

Much of the light seemed to fade from the woods

around them. Richard looked up at Rick. From the flustered look on his face, he didn't seem to recognize what he had just said. "You arrogant—" Richard's voice was tense, and it came out in little more than a whisper. He stopped when he felt John's hand on his wrist.

"The doctor was right about that now."

Richard looked down at John and stared into his face. His eyes were closed, and the muscles seemed to be slackening. "We have to do something for him," Richard said.

Instead of responding to him, Rick leaned over John and yelled, "What do you mean, 'The doctor was right?' "

John's lids fluttered open a moment. He looked at Rick, and where Richard would have expected an expression of anger or pain, he only saw a residual curiosity. "The nature of consciousness is to define what it calls reality. It's all your observations that combine to form what it is you think reality is. God plays dice with the universe, and you be the dice, man."

Rick squatted and said through clenched teeth. "What the fuck are you talking about?"

"This *is* your world. Richard Brandon's world. What John Waters' world is, I don't know, but I'm going there. . . ."

His voice trailed off, and his face lost its animation. It took a while for Richard to realize that John Waters, Doctor Richard Brandon's grad student assistant, was dead.

"Come on," Rick said. "There's nothing left here."

Richard stayed by John's side, looking into his face. All this time he'd been driven homeward. What if there was no home there? Could his first fears that his entire life was a convenient fiction be right.

If that was true, if his life was some distorted misperception, what about Rocky, Richie, Rick . . . ?

Rick yanked him up, away from the body. Richard didn't resist. He felt that he had come close to some sort of truth.

CHAPTER 46

RICK

RICK could feel his destiny pulling him. He had long since passed any point where he could reconsider his actions, even if he had wanted to. He might have changed course before he had taken the Sword, but after that he could only feel a certain inevitability.

Paradoxically, the feeling of predestination made him feel more in control than he ever had before. His destiny was to face the Adversary, and to accumulate the power necessary to defeat him, perhaps even to succeed him in the place of absolute control of this realm.

What he needed was for Richard to claim his Artifact, the one Vitus' divine providence had ceded to him. When he fell, as Citas' prophecy said he must, Rick would be there to claim the Horn as he had claimed the Sword from Rocky.

It was clear to Rick that he was the one that Citas said would face the Adversary, so it would be he who would bear the accumulated power of the Sword, the Horn, and the Cirque—and he would take the Ring from the betrayer. He did not have to wait for Richie, for he saw that each Artifact had a divinely assigned bearer to take it from its resting place. Even the Adversary must have been divinely chosen to take the Staff—

But Rick had been given the prophecy, so it was he who would bear all in the end.

He thought about saying all this to Richard, to call him away from the body by explaining how it was all for the best, how things were happening just as they were meant to. He only thought about it. He could tell from

Richard's confused expression that he was not ready to understand.

Rick pulled Richard away from the dead man, and led him to the path he saw, wending deeper into the sunless woods. Rick could feel them slipping into a world slightly removed from the one they had been inhabiting. He had felt it when they had followed the gnome king under the hill, and when they had boated to find the Sword.

He felt an awareness creeping in from the Sword, giving him a preternatural awareness of the woods around him. It was a constant pressure that would have overwhelmed his perceptions if he had not had such a tight focus on his own destiny.

After a short walk beyond the body—Rick avoided naming the corpse, even in his mind, because his presence was so disturbing—the forest opened out around them, into an impossible bowl-shaped valley.

The rim of the valley rose far above the horizon, leaving only a tiny circle of sky above them. They emerged from the mist near a clearing on the bottom of the bowl.

From the feeling of the Sword, Rick knew that they'd been anticipated.

He turned to look at Richard, and realized that the man was talking to him. ". . . pause to think a little. What if your assumptions are wrong?"

Rick could feel the press of other beings around them, anticipating some sort of confrontation. He turned away from Richard and said, "Quiet."

He inched his way to the clearing which, to the eye, was empty. The foliage around them had turned colors, like the woods around the place where Rocky died, but the reds and yellows were too vibrant, too odd. The appearance was of a black-and-white film hand-tinted by someone slowly going blind.

Richard hadn't stopped talking. "What if John is right? What if this is some manifestation of our own perceptions, our own minds? What if *everything* is?"

"*Shh!*"

The other presence waited until Rick and Richard had stepped a few feet into the clearing. At that point, Rick could tell that they'd been surrounded. What he had first taken to be a line of trees encircling the clearing, had resolved into rank upon rank of red-and-brown humanoid forms. Their coloring and the texture of their skin blended in with the surrounding trees so perfectly that it was impossible to define a point where the crowd stopped and the forest began.

One pale form did stand out when she stepped clear of the tree line.

"Leave this place," Daenan said. "Leave before more harm is done."

Rick placed his hand upon the Sword and he heard Richard's intake of breath, "What are you doing here?"

She turned to face them. "I do not wish the world to end."

"This world . . ." Richard hesitated, as if trying to think his way out of a difficult problem.

"Leave this place. The world is wounded, but alive—"

Richard whispered, "Rocky."

Rick paid little attention. He inched the Sword from its sheath. As he did so, he could feel the shape of the coming conflict, in all its permutations. He could sense every act and every possible counteract. He felt the sense of destiny moving when he realized that every permutation led inevitably to a single conclusion.

"It is you who should leave this place," Rick said. "We are here for the Horn, and we shall not leave without it."

Daenan shook her head. "With each Artifact that enters the world of men, the end of things comes closer. Three already is too many."

Richard placed a hand on Rick's sword arm. Rick almost winced at the impertinence. They had a destiny here.

Richard's voice was barely audible. "When Rocky died—"

"A great part of the world died with him."

"But why fight us, then? If we're part of the world—"

"No, you don't see what you do." Daenan spread her

arms and her eyes took on an unnatural glow. "You would bring together the body of Chaos and reform the universe to your own vision. My fey brethren would see you bring the fragments together with no center, and let the universe tumble into the void. Neither is acceptable. Better that the fragments die with the center intact—"

Rick finished drawing the Sword. The small circle of sky had darkened above them. Shadows draped the clearing, carving Daenan's pale form in relief. She was tall and spectral, imposing but somehow not entirely there. Nothing seemed truly there anymore. The Sword had taken on more than its share of the surrounding reality, making everything fade a little in its presence.

"We are called to face the Adversary," Rick said. "I shall face him and defeat him."

"You intend to defeat yourself," Daenan replied.

An evil wind seemed to carry through the clearing. Richard stared at Rick, and the Sword, and interposed himself between him and Daenan. "Wait, Rick. Think, *please*."

"Move aside, Richard," Rick said. "I've heard quite enough from her." He looked across at Daenan and said, "You cannot win this fight. The gods have already decided the victor."

Richard didn't move. "This place is a part of us—or vice versa—what if she's right?"

Rick stepped up to Richard and placed a hand on his shoulder. The hand was shaking, and Rick could feel the flush in his face. Anger was a pressure right behind his sinuses, burning his skin, making his breath taste like blood. *"Move!"*

"We're all a part of each other and this place," Richard said, holding his hands up defensively, his speech frenetic. "What if the Adversary's one of us?"

"Move!" Rick shouted, and he shoved Richard aside with the flat of his blade. He was gripped with a blazing fury. The time for discussion was over. He dove at Daenan, striking with Heros' weapon. She dodged him with an agility beyond any mortal creature's, but Rick

could see defeat in her eyes. Once battle was joined, the Sword decided the outcome.

It ended with the Sword buried hilt-deep in her sternum. She stared at Rick, their faces only inches apart. Her expression didn't register pain, only something that looked like an alien sadness.

"We have both lost," she said to him.

The Sword shuddered in his hand, and Daenan's body slipped away, collapsing in a heap. Rick stepped back, shaken.

Rick gazed blankly at the body. "I thought they couldn't die," he said in a shallow monotone. He waited for Richard to answer him, to tell him what he already knew, that the Sword could sever the life of an immortal creature. . . .

Richard didn't answer him.

Rick felt an uneasy sensation. Above, iron-colored clouds scudded across the sky. In the distance, through a quickening wind, he could hear birds cawing, as if in pain. Dried leaves blew across the clearing.

Rick looked down and saw the forest more worn and haggard. The trees had shed much of their foliage, leaving more than their share of naked branches. Too many of those branches were bone-white and dead.

His gaze continued down until he saw Richard, on the ground where he had fallen after Rick had struck him. Rick had thought that he had used the flat of the blade—

The Sword knew. *It knew that Richard would have interfered with the combat. The Sword insured its victory.*

"What have I done?" Rick exclaimed. He kept stepping away. The enormity of what had just happened was still sinking in.

At his feet, Richard's corpse bled into the clearing, next to Daenan.

He had killed someone. Not just someone, but someone as close to a brother as he would ever have.

Daenan's blood, too pale and anemic, slid down the blade to merge with the few traces of Richard's.

"He tried to block destiny," Rick whispered, trying

to force himself to believe the words. He had to now; what else did he have left? If he abandoned his vision now, it would be worse because then the deaths would be pointless.

Now he *had* to kill the Adversary.

He heard movement and looked up at the edges of the clearing. The wood-people were there, still, but they were drawing aside, revealing a path in front of them. It was as if the forest itself had parted for him.

It wasn't quite what Rick had expected. His heart was racing, expecting a battle, anticipating it. Nothing could stand against the Sword. Maybe the wood-people sensed that too, and that was why they moved aside.

Rick strode down the path. Everything inside him had drained, leaving him a Thrall, a husk emptied of everything but purpose.

The path was broad and straight, but it curved up so that the destination was lost behind a canopy of leaves. Rick practically ran through the aisle of dappled shadow, he could feel that what he had come for lay ahead. All around him the woods were alive with the sound of whispers, like wind through leaves.

Rick emerged into a clearing that was the inverse of the prior one. Here he stood on a round hilltop, bald of trees, where the horizon fell away at all points around it. It was as if this entire woods might be bounded by the two clearings, and any path straight away from this hilltop would end in that first clearing.

The other thing that marked this place was a ring of stones on its crown and an old woman who stood next to the largest of them. She was stooped and leaned upon what at first appeared to be a walking stick. Something about her, some atmosphere around the site, made Rick approach very cautiously.

He walked slowly toward the woman, and the circle of stones.

As Rick came closer, what had appeared to be a walking stick now seemed to be more of a small tree. Roots snaked from its bottom to seize purchase from the stony ground, and above the woman's head, it split into boughs that turned a few leaves toward the darkling sky.

The old woman herself seemed more and more treelike as he drew closer. What he had seen as a rumpled cloak from a distance resolved into skin the color and texture of bark. Matted green hair extended to her ankles, like ivy. As he came to stand a few yards from her, he saw that her moss-covered legs, like her staff, snaked into roots clutching the hardscrabble ground.

At first she didn't move, and it was easy to believe that she was nothing more than a mutant tree. Merely a signpost set to mark a sacred place. But when Rick started toward the circle of stones, she spoke.

"You must face me, Richard Brandon," she whispered. She talked with less breath than it would take to extinguish a candle, as if she spoke with the small breeze that crossed the clearing.

Rick turned to look at her. While she had seemed immobile at first, her posture had shifted to face him.

"Who are you?" Rick asked.

She laughed. "You have seen me before. If you do not know me it is because you choose not to remember."

Rick shook his head. "That doesn't matter. I'm here for the Horn."

"Look." The tree-woman pointed a wooden finger out toward the horizon. Rick turned and saw wide random swaths of bone-white scarring the forest. All the vibrant reds and yellows had gone to a crumbled brown.

Rick turned around to face her. "What is happening?"

"I am life, the earth beneath your feet, the axis around which the world turns. I am dying. You would take the Horn from me?"

Rick felt a knot of anger grow in the pit of his stomach. "I've been charged to take it from this place."

"You? Who has charged you?"

"My god. You cannot deny me."

"What are gods but your own passions writ large?"

Rick's hands trembled on the hilt of the Sword. "I've been chosen to face the Adversary. To defeat him."

"You are the Adversary," she said. She looked at him and shook her head. Pointing inside the circle she said, "Take it, it cannot keep me alive anymore."

For a long time Rick stared at the tree-woman, but she had said all she was going to. She slowly sank back into immobility.

Rick walked inside the circle of stones, and retrieved the conical Horn from where it lay on the ancient stone. As he looked up from it, he could see the dead spots in the woods outside the circle. The swaths of gray had doubled in size.

CHAPTER 47

RICHIE

AS Richie returned to Quinque, the world disintegrated around him. On the opposite side of the road from him was an endless file of refugees walking away from the city. Their expressions were dead, and they did not talk among themselves, or pay attention to Richie as he passed them. They moved as if they were merely automatons, and they paid no attention to the chaos through which the road passed.

Richie paid attention.

It had started with a car. At first it seemed merely a shadow off in the grass, but it had caused Richie to pause. He had stood for a long while staring before he had run off toward the shape in the grass.

It had been the rusted-out frame of an ancient Oldsmobile, a gas-sucking behemoth from the early Seventies. Grass grew through its seats and the engine. Everything plastic had been worn away, and everything metal had oxidized to the same color midway between brown and black.

Richie had run from the car, but there were others, all parked parallel or perpendicular to the road, as if making a city grid that didn't exist any more.

When he passed refugees, they paid no attention to the wreck-age from another reality. He watched as the ghosts of buildings tried to emerge from the shadows of their foundations.

The fractures were invisible, the alien things appeared as if they belonged there. Richie suspected that if he grabbed a passing refugee at random, he would express no surprise at the artifacts they passed, and would maintain that they had always been there.

Richie knew that these things hadn't always been there, and were a symptom of some fundamental breakdown. Quinque *was* breaking down, and other things, random things, were filling the gaps, placing half-buried asphalt under his feet.

He walked on a constant edge of vertigo, a feeling that matched the endless ghost town he walked beside.

The refugees finally pushed him off of the road entirely. Trees crowded around, but not on the treeless aisle along which he walked. He passed occasional dead cars, flanking him, and an occasional slab of concrete would emerge from the soil.

Once he kicked a metal sheet that was half-buried in the sod. The metal was solid rust, but the oxidation had painted the surface in patterns of light and dark, a negative of the original markings on the sign. It was directing him how to find Interstate 77.

As he walked, he would occasionally stare into a shadow and picture reaching for a skyline separated from him by a window of leaded glass.

He still carried the Ring. In his pocket, not on his finger. He never forgot it was there. Its presence seemed to weigh more than the gun he carried in his opposite pocket. It was a mental weight that was always there, so he felt its presence even without seeing it.

He was taking Lucian seriously, taking the Ring to the city, but he wasn't sure what he was going to do when he got there. He wasn't sure what was happening, and he had the feeling that his ignorance was only his own self-deception. The Ring was supposed to draw aside deceptions, and Richie had some idea what lay behind his own self-deceit.

He may have read Tolkien one too many times, but he wasn't going to put the Ring on until absolutely necessary.

It was deep evening when he reached the boundary of the city—about where Euclid would have hit East 20th if his fragmenting memory served right. Quinque, the eternal city of Richard Brandon's childhood imagination, was changed. It was not only the fact that refugees had finally begun to empty the city, anticipating a siege. Richie could see the changes from a distance, as if the city were dying from a malignant tumor.

The defenders had raised up ramparts of earth that did little to shield the city against the unreal malignancy. The bodies of automobiles made up part of the ramparts themselves. From where Richie stood, he could see fragments of another city pressing into the center of Quinque. Threads of concrete, steel, metal, and glass snaked through the old city, spiraling like traces of black ink caught in a vortex, not yet quite embracing the ancient palace at the center.

Richie walked down, into the frozen whirlwind, against the flow of refugees. At the moment the gates were open, and if he kept to the center of the flow, the defenders could not prevent him from entering the city.

There was a feeling, and he could see it in the guards' faces, that soon the gates would close, the earthen ramparts would be manned, and no one would enter until the city fell. As if in anticipation, the western sky was darkened by what looked like an oncoming storm.

Once clear of the gate, Richie broke free of the exodus, and the smell of exhausted humanity, and wandered into the dying city. He roamed, light-headed and looking for somewhere that would offer food and a place to rest. The streets he walked on were cobbled, but in places the cobbles were replaced with asphalt, as if patched by some mad interdimensional road crew.

The buildings near the gate wore the same Tudor faces, the same blind leaded-glass eyes, that he remembered. However, he saw fragments of anachronism. Tar paper and black shingles over one gable, a peeling sheet of siding on another. On one building's corner, dangling and broken, hung a metal bracket bearing empty porcelain insulators designed to hold incoming power lines.

Before, when he and his fellows had come here, the problem had been finding a free room. Now the problem was the opposite, finding a place that was open and not deserted. He pounded on several doors that never opened; he wandered into more that led into buildings that'd been stripped bare.

"Come on," he muttered, leaning on the doorway of the fifth abandoned building he'd come across. "The siege hasn't started yet. There's got to be a place where someone can get something to eat."

He looked out at the road where he found himself. This inn seemed more abandoned than the others he'd passed. Other streets had been flanked by buildings that were occupied, if not open to strangers. In this one, Richie could see no sign of people. The exodus was long behind him, and the sounds of the surrounding city seemed muted and distant.

Richie raised his gaze above eye level, to look beyond the rooftops of the buildings across the street. He could see now why this place was emptier than anywhere else. He was barely a block away from one of the dark metallic spirals that swept their way into the city. He could tell simply by the ranks of telephone poles, wires sagging under masses of creeping vines. They seemed to mark the boundary, and obviously no native wished to be near such a thing.

Richie stepped out of the doorway and walked toward them, and into a world that seemed long abandoned.

The spine of the asphalt road was broken. The cars parked on its shoulder had been weathered to a uniform gray. Telephone poles, weighted by vines and pushed by ages of wind, rain, and ice, leaned at odd angles into the road, as if reaching for him. Houses flanked him, old two-family dwellings overrun by plants and weather, their flanks a lighter gray than the cars.

The sounds of the city he had just left were gone completely. The street was cloaked in a deadly silence. He walked toward the east, where the palace should be visible.

Instead, against a blackened stormy sky, he thought he could see fragments of a broken skyline.

Richie stopped at a brick shell, whose door was blocked by a collapsed and disintegrating sign that said in four-foot letters, "Hienens." Hunger driving him, Richie stepped through one of the holes that used to be plate glass windows.

Once inside the dead supermarket, it took time for his eyes to adjust. Even though he knew that this could not have been here when he had last been to Quinque, he could see that it had been abandoned for a very, long time. Long enough for the smell of fresh rot to become dry, dusty, and almost subliminal. The atmosphere made his skin itch.

Something here would still be edible. Just by looking he could tell that it had not suffered some disaster-spurred panic. The shelves had been stocked, the store had closed, and had never reopened.

He wandered the aisles, first through what was left of the dry goods. Those had disappeared in a flurry of rats' nests. Shredded paper lined the shelves where there used to be cereal boxes. Both food and rodents had disappeared some time ago.

In other aisles, bottles had burst under the pressure of their contents. Everything had melded into a glass-sprinkled, tarlike mass coating the metal shelves.

He went nowhere near the fresh fruits or the refrigerated containers, even though time must have drained any impact from the omnipresent rot.

The cans had survived. A few had swollen, gone rust-spotted, or had exploded, but most seemed intact. It wasn't a sane thing to do, but Richie started grabbing cans. He was too hungry to care how safe the food was. If a can retained its original shape, he assumed it wouldn't kill him.

The cans shed their labels as he grabbed them, their adhesive gone to dust.

He stumbled out of the ruins of Hienens with an armful

of spotted metal cans. He scattered them on the asphalt when he reached the light, and sat down in their midst. He pulled the knife from his belt and began stabbing the iconic metal cylinders.

He emptied two cans of metallic-tasting Spaghetti-Os before he began to worry about the safety of what he was eating. The cans themselves didn't inspire confidence. They were labelless, spotted with rust, and their seams had begun to discolor.

He dropped the second empty can and wiped his knife on the overgrown grass growing between cracks in the asphalt. "What the hell is this?" Richie spoke aloud to the deserted buildings around him.

He stood and shouted, "What the *hell* is this?"

His voice didn't even echo against the silent landscape. The wind didn't move. The only clouds were stationary, darkening toward the western horizon. Everything was as motionless and silent as a photograph, or an empty stage set.

"This ain't my world," he yelled up at the sky. "I got the damned Ring, and if this is your idea of sending me home, this is one hell of a fuckup."

He stood there waiting for something, some sort of answer, if only a distant bird call. Even the bark of a dog would be welcome in the sterile landscape. But there was nothing, no response. It was as if he had, again, slipped into another reality, leaving Quinque behind.

"One *hell* of a fuckup."

He turned back to the Hienens. The food made him feel less dizzy, at the cost of a slight nausea. He wanted to know how old this stuff was. Again he felt the protest of logic, this place had not been here when last he walked through Quinque.

But here was here, and everything around him said that this was no longer Quinque.

He stepped through the window of the dead supermarket one more time, for a more methodical search. Richie soon found what he was looking for. Near the entrance was another rat's nest that used to be a pile of newspapers. The stack had been thick enough that the papers at the bottom had mostly escaped destruction. He reached down and pulled a yellowed copy of the *Cleveland Press* from the bottom of the stack.

The date on the paper read July 4th, 1970.

CHAPTER 48

RICK

RICK walked north.

With no one to accompany him, his memory faltered from one moment to the next. He was unsure of where he was at any given time. All he had was an iron sense of where he had to go. Destiny had evolved into predestination, and then into a rigid determinism that gave him no choice but to walk forward, toward the Cirque he'd been charged to carry. His movement was inevitable, drawn by a gravity only intrinsic to him, and the Artifacts he bore.

He walked north, accompanied by a bizarre amalgam of imagery. He passed, untouched, across a battle-scarred plain. Bodies fell across his path, their blood draining into the cracked mud. When he walked over them, the cracks in the mud would sprout tiny black flowers.

Armies surged north and east, while Rick picked his way across the trail of wreckage the war left behind itself. Sometimes forces would confront him, and the Sword would cleave all opposition until Rick could continue on his inexorable northward journey. Sometimes he was cut, or burned, or mauled, and then the vital force of the Horn sustained him.

Rick passed silent places where corpses had been scattered on the rocky ground, the war long past; bodies abandoned long enough for vines to envelop their tawny bones.

Rick walked along wounded hillsides that smoldered in the aftermath of battle. Tarlike smoke cloaked the twisted woods he passed through and monstrous shadows flitted above the level of choking smoke, flying toward the unseen eastern horizon.

When color leeched out of the rocks beneath his feet, and smoky shadows cloaked him in a perpetual dusk, he had reached the foothills of the mountains upon which his glory rested. He had left Quinque again, for no such mountains existed within its boundaries. He had entered the fey realm where the Cirque was kept.

When he reached it—when that chief of all the Artifacts was upon his brow—he would face the demon infecting this land. He would defeat the Adversary. In that he would find the justice of all that had happened.

Rick climbed.

He climbed from blurred phantasmagoria into a dead world. Ice bit through what clothing he had left, the wind scouring his skin. Rocks tore into the meat of his hands, scraping bloody patterns on his palms. Every breath sliced into his lungs, sucking heat from the flesh of his throat. His eyes watered, and his tears froze, burning, on his cheeks.

Still he could not stop. It was as if he were no longer capable of forming the concept of stopping. His progress slowed as the way steepened, but it never completely ceased. Rick ascended though a gray twilight erased of any detail. The roar of the wind washed away any other sound. The cold numbed his skin.

With almost everything wiped from his perception, Rick felt as if he were floating, even when he was dragging himself upward with bloody, clawlike hands. His spirit felt decoupled from his body, floating somewhere dark and quiet, where the efforts of his body weren't felt.

After a timeless effort, Rick ceased climbing. He stood at the summit for quite some time before he was aware that he had stopped. The ascent was over, he had reached his goal.

And, as if his realization dictated the world around him, the endless wind ceased, and the blowing ice settled. The gray world resolved itself into a peak amid peaks. Above him was a black, starless sky, a sky erased of every feature. The void above sparked a deep vertigo in him, and he had to lower his gaze.

On the peak with him was a small building, a tiny brick structure that was little more than a niche standing alone. He could feel that he was almost to his goal. What drew him sat within the wind-scoured niche. His smile cracked his lips so they bled.

Rick slowly walked to the tiny temple. "What guardians are there for Citas' Cirque?" he whispered to himself. His voice was hoarse, it was the first time he had spoken since the woods.

A voice came from behind him, "The most noble guardians of all, my Adversary."

Rick turned and faced a ring of tall, pale forms; every pale face had the same inhuman cast to it as Daenan's had. Their hair blew free in the wind, and their irises glinted like precious metals. They wore elaborate silks that bore patterns so intricate that they inspired almost as much vertigo as the sky above.

He held the Sword and the Horn; armies couldn't stop him. He should not be afraid of these elves. He had seen that even their immortality could not stand before him. He should not be afraid.

But he was.

When he finally spoke, he said, "I am the enemy of the Adversary." He put a nervous hand on the Sword, "I am here to defeat him."

The tallest one strode forward, arms folded and a half-smile on his face. "You should slay him, then. Shouldn't you?"

"You are allies of the Adversary," Rick insisted, clutching the hilt.

"We are the allies of any who serve our purposes."

"I am here for the Cirque."

"We know why you are here."

Rick nodded, he still felt uneasy, "Then allow me to take it."

"Of course—"

Rick turned to go to the small building; he stopped when the lead elf said, "But first you must be shown."

"Shown what?" Rick turned to face the speaker, who had extended a long arm toward the edge of the mountain.

"Come," he said to Rick, walking to the edge of the precipice. The others parted to let him through. Rick followed, too aware of the edge of the precipice so close by.

"There," the elf extended an arm over the panorama below.

Rick looked over the vista, catching his breath. At first he could make no sense out of what he saw. There was just too much in the view, too much crammed within a too-close horizon ringed by the boiling black void. Only the center of the view, directly west of the mountains, was clear.

It took a moment to understand what he was seeing. The land itself was a vortex below him, spiraled slices of an infinite number of landscapes turning around a central axis. Near the horizon, the vortex swept by too fast for Rick to see any features, the changing, mutating landscape turned gray and fragmented into black at the horizon.

It was as if reality itself were swirling about the gates of Quinque. Even from the distance of the mountain, with a clarity of vision that seemed impossible, Rick could see that the great city had been itself breached by tendrils of alien realities. He could even see their creeping motion, much slower at the center than at the edge. The shadows twisted and spun throughout the whole universe below him, like threads of ink spinning toward a drain.

The center, the axis of all this, was the great palace of Quinque. He also knew that central to that would be the sacred garden, where he had arrived here with his destiny.

"The shadows, the dreams of Chaos," Rick whispered. He was beginning to understand some of what was happening.

"The Dream from which you sprang," the elf next to him whispered seductively. "All of it, every possibility, is down there."

The Thralls had existed to protect the boundaries of dream and dream, dream and reality. *Had their destruction spawned this?* Rick stared at the boiling horizon, and—almost too dim to see—saw what seemed to be fragments of the fluxing grayness flying off into the darkness, bringing the void of the horizon that much closer.

"I have to stop this," Rick muttered. For the first time in a long while, he began to wonder if he was right. Could what he saw as destiny be something else—?

"The Adversary is responsible for this," the elf said, smiling.

Rick turned to him, "The Adversary?" he whispered. "Not me, not my companions?"

"Our race does not lie," the ancient elf said. Rick could suddenly hear the age in the voice. It was perceptible nowhere else, but in the voice the age was immeasurable. As old as the world itself. There was also an unnerving hint of irony in the statement, which Rick ignored.

"How can this be stopped?" he asked.

"You come to slay the Adversary?" the ancient said. He smiled then, a wise smile that almost became mocking. "Then you must slay the Adversary."

Rick looked at the swirling mass that had once been the private land of his childhood. The place of his dreams, overrun by dreams of its own. He felt fear and doubt in his gut. For all the Power the Artifacts had given him, it was nothing compared to the maelstrom below him. He shone as bright as the sun, but what was the sun when the galaxies themselves were disintegrating?

"How can I defeat the Adversary?" As he spoke the words, he could feel the renewed force of destiny upon him. He was here to set things right, to slay the one responsible for the travesty below, before the universe itself was snuffed out.

"The one you call the Adversary carries only the Staff, that Staff controls the magic of this land. You must bear all else before that, the life of the Horn, the might of the Sword, the authority of the Cirque—the one bearing the Staff cannot prevent your approach then. When you face the one bearing the Staff, sever his connection with it, take it for your own, then destroy him."

"What about the Ring?"

"Take it afterward from your betrayer. You do not need it to do as I describe."

Rick looked out at the maelstrom. He still feared it. "Shouldn't I take the Ring first?"

The ancient grabbed Rick's arm, and said forcefully, "No!"

The move was sudden and unexpected enough for Rick to raise the Sword. He did not bring it down, and the ancient backed away from him.

"No," the elf said, "You must take the Ring *last*. You must pledge this if you wish to take the Cirque from us."

Rick backed away from him, toward the temple. "A moment ago you were just going to give it to me."

The ancient shook his head. "We were never going to 'just give it.' We have not even brought you fully into its presence yet." He waved a hand back toward the vista. "The Cirque will give you ultimate authority over all you see down there. You would be higher than any king. The wealth and power of all nations will be yours—"

"Once I kill the Adversary."

The elf only smiled. "Our price is merely the pledge that you do not take the Ring from your betrayer before the Adversary is slain. Is that too high a price to become as a god to this world?"

Rick stood there, and after thinking for a long time, he said, "Agreed. I shall take such a pledge, and bind myself to it."

The elf smiled.

CHAPTER 49

RICHIE

QUINQUE crumbled as Richie waited for the siege. He stayed within the deserted swath of Cleveland. The deserted landscape at least seemed stable. When he walked out in the midst of what was left of Quinque, buildings were likely to change while his back was turned, people were likely to disappear. Quinque had lost its cohesion, almost as if it only had a solid definite form when he was looking upon part of it.

Taking refuge in the ruins let him hide from the changes, though not completely. The deserted city mutated as well, in ways subtle and profound. Richie didn't realize that until, on the third day after his arrival, he began to find bodies.

Until then the city had been clean of any sign of prior inhabitants. But when he woke and started searching for food, he discovered skeletons in the buildings. The first find was a grinning skull staring at him from a curled form behind the counter of a drugstore. Richie ran out of the store, gasping.

There was nothing particularly vile about the remains, it was the shock of stumbling across them that stole his breath. He stood there, and began to notice the other changes around him. He could hear the calls of insects, and above, he could see the shadows of black birds sailing against the cloudless sky.

The sky itself was the most disturbing change. The sun had risen, but only the sky above was pure blue. As the sky arced to the horizon, the blue leeched out of it, turning a gray, that darkened to black at the horizon.

The horizon was black on all sides now, boiling like a thunderhead, but the roiling was of something more fundamental than cloud. It reminded him of his dreams.

Looking at the turbulent horizon, Richie had twin thoughts, that something irrevocable had happened, and that the siege had begun.

Richie ran toward the center of the city, which stood in the same location both in Quinque, and in the deserted city with its ghostly skyline.

The ruins had grown nearly to the castle. New bridges spanned the river, reminding him of the Underworld the gnome king had led them to.

Shadows snaked and spun around the skyline. The view between the twisting shadows alternated between the buildings of a long abandoned downtown Cleveland, and the ancient palace of Quinque. Space and distance seemed to twist and distort as he watched, something close by could be far away. . . .

He looked past the buildings, toward the horizon, and saw the roiling black horizon where the lake should have been. Richie reached into his pockets and pulled out his gun, and the Ring.

He wondered if it was time to put on the Ring yet. Then he put it back into his pocket.

As he closed on the palace, he kept looking behind him. It was hard to understand what he saw, since it seemed to change every time his gaze shifted slightly. A blackness was spreading throughout the city, the abandoned one, and what he saw of the fragments of Quinque. It was as if tiny motes had freed themselves from the boiling horizon and were splitting north and west, toward him and the palace.

He was watching the Adversary's army breaching whatever defenses the city had—which was none. Looking back east, Richie could see the black army marching in through the cracks in the city's reality. They moved through the abandoned city, and quickly overwhelmed the inhabited remains of Quinque. As they spread, the parts of Quinque they invaded ceased to be Quinque. The last remnants of the fantasy realm dissolved as the invaders crossed into it.

Richie looked up and saw that what he had taken for birds were demonic outriders of the invasion, flying against the edge of the palace, swooping around the twisting shadows following them around the center of the city.

"My God," Richie whispered.

If it were possible, when he came to the edge of the palace, the chaos was worse. Shadows tore at the heart of the city, whirling strips of blackness, miles in length. As he closed toward the whirling mass, the matter of the abandoned city seemed blurry, unsure of itself. His eyes couldn't find the edges of objects, his vision began losing the ability to tell where one object ended and another began.

The sky itself faded as he approached the center.

Beyond the whipping shadows, Richie could see glimpses of the palace. First he could see a wall, or a window, then the shadow would tear by, leaving the surreal vision of blurred abandoned city in its wake.

Far above him, dark avian forms circled the vortex that centered on the palace. They seemed no more substantial than the shadows themselves. He had a feeling that the city itself, this close to the edge of the vortex, was even less so—as if it didn't quite exist yet.

The wind pulsed with the oscillating shadows, roaring alternating with dead-still silence. It was cold here, a cold that sank into the flesh and drained the marrow from the bone, a cold Richie couldn't do anything about, because it was more mental than physical.

He approached as close as he dared to the edge of the violence, the perimeter defined by the twisting shadows. This close, Richie could see them clearly. He didn't want to. They appeared to be tears, rips in the fabric of . . . *everything.*

No light penetrated them, and none was reflected from them, but Richie could sense that these rippling forms weren't flat. Richie saw in them an infinite abyss that contained nothing, no light, no matter, only void. Each time one of the shadows snaked by him, the wind would pulse toward it, carrying air and heat into the void, as if it were hungry.

Every four seconds, one would stream by, twisting a path like a tornado, leaving change in its wake. Buildings would shift, become more or less substantial, change color or size. Every half-minute or so, one of the shadows would twist by and erase the changes, leaving a clear view of the palace, the last concrete remnant of Quinque.

It was all Richie could do to stand upright. He put his hand in his pocket, and squeezed the Ring. He was still afraid of what would happen when he put it on.

Even the Ring felt cold here. It pulsed in his hand, as if it wanted to be used.

A shadow tore by him, and the wind roared, the air itself sounding like a wounded animal. The roar rose in pitch to become a shriek, a shriek coming from above him. The shriek wasn't the wind.

Richie looked up into a dead-black sky and saw a piece of lighter blackness diving toward him. One of the flying things had noticed him. For the first time he could see the thing, and it looked like something out of a painting collaboration between Salvador Dali and Hieronymus Bosch. It resembled, distantly, a bat whose features were all misproportioned and in the wrong places. It had claws, and tentacles, and fangs, and more eyes than it needed.

"Shit," Richie said. Even his voice was distorted here; above the screech of the flying thing, it sounded choppy and staccato, "Sh-h-hi-i-it!"

He raised the Beretta and pointed up at the diving creature and quickly fired three shots at it. The sound of the nine-millimeter seemed to rattle on forever as a throbbing echo. Above him the thing tumbled with the impact, turned gray and dissipated in the wind.

"It worked?" Richie looked at the space where the creature had been. It now only seemed a cloud of fine ash. The thing didn't take bullets very well.

Another tear roared by him, and this time it didn't degenerate into one shriek, but at least half a dozen at various pitches and volumes. All of them rising and increasing in volume.

Richie looked up, and saw a flock of the flying things descending toward him.

"Oh-h-h f-fu-u-uc-c-ck. . . ."

Richie popped the magazine out of the Beretta and checked the number of shots he had left. One in the magazine, which meant he had one more in the chamber—

At least six of the things were diving toward him.

He couldn't outrun the things, and he didn't have enough shots for them, so he only had one real choice. He looked down at the tearing shadows. One whipped by him as he watched. Behind it, he could see part of the palace.

He held his breath and dived through.

He rolled, got up, and ran. The area traversed by the shadows was at least a hundred yards wide, and one was racing toward him from his right. He dodged it, diving to hug the wall of the palace. It missed him by inches, sucking the warmth from his skin. Its near-touch was like ice on the back of his neck.

He hugged the wall, his face buried in fresh moss, waiting for the end. It didn't come. The shadow had missed him, and his guess was right. The flying things couldn't, or wouldn't, pass across the frontier he had just traversed.

He turned to face the opposite side of the frontier, and found himself looking at a much stranger view. The shadows would pass and change the landscape beyond the frontier, a frontier that ended about six feet from him, but the changes he saw beyond them were grosser, more profound than he had seen from the other side. On some passes he would see Quinque, and on some he would see the abandoned city, but more often the view would degenerate into random patches of light and color, or into the same boiling void that seemed to be swallowing the horizon.

Richie turned away from the chaotic view, and made for the closest entrance to the palace, which seemed to offer at least a temporary haven. He expected it to be difficult to get inside. After all, the place was under siege.

To his surprise, he found a heavy oak door standing wide open to the chaos. Richie hugged the wall up to the edge of the entrance, and carefully peered inside, expecting some sort of ambush.

There was nothing beyond but a small, nearly empty, anteroom. Richie slipped inside.

There were no guards, no people at all, beyond the door. In one corner of the room, a log table had been overturned, shattering a pitcher on the flagstone floor. One of the guards' polearms leaned in the corner of the room, abandoned.

The room felt charged by recent panic. Richie looked behind him at the storming reality six feet from the door. He could understand the panic, though he suspected that the guards who had run had run in the wrong direction. While the palace seemed to be the focus of what was happening, Richie suspected that the world beyond the castle was in much worse shape now, if it existed at all anymore.

Richie slammed the door shut, and barred it, as if it would do any good.

"Okay," he muttered, "you're the tactical genius, what now?"

He only had one real answer to that. He started to head toward the sacred garden at the heart of the great palace.

He ran through the halls, accompanied only by the sound of stones and timbers creaking in unnatural winds. Everyplace was empty of people, the whole population had abandoned the palace, making it an eerie extension of the city he had traversed to come here.

He wasn't quite sure of where he was, but he ran by instinct, away from the sounds of chaos which seemed to be increasing behind him. The palace was a huge building; he ran for ten minutes, the sound of the storm rising behind him.

The shadows reached the outer wall before he reached the garden. He knew when it happened, because the stones in the walls screamed in protest, and the ceiling rained dust on him. The air pressure dropped in the corridor, popping his ears and bringing a chill wind that rustled tapestries and sucked the life out of his skin.

Richie redoubled his pace, running for the garden. He had no idea how that could help him. He doubted that any place was safe when reality itself was being chewed apart behind him.

Finally he reached the sculpted arch that led to the garden. The door was closed, and barred from the other side. Richie slammed his shoulder into the door, and cursed.

"Fuck it," he shouted at the door. "What the hell's the point?"

The walls around him were vibrating. He could smell something like electricity in the air. He looked up, and saw cracks appear in the ceiling, shedding dust that made his eyes water.

Richie smiled grimly. The whole world might be on the verge of breaking apart into the void beyond those shadows, but if he knew anything, he knew how to get past a locked door.

Around it, anyway.

Richie ran down the passageways, paralleling the garden's walls, looking for stairways leading upward.

It wasn't long before Richie emerged on a roof overlooking the garden. He stepped out on a walkway along a peaked roof that fell away to either side of him. Cold wind slammed into him as soon as he emerged onto the narrow path, so he couldn't stand upright, and had to crawl out on the roof.

What he saw first were the shadows spiraling around the palace. They were grinding through the edges of the palace itself. The shadows were less snakelike now, more like tattered black curtains. When their black forms brushed across the outbuildings of the palace, the substance of the palace seemed to take on the fuzzy unreal quality he had seen on the other side of the maelstrom. As he watched, a massive sheet roared by, and the bits of the palace seemed to turn gray and fall into the shadow, spinning into an abyss.

"*Goddamn!*" Richie shouted, barely audible over the wind.

From his precarious position on the roof, he lowed himself down the side opposite the destruction. As he edged downward, the wind became worse. Leaves and branches began sliding by him and up the side of the roof. He descended into a cloud of blowing detritus.

He gained the inner wall, and climbed down a stone trellis that almost reached to the roof. The plant that used to occupy the trellis was thorny and bit at him, but Richie was beyond paying attention.

He pulled his gun as soon as he reached the ground. There was nothing immediately obvious to shoot.

The garden was dying, if it wasn't dead already. All the plants were leafless, and brown grass occupied whatever ground wasn't completely bare.

Richie edged along the wall, trying to find a path. When he did, it led him to the courtyard of the statues. He stopped a moment to see what had happened to them. It wasn't encouraging. Two of them had toppled to shatter against the flagstones. Heros had broken apart on his sword, and Vitus no longer held his arm up in a toast.

The statue of Citas, the throned god, had canted to the side, and had blackened and corrupted almost as much as the statue of Magus. Only his own statue, Lucas the trickster, remained unchanged, still grinning evilly, as if the wrath tearing at the palace gates was nothing more than he had expected.

Richie ran for the center of the garden, where he had entered this nightmare. In a few moments he stood before the twin oaks that were the axle of the world.

The oaks were unquestionably dead. Richie had to suck in a breath when he saw that. He knew Quinque, had lived with it for years, and he knew what it meant when those trees died.

The universe itself was going to die.

Up until then, there was some vague streak of hope in

him. He had thought that he would find some way out. There had to be some last minute fix that could be pulled off, just like all the legends he'd been seeing reprised around him.

But this was final—he knew it, felt it—and it was like a blow to the groin.

It took a moment for him to notice that there were two figures huddled by the trees. Richie stepped closer and realized that they were Alveron and his uncle. He raised his gun, and stopped when he saw that both were dead.

Uncle held his nephew's head in his lap, his hand resting on his forehead. From the look of things, he had used the other hand to slit his own throat.

As Richie lowered his gun, the sky darkened. He looked up and saw all the streaming shadows join above him, tied together at some point above the dead oaks. The spinning shadows began to erase the light from the sky. Everything above became a black, boiling void.

The sound of splintering wood came from the direction of the garden entrance. Richie looked off in that direction. He could tell that the shadows had not reached the edge of the garden—yet.

Something else was breaking into the garden.

"The Adversary," Richie whispered. He finally reached into his pocket and slipped the Ring on his finger. As Lucian promised, it unveiled all deception to him, even his own. That knowledge confirmed his worst fears.

"Oh shit," Richie said, and ran off to the garden entrance.

CHAPTER 50

RICK & RICHIE

RICK wore the Cirque. The power of command was within him. He crossed the broken land, and whomever occupied it parted to let him pass. No words needed to be spoken. He had become a natural force, a wind from the mountain that no one could stop.

Chaos followed in his wake. There could be no turning back, because there was nothing behind to turn to. He traveled to Quinque, because he felt that the Adversary traveled there. There was where he would defeat the Adversary. There was where he would save the world from the storm that tore it apart.

Shadows followed him, dark voids, hungry, pacing. More darkness spread behind him as he walked. It was as if every step he took drew a shadow from the ground he trod and loosed it to add to its brothers.

It was not long before he led a body of darkness more substantive than anything he walked among. The landscape changed as he walked; hills became valleys, rivers became deserts, farms became swamps, and mountains became glittering skyscrapers. The transformations accelerated as he walked, the universe itself writhing in pain.

Without fail, whatever he passed on his journey—skyscraper or farmhouse, tree or rock, the sky and the ground itself—fell into the abyss that followed him. A cold wind blew past him, draining the heat from everything but him. His destiny moved him, and nothing could stay his progress, not even the disintegration of the ground beneath his feet.

He had no fear, nor any thoughts beyond reaching the

culmination of his purpose. Whole realities rose and fell beside him, but his gaze was on his unchanging destination, visible to him through the vortex of shifting imagery, the great palace of Quinque. It shone to him like a jewel in a bonfire.

There were barricades on the road to Quinque, but they had been abandoned before he reached them. He didn't need to change his path, or even slow his progress. The great earthen mounds, spiked with logs and other debris, drained into the abyss on either side of him. The shadows spun, releasing tendrils of darkness that touched the obstacle and turned into blurry insubstantial light that faded into the deeper darkness. It was as if the shadows themselves were helping him.

Rick smiled. Nothing could withstand the force of destiny.

Nothing.

The great city was a blur around him, a shimmering light image indecisive about what form it was trying to represent. The light, all that was left of the city, drained into the shadows as he passed.

When he reached the whirling maelstrom around the palace, the shadows swirling around it slipped around him, draining into the darkness behind him. The darkness arched above him, extending to engulf the sky in an endless void.

The Adversary had preceded him here. Rick could feel his presence in the Artifacts he bore. The Staff was here, as was the Ring. All five in proximity for the first time since the death of the Chaos that birthed them.

He saw it in the Sword in his hand, which appeared more solid, more real, than ever. Beside it, everything before him seemed less substantial than a reflection of mist. He felt it in the Horn on his belt, which strengthened his body and made him more alive than anything left in the world. He knew it from the force of the Cirque on his brow, giving him an authority that made matter itself yield before it.

The power, the essence of the Artifacts increased the

closer they came to one another. When someone bore all five, his power would be infinite—

Rick smiled, raised the Sword, and the wall before him collapsed, the stones tumbling into shadow. He walked into the palace, darkness at his heels, and closed upon the Adversary.

The great palace crumbled away as he passed, bricks, mortar and timber blurring and falling behind him. He walked slowly toward the center of the palace, toward the garden.

Things filled the palace corridors, dark twisted things that would not make way for him. Rick knew they were remnants of the Adversary's army, and he cut them down as he passed. Whatever they once had been, they all fell before the Sword.

Rick carved a path through the halls of the crumbling palace, and to the doors of the garden. The doors had been broken away, leaving the way open to the sacred garden. Beyond the doors, under a black sky, an armored figure stood in the courtyard, flanked by statues.

The figure wore a cloak, and its face was hidden in shadow. But Rick knew the figure at once; it was the shadow that haunted his dreams.

It raised a staff as he approached. *The* Staff.

Rick attacked.

A glow suffused the courtyard, centered on Magus' Staff and draining into the statues. As he ran toward the Adversary he heard the sound of grinding stone. The statues, larger than life-size, were moving. Tons of corrupted, green-veined marble, reached for him as he charged the Adversary.

The figure of Citas tried to pummel him with a fist that used to grant a benediction, but he carried the Sword, and he could not fall in battle. He knew where the blow would land, and how to avoid it. He moved to the side, and ducked again to avoid the sweep from Magus' marble staff.

Three statues stood between him and the Adversary, raised by the Staff's magic. It meant little to Rick, they were only so much stone, animate or not. He raised his sword and broke Citas asunder just as he had laid low the walls to the palace. The statue fell into fragments that scattered around him, the head falling into the Abyss behind him.

His next blow shattered Lucas' legs, sending the statue tumbling headfirst into the dead trees surrounding the courtyard. Magus fell afterward, his staff shattered into infinite fragments. Now nothing stood between him and the Adversary.

Then came the laugh, that hideous laugh from his nightmares. The Adversary raised the Staff toward the sky, and kept raising it, and raising it. The Adversary's arms reached for the sky, extending his shadow until he stood taller than the statues had, taller than the walls of the courtyard, tall enough so his shadow was lost in the boiling black sky.

The laugh boomed out from the shadow, and Rick could feel the world tilting under him. Just like the nightmare, the ground was about to open under him. He couldn't let that happen. He knew he had to strike the Adversary down, and he knew that the Sword's aim could not be checked.

He threw the Sword at the giant figure's heart. It sailed true and pierced the Adversary's chest. Rick heard an agonized scream and the figure collapsed at his feet.

He stood there, dumbstruck for a moment, not believing that he had done it. He had defeated the Adversary. He had done it.

Hadn't he?

Something felt wrong. Rick walked up to the crumpled body, a tattered pile of cloak and armor. Where was the Staff? Where was the *Sword?* Rick looked down at the body and saw the violence torn out of the chest and wondered if the weapon could have passed completely through the Adversary's body.

He knelt down next to the corpse. Its face was still shadowed by the hood of its cloak. Rick reached out and pushed the hood aside. He saw the Adversary's face.

No. His mind shouted the word. All the breath had left him, and he couldn't speak. He stumbled back from the corpse.

"No—what?" Rick could not understand what he had seen. The Adversary had the face of a ten-year-old boy. As he watched, *stared* at the body, it melted away into nothing.

Richie watched as Rick kept backing away from the illusion.

Richie almost felt sympathy for him as Rick felt down for the Horn that had been on his belt. It wasn't there. It was safe inside Richie's jacket, where he'd stashed it when he lifted it.

There was panic in Rick's voice, but Richie couldn't bring himself to be gratified by it. *"What?"* Rick asked almost plaintively.

He spun around to face Richie. He looked worse off than Richie did. His clothes were tattered, his skin covered with filth, leaves and twigs were tangled in his hair above the Cirque. Richie raised the Beretta with his left hand, his right still hurt from the beating Daenan had given it.

"You?" Rick yelled at him.

"Yeah, me. Just in time, too."

"What are you doing? We've got to defeat the Adversary—"

Richie shook his head and started circling around Rick, keeping the gun trained on him. "You don't get it. *We're* the goddamned Adversary. You've already destroyed whatever reality existed here before we came."

"You're lying."

"Look behind you, you twit."

Rick looked around with a wild gaze, his expression confirming what Richie had known for a while now, Rick was nuts. Maybe he was the part of him that had always been nuts. He stared back at the swirling black shadow at his heels and muttered, "The elves."

"Fuck the elves," Richie spat. "They want nothing better

than our own suicide." What were they, Richie wondered? Probably some festering guilt about the accident. "You see this?" Richie held up his hand, showing the Ring he now wore. "It's the master of truth and deception. I know what's happening. Do you want to know how badly you fucked up?"

Rick turned around.

"We weren't supposed to kill the Adversary, we're supposed to *face* him. We're supposed to face the part of us that's common to all of us. We're *all* the Adversary: you, me, Richard, Rocky—"

Rick shook his head. "Lies," he muttered.

Rick looked around the courtyard. Richie could see that the illusion part was sinking in. Rick was staring at the statues, which had never really moved, and at the spot where the ersatz-Adversary had fallen, an Adversary that was never really there. Richie couldn't tell if anything else he was saying was making an impact.

"Kill him," Richie said, "And we *all* take a header into that void out there, with the rest of Quinque."

Rick turned to face him and said coldly, "Give me the Horn and let me pass."

Richie could feel the compulsive power of the Cirque that Rick wore, but it washed against the Ring before he felt more than a slight tug. He wasn't getting through to him. He shouted, waving the gun, "Fuck, Rick, can't you see it? The Adversary is *us*. He's the Richard Brandon that never woke up from that accident. We're the pieces, what's left of him. You, me, the doctor—" Rick was scowling at him, fumbling at his belt. "—Quinque was all we had to pull us together. This stupid adolescent fantasy. And for every one of us who died, we lost a little more of it. The garden's all that's left."

Rick jumped at him. Richie jerked back as he saw the knife in Rick's hand. He had fired both shots before he knew what was happening.

But he did know what was happening. That was the point of the Ring. He had known that Rick had to die the moment he'd slipped the Ring on his finger.

Rick hadn't known any such thing. The knife flew from his hand as he fell backward, an idiotic expression of surprise on his face. He collapsed on the ground, blood pooling around him from holes in his chest and his gut.

"*Fuck!*" Richie said. "You crazy shithead asshole! You couldn't listen."

The world seemed to twist. The shadows lost their regular swirling motion, and became random, chaotic. Richie tossed the gun aside and grabbed Rick's collar. Rick didn't resist.

Rick muttered, coughing blood, "This wasn't supposed to happen."

This is it, then, Richie thought. They'd been supposed to assemble all the fragments and form some sort of a whole out of them, before this mental world disintegrated around them. What he had was himself, and the five Artifacts.

He hoped the knowledge the Ring gave him wasn't bullshit, or the next few minutes were going to finish off the show.

Richie dragged Rick over the ground, toward the trees in the center of the garden. The shadows followed.

The Adversary was there, waiting. Richie shook his head when he saw him. *Just a kid who dreamed up this mess.* He supposed that, if he'd spent twenty-five years here, he'd want to do something about it, too.

He deposited the unconscious body at the base of one of the trees, and removed the Cirque from his head. Rick immediately seemed to lose some of his substantiveness.

The kid was looking at him with wide eyes. In one hand he held Magus' Staff, in the other he held Heros' Sword. Both items were too large for him. The Sword dragged on the ground, and the Staff swayed back and forth in his grasp.

Richie dropped the Cirque on his head; it fell at a cockeyed angle.

"I'm frightened," the kid said.

"You ain't the only one," Richie said. He glanced out at the garden. The shadows were bearing down on them like a Mack truck.

He took the Horn out of his jacket and shoved it into the kid's shirt.

Above them the shadows pulsed and came closer. The top of the oak tree began to fragment, branches blurred and tumbled upward to be lost in the darkness.

Richie pulled the Ring off of his finger. Knowledge faded from him as he did so, and with it his own fear grew. But he was long past turning back, even though all he knew now was that bringing together the five Artifacts would resurrect Chaos itself.

"Never liked the idea of being someone's effing dream," Richie said as he slipped the Ring onto the kid's finger. He held on to the kid as the shadows dropped down upon them and the world disintegrated.

EPILOGUE

JULIA

JULIA sat in a waiting room, preparing herself for the worst. It was bad. She knew it was bad even though Dr. Kavcheck wouldn't quite admit it. She had seen him, briefly, before they ushered her out of the ward.

Richard was having seizures. Intense, horrific episodes that were much worse than the paralysis had been. She had seen him caught by one, his muscles spasming, back arching, and his face contorting into a nearly obscene expression. The paralysis had stolen what identity was left to him, but the seizures were a possession by something else, something evil and chaotic.

Dr. Kavcheck wouldn't say so, but Julia was convinced that Richard was going to die. So she sat, afraid to move, to talk, or to think, waiting for the doctor to come and tell her it was all over.

The room was a perfect place to picture the darkness eating away inside Richard. The room itself was a sterile void, empty of any emotion in its abstract prints, pastel colors, and plastic plants. It was too trivial a place to wait for someone to die.

Julia buried her face in her palms because the fluorescent lights gave her a headache.

More than anything else, she wanted to leave. She wanted to return to the point in her life when she was at college, and family was only a distant thing she thought about on holidays. . . .

It was like Mom; someone's death forced you to take over part of their life. With Richard, there might be less to carry, but somehow the impending weight seemed just as heavy.

Julia wanted to leave, but she stayed, wondering how much less of Richard there would be when his heart finally gave out. She stayed until Dr. Kavcheck came for her.

She knew he was there when he tapped her on the shoulder. She looked up from her hands, expecting to read the worst in his face. She was irritated when she saw the same composed expression that he always wore.

"How is he?" Julia asked.

He paused a moment. There was something in the pause that wasn't what she'd feared. It wasn't the hesitation of someone trying to break bad news, it was the brief silence of someone who was fumbling to find the words to describe something. In the end, he said, "He's managed to recover."

A weight lifted from her. She straightened up. Richard hadn't died. "That's wonderful," Julia said. "How much of his movement has he gotten back?" She kept thinking of Sister Magdalene's uncle, who had a stroke and was left with a limp. Even if Richard hadn't been suffering from "real" strokes, she was worried about permanent damage in the areas of his brain that still worked.

Dr. Kavcheck was shaking his head, more in bewilderment than in negation. "Julia," he said. "I mean more than just from the attacks he's suffered over the past few days."

She straightened up, feeling a fluttering in her chest next to her heart. "What do you mean?"

"I mean he's recovered," he said. "Considering his prior deficits, he's made as close to a full functional recovery as not to matter."

Julia stood. "You mean . . ."

"He sees people." Dr. Kavcheck's voice had become breathless and rapid, the words spilled out of him. "He *hears* us, reacts, understands, has motor control."

Julia placed her hands over her mouth. She could feel tears forming in the corners of her eyes. She had thought she had cried herself out. "Can he talk?"

"Not well," Dr. Kavcheck admitted, but he rushed to add, "but that's probably a matter of physical therapy. He hasn't said a word for two decades, and his vocal cords have atrophied. We gave him a pad of paper and his command of the written word seems—"

"Can I see him?"

"Yes, of course." Dr. Kavcheck smiled, "We told him his sister was here, and he wanted to see you immediately."

"He wanted to see me?" Under her hand, she felt a goofy smile that hurt the sides of her face.

They had moved him back into the semiprivate room when she hadn't been looking. Dr. Kavcheck took her there. Richard lay in the bed as if nothing had happened. But Julia could see something *had* happened even before Richard turned his face to them.

Something in his expression had changed by an order of magnitude. There was the light of intelligence there, behind his eyes, and his eyes moved. Julia could actually see him taking in his environment. He found something even in an environment as emotionally dead as his hospital room.

Then he turned his head to face them as they entered. The motion was so unexpected in Richard that Julia gasped and felt a chill. It was as if a corpse, or a statue had suddenly moved.

Richard wheezed and coughed something, and waved. It was a moment before Julia could interpret the sounds as being, "Hi, Doc."

The speech seemed a reflex, because he ended with a cough and a brief expression of pain. Julia felt a wave of sympathy for him.

Richard, however, had forgotten the wince of his voice, if he had even noticed it in the first place. He bent over to the bedside table and grabbed a clipboard. It was one of those ubiquitous hospital clipboards, but instead of medical records, it held a blank yellow legal pad.

Richard grabbed a pen and scribbled for a second and turned the pad to face her. It had one word, *"Sis?"*

Julia nodded, felt the tears finally erupt, and said a choked, "Yes, yes." She took two steps and hugged him.

For a moment, Richard froze, as if he didn't quite know how to react. Then he relaxed, reached around, and patted her on the back as she cried into his shoulder. She heard a very hoarse whisper, barely a voice at all, say, "S'okay."

"Oh, Richard," Julia said into his shoulder, "I thought you'd never know I was here."

After a moment there was a wheezing noise from him that sounded like, "Eee."

Julia stood up and looked at him. "What?" she said.

She saw a brief flash of frustration on his face, but he grabbed the yellow pad and scribbled again. Then he gave her the pad. *"Call me Richie,"* it said. *"Richard is someone else."*

Julia chuckled and nodded. "Sure, Richie."

Richard—*Richie*—took back the pad and scribbled on it again.

She read it, *"Didn't know I had a sister."*

She thought of telling him how long she didn't know she had a brother, but she decided she could get into that with him another time.

"It's all right," she said, patting his hand. "It wasn't your fault."

Dr. Kavcheck tapped her on the shoulder, "Richard is going to need to rest. You can come back during normal visiting hours."

Julia wanted to object, there was just too much that she had to go over with Richie. But Dr. Kavcheck was right. There was no way to do it all tonight. They would have time later.

She turned to Richie and said, "I have to go. We both need some sleep."

Richie was scribbling something more, and at first Julia thought it was a farewell. But when he handed it to her, she read a question that she would have never expected.

"Well, okay," she said. "Johnson, Kennedy, Carter, Reagan, Cuomo, and Powell."

Julia felt a little confused, but she could always ask him about it later. "Good night," she said, and kissed him on the forehead.